I0649577

Cyberhawk - *Rise of Heroes*

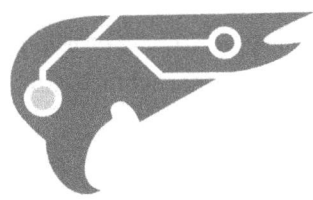

by Gretchen L. Winkler

Copyright 2025

Disclaimer

All characters in this book are fictitious. Any resemblance to actual people, living or dead, is purely coincidental.

Copyright 2025 Gretchen L. Winkler

This book is protected under the copyright laws of the United States of America. Any reproduction or unauthorized use of the material or artwork contained herein is strictly prohibited without the express written permission of the author.

All rights reserved.

No generative artificial intelligence (AI) was used in the creation of this book.

An original story by Gretchen L. Winkler.

Visit our website at www.cyberhawkheros.com

Library of Congress Control Number: 2025927207

Original cover concept by Gretchen L. Winkler

Graphic design and artwork by Andrew McCall

Published by User Friendly Media Group, Inc.
UserFriendlyNation.com

Special thanks to William Sikkens, Jeremy Winkler, and the engineers, scientists, and test pilots at Cyberhawk Research & Development. You know who you are and how your dreams of cybernetic equipment and enhancement are moving Humanity towards a better world. Let's keep your goals close to our hearts and work towards a positive outcome in the future. Your tech inspired Bill, Jeremy, and me to dream about what a world like that would be and how it would shape the future of Earth.

CHAPTER 1

The early spring afternoon sunlight was pleasant as he waited on the rural, isolated airstrip not far away from Eugene, Oregon. Weather in the Pacific Northwest could be mercurial. One minute, there was a bank of dense, chilling fog with a light rain, and next, cheerful sunlight warming one's shoulders, bursting through big, puffy clouds. The air was fresh, and the landscape was pleasing and easy on the eye. Rolling green hills with trees, farmland waiting for their next crop to sprout, and refreshing moisture that assured that there would be things growing soon were all around.

Robert Justice had recently agreed to take on this position with the hope of being part of making the world better. It was hard to leave his old position as Chief of the Fire Department back in Carson City, Nevada. He had good friends back there, and his wife and son had been happy there as well. It was a small city with big responsibilities as the state capital. However, despite the fact that he enjoyed living there and had many fond memories, he found the offer to captain an elite team of emergency services personnel hard to pass up. The pay was good, and the location was also fine. So, he talked with his wife, Jessica, about moving and taking on new responsibilities. How could she say no when she saw the excitement in his eyes?

So now the thirty-four-year-old stood on an isolated airfield as he waited for his new team members to arrive. This would be very different in that they would not all be firemen. This new team would be composed of emergency services personnel from various fields of expertise. The Cyberhawk Team was to be the first of its kind. A new way of thinking of rescue operations with all the best tech, and hopefully, the best people. The headquarters for the Cyberhawk Team was a private section of the rural airstrip, neatly hidden among the typical airfield-type warehouse structures. Their main building was at the end of the row, tucked back just a little up against the forested area. A stranger would have no idea that anything unusual or special was in this area. Their building just looked like a nicely upgraded avionics shop with nice offices upstairs.

Robert stood outside enjoying the sunlight as he waited for his new team members to arrive. He watched a small Cessna take off and head into the southern skies. The little plane popped up with ease over the blackberry jungle that was on the far south end of the strip. He hated waiting and tried to get himself to be focused, calm, and professional. He started to glance through the folder full of paperwork he had on each of the new people who had been selected.

"So many of these people are from all over the world...," he mumbled to himself. "I had figured that this was a State of Oregon project. It seems strange. I hope they all speak English because I do not speak Spanish or.... Swiss?"

Then, a noise caught his attention. A car door slammed shut. Back towards the tree line behind the buildings, where the parking lot was located, seven people were walking together from the parking lot. He took a mental count of the people and realized that some were missing. Robert pulled in a deep, long breath. Life was filled with unexpected situations, he told himself. He quickly glanced at his smartphone. There were several messages, some of which stated that a few team members would not be able to arrive until the next day. He would have to do a second introduction for those who would be late. He quickly rifled through the paperwork to guess who was approaching and set aside those who had sent him messages. Each of the resumes included a profile photo.

One of the male applicants, wearing blue jeans, ranching-style lace-up boots, and a big smile, strode directly towards him, extending his hand out and said, "Hello there, I'm Rafferty Lewis. Are you the fellow we're supposed to speak with about the Cyberhawk team?"

Robert accepted the extended hand from the young man with the cowboy-style drawl and replied, "That would be me. I am Captain Robert Justice. You can call me Captain Justice or just Captain for short. And ....you are a fireman from Wyoming?"

"Well, heck yes! That would be me, sir. I mean…. Captain," replied the thin but muscular white man of twenty-five years. He ran his hand back through his wavy, sandy blonde hair and then stuffed both hands deep into his pockets in a boyish type of fashion.

"It says here that you have received many accommodations while in service to your department, but I also see several arrests. Hmmm. But... you did pass the clearance requirement," Robert addressed the younger man.

Rafferty grinned broadly and replied, "Well, that was just because my fire-fightin' pal, Chris, and I were in a couple of bar fights. His granddad was a cowboy a long time ago, and his heart was set on working in the areas where his granddad used to work as a ranch hand. So, he loves country music and dancing, which I thought was surprising for a black guy, so we like to go to the taverns once in a while....and well, some of the guys just get bent out of shape when Chris shows up there. So, he and I would teach those shit sniffers a life lesson."

"I see. A life lesson....??" Robert raised an eyebrow, wondering exactly what the younger man meant.

"You know...that being a piece of shit racist isn't the American way. We're a melting pot, like my dad used to say. So.....if you don't think that's a good enough reason to get into a bar fight defending your best pal.... well... I might not be the right guy to serve in this Cyberhawk team," replied Rafferty. He stood defiant as if there might be a conflict coming his way.

Robert had to repress a smile.

"Oh no, I think you will do fine. Loyalty, as well as...clear level-headed thinking, is what we need to make a good, solid group. I approve of loyalty and the ability to see beyond old, outdated ways of thinking," Robert replied as he looked at the rest of the group observing their reactions to Rafferty's statements. No one appeared to have any problems.

A middle-aged man of modest height seemed to be evaluating the conversation and stepped forward to ask a question. He spoke with a thick European accent that was not Austrian or German. It was Swiss.

"What is the plan here? I was not expecting to be sent to a location that was so rural, unless we have a humanitarian need in this area, which, from the looks of things,… I doubt."

Captain Justice quickly rifled through the papers in the folder and found one that matched the man's appearance.

"Are you Dr. August Hanni?" he asked.

"Yes," replied the shorter man, with grey-blue eyes and neatly trimmed wavy brown hair.

"It says here you are a medical doctor with very high credentials and… several international awards to your name. Impressive," Robert paused for a moment, wishing that the rest of the team had been present. "Everyone selected for this project was chosen for their expertise, experience, and reputation. Dr. Hanni, you were selected because you will be needed."

Robert looked up at the others who had assembled as if they were part of an audience and said, "We are missing some of our team members, so we are going to go through this process again when they arrive, but… let's start now to get to know each other. Janet Hallmann?"

"Present," said the athletic-looking woman with pale skin that was accentuated by her shoulder-length auburn hair. She spoke with a French-Canadian accent.

"You were part of the Royal Canadian Mounted Police, right?"

"Yes, that is correct," replied Janet Hallmann.

Robert Justice nodded to her and read the next name.

"Is Fernando Sanchez here?" asked Robert.

"I am here," replied the man, with tan skin and of average height, smiling with enthusiasm. "I was a fireman, and then I worked for FEMA for ten years. I can't stay away from a good disaster. I like helping people."

"Then you have joined the right team," replied Robert as he called for the next person, whom he thought he recognized. "Sandra Ridgestone?"

"Present," replied the tall, slender woman wearing sunglasses. She appeared to be about thirty-five years old and had that typical cop sternness about her. She wore her naturally long blonde hair pulled neatly back into a ponytail.

Robert nodded to the woman and proceeded to the man, whom he presumed was the pilot of their team.

"Chris…. Takahashi? I hope I said your name correctly," said Robert.

"That's me, Captain. And you said it correctly," replied Chris Takahashi. "I have almost two thousand hours of flight time. I started learning how to fly as a teen."

The Captain took note of the confident young man who also dressed neatly and wore the latest tech gadgets.

"And Raven Smith?" asked Robert, catching the attention of a Native American male.

"Present. I am an experienced paramedic with EMT disaster training, and I worked for the American Red Cross," answered Raven Smith.

Robert Justice smiled, observed his new team members for a minute, and glanced about the airfield.

"Welcome to the Cyberhawk Team, ladies and gentlemen," said Robert. "This will be the beginning of a brand-new, innovative way of looking at emergency services. I will start getting everyone familiar with our base of operations. Each of you has already been emailed our rules of conduct and has signed a non-disclosure agreement. This facility appears to be a small, private, typical airfield, but in reality, it is a highly advanced, hidden facility. We also have quarters on-site for those who need or wish to have residence here. Human Resources should have already assisted those of you with families, but if not, let me know." Robert started to stroll about, making gestures to the location with the group following him. "We are going to be the very first to operate as an elite team for emergency services using technology that has not been made available to the general public, ...ever before.

Everyone here has been selected for the skills or experience that they bring, which will make an effective team. Does anyone have any questions so far?"

Captain Justice looked about and noticed a hand-raised gesture from Chris Takahashi.

"Yes, Mr. Takahashi."

"When do we get to see this technology that you are talking about?" asked Chris.

"Right now. I want everyone to follow me this way to the hangar bay at the end of this row," said Robert as he started walking towards the building. Everyone followed along as they surveyed the site. "Since we have located our base of operation at this airfield, we can easily leave at a moment's notice. If we are needed at a location that requires us to travel far, we have two airplanes and one helicopter stored on-site. The rest of the space is used by local pilots who house their planes in the other buildings here. This is an economical and practical use of this property."

"I thought we were required to have clearance to be able to set foot on this property?" questioned Sandra Ridgestone, thinking about the civilian pilots who would use the airstrip.

"Well...Ms. or Mrs. Ridgestone?" Captain Justice inquired.

"I prefer to go by Detective Ridgestone.... which I guess is ....no longer the case here...," replied Sandra with a slight shrug.

"Well, ...Detective Ridgestone, the airfield is open to private users of this strip, but our buildings and technology require a security clearance. Not to mention, being part of this team also requires clearance. As far as titles go, everyone who has earned a title of respect may continue to use it if they wish, but I am the captain, and I oversee this operation regardless of what rank you may have had before," answered Captain Justice.

"What if we don't have a title or don't want to use it?" asked Raven Smith.

"It's up to you. Most titles are for the chain of command and ease of knowing who is responsible for decisions, both good and bad. We are a team of experts, and respecting each other is key to making this project work well," Captain Justice explained. "For example, Dr. Hanni earned his title through education, and Detective Ridgestone earned hers through work experience and training. We have no problem using these."

"I'd like to be referred to as a flight demi-god," said Chris Takahashi, turning to Fernando with a big grin. "But I doubt anyone would want to refer to me as such."

Fernando had to repress breaking out into laughter and said, "Yeah,….. a cool title like Master of the Universe would be fun."

The group stopped in front of a security door positioned at the north end of the structure, near the southern end of the aerodrome. The group's attention was momentarily diverted as they observed a brightly colored vintage biplane speeding down the runway, preparing for liftoff. The airstrip was oriented north-south, with mowed grass all around, except for the small forest on the far east side of the property. The unique-sounding motor held everyone's attention as the plane gently lifted itself up into the air. The far south end was a dense area of blackberries and a few smaller trees, while the north end of the strip was completely flat and open, with small farms scattered throughout on the other side of the roadway. Christ Takahashi broadly smiled as he watched the old taildragger plane.

"You have to have a special endorsement to be able to fly one of those," he commented to no one in particular.

Rafferty grinned at him and said, "Looks like fun with the wind blowing across your face."

"Yeah......gotta wear goggles though," Chris added. "The wind will dry your eyes out."

"You will have plenty of time to watch airplanes," remarked Captain Justice.

Those standing near the captain watched as he pulled out a card and slid it into the secure door locking system, which was made of reinforced materials. The frame looked sturdy, too. The door made a chirping sound before the locking mechanism disengaged. The building appeared to be three stories tall and had a typical metal exterior, similar to what one would find on an airfield, housing airplanes and offices. Inside was unexpectedly different.

"Come on in. It's time that you start to get accustomed to what might be considered your second home. All of us will be spending a lot of time here. Especially those that plan to live here on base," said Captain Justice as he entered the building.

Inside was a clean, high-tech design for comfortable living, featuring a large kitchen and dining area, a recreation area, and a workspace, all located on the main floor. A large roll-up door was available for bringing in equipment that exceeded the size of the door frame. Secured storage spaces were neatly hidden behind cabinetry.

Looking up at the vaulted ceiling, one could see that there were two additional stories of space, where bedrooms and baths were located, along with couches for relaxing, watching TV, or working on a computer. The design was bright and cheery. Towards the top of the ridge of the roof were skylights. On the outer northern wall, where the roll-up door was located, there were four huge windows high up that allowed light to enter the upper levels of the space. The upper levels had a steel railing, allowing one to peer down to the main floor. A transparent elevator system went all the way up, and a set of stairs on the other side only went to the second floor. High in the ceiling was a large, strange-looking hatch above the lower workspace area. It looked mechanical and automated. Everyone seemed excited or intrigued to look around the facility.

Chris gazed upwards and asked, "Captain, what is that hatch for?" He gestured to the ceiling.

"That is an automatic hatchway," answered the captain as he strode over to a control panel. He slid his security keycard through the device and then typed in a code. Suddenly, a rumbling sound filled the room as the hatchway door opened. The group could feel the air flow into the building and see the blue sky above.

"Why is that there?" asked Dr. Hanni.

"You know...I actually ... don't know. I was just informed about it and assured that it is waterproof and can withstand snow and ice, just like the solar panels and skylight windows located high up on the ridge. I was told that efforts had been made to make this place as eco-friendly and secure as possible. Everything has a purpose," replied Captain Justice. "If...I wasn't married, I think I would have liked very much to stay here."

The group gazed contemplatively for a moment.

"Damn! Have any of you looked in the kitchen?! This is a top-grade chef's kitchen with all the cool toys. And not the cheap stuff either. My mother would be envious. Makes me want to take up baking," remarked Raven Smith.

"I'm not a bad baker…, but I am not going to be living here," commented Sandra Ridgestone, peering over at the kitchen area.

"Why?" asked Raven.

"I have two kids who need me to be around. But I think they would like this place. But I seriously doubt you all would want pre-teens running about getting into things," Sandra replied with a laugh.

"Well, this certainly is not a military style barracks. So, why the effort to make the workspace and living quarters so desirable?" Dr Hanni asked Justice.

"That, I can answer. Our employers want people who wish to stay. We all went through several screenings and a couple of interviews, right?" asked Captain Justice, quickly looking around to see heads nodding. "They are planning on investing a great deal of money and time into the training of our team and want dedicated individuals. That was made very clear to me when I accepted this assignment. Currently, the cost of living has skyrocketed, making it difficult to find an affordable place to live. Therefore, they wanted everyone to be comfortable and feel at home. So, I guess I will ask….is there anyone having second thoughts?"

Everyone except Dr. Hanni seemed to have no doubts about the project. Captain Justice gave the doctor a look.

Dr. Hanni took a deep breath and said, "I am always having second thoughts about… situations. I want to be in a place where my medical training can be of the most use. I made an oath to heal others, and …that is what I want to do. I do not wish to be a slave to insurance bureaucracy or some private industry's money-making scheme. So… if I find myself not contributing to the well-being of others, I may want to leave."

"Understood. And I appreciate your honesty. If you start to feel like you are not living up to your personal goals, let me know, and together we will work towards repairing that situation," said Captain Justice.

"Thank you. I will do so," replied Dr. Hanni.

Several of the new team members found themselves feeling restless as they looked about. Fernando and Chris stood together appraising the place. Finally, Fernando could not wait any longer and asked, "Can we look around? Have we been assigned rooms already?"

"Certainly. Make yourself at home. And no, the rooms have not been assigned. Everyone, please feel free to explore the facility for about fifteen minutes, and then we shall all meet downstairs in the dining room," suggested the captain.

Fernando, Chris, Raven, and Rafferty all looked at each other and then quickly headed towards the transparent elevator like eager children. They all enjoyed watching as the machine's mechanisms lifted the device upward.

Dr. Hanni exhaled in disgust, "They are grown men, ... and act like children."

"Well, they are grown men, ... but .... they are all .... *young* men with a lust for life. That's good. Enjoy it while you can, I say. I would if I were in my twenties again," Sandra remarked to Dr. Hanni.

"I suppose. I don't think I was ever young....at least not like that," said the doctor.

"Come on, Doc. You had to have had a few young and crazy years at college," said Sandra, hoping to draw out a funny story from the very serious European gentleman.

"I started university at age thirteen and graduated with honors and immediately was accepted to start my studies of premed, which I also excelled at, and graduated with honors to go on to my doctorate.... I don't recall any childish moments between studying. I had very little time for friends. I was expected to make my family proud of my achievements," replied Dr. Hanni.

The tall, lean blonde woman, still wearing her sunglasses, eyed Dr. Hanni with an investigator's critical eye and then replied, "Alright, Dr. Hanni.... you win. You were never young."

Moving smoothly upwards, the transparent glass elevator made its way up to the second floor. Raven Smith found himself fascinated with the idea that the elevator was transparent. The design eliminated the claustrophobic feeling that elevators often gave off. It was a nice aesthetic change unless you had a fear of heights. There was no need for conventional decorating, as the environment itself was the decoration, including the lighting.

"I wonder if there was a reason for making the elevator see-through. Not that I mind," Raven pondered aloud to no one in particular.

Rafferty Lewis just smiled with his hands still jammed into his front jean pockets. He looked about, evaluating, and said, "Probably to look nice. This is pretty swanky for a clubhouse for a bunch of rough guys like us."

Chris gave an appraising smile and replied, "Yes, but we are not all rough guys. Some of us like the finer things in life. This team comprises a diverse range of experts. Are any of you pilots?"

The guys shook their heads as the door opened to the second floor, and they all got out. Each of them scanned the upstairs and eventually found their way to the balcony to look up and down. Finally, Fernando turned to Chris. Chris had Japanese heritage, with black hair and a medium build, and possessed one of those knockout smiles. He dressed fashionably, wore cool gadgets like a fancy smartwatch, and his hair was perfectly styled.

"So, you are the pilot. What do you fly?" Fernando asked.

Chris smiled broadly with confidence and replied, "You name it, I can probably fly it. You see, I was hired to fly the two planes and the helicopter that the Cyberhawk program owns and has stationed here. I began learning to fly when I was a teenager. I am also an expert at flying drones."

"Drones...," Fernando nodded appreciatively. "Those were very useful during the last Hurricane relief I worked on. We saved a lot of people by using those. I wouldn't mind learning how to fly some of those...geez...I think it would be fun even to learn how to fly a plane."

Rafferty came strolling back towards the others after being in the bedroom areas.

"This place is awesome," he declared. "Top-notch bedrooms and private bathrooms for each bedroom set. They really put the bucks into this place. Check out the comfy couch and big HD8 TV!"

"And video games…. they do want us to stay," added Chris.

"I think we could use some art. I wonder if they would allow me to hang some of my paintings in my room," commented Raven as he looked about. "Perhaps even out here if nobody objects."

"Art is cool with me. But I need to know if the beds are comfortable," replied Fernando as he headed for one of the bedrooms. The others followed him since that was a reasonable concern. Anyone who worked hard for a living needed a good place to rest and recover. He sat down on the lower bunk and then reclined, putting his arms up behind his head. "Hey, this is nice! I could easily see myself relaxing here."

"Those…are the new smart mattresses. You know the ones that change temperature and elevate when the sleeper starts snoring. I love this! Take a look at all the cool tech that has been incorporated into the bunk area, as well as the bathroom. This looks like an Alexa system…. hey Alexa, turn the light on," Chris requested.

A glowing blue light activated, and then the voice of the AI proceeded to ask, "Please specify which light."

Chris looked about the room and then peeked outside at the number on the door. "Alexa, turn the light on in bedroom three." The light in the room came on after the request was made. "Gentlemen, we are now living in high-tech luxury."

The four young men grinned at each other.

"Well, that's different. I haven't ever lived in a place with smart tech in it. We all got up and used the light switch, you know, the old-fashioned way," said Rafferty. "I guess I will need to learn to adjust."

"This is sooo…. cool!!" exclaimed Chris.

"Dang! You're really into this geeky stuff, huh?" commented Rafferty after seeing Chris's eyes light up with joy.

"This is the way all homes should be made. It is the way of the future. I have always been fascinated by technology and shows about it. As a kid, I wanted to be a crew member of the Starship Enterprise," replied Chris.

Fernando leaned towards Rafferty.

"Rafferty, remember this guy flies drones and pilots planes. He's all about the tech," commented Fernando. "And air…even if some of it is…a little hot."

"Yup, that's me," replied Chris with a satisfied smile, not taking offense at Fernando's mild jibe.

"The balloon doesn't rise without hot air," said Chris.

"Point taken," answered Fernando.

"You know," commented Raven, looking around. "There aren't enough rooms for us each to have a private space of our own. We are gonna have to share. I want to hang my paintings on the wall. It's important to me. I need someone who isn't going to mind."

"What kind of pictures do you paint?" asked Rafferty.

"Mostly spiritual images from my culture. I am very close to Raven. He's a very powerful protective spirit that flies about the Columbia Gorge. At least that is where I discovered my connection to him. So many of my paintings are inspired by Raven," he replied.

"Your name, too," remarked Rafferty.

"My name, too."

"How did you get your name? Is it a family thing?" asked Rafferty.

Raven gave a half smile and replied, "My father is a truck driver. You know, the big rigs. He has a route that he often takes through the Columbia Gorge on Interstate 84. One night, he was coming back, and there was a bad thunderstorm. He said that he had a vision of an enormous raven flying alongside his truck and over it, as if guiding and protecting him from the storm. He said the bird spirit stayed with him until he was safely out of the Gorge and the storm. He told me that he knew in his heart that if Raven had not protected him, he would have died in an accident, never to find out that his wife was pregnant with a baby boy, who was me. I am named after Raven."

"Wow, that's a really cool story," remarked Rafferty.

"Where did your name come from?" asked Raven.

"I was named after my great-grandfather," replied Rafferty.

"Oh. That's good to be named after an ancestor," replied Raven.

Rafferty just smiled as he dug his hands deeper into his pockets.

"Well, not as cool as the story around yours. Alright, I don't mind having some art on the walls as long as it isn't like a bunch of messy colors slapped on a canvas...or gory stuff," replied Rafferty. "I like subjects that I can look at and... it makes me feel good. Like my mind can wander there peacefully. Hopefully that makes sense."

"Nothing gory and *none* of my artwork is...*slapped* on a canvas," replied Raven, somewhat disdainful of the idea. "My work should uplift the spirit. I have pictures of some of them on my phone."

"Great. Let me see," replied Rafferty, getting closer to Raven to view his cell phone.

Raven flipped past a few images and then began showing the colorful designs, all of which had ravens somehow intertwined within the theme of the painting. Rafferty asked for several to be zoomed in to see the details.

"Hey, I like those. It's a deal. You and I can be roomies," Rafferty concluded.

Fernando turned to Chris after Rafferty and Raven decided to become roommates.

"So, I guess you and I can share a room. I like tech stuff too. How do you feel about superhero movies?" Fernando directed his question to Chris.

"Love them. Can't get enough of them. Some say I am a bit of an expert on the topic," replied Chris.

CHAPTER 2

The large primary bedroom was filled with furniture and boxes strewn about, with small open trails leading to the exit and the bathroom. It was still dark out in the modest west Eugene neighborhood filled with neatly organized middle-class homes with tiny yards and architecture that appeared to be "xeroxed" in sets of three. This basic single-story house was light grey with a slightly upgraded stone accent, white trim, and a two-car garage that was also filled with boxes. The neighborhood had neat little straight streets, level yards, and sidewalks. It was all quiet, except for the cell phone alarm, which was slowly growing louder and louder as the owner ignored each passing minute.

A grumbly moan came from the queen-sized bed and its single occupant.

"Oh, crud, I gotta get the kids going!" exclaimed a voice from under the covers.

The tall, sandy blonde woman quickly extracted herself from bed while turning off her cell phone alarm. Moments later, she was already in the shower and getting ready. Sandra Ridgestone hated being late, and her cell phone worked as her backup wake-up call. She would have to hurry and get the twins going as well.

Back at the airfield base, a buzzing alarm went off as well. One dark brown eye popped open and gazed at the digital clock.

"Ugh....I thought I just went to bed. Okay, it's gonna be one of those days," said the former member of the Royal Canadian Mounted Police.

With a yawn, Janet sat up and looked around at her modest new quarters. Her two suitcases and three boxes of personal belongings sat in the walkway. They were fine there for the moment, but she would need to make time to get her stuff stowed away properly. She and the guys, who were now housed at the airbase, spent time last night watching TV, drinking beers, and getting to know each other. So, she did not organize her quarters, unlike Dr. Hanni. He seemed a bit uptight to her, but every team needed someone who followed the rules and paid attention to details. She just didn't want to be that tightly wound person. She wanted to enjoy life again after feeling so sick and then having her heart broken. Camille was a person of the past with selfish expectations and was no longer in Janet's future. No more serious relationships with anyone was Janet's new motto.

"And I am here...now...at the new job site...I had better get myself going," Janet said, pulling herself out of bed and heading towards the bathroom. Turning on the cold water and splashing it upon her face felt good, and so would a nice hot shower. "I hope the guys haven't stolen all the hot water. I wonder how long this will be, just *my* bathroom. I guess I had better enjoy it while I can."

Back in the West Eugene neighborhood, Sandra was ready and making sure her twelve-year-old twins had their lunches and school gear. Both had blonde hair, like their mother, but they were very different from each other in terms of desires and interests.

"Mom, going to a new school is gonna suck. I won't know anybody there," complained the girl.

"Tessa, your brother won't know anyone either, so... you will have each other," replied Sandra, adjusting her sunglasses a little.

"Really? You want me to hang out with Mr. Star Wars nerd? I said I wanted to have friends and not be alone with losers for the rest of my life," retorted Tessa.

"Hey, I like Star Wars and sci-fi stuff," replied Sandra.

"Yes, but you are old-fashioned," replied Tessa without hesitation.

"Gee, thanks for making me feel...old," replied the detective, who was also a single parent since her ex-husband had disappeared.

"Well, Mom, you are old. Look at the clothes you wear and how your hair is. We seriously need to get you a makeover. You would look so much better if you wore some heels, skinny jeans, and a cute short leather jacket. Faux leather, of course," chided her daughter concerning fashion choices.

"I like my...flat shoes and normal-fitting jeans, I can move in them. You do remember that I am a detective, and I investigate locations of crimes, right?" retorted Sandra as she gestured for everyone to head for the front door.

Tessa rolled her eyes in disgust and grabbed her stylish backpack.

"Mom, you look fine. She's just going through…some kind of weird selfish phase," stated Michael as he stared at his twin sister, wondering if she was his twin anymore. He was already wearing his coat and backpack. "I am starting to suspect that she is some sort of changeling."

"I think it is called hormones, dear," Sandra replied as she locked the front door. Michael was lingering by the front porch area while Tessa was already on the sidewalk. "Hey, when you two get home, I want you to finish unpacking your stuff. And if you get done, please start unpacking the rest of the kitchen boxes."

Tessa was already walking towards the bus stop that was located just down the street, and acting like she was out of earshot. Michael turned to his mother.

"Sure, Mom," he said and then took off to catch up to his twin sister.

Sandra was already driving to the base when the rain started to fall. Her wiper blades failed to clear the windshield completely, which was irritating. New wiper blades were just another item she needed for her aging automobile. Sometimes she felt like Lieutenant Columbo with her old car, but what was a single mom of two supposed to do? She hoped this new job would work out. The pay was quite reasonable and would allow her some financial security. The frustration and stress slowly led her mind to wonder what happened to her ex-husband, Karl. It was not like him to disappear and ignore his responsibilities to his children. He loved them. At least Sandra thought he loved them. She also thought they had parted ways in a reasonable fashion, which felt more like a directive than a breakup. At times, she wished that they had been able to work through whatever the problem was. She still could not understand what prompted his change of heart. She did not hate him, but she felt deeply hurt by his change of heart. And then the strange letters came from the military. It was all very much a mystery, which she did not have the clearance to investigate.

When Sandra arrived at the small airfield, the clock on the car dashboard gave her the embarrassing news that she was late. She hated being late, and this was technically her first day on the job.

"Just wonderful, Sandra. Way to make a good impression by being late," she chided herself. Sandra took a deep breath as she strode towards the entrance and put on her calm detective face. She opened the door and said, "Good morning, everyone! My apologies for being late. Did I miss anything?"

"Coffee," replied Captain Justice, raising an eyebrow. "We all have our morning coffee and have been introducing ourselves to each other. So, it's your turn now."

"Okay. Uh…I am or was…. Detective Sandra Ridgestone. I was an officer with the Los Angeles Police Department for fifteen years. Got divorced. Have two kids. I love being a detective… but I have had several close calls with death that made me think twice about my occupation and having children who rely on me. I enjoy working to protect others and serving the general public. I think we need good people out there keeping the crazies off the streets. And this Cyberhawk project sounded like a step in the right direction for my children and me."

Fernando came from the kitchen area carrying two full cups of steaming hot coffee. He offered one to Sandra, which she gratefully accepted.

"Thanks. You're a lifesaver. I guess I missed everyone else's introduction," said Sandra apologetically.

"No, I just made you go first because you came in late. Nice intro. Next," replied the captain.

"I'll go," said Fernando, still standing with his cup of coffee. "My name is Fernando Sanchez. I began my career as a firefighter as a teenager during the summer months. They needed help because the drought was so severe throughout the West. I am from Sacramento, California. After doing this for several summers, I realized that I wanted to continue being a firefighter, which pissed my dad off. He wanted me to go to college and become like Dr. Hanni." Fernando gestured towards the European doctor. "But I like being outdoors and being with people. I worked with FEMA for a couple of years and participated in several rescue operations during the hurricane season. You see a lot of stuff doing that kind of work. Some of it is sad, but also...... Americans actually love each other. Don't believe the crappy news and social media. I saw all kinds of people working together to help their neighbors and total strangers. That's what America is about. That's what I am about. I am here to become a better man. I want to do more. And I was told that the Cyberhawk program is about that. I want to dive in and get going."

"Well, I guess you should be on our PR staff… if we had one," said Captain Justice with a smile. "That was a very positive testimonial."

Fernando just grinned and then took a sip of coffee.

"So, Captain, Fernando brings up an important point…when are we going to get started? I was told that I needed to fly missions. I want to see the planes and the helicopter," commented Chris. "If we need to go somewhere, I want to be familiar with the aircraft…ahead of time."

Captain Justice eyed the eager younger man.

"I was hoping to have the whole team here for the start of the training sessions, but Chris has just given me an excellent idea. Let's take a look at the planes our team gets to work with. You will see that Cyberhawk is not sparing any expense. We have what we need to reach locations where we are needed most. That means we have a small plane for short missions, a larger cargo-type plane for when the whole team is needed at a location, and for those difficult-to-land places, we have a helicopter that can hold up to six people and their gear, plus emergency provisions. Let's all go out to the hangar."

"What about locations that are not that far away?" asked Rafferty.

"Cyberhawk has three state-of-the-art SUVs fully loaded for the transport of gear or towing of smaller vehicles. They are all stored away in our private hangar," replied the captain. "Let's go take a look at these items right now."

Everyone got up to follow the captain outside, grabbing jackets and gulping down coffee. They went directly to another large building that was closer to the airstrip's tarmac. Captain Justice opened the secured side door and turned on the lights, revealing the Cyberhawk vehicles emblazoned with the blue and gold hawk, accompanied by blue and gold lettering above, which read 'Cyberhawk.' The logo conveyed the impression of the desire to go fast like a fighter jet. Behind the vehicles in the back center space of the building were workshop cabinets and benches with tools and machinery. Everything needed to make repairs in-house was available. The place was a shop junkie's fantasy. Chrome and paint sparkled; the vehicles drew everyone's attention like a ride for a superhero. Thoughts of Batman and the Bat Cave came to mind.

The group stood in awe or appreciative silence for about two minutes.

"So, Takahashi…. these are the birds that you will fly and get to know very well," said the captain. Chris was already standing close to the small plane, which had the Cyberhawk paint scheme, and had started to examine the struts, wheels, and welds. Just as Chris was beginning to fall in love with the plane, the captain's phone buzzed. Robert Justice quickly looked at the phone. "While Mr. Takahashi discovers his next true love, why don't we have..." The captain looked around and then said, "Raven Smith, tell us about yourself."

The young Native American male made a facial expression of surprise and responded with, "There isn't much to tell. My name is Raven Smith, and I enjoy painting in my free time. I was recruited from the Red Cross. I did relief work with them for natural disasters... like Fernando described. One sees the true nature of others when times are bad."

Fernando nodded while everyone else realized that they would have to say something about themselves soon.

Janet volunteered, "I'll go next. I am Janet Hallmann, and my rank in the Royal Canadian Mounted Police was Staff Sergeant. I was born and raised in Quebec, which is the French-speaking province. That means I speak English and French fluently. I love Hockey and cheese." She paused and sighed a little. "I came here for a change in life. I loved serving the public, but...I needed to be someplace... else." Janet started to look a little uncomfortable, as if speaking of such matters made her feel bad. "I had a very painful breakup, and ...... I need a new family, friends, and scenery. I need something new and challenging. I want to be focused on the future and not the past."

"By the way.... I love cheese and speak French as well," Dr. Hanni said to Janet, making her smile.

Everyone seemed to understand Janet's desire to start something new. Then the Captain's phone made a weird sound, breaking the introduction spell and everyone's nervousness. He looked down momentarily at the device and then looked back up at everyone.

"Well, thank you, Mr. Smith and Ms. Hallmann...I just got a message that the man in charge of the maintenance and redesign of the planes will be at the hangar bay in a couple of minutes. So, everyone except Mr. Takahashi will come with me back to the Cyberhawk base building," said the captain, then turning to Chris. "If you want to have a full introduction to the planes you will be operating, Roy and Chester will be here in a few minutes. Do you mind waiting?"

"No, I am just fine checking out these babies," replied Chris. "I'd like to meet the man who takes care of them. I already have questions about some of the modifications that I am observing."

The captain nodded and smiled, leaving Chris to wait for Roy and his pal Chester. He led the others back inside the building and drew everyone's focus to the area near the roll-up door, where there was concrete flooring. Equipment had been set up with a VR system and two robotic units that were firmly attached to sturdy stands. Everyone seemed excited except for Dr. Hanni. Captain Justice strolled toward the two industrial-looking units.

"These two high-tech-looking devices, called XTs, can be controlled by VR headsets. These will be used for the beginning of the training for equipment that is part of the Cyberhawk

program. Who wants to be one of the first ones to try them out?"
asked the captain.

Fernando and Rafferty both raised their arms like eager
schoolboys.

"Alright, gentlemen, take the seats provided. And I will get
you started since the LabCoat Crew is busy today," the captain
gestured for them to sit on the chairs that had VR headsets sitting
upon them. "I have had a fair amount of training already on these
devices."

"What is the point of the VR setup? Why not have a
software program do what you want?" asked Dr. Hanni. "These
look like typical industrial machines used in assembly lines."

"Good question. Not all software can be ready for the
various situations that we may be called to handle. We can't wait
for a programmer to write software procedures in an emergency.
That would require an AI of very advanced capability, and right
now, such a capability is rare, and it is being utilized for other
purposes. So, having experienced Humans handle this process is
the best way to deal with this," Captain Justice replied as he got
Rafferty ready with the headset. Fernando, seated in the other
chair, watched closely and began performing the same
procedures. The captain made sure that Rafferty had all the
straps correctly fastened. "How does that feel? You don't want it
too tight or too loose."

"Feels fine. It's dark," answered Rafferty.

"It should be. Put your right hand up on the right side of the headset. Feel for a button. Press it once firmly. You should see some light flash and messages of the software beginning," the captain advised.

"Yup. I see it," replied Rafferty.

"Good. There is a set of hand devices, which I should have had you put on before the headset," said the captain as he picked up the devices and started to help Rafferty put them on. Janet came over to assist with Rafferty's left hand while Fernando, observing from the other chair, started to work with the hand devices for his system.

"Thanks, Janet. The person who was recruited to be my Logistics Assistant has not yet arrived," the captain said to the former Mountie.

"No problem. It's all part of being on the team," she replied.

"Well, shit, I feel like I am the center of attention. I like that," commented Rafferty with his cowboy drawl coming through strongly. He had a big, cheerful grin on his face.

"In a moment, I will be there right alongside you, pal. I figured out how to put the handpieces on myself," bragged Fernando.

Raven and Sandra both found this funny as the captain made his way over to Fernando to help him put the headset on correctly.

"So, both of you... by now should see the startup menu with a prompt to do the quick hand device training, select that, go through the training exercises, and at the end, put your names into the software when prompted. The computer will keep track of your progress. This is an important start to your training," said the captain as he walked over to the table where a laptop was set up. "I need someone to monitor this."

"I will do it," volunteered Dr Hanni.

Meanwhile, the rest of the group remained focused on Fernando and Rafferty.

"You done yet?" asked Fernando. "I have already completed the training exercises."

"Yeah, I'm almost done. It's weird typing my name without an actual keyboard to use," said Rafferty.

"Really. Obviously, you don't play video games much, huh?" commented Fernando.

"Not really. I'm more into the real world," he replied.

"Okay, gentlemen, we are about to test your ability to use the static manipulator units. Go to the training menu and select static manipulator exercise," instructed the captain as he turned towards the others. "You will all want to keep your distance from the units because...sometimes this can get ......wild."

Rafferty suddenly could see through his XT's point-of-view camera. He was much higher up off the ground and could see the room where he was currently sitting. He raised his right arm up and could see the robotic limb come into view.

"Hey! It's like the robotic arms are mine, and I can see from… his point of view. It's like he is me," commented Rafferty as he turned a bit, making the XT look in his direction. He chuckled, "And I can see myself sitting there! Shit! This is fun!"

Fernando started doing the same to see himself from the XT's point of view as well. He could also see other objects placed within the machine's reach. There was a ball, a broom, and a coffee cup. Fernando looked down, watching as he gestured for the arm to go towards the ball. He tried several times to pick it up, but realized he couldn't. Discovering this, he tried to pick up the ball with both appendages. The large, semi-soft beach ball could be lifted with both robotic arms working in unison.

"Hey Rafferty, there is stuff on the floor that we can pick up with the robot arms. Try that," he suggested.

"Alright. You're working on the ball, so… I will pick up the broom. Ah, heck, I picked it up wrong. I have the bristles sticking up."

"Yeah, well, I got the ball fine," Fernando chuckled. He moved the robot arms in a gesture to throw the ball at Rafferty's XT. "Heads up!"

"Hey?!" cried Rafferty as he instinctively used the broom to block the incoming ball. He successfully deflected the beach ball and started laughing. "I blocked the ball!! Throw another one!"

"I can't. I only had one ball to play with, and it is now out of reach," replied Fernando, looking around with the XT.

"Try the cup," suggested Janet. "To pick up…. not throw."

Fernando paused to turn and find Janet standing and watching.

"Alright, I'll try picking up the coffee mug," replied Fernando, focusing on the much smaller item in front of him while Rafferty was using the broom to move the beach ball placed in front of him closer to Fernando's reach. "Watch it, you nearly knocked over my cup."

"I was just trying to send another ball over to you," replied Rafferty.

"Hey, Rafferty, try picking up the cup. Let's see if you can do it," Janet said as she found her enthusiasm for the devices. The more she watched, the more she wanted her turn.

"Sure thing," replied Rafferty as he let the broom fall away from the cup and turned his focus upon the fragile-looking item. He started to wonder how much pressure he could use safely to lift the object.

"I have it," said Fernando, holding his cup up by the handle loop.

"Fernando, the liquid would have spilled out of it if you held it that way," commented Raven.

"Guys, I can do it," Rafferty asserted as he grasped the cup with the robot hand appendages, but he held it too tightly. The cup broke under the pressure. "Aw, shit. I'm sorry."

The others laughed a bit and speculated on how they could do better as Fernando and Rafferty removed their headsets and let two others take their place.

"Captain, I'm sorry about breaking the cup. You can dock my pay if you need to," said Rafferty apologetically.

Captain Justice shook his head and went to a box and pulled out another cup that looked just like the one Rafferty broke. He then placed all the objects back where they had been for the next set to train with. Captain Justice made sure that Janet and Raven were situated before he returned to the computer, where Dr. Hanni was already monitoring the laptop. Streaming videos and data were being collected from the machines and designated into performance files for each team member. Dr. Hanni looked up at Justice as if to ask if he should start the next simulation. The captain nodded.

"What is the point of this? This is factory work. You don't need someone like me to be part of this," Dr Hanni questioned the captain.

"Actually, we do. Just try to be patient. I am missing my assistant. She would ensure everything went smoothly, and I'm trying to make sure a rather diverse group of people gets an introduction to what the Cyberhawk program is all about. I need you to be a part of this," replied the captain.

"But all of this seems juvenile...and a waste of time," replied the doctor.

"Okay, ... imagine if those robots over there need to be controlled by a skilled engineer in a location that is too dangerous for the engineer to go. Or... perhaps a machine far more delicate and sophisticated in a location where a highly skilled doctor like yourself is needed for an emergency operation, but you can't get there. You could put on the VR gear and control a sophisticated robot and save someone's life far, far away," Captain Justice countered.

Dr. Hanni paused for a moment in contemplation. The man looked around at the people present in the room. They were primarily people who risked their lives every day in their former occupations.

"Alright. I see potential there. I can be somewhat …. restless and impatient. I will amend that …….as long as I see… more that has that level of potential. How far away are we from that kind of work? Months? Years?" questioned the doctor.

"We are closer than you think. I need everyone to be prepared for what it means to be part of Cyberhawk. We will be the premier emergency services team for this whole state, and what we do here will lay down the foundation for other groups like us across the country," replied the captain, expressing his hope for a better future. "Perhaps someday……….the entire world."

****

Two women stood together waiting to go through the security ticket door to attend the rifle and outdoor sporting event. The older woman had her dark hair neatly pulled back into a ponytail with a camouflage ball cap stylishly placed upon her head. She wore a matching, lightweight outdoor jacket with pockets, simple, green-colored trousers, and sturdy, clean hiking boots. The younger woman was similarly dressed, but she did not exude the same confidence as the older woman. Once past the ticket gate and through the event hall doorway, the vast and almost overwhelming room with high ceilings assailed their senses. So many sights and sounds to comprehend.

"How do we do this, Vanna?" the younger woman asked. The room was full of echoes and the sounds of many people talking and moving around.

"Just follow me and listen and learn," said the older woman.

The younger woman silently nodded in obedience.

They started walking through the stalls and displays of outdoorsman-style clothing, where sellers offered knives for all purposes, book vendors provided manuals on building the perfect log cabin and cooking over an open fire while camping, and another booth sold rifles and ammunition. The tent display was a plethora of happy colors amidst the more somber, camo-style themed booths. Along the sides of the event room were camping trailers of all kinds that attendees could explore and dream about their ideal camping trip. The older woman paused for a moment as if gathering her bearings. She then walked over to a large table display where the vendor was selling a variety of items suitable for campers or hunters. She started to browse the table with the younger woman keeping close. She eased her way up next to a man who was asking the seller a question about a particular type of pocketknife and asked which kind would make a good gift for a child who had now become a teenager. The man wanted the knife to be useful but not necessarily easily construed as a weapon. He wanted the child to be prepared if an emergency were to happen.

Vanna, the older woman, listened carefully to the man next to her while continuing to look at a personal set of camping utensils that came in a neat little box. *The man was full of fear and uncertainty.... the man had learned these worrisome habits from his family......he feared that people he did not understand would take his livelihood......he fears strangers would corrupt his children into becoming bad people.... he does not want to be guilty of neglecting them...he wants them to be safe and happy.......* The man waited patiently while the vendor retrieved an item to show.

"It is so nice in this day and age to hear of a father caring so much for his children," Vanna said to the man.

"Yeah. I love my family very much," replied the man, seeming a little surprised by her suddenly talking to him.

"I truly admire a man who dedicates his life and very being to do what is right," she said and paused for a moment. "I lost my dear son....to those who did not believe in doing the right thing.... people that were influenced by non-American ideals...... I miss him so much. He was such a good boy. He had wanted to serve in the military... had he survived," said Vanna.

The man turned to her and said, "I am very sorry to hear that. I have a son, too, who is just becoming a teenager. I worry about him. The world seems crazy now."

"It does indeed. I hope your son survives and becomes a great man," replied Vanna. "What are you doing to help?"

"What do you mean?" he asked.

"Oh, there are lots of ways to help. Some pray… while others join charity groups to assist those in need. Strong individuals with great conviction join groups like the Action Men, who work to protect the American way of life," said Vanna.

The man nodded as if taking in her words.

"You know, that gives me something to think about. I may not be doing enough," he replied to her.

At this point, the vendor returned with the pocketknife set that the man had asked about. Vanna gently moved away with the younger woman following, listening, and learning.

CHAPTER 3

It was midday when Chris Takahashi came strolling into the Cyberhawk base with a big grin on his face. He found the group on a break and having lunch. Chris selected a portion of a sub sandwich and settled down with the others who were chatting about robot VR exercises. Chris was feeling pretty good after having a chance to look over the two planes and the helicopter, not to mention being taken up for flights in each. He was extremely pleased about landing his position on this team. He had no doubts. He liked the people he would be working with, which was also a big bonus.

Chris sat down next to Fernando at the large dining table, which was not too far from the kitchen.

"So, the mechanic here is a pilot; he doesn't just fix things, he also knows how to fly and can test the craft that he repairs and modifies. The guy is brilliant," said Chris, putting his plate and drink down.

"What was the guy's name…Chester?" Fernando asked before taking another bite of his sub sandwich.

"No, Roy Ekstrand. Chester is the robot cat. You will eventually meet both of them. Roy also knows how to repair all the land vehicles. He's brilliant. And really tall like some big Viking dude out of a movie," replied Chris. "He could take Chris Hemsworth's place in the Marvel movies."

"Really? Is he that good-looking? I wonder if he can fix my car…stupid thing acts like it has a poltergeist in it…." grumbled Sandra as she toyed with the remaining portion of her lunch.

Rafferty watched her show a profound lack of interest in her meal.

"Hey Sandra, …...this is good grub, don't ya think? If you don't want to finish that side salad, I will," offered Rafferty.

Sandra sighed. She refocused her thoughts.

"The food is good. I am just grumbling about my own problems. Thinking about my kids, my new mortgage, and the old car…" replied Sandra. "I am just being a grumpy old cop."

"I don't think you're old," remarked Rafferty, trying to win over the worried woman. "Perhaps five years older than me?"

"Seriously, guys? No one is curious about the robot cat?" Fernando wondered aloud, listening to the conversation going on around him.

Sandra shook her head and said, "A little more than that."

Chris finished his mouthful of food as he listened.

"Sandra, are you worried about stuff here? I think this place is great. All the cool toys we get to play with, and nothing is cheap or duct-taped together. It's nice to be asked to be a part of a top-notch company. I don't think this is going to fall apart," said Chris. "It feels like the real deal."

Rafferty nodded in agreement with Chris and then looked at Sandra.

"I am assuming you are getting good pay too, right?" Rafferty whispered across the table to Sandra as he glanced quickly at the captain, who was busy in a conversation with Dr. Hanni. "I know we aren't supposed to talk about that stuff, but you're getting full benefits, right?"

"Yes, actually…. for once, I am getting paid with benefits that in the long run will get me out of debt," she replied. "I think I am just not used to something going right. I'm a detective. I look for stuff out of place. Bad stuff always seems to happen." She sighed. "I also miss having that special someone who understands me and works with me to get life tasks done. I miss that companionship."

"I get that," said Rafferty sympathetically.

Fernando turned to Chris and asked, "So, you got to fly one of the planes? What did you think?"

"It was great," replied Chris. "It's a modified Piper Cherokee 6…… and …...the modifications allow it to do a few more maneuvers than the normal one can. So, in case something odd happens, I can take action. It also has all the nighttime …IFR gear and some other impressive stuff. Excellent communication equipment that will interface with a heads-up display, which I was told everyone will receive at some point. We all have to be fitted for the glasses and helmets."

"Helmets?! What do we need helmets for?" Janet asked, overhearing that part of the conversation.

"We will need helmets for other gear that we will be training with later. First, everyone will be fitted with the HUD glasses. That will be tomorrow's agenda. And Chris, you will be training on the big plane tomorrow after you get fitted," answered Captain Justice.

"Great! I haven't had much of a chance to fly a twin turboprop aircraft. Soooo...... I am excited about that. It has also been modified for the Cyberhawk program. At least that is what Roy told me. He's a pretty good pilot, too," commented Chris, revealing his feelings of exuberance.

"Seems like all the equipment here has been modified in some manner. I wonder why? Captain, why is everything customized?" asked the former Mountie.

"Because we are branding an elite team of emergency services experts, and our employers want us to have the best. They want you to have confidence in the equipment you are using. Each of us has risked our lives in some form or another...and perhaps paid a price for it," replied the captain.

Everyone at the table seemed to take this comment with a particular poignancy that resonated deeply within them. The powerful moment was interrupted by Roy Ekstrand, who had just arrived, escorting the four additional team members. The captain immediately got up to shake everyone's hand and introduce himself. Roy gave the captain a nod and then headed back out the door with a large, robotic black-and-white house cat. ·

"Glad to see that the rest of you have been able to arrive. I am Captain Robert Justice, and these folks sitting at the table are the other members of the Cyberhawk Emergency Services Team. I want to introduce Rafferty Lewis, Janet Hallmann, Fernando Sanchez, Sandra Ridgestone, Chris Takahashi, Raven Smith, and Dr. August Hanni," said the captain as each individual made a friendly gesture of acknowledgement when mentioned. "Come take a seat at the table. Have you all already eaten?"

The new group of four all made gestures and said that they had already had lunch and were fine. The captain sat down and encouraged the others to do the same.

"Do you have coffee? I would love a cup of coffee," said the handsome young man with chiseled features in his mid-twenties. It was clear that Daryl Crane took good care of his body and worked out regularly.

"Certainly. Go ahead and…," said the captain as Sandra got up and headed for the kitchen area.

"I'll get it for him," said Sandra as Daryl followed her.

"Thanks. But you don't have to serve me. I can do it," said Daryl.

"Hey, I can smell a fellow cop a mile away. We live on this stuff down where I come from," replied Sandra as she handed him the full cup of dark brown liquid.

"Us too," replied Daryl with a grin as he smelled the rich aroma of the dark coffee.

"You are Daryl Crane, the officer who was given that big award last year," she said.

"Uh, yes. You must be a detective, or you have a really good memory," Daryl said, looking a little embarrassed.

"Yes, I was a detective back in my old department. But I saw you at the awards ceremony. You made quite an impression on everyone present. Good to see a brother police officer here. Most of these guys are firemen. Nothing wrong with that, but they have a different mindset," Sandra commented to Daryl.

"Agreed."

Captain Justice noticed that the two had not come back and requested, "Come on back over to the table. I want our new additions to introduce themselves."

"Of course. I'm Daryl Crane, and just like Sandra," Daryl paused and looked at her, and then continued. "I was a police officer before I accepted this assignment. My specialty was serving on the Port of Seattle SWAT team. I had been injured in the line of duty and have been lucky enough to get amazing medical care. I want to be part of something big, not large like a big company, but big… as in something meaningful. Cyberhawk seemed like it was the pathway to that goal."

The new dark-haired man with tan skin, who appeared to have Mexican heritage, took notice of this and stood up to introduce himself.

"Well, I am also an officer of the law. I am Alejandro Luis Morales. My family and I have moved here from Mexico. It's all about family, you know. That's why I am here," added Alejandro, revealing his thick south-of-the-border accent.

The woman with the long black hair and coffee-colored skin gave a mirthless chuckle and said in her strong British accent, "Well, I am far from being a police officer. My name is Diana Aanya Thomas. I am an expert in logistics, and I was recruited to serve as Captain Robert Justice's logistics assistant. I make sure that things run smoothly. If something needs to be done, tended to, supplies ordered, groups coordinated...... I take care of those things."

"Nice accent," commented Rafferty.

"And boy, have I needed you these last couple of days. So glad to have you here now," the captain said warmly.

This left the young woman in her mid-twenties with wavy, sandy blonde hair, dressed in feminine-oriented attire of pinks and aqua, to step forward and speak about herself.

"And so, I guess that leaves me," she smiled sweetly. "I am Ellena Schmidt, and some people call me the Mermaid because I love everything that has to do with water. I am a professional scuba diver and.... I even wanted to be part of the Navy SEALs, but there were a few tests that I couldn't pass. However, I was accepted into the Coast Guard. Which I just loved. I loved being out on the patrol boats, helping people, and protecting our country's wildlife and borders. I hope to be a valuable asset to Cyberhawk. I also got my undergraduate degree in Marine Biology from OSU... go Beavers!"

****

Later that evening, all the team members who were staying on base had just finished up their dinner and were cleaning up. A total of eight people needed to learn how to get along with each other in their new home. The evening meal together was a good start on that process.

"Thank you, Fraulein Schmidt," said Dr. Hanni as he got up from the table and walked over to the sink to clean off and put away his plate and utensils. "That was a wonderful meal. Have you always been such a good cook?"

"No, not until I got into the Coast Guard, and... my specialty is seafood. So, you probably should not ask me to make any desserts or... food that doesn't involve seafood," Ellena replied cheerfully.

"Oh, okay," Dr. Hanni replied. "Well, that was very nice. I'm a fairly skilled baker, and I'll see if I have time to pitch in and help with preparing some of our meals. I understand the premise of adhering to the required ingredients, followed by the correct temperatures or heating processes. I make excellent quiche and several kinds of bread. I discovered that baking was a stress reliever for me."

"Hmm. Homemade bread. That sounds yummy," commented Ellena.

"I will second that! However, my strong point is eating, although… I am pretty good at barbeque. Give me an open fire, a good cut of meat, some herbs to season with, and I can make it," Rafferty added, overhearing Dr. Hanni and Ellena.

Janet gave Rafferty a big smile and patted him on the arm, and then turned to Ellena.

"That was a great meal, Ellena. Thank you. I guess everyone here will have to help with the cooking. Maybe we can all sit down and share what we like to cook and see if that fits in with everyone's needs," suggested Janet as she turned to Rafferty. "And I also like barbeque…and eating."

Rafferty laughed.

"Thinking about a schedule… well, we are all grown-ups and can make our own breakfast, so no one has to get up early. The kitchen is well stocked. Perhaps we can take turns with evening meals," said Dr. Hanni.

"I like that idea," said Janet as everyone moved towards the kitchen area to clean.

"Although I do make a mean breakfast of scrambled eggs and bacon," said Rafferty. "I don't mind getting up a little early to treat my pals once in a while."

"I am not much of a cook. You would not want to eat anything made by me, but I could help someone else," offered Raven.

"Yeah, I am right there with you. I don't cook either. I'm well known for making bad coffee and burning water," added Daryl.

"Me too," Raven shook his head and then nodded to Daryl. "So, you said you got hurt in the line of duty. What happened?"

"I got caught in a crossfire. We didn't have enough intel to realize that our hostage situation was a bit more than that. We walked into a gang war shootout, and I suspect that we were called to cause chaos and buy time for someone to get out of the way with a lot of illegal merchandise. I got hit multiple times, and it screwed up my back," answered Daryl.

"You look fine. Where did you get hurt?" asked Dr. Hanni.

"Actually, he looks amazing," Ellena whispered to Janet.

"I was hit in the spinal column several times. I had excellent medical treatment. I would be paralyzed if it were not for them," replied Daryl.

"Hey, that's funny, I had somethin' like that happen to me as a kid. I fell off a horse, and my parents got talked into having some experimental treatment done to my back. I would have been crippled if they had not agreed to it. I used to visit the doc every year since I was the youngest person ever to receive that treatment," said Rafferty, holding his bottle of beer up as if he were about to toast someone. "They told me that they learned a whole bunch from my injury and healing process, which helped other folks."

"That is fascinating. Do you recall the organization's name? Perhaps I have heard of them," said Dr. Hanni, taking a serious interest in the conversation.

"Strangely enough, the group that helped me was called Cyberhawk Research and Development. That was one of the reasons why I applied for this job. Made me think of those who helped me when I was a kid," replied Rafferty. Everyone stopped what they were doing, and they all stared at Rafferty. Rafferty noticed the silence. "Did I say something odd? Y'all are lookin' at me."

"Cyberhawk Research and Development…. I know of that company," said Dr. Hanni.

"So do I," said Janet.

"Me too," added Ellena.

"Yes," said Daryl.

"What are the odds?" asked Chris.

"This is crazy shit. We… *all* have heard of Cyberhawk Research and Development?!? I thought it was a little-known company that did… stuff…quietly," Fernando speculated.

"That was my impression of them, too. So, Dr. Hanni, why do you know about them? Did you work for them?" asked Raven.

Doctor Hanni let out a mirthless laugh.

"No. I had a heart attack at age twenty while at a medical conference, and some of their people were present. I was dying, and their technology saved my life," answered Dr. Hanni.

"Wow, they saved my life as well. I was in a bad plane crash," said Chris.

"My situation was not as life-threatening, but I would have lost my ability to hear," added Ellena.

"And I would have lost my ability to walk and my lower right arm if I had not had the opportunity to work with them. This can't be a coincidence, right?" wondered Raven.

"Wow, just like Anakin Skywalker...," said Chris.

"Yeah...uh... but I didn't turn into a Sith. And didn't he lose both arms?" replied Raven.

"Well, he lost his other natural arm after that epic fight with Obi-Wan," conceded Chris.

Shaking his head in disbelief, Dr. Hanni turned to the others and said, "This is extraordinary. We are all tied to Cyberhawk in some fashion. We will need to ask the others if they benefited from Cyberhawk Research and Development at some point in their lives. This is no coincidence."

"I agree," said Janet.

"But then....my next question would be.... why? Why are we all here now?" asked Rafferty.

CHAPTER 4

After a few days, the Cyberhawk team was coming together, and everyone was settling into their new positions and slowly building relationships. Part of the group was assembled in the Cyberhawk hangar bay and was preparing for a few drills on how to board and disembark the plane quickly with gear. Captain Justice stood with Diana Thomas, who held an Android tablet and added information to the computer system as needed. She was organizing Captain Justice's schedule to make the most efficient use of his time. Daryl, Ellena, and Alejandro had gone to bring the equipment in for the training exercise. While waiting for the equipment to be brought in, Chris, Fernando, and Roy discussed the attributes of the smaller plane and the complexities of balancing the load correctly for successful flights. The remaining team members stood patiently.

"Alright, what is this about everyone being somehow linked to Cyberhawk Research and Development?" Sandra asked the group that was waiting.

"Well, Detective Ridgestone, you are the last one that we have not spoken with… besides Captain Justice," replied Dr. Hanni.

"What?! You mean everyone else has been asked except me?" Sandra asked, a bit exasperated.

"Well, you did need to leave the other day before we could talk with you," the man replied, his European accent making it sound perfectly civil and acceptable.

She sighed in acknowledgement.

"I have children and... sometimes a parent cannot let them wait. So, what's the deal?" Sandra asked, adjusting her sunglasses, which she always wore.

"We just wanna know if you had any special connection to a company called Cyberhawk Research and Development. So far, we all have some interesting stories," said Rafferty in a lowered voice.

The former detective shook her head, making her long ponytail wave back and forth a little.

"I'm not sure I should be talking about any of this," replied Sandra.

"Are those prescription sunglasses? You wear them a lot," commented Dr. Hanni.

"Personally, I think you look nice in them. Gives you a kinda cool and mysterious look," added Rafferty, standing with his hands jammed into his jeans pockets.

Dr. Hanni turned to give Rafferty an incredulous look.

"She is hiding the fact that her eyes are two different colors. A rare anomaly, but it does happen to Humans," remarked Dr. Hanni.

Sandra had her arms folded across her chest and made a face.

"Except that my left eye is artificial. The color is different from the right eye and…. I get tired of people asking about it. So, I wear sunglasses a lot," replied Sandra. "It was an emergency repair…. and I never got around to requesting a different color. The idea of having my eye operated on is…icky."

"Well, I have a feeling that we all understand. You don't have to worry about us asking too many questions and not understanding," replied Dr. Hanni.

"Well, I just explained it to you. And yes, it was Cyberhawk Research and Development that did the implant…amongst other things…..," she replied in a hushed tone.

"That means all of us have had work done by them. We should chat with Captain Justice. There's somethin' going on here," said Rafferty. "And I don't like keeping secrets from the person whom I am supposed to trust in the leadership role."

"Agreed," said the Swiss native.

"And I was worried that working here might be too low-key and boring," remarked Sandra, rolling her eyes.

"Why don't we plan to talk about it with everyone present? That way, no one feels left out, and if there is a problem, we can deal with it. Personally, I like Captain Justice, and I think he would prefer us to be open with him about what we have discovered," Janet added.

"Well, he is the person in charge of the team, so that makes sense. Let's do this," agreed Sandra.

Just then, Daryl, Ellena, and Alejandro pulled in some robotic-looking equipment on industrial-looking carts. The devices looked like a cross between Mandalorians, Transformers, and Iron Man. The two devices had some similarities to the static XT devices that they had practiced with when they first arrived. Captain Justice smiled broadly when they brought them into the hangar bay. The entire team seemed impressed and fascinated by the new equipment, looking hopefully at the captain for an explanation.

"This device is called an XO, at least for the time being, and it is one of Cyberhawk's foundational pieces of technology. Everyone on the team will learn how to use it, but some will receive more training on it than others. This is one of our premier pieces of rescue equipment. For example, Diana will not need to use this piece of equipment regularly; however, it is essential that she understands how it functions and why other team members will need to use it. Chris will also need to learn how to use it, but his primary function in the team will be to use his piloting skills for aircraft and drones. Ellena will also need to learn how the XO works, but her focus will be on a different piece of equipment that complements her strong points and understanding of how to interact with water. This team is not about rivalries, but everyone excelling at what they are best at," said the captain proudly.

Dr Hanni's body language and facial expressions caught the captain's attention.

"Yes, Dr. Hanni, you will need to learn how to use it, but your focus will not be on this piece of equipment," remarked the captain, having learned to notice when the doctor looked uncomfortable.

"Uh, I understand and appreciate that, Captain. But that is not what I want to bring up," the shorter man who was older than most of the team said, looking at everyone. Several of the others nodded to him, which the captain noticed right away.

"Okay, what is going on?" asked the captain.

"We all would like to know how Cyberhawk Research and Development fits in with this team. We have discovered that each one of us has had some relationship with that company... and well, it can't be a coincidence that this team is referred to as Cyberhawk," said Dr. Hanni.

Captain Justice was surprised and found himself at a loss for words.

"Hey, Captain, have you been helped by Cyberhawk Research and Development?" asked Fernando.

Everyone was now wholly focused on Robert Justice, including Roy, who kept quiet and waited to see how things would unfold. The captain nodded and then pulled out his phone, starting to tap on it. As he waited for a response, he looked at everyone, knowing that this was a pivotal moment in trust. He took a breath to calm his surprised feelings.

"Okay, ...this was not the topic I was expecting to discuss right at this moment," he paused, collecting his thoughts. "I am required to get permission to discuss this topic openly. And I am waiting for a response from the person who can grant me that authorization."

A few moments later, an older man entered the hangar bay. He purposefully strode towards the group. He was dressed like a regular person that you might run into anywhere. He wore a neat button-up shirt, dressy cargo slacks, and sturdy but nice sports shoes. The man made casual clothing look almost military sharp. It was evident that the captain knew the man.

"Mr. Knight, you didn't have to come," said Robert Justice.

"Yes, I did. You have assembled a smart group of people here. And smart people figure things out. Hello, Cyberhawk team," Mr. Knight addressed the assembled group.

"Everyone, this is Mr. Lukas Knight. He is one of the founders of the Cyberhawk program. He has dedicated a lot of his time, money, and creativity to making this project a reality." Captain Justice introduced the man, who appeared to be in excellent health, despite being significantly older than the rest of the team. He had light grey hair and eyes that twinkled with tenacity.

"So, you have all discovered that you have something in common. Captain Justice also shares that with you all, but we had asked him not to discuss it. Some people are very uncomfortable talking about injuries or illnesses. Some people are afraid that if others know they are different, they will not be accepted. That issue of concern has surfaced with those of us who put the

Cyberhawk program together. Some religious groups might find you unnatural. However, what is unnatural is not caring enough about another person to ensure they are allowed to receive the help they need. And sometimes that requires technology," he paused for a moment and started to roll up his right sleeve. As he did this, it began to reveal an obvious mechanical lower arm.

"I was the second person to have an artificial arm like this installed. The first one was a military veteran who lost his limbs serving our country. He volunteered for the process in the hope of gaining more control over his life and helping the researchers learn how to make replacements a reality. He wanted to help so that others would not have to suffer. I was the first lucky one that benefited from his bravery," Knight continued to explain.

"So was I," chimed in Raven, patting his artificial arm, which had a natural skin-like covering that hid the mechanical attributes inside. No one would have realized it was an artificial limb.

"May I look at your arm more closely?" Ellena asked Knight. "I didn't know they could fix limbs, too." Knight gestured for her to have a closer inspection. He was used to having his arm be an oddity to marvel at. Ellena came over to see how Knight's fingers and wrist work, just like a regular person's. "That is amazing!"

After a few minutes of wonder and awe by team members, with Roy just hanging back as if this was like having a coffee at

Starbucks, the revelation started to sink in as to what kind of company they had all joined to work with.

"Now you all can see why it is important to start having this level of technology available for the emergency services teams around the country. Perhaps accidents can be prevented, or injuries made less severe by having the right kind of equipment available," said the captain.

"You don't have to convince us. We are all on board with the whole concept of safety and cool tech that makes life better," replied Fernando.

"I am just glad that I got the chance to work on something like this. So, what does this thing do?" asked Raven as he strode up to the XO to inspect it more closely.

"It is a powered exoskeleton that will enhance strength while protecting the user from physical strain. It is ideal for heavy lifting tasks, and in emergencies, can assist the user to lift up to five hundred pounds," answered Captain Justice.

"Holy cow!! How many times have y'all wished you could lift somethin' heavy to extract some poor soul from burning wreckage?! I think I will love this machine. When do we get started?" asked Rafferty.

"Get in line, pal. I want to be the first to try," said Fernando with a gleam in his eye.

The captain just smiled. He knew that a team already excited about the equipment would be even more excited about using it to save lives. Dr. Hanni eyed the mechanical monstrosity.

"Are we just going to shelve the other topic?" asked the doctor.

"Don't worry, Dr. Hanni. We shall make time to have a serious discussion about the connection between all the team members. The captain just really wanted to get started on introducing the team to the technology and the goals behind it," Knight addressed the doctor's concerns.

Dr. Hanni sighed a little and took a second look at the XO with an appraising look and said, "I have only seen the passive exoskeletons in use. This looks very industrial. Does this one have connectivity?"

"Yes. And it will adjust its movements to the individual using it," replied Knight.

"This XO is just the tip of the iceberg of the tech that we want to train the team on. Someone like you can help ensure our team members are safe. Perhaps you can suggest some innovations that will make it better," the captain added.

"I would just feel better if we discussed all of us being connected through Cyberhawk Research and Development. And I think others would agree...... once.... they get through being excited about the big toys," remarked Dr. Hanni.

Lukas Knight nodded and turned to the captain and said, "He's right. Let's plan for a formal discussion tomorrow. And I will be here with a few others."

"As you wish, Mr. Knight," the captain turned to Diana. "We need to modify tomorrow's schedule for Mr. Knight and company to make a presentation and discussion with the team about Cyberhawk Research and Development."

Diana held her tablet and started tapping on things, and asked, "Is this an all-day event?"

The captain turned and looked at Lukas Knight.

"Yes, we should schedule for the full day. This requires conversations with team members that may take more than just a briefing. Some of these individuals have experienced extreme, life-changing events as a result of Cyberhawk's involvement. I don't want anyone to feel pushed aside due to time constraints," replied Knight.

"Alright....Diana, please arrange a catered meal with delivery for everyone as well. I don't want anyone to feel they have to prepare food while others are discussing important matters. Make sure we have enough for Mr. Knight and the experts he plans to bring," requested the captain.

"Do you know how many?" asked Diana, making notes on her tablet.

Captain Justice turned and looked at Lukas Knight. Knight just sorta smiled and shrugged.

"This is the LabCoat Crew... they are always present, but some of their projects require timely interaction. I will bring as many of them as possible. The Emergency Services Team needs to meet them all anyway," replied the older man.

"Sounds good. Then I guess I can count on seeing you tomorrow... bright and early?" asked the captain.

"Bright and early," replied Knight as he headed out the door.

The rest of the day was spent taking turns learning how to use the XO devices and loading the different aircraft with the necessary gear for emergency response missions. Roy took over instruction on the various aircraft, emphasizing that Chris should memorize all the details and later have authority over aircraft procedures when the team was required to use them for missions. The team members were given basic knowledge of emergency procedures in case they needed to fill in for another team member who may be incapacitated. By the end of the day, everyone was exhausted from loading and unloading the aircraft several times. Roy enjoyed putting them through their paces to see how they handled the stress of needing to perform quickly and correctly. Captain Justice also participated in these drills and worked alongside those he commanded. By the end of the day, the team members were glad to go to bed and get some rest, but none of them forgot that each one had something in common from their past.

No one was late the next morning.

Lukas Knight arrived at the Cyberhawk airbase along with his assistant, Trevor Howard, who was the sharpest-dressed man that any of them had ever met. He looked like he had just stepped off a fashion show runway. The CEO of Cyberhawk also brought three others with him, one of whom did not look happy about being there.

"These three individuals here are members of what we affectionately call the LabCoat Crew. This is Kendra Boisen, an accomplished engineer who works intimately with the robotics aspects of our work. This is Dr. Idunna Eirstone, who is an expert in neurology, chiropractic, and herbal medicine. And this irritable-looking man is Dr. Elgin Cross, the team leader of the LabCoat Crew. He is an excellent engineer, an expert in computer science, and a physicist."

The irritable-looking man ignored Lukas Knight's friendly jab. Dr. Elgin Cross appeared to be about fifty-five years old, with short, dark hair, pale skin, a neat goatee, and a mustache. He wore a lab coat, but what caught everyone's attention was the high-tech glasses he wore and the agitated state he seemed to be in. Then there was Dr. Idunna Eirstone, whose confidence and demeanor made her seem to be older, but her age was unfathomable. Her skin was very pale, her eyes were a lavender shade, and she had bright green hair. In contrast to her peers was Kendra Boisen, who was short, blonde, and a little plump with an infectious, cheerful attitude. Everyone could tell that she would be the most approachable.

Dr Hanni eyed Dr. Elgin Cross, feeling that he had seen or met the man before.

"We know each other from somewhere," Dr. Hanni declared as he walked up to Elgin Cross.

Elgin Cross twisted his mouth a little and then replied slowly, "You are... the heart repair... about twenty years ago."

"Yes, that would be me. I was at the conference in Seattle, Washington. I became very ill and passed out. When I woke up, I was in an extraordinary state, and I had been told that I had been operated on by an experimental team of scientists and doctors who had saved my life with a new technology. I was informed that I would need to be monitored for a period of time because I was the first person to receive such a device. The procedure was done in a mobile lab belonging to Cyberhawk Research and Development, and then I was transferred to a traditional hospital setting. That is where I recovered. But I remember you... you have not changed much," replied Dr. Hanni.

"Yes, well, one does not mess with perfection," Dr. Elgin Cross replied.

Kendra Boisen overheard the conversation between Dr. Hanni and Dr. Cross. She stepped in cheerfully and said, "Dr. August Hanni! I have read so many wonderful things about your work. You were at the top of our list of hopeful medical doctors to join our Cyberhawk Emergency Services Team. We need someone with your background and experience. This is Dr. Eirstone. She is a specialist in neurology to assist with complications involved with certain aspects of our technology, such as delicate operations to tie cybernetic equipment in with the Human nervous system."

Kendra deftly pulled Dr. Eirstone over to speak with Dr. Hanni as Elgin Cross made his way elsewhere.

"I read about your recent work with the victims in that earthquake in Temuco, Chile. The devastation was profound, and the team of doctors that you worked with did amazing work on the injured," said Dr. Eirstone. "You have impressive skills."

"It was very gratifying to take the skills I have to assist people in need. There are so many doctors these days who forget that the true calling of medicine is not the golf course," replied Dr. Hanni. "So, how will I be able to continue to help others in this setting?"

Kendra smiled, seeing that Dr. Hanni and Dr. Eirstone seemed to find some common ground and headed for Dr. Elgin Cross.

"Why are you being such a jerk? We need these people to be part of the Emergency Services Team, and Dr. Hanni is a crucial part of that team. We all need to be able to work closely with him. He will ultimately be the one to test the remote surgery equipment. Stop making unnecessary enemies," chided the young woman.

Elgin Cross just twisted his mouth and rolled his eyes a bit and then replied, "I hate doing this PR stuff. I should be back in the lab working on my calculations."

"Miss Boisen is correct," said Lukas Knight, coming up from behind them as he made his way across the room to speak with Raven Smith and Rafferty Lewis. "Go chat with Robert Justice and the young pilot," Knight suggested to Cross.

Elgin Cross made a face, folded his arms, and then turned to look for where Justice was in the room. He was standing next to a young man of Japanese descent, discussing something that Elgin presumed would be mundane.

As Dr. Cross neared the captain, he could hear the man speaking.

"So, after the fire and the fact that those bones were crushed, the doctors brought in several people from Cyberhawk Research and Development and proposed the idea of cybernetic repair that would replace the crushed bones. I would not be able to walk if they had not done that for me. That was nine years ago," said Captain Justice. "And the recovery period was remarkably short compared to traditional medicine."

"My surgery was seven years ago, and it basically …saved my life. My parents made the decision. I think they were initially concerned that I would be unhappy about having artificial parts, but I love technology, and the fact that something like this can save a life is phenomenal. The surgery they did for me…. I am so grateful that it was done. Now, I can be here working with all of you, flying planes, and doing the stuff I love," replied Chris.

Captain Justice nodded to Chris and turned to Elgin Cross, who had come over.

"Chris, this is Dr. Elgin Cross, who most likely oversaw both of our surgical repair processes. Dr. Cross, how may I help you?" asked Captain Justice.

"Knight wants me to mingle. So, I am mingling and answering questions. Do you have any?" he asked.

"Actually, I do have a question," said Chris, pausing and looking at both men momentarily. "Where do you work? Is there some big office building that you are located in?"

"No. That would be Knight. We are tucked away in the hidden basement facility," replied Elgin Cross with a gleam in his eye. "Which is where I would like to be right now."

"A hidden basement facility?" both Chris and Robert Justice said together.

"Yes......would you like to see it?" asked Elgin Cross.

"Oh, hell yeah! Is it far?" asked Chris.

"Oh...perhaps sixty....... paces from here," replied Elgin Cross with a mischievous grin.

"What?!" exclaimed Robert Justice. "The lab...... You work out of ... is on this property? Where?!"

"The building behind your large hangar that looks like a small private hangar bay is a garage bay and secured entrance to the underground facility," replied Dr. Elgin Cross.

Robert Justice had to keep his reaction under control in front of his team. He felt a bit betrayed by not being told that such an important facility was so very close.

"Well, I am with Mr. Takahashi here and would like to see the hidden...facility," replied Captain Justice. "When would that be possible?"

"Oh, let me go ask Lukas Knight," said Elgin Cross with a grin, making a beeline for the man.

Takahashi and Justice followed along. Lukas Knight, seeing that Cross had two of the Emergency Services Team members in tow with a smirk on his face, caught his attention immediately.

Lukas Knight let out a sigh and asked, "What can I do for you, Dr. Cross?"

"Captain Justice and the young pilot want to see the Laboratory facility," replied Elgin Cross.

"It's a little early for that. We just started their training and introduction to the technology that they will be using," remarked Knight, feeling less than amused.

"Well, you asked me to mingle, and the question was about where I do all the wonderful things that I do. So, I answered the question," replied Elgin Cross.

Lukas Knight gave the eccentric scientist a stony gaze.

"Alright, but I want no complaints if any of your projects get delayed or damaged. No drama," replied the older man firmly. Lukas Knight then turned and looked at the room full of people and drew their attention, and announced, "Hey! Does everyone want to see where the LabCoat Crew does their amazing work?"

There was a resounding positive response to his upbeat question, resulting in everyone following his lead towards the unknown location hidden underground. As the team followed the three scientists through the secured doorways, Lukas Knight walked alongside Captain Justice.

"Within the next couple of weeks, you will be given a code to be able to access the underground facility when needed. Our original plan was to give you time to focus on getting your team members more comfortable with the technology. Your people's ability to realize and discover that they all had something special in common has changed the timeline a little... not to mention that Dr. Elgin Cross can be an irritating drama queen."

"I noticed that," replied the captain. "I am glad that he is not my problem."

Knight chuckled a little and said, "Yes, I wish I could say that. However, he does good work and is trustworthy. Just a bit of an asshole at times."

The entrance to the lab was located inside the secured garage bay, which housed approximately ten vehicles with room for twice as many. Some of these vehicles belonged to the LabCoat Crew. There were two types of access points: stairs and an elevator. Both required special security codes and cards to work. The group divided, with half taking the elevator and the other half taking the stairs, which led one level below. Kendra Boisen led the group downstairs.

"Nice place to park your car. You never have to come out of the office to a spooky parking lot with snow all over your car," commented Ellena as she glanced about, wondering if there was room in the elevator or if she should go down the stairs.

"It is a nice perk. No more wondering if creepers are lurking. I love being a part of the LabCoat Crew," said the engineer in her late twenties cheerfully. "My father always says I talk too much and am too animated. He's hardcore Danish, but I'm happy being my cheerful self. Does anyone else have opinionated parents?"

"Oh yes, my parents have lots of opinions about things," replied Chris Takahashi. "But they mean well. They are hardworking people."

Kendra smiled, "Nice to know that I have someone around who understands what it is like."

"For me," said Raven. "It's my grandparents. My parents understand that I want to see more of the world, but my grandparents are always saying, *'Raven, you should come back home. We need the young people to be here and continue our ways.'* I get that, but I want some time to learn more about the world around me. I think if I understand more about other people, then I can be a better asset to my tribal community."

"Family expectations can be a bronco ride. My uncle did not want to take up the family ranch, so it fell upon my dad to do so. Luckily, he seems to like it. My parents are pretty easy going about what I want to do," replied Rafferty as he and the rest of the group trotted noisily down the sturdy steel stairs.

"Just be glad you all have family to annoy you. My parents died four years ago in a car crash. I still find it hard at times to think I will never get to tell them about my studies or the training I was doing with the RCMP," remarked Janet Hallman as they all reached the secured door that Kendra passed her security device over.

"I'm sorry to hear that," said Rafferty, along with the others voicing similar feelings.

"It happens. We all know it from the jobs we do to help other people. People die. I just miss them sometimes," said Janet as Kendra opened the door, revealing a pristine and very busy-looking industrial lab.

The others from the elevator were already standing in awe of the facility's size and complexity. There were hallways that divided sections into private areas and other spaces designed for testing and fabrication.

"Dang! And they have all this... neatly hidden below the ground," remarked Rafferty.

"And it's all white and pristine like a Star Wars medbay," commented Chris, wide-eyed.

"That was done to encourage cleanliness along with bringing more light into an area that is light handicapped," replied Kendra.

"What happens if the power goes out?" asked Sandra as she took in her surroundings.

"That's what backup generators are for, along with some special paint that glows in the dark for twenty-four hours," replied Kendra.

"Most glow-in-the-dark paint only lasts for a short time," commented Sandra. "I know this because my son wanted glow in the dark paint to create the universe on his bedroom ceiling and walls…...and ……. much to his dismay, it did not last all night long."

"Oh, we have some special paint... that your uncle invented," said Kendra, turning to Rafferty.

"Uncle Benjamin?" said Rafferty.

"Yes, and as a matter of fact, he is here... somewhere. I am sure he would love to meet you all," said Kendra. "Let me go and find him. He's probably in the chemistry room or perhaps in his office."

Kendra dashed off.

"You have an uncle who works for Cyberhawk?" Sandra asked, turning to Rafferty.

"Yeah. He didn't want to be a rancher, and well, he is the reason why I got a second chance to be able to walk," replied Rafferty, stuffing his hands into his pockets.

"That makes sense," nodded Chris.

"Rafferty was the youngest person to receive cybernetic implants," remarked Dr. Eirstone.

"We don't normally test technology on children. Their growth process is very complicated to compensate for," added Dr. Elgin Cross. "We did amazing work with young Mr. Lewis."

Rafferty smiled and then pulled his hands out of his pockets.

"And look at me! I turned out just fine," said Rafferty.

"Except that you are a goofy cowboy guy," said Fernando, nudging his new friend.

"I don't wear the hat all the time," replied Rafferty. "Only when I go riding."

"But you do wear those rancher boots and…...it's the way you talk," replied Fernando. "You have the cowboy accent."

"Okay, Mr. Mexican ancestry that does not speak Spanish," retorted Rafferty, nudging him back.

"Hey, I am an American. Don't lay that grandparent's guilt trip on me…. 'Fernando, you need to learn your ancestors' language or else your cousins will think you are a gringo.' I am an American, and this is my home. But I do get that a lot. People assume I speak Spanish."

It was at this point that Alejandro Morales just eyed the other man and finally said, "I do speak both languages…Español fluently, and my English is getting better."

"Well, if this is a contest about who can speak multiple languages …I can speak Romansh, that is Swiss, German, French, Castilian Spanish, English, Italian, and some Latin," said Dr. Hanni proudly. "Anyone else?"

"No, I think you have most of us beaten. I was required to learn English and French," replied the Canadian-born Janet.

Before any further comments could be made, Kendra returned with Dr. Benjamin Lewis and Dalen Hughes.

"I want to introduce two other members of the LabCoat Crew. This is Dr. Benjamin Lewis, one of the founding members of the crew. He is an engineer and an expert in chemistry... he is also," Kendra paused as Dr. Lewis went to greet his nephew with a kind hug and pat on the back. "He is Rafferty Lewis's Uncle." She then turned to the short black man wearing a lab coat and said, "This is Dalen Hughes. He is a practical engineer, and his expertise focuses on airplanes, rockets, and cars; he is our main jetpack engineer. He and Dr. Lewis work closely together on the types of fuels needed for such projects."

Everyone gathered closer together to chat with the new people introduced, while Dr. Elgin Cross disappeared into one of the rooms down one of the hallways.

"I heard the word jetpack and, well, I knew you were the first person I had to say hello to," said Chris, extending his hand out to shake Dalen Hughes's.

"Uh, thank you," said Dalen. "I suppose you are probably the talented pilot hired to be a part of the Emergency Services Team."

"That would be me," said Chris, opening his arms in a gesture of 'here I am'.

"And the rest of us are excited about the idea of jetpacks, too," added Fernando with Raven, Rafferty, and Daryl Crane crowding around.

"Well, I am very pleased to hear that. There will be a point in the future when our latest version of the jetpack will be integrated into the Emergency Services Team. We will need brave, healthy individuals like yourselves to be willing to learn how to use these devices. I feel very strongly that the addition of a jetpack to your team is essential to making your jobs more successful," replied Dalen, feeling his enthusiasm swell as he realized that he had people who were also excited about the prospect of flying a jetpack.

Sandra Ridgestone joined the group surrounding Dalen Hughes and listened to what was being said.

"A jetpack. Like… a Mandalorian or …. Iron Man?" she asked. Her detective's doubt-filled side came through strongly in her tone.

Dalen turned to the slender, tall woman who wore sunglasses inside and replied, "Well, sorta. Those versions are more favorable and currently more steeped in fiction than science, but ideally, those are the desired type of outcome for our end product."

"Hmm, that's interesting. How do you see that being helpful for our team?" she asked as the guys all listened to her intently and then waited for Dalen's response.

"I have proposed to Mr. Knight that Emergency Services Team members could have an advantage with this additional resource. For example, may I assume that many of you are experienced firemen or perhaps police officers who have had to chase down criminals?" said Dalen, pausing to see affirmative reactions from those listening to him. Seeing their reactions, he continued, "A police officer with a jetpack could locate a criminal on the run quicker and without endangering the public with a vehicle pursuit situation. Additionally, when firefighters are dealing with large uncontrolled burns in areas that are difficult to maneuver through, scouting techniques to search for individuals in danger from the fire could be located quickly through aerial means, thus not wasting valuable time that may be required to rescue those in danger."

"Okay," nodded Sandra, thinking about what he said and how it could be advantageous. "So, I take it that these jetpacks come with gear that also helps to protect the wearer."

"Oh yes. That is an essential component of their design. We manufacture all our prototypes in-house and test them to meet a wide range of quality requirements. Have you had time to become proficient with the XO or CyberSkeleton?" asked Dalen, looking at Sandra and then the guys.

"No, we have only seen the device. We have been practicing with the stationary units to get used to the software," replied Daryl.

"Oh, I see. Well, I could show you around the lab, where we test and create the prototypes. Would you like that?" asked Dalen.

"Hell yeah," replied Rafferty.

"I love tech," answered Chris.

Hearing enough from those listening to him, Dalen Hughes led this part of the group back into the areas where a CNC machine was located and was currently working on cutting something out of a sheet of copper. Not far from it stood a group of 3D printers of various sizes and designs, some of which were actively building something. He pointed out another machine as a laser etcher, along with a row of computers that were all set to work with the devices in the room. The group saw other people whom they had not been introduced to, who were busy working on various projects. Dalen avoided bothering these individuals as they appeared to be very focused on what they were doing. They walked past a door to a large chemical laboratory, a testing laboratory, a clean room entrance, and another section that had offices and presentation spaces.

"There are some places where we should not enter unless it is absolutely necessary. Like the clean room. They build stuff in there that has stringent requirements," Dalen paused for a moment and then said, "Ah, but I do know of two locations that you might find more engaging, and you may even be asked to assist with some of the experimental processes."

"Like what?" asked Raven.

"The practical test room and the holography department room," answered Dalen with a smile. "Follow me."

Dalen led them all first to the practical test room, which was akin to a spacious warehouse with high ceilings and concrete floors. There was an assortment of heavy lifting equipment, ladders, and an enormous treadmill that resembled a training device for small dinosaurs.

"Whoa, what is the treadmill for? You don't have an Incredible Hulk hiding somewhere, do you?" asked Fernando.

Dalen chuckled, "Ah, no, we do not. That is for testing some of the equipment for speed, gait, agility, and endurance. It's also great for a quick stress workout when a project is driving you crazy, and you can't go outside for a brisk walk because it is raining."

"You could run a whole group of us on that or even a horse," added Rafferty, seizing up the device.

"Have you ever used it for RC plane takeoffs?" asked Chris.

"It's not very good for that. Several others tried that a while ago. It is better to take the plane outside and request airfield time," said Dalen.

Just then, Lukas Knight came in with the rest of the group.

"Dalen, I am about to take the rest of the team to see the Holographic Lab. Would you like to join us?" asked Knight.

"That would be perfect, Mr. Knight. There is only so much to show them here without anything being tested," replied Dalen, gesturing for his group to follow the others off to the Holographic Lab.

"You know I am hoping for Star Trek, but it's not gonna be that cool," Chris remarked to Fernando.

"You never know. I wasn't expecting to find so much tech being used for rescue operations. I figured that some good computers, sturdy vehicles, and advanced communications equipment would be used. I wasn't expecting to learn how to use an exoskeleton. Were you?" Fernando asked Chris.

"Well, no. I was hired to be a pilot," replied Chris with a grin. "And I am a good pilot. A very good pilot."

The group of visitors slowly filed into the Holographic Lab, a generously sized, dimly lit room with computer workstations and three tables positioned in the center of the space. One of the tables had a technician working with a holographic projection of the human body, and she was manipulating it in mid-air against the image itself.

"Let me introduce Renata Washington," said Lukas Knight, gesturing towards the tall, lean, dark-skinned woman with tightly curled hair that cascaded down her shoulders.

"Hello, Mr. Knight," she paused to look at everyone. She had a slight German accent, which caught Dr. Hanni's attention. "How may I assist you and your touring group?"

"These people are the members of the Cyberhawk Emergency Services Team. You will see them around the base since some are living on-site and working here. From time to time, some of them may require the assistance of the LabCoat Crew. They will also be available after training to help develop some of the new equipment," replied Knight.

"Very well. Glad to meet you all. This is the Holographic Lab. This table is designed for a project we have been working on, which displays three-dimensional objects. Our goal is to work with the objects and explore the various layers. This example is of the human body, and I can spin it around to see different angles and request that only certain layers be available," said Renata. "This is somewhat like an ArcInfo layering system for geological structures, but in this case, it is the human body."

The human image suddenly became just the pulmonary system, with the veins and heart being displayed. Captain Justice spotted Dr. Hanni smiling with appreciation. He took note of that for any future conversations he may have with the medical doctor. It was good to see the man getting excited about some of the technology that would be available to him and the other team members.

"This is like Iron Man," Raven remarked quietly to Chris and Fernando. Both nodded in agreement.

"This table over here," said Renata, walking away from the first one to another. "It's for a communication project." She turned to Kendra, who nodded and instantly knew what Renata wanted. Kendra exited the room through an unknown doorway. "If I turn this device on, it projects an image transmitted from another location."

Renata pushed a few buttons, and in a minute, gradations of blue light composed the form of Kendra standing somewhere.

"Now, you all may think this is a static image of Kendra that has been scanned. We've seen such images throughout the years on film and social media. But this is a live transmission of her from another computer source," said Renata as Kendra waved to everyone and smiled.

"Can she hear us?" asked Diana Thomas, who seldom left Captain Justice's side.

"Yes, I can," said Kendra's image.

The members of the Cyberhawk team were thoroughly impressed.

"Now, this is like Star Wars," Sandra commented to Chris, Raven, and Fernando. They chuckled in agreement as they continued to view the technology with appreciation.

"The third table is currently not in use. We have several rooms in this lab that can be used for holographic experimentation, but the one we are about to see is one that we are very proud of," said Renata, pointing to a door. "And I am assuming ...... that Mr. Knight would like to show you what is in there."

"I would be delighted. Thank you so much, Miss Washington," said Lukas Knight as he led the way.

He opened the door and revealed a room with an exceptionally high ceiling and a strange, grid-like pattern that covered the walls, floor, and ceiling.

"Alright, I want everyone to come in and stand together in the center of the room," Lukas Knight instructed. "A bit more in a row, like you are waiting in a line," he said, and then, after watching everyone find a place to stand, he asked, "I want everyone to close your eyes. Do not open them until I say so."

"This is odd," Dr. Hanni mumbled to himself.

Ellena was standing next to him and replied, "Just have fun with it. You need more joy in your life." She then patted Dr. Hanni on the arm.

"Alright," he replied.

Once Lukas Knight saw that everyone had closed their eyes, he went to the control panel area in the entrance way of the room and tapped in a few commands. Within a minute, the whole room changed.

"I hear birds," said Janet Hallman.

"So do I," said Captain Justice.

"I hear water and insects too," added Raven. "And I can tell that the lighting in the room has changed."

"Alright, everyone, you can now open your eyes," said Lukas Knight.

To the delight and somewhat shock, the Emergency Services Team found themselves all standing on an arched bridge that put them before the beautiful Multnomah Falls of Oregon. They could now hear the roar of the falls and see the large pool far below, into which it poured. Rocky formations jutted skyward, surrounded by trees, shrubbery, and a diverse array of life forms, including birds and insects.

"Oh, my goodness," said Diana.

"Madre mía," said Alejandro, who often remained reserved and quiet.

"This …is…amazing!" exclaimed Rafferty.

The group broke out into numerous exclamations and observations about the room's details and how realistic it felt.

Finally, Raven turned to Lukas Knight and said, "It is missing the smells, the moisture, and the wind. But it is fantastic."

"I am glad that you appreciate the work that the LabCoat Crew has put into this project," replied Knight. "Maybe someday we can add those other variables."

"It is gorgeous, but how can this be put to practical use?" asked Dr. Hanni.

"There he goes. The man hates fun," commented Fernando.

Dr. Hanni turned and gave Fernando a frustrated look and then turned back to Lukas Knight and said, "This is brilliant technology, but what applications other than... just being beautiful does it have?"

"You are not the only one who has voiced that concern. A significant amount of funding and man-hours have been invested in this project. The value of the holographic room is something that will present itself as more useful in the future. We have to start somewhere. The room has already proven to be beneficial for trauma patients. One cannot always easily go to places like this to feel calm or be distracted from stress. Another application has been discovered recently with the new Webb Space Telescope. One of our engineers, Trevor Vermeulen, has started working with the images from the telescope to build a space experience." Lukas paused to look at everyone in the room to make sure they were all paying attention. "I am going to change the selected program, and this can be disorienting. Be prepared, or perhaps close your eyes."

He went over to the control panel on the entrance wall and tapped in some new commands to load the other program. The walls, floor, and ceiling slowly started to fade from the lush forest waterfall park setting.

"And this is like Star Trek," Chris said to Fernando and Sandra.

"Agreed," said Fernando. "A little like the holodecks on the Enterprise."

Slowly, the room grew darker and darker until it was pitch-black. Then, one by one, small pinpoints of light started to appear all around them. A vastness of stars, nebulae, and galaxies began to appear in an awe-inspiring complexity, variety, and number.

"Wow," said Janet softly.

"I feel like I am floating in space," remarked Captain Justice.

"We are still researching this one, and it is updated as we get more information from the Webb Telescope. This project will be useful for educational purposes. It would be nice to include sound. We want to learn if there are any sounds that humans can perceive. We know that sound waves do travel through space, although we cannot hear them, so can we feel them?" Knight postulated.

"Mr. Knight, this is glorious. So beautiful and... awakening. I feel so small," said Raven.

CHAPTER 5

The university library was quiet as usual. Certain areas were designated for students to study alone or in groups, provided they kept the volume level down. It was early evening when most students were off having dinner or a well-earned break from their studies. But she was not here to study and did not need a break. It was her mission to find weak-minded females suffering from stress and, hopefully, male oppression. She spotted a table of three female students sitting together at one of the large tables. She sat down at the table next to theirs. They all stared at her with secretive, judging glances. She wore dark gothic clothing, which heralded that she was into darker things. She looked edgy and forbidding, like a character out of a Halloween tale, with jet-black hair and bright red tips worn in a chaotic fashion. She had the prerequisite piercings and tattoos, as well as black fingernail polish, all proclaiming her defiance against the establishment. She was the stereotype of a bad girl. She was amused by how easily she could portray a character, and everyone would believe it.

She set her backpack down, pulled out her books and tablet, and began to read… and listen.

Once the other young women had regained their composure after eyeing the new student at the table next to them, they returned to their project.

"Okay, so we will need to be able to identify an alluvial fan when it comes up in the series of slides. I made quick drawings of the slides the professor presented," said one of the three.

"I just don't know if I can remember all of this," complained one girl. "I just miss Jeff so much. He is all I think about."

"You need to put him out of your head," said the third girl wearing glasses.

"Well, I can't," said the girl, missing Jeff.

"You're gonna fail. And you will prove your parents' attitude that you should just get married to some guy in your church. You need to focus," said the first girl with the notebook.

The unhappy girl frowned.

"Hey, I could not help but overhear you are having guy trouble… not to mention unsupportive parents," said the girl on a mission in dark clothing.

"I just really thought Jeff liked me for real. He seemed like the perfect guy. We both want to become schoolteachers. We would have the same hours and similar interests, but not be competitors. He wants to be a math teacher, and I want to teach elementary school kids," replied the heartbroken girl, seizing the moment to talk about Jeff.

"Yeah, I get that, but all guys are bastards. They just want to use us. It's part of the system," said the Gothic-looking girl.

"Well, you don't look like you are having any trouble. How would you know?" asked the girl with the glasses.

The Gothic-looking girl looked over at them with a smug smile on her face, making her dramatic makeup look even more shocking.

"That's because I am an empowered woman. I take what I want from guys, and that's it. I use them the way they use us. I also have extra help," replied the girl, slyly enticing the others to want to know more.

"And what is that?" asked the girl with the glasses, sounding a bit skeptical.

"I have... a special connection with... let's just say... powerful people. Women who care about other women," said the dark girl.

"So, you are a Lesbian?" asked the girl with the notebook.

"I like guys," said the brokenhearted girl.

"No, it's not like that at all. These powerful women care about all women. It does not matter who you sleep with or what you look like," said the dark girl, setting down her book. She sat up and leaned out of her chair towards the other table. "They have ways of making you more confident, successful, and in some cases ....more appealing."

The three young women all looked at each other with curiosity.

"Oh my, you're a witch," said the heartbroken girl.

"Such a nasty word... placed upon any woman that would do stuff better than a man. A midwife helps deliver a baby, but she gets labeled a witch because she is taking money out of a male doctor's hands. And the herbalist gets called a witch because she is healing people, and those in power do not get a part of the action, so she is labeled a witch and killed. How is that justice?" asked the girl with the tattoos of magical symbols.

"Well, ...that is not justice. It is not based upon fact or evidence," said the girl with the notebook.

"Seems rotten," said the girl with the glasses.

"And so is how......Jeff is treating her. She can't study to be successful because he has lied to her and used her. He probably subconsciously thinks she is competition," remarked the girl in the Gothic clothing.

The heartbroken girl just frowned and stared down at her books. A few tears dropped onto her open geography book.

"I don't want to be a victim anymore. My family is always treating me like I am stupid. Like, I need a guy to take care of me. I want to show them that I can do this.......," she broke off into tearful sobs.

The girl with the glasses put an arm around her and hugged her, and said, "It's gonna be alright."

"Is it?" said the dark girl, standing up and moving to crouch down at their table. "I think she needs a little help from my friends. We are all about helping each other and being supportive."

The girl with the notebook and the girl with the glasses both turned and looked at the girl with tattoos and piercings wearing strange clothing and said, "What do we need to do? We want to help her."

"Follow me. Let's go back to my dorm room, and I will do something that should help her push off all this negative energy from that Jeff away," said the dark girl, turning away from them, smiling. She started to pack up her backpack. Her mission was going well. Soon, she would have three more new recruits. College was going to be easier than she thought.

****

It was evening, and those staying at the Cyberhawk base had just finished dinner cleanup and were settling down for the rest of the evening. Dr. Hanni was in his room, using his computer to write messages to his family back in Switzerland. At the same time, everyone else relaxed in the upstairs lounge area, watching TV or playing video games. Ellena was playing an in-house game designed to train people how to use the water-based XT device. She had the VR headset on while the others watched her progress on the large, flat-screen smart TV.

"No! More to the right!" a couple of the guys yelled.

"You missed the purple crab. He was worth fifty points," commented Janet.

"I didn't see him. It is so strange to use VR instead of being in the water, but I need to get used to this just in case I need to do underwater rescue work," replied Ellena as she stood with arms extended out in her pink and aqua hoodie.

"Huh, I take it that this stuff is different from real diving," commented Daryl.

"Oh yeah! Completely, ...but ...Cyberhawk has these cool underwater machines that can do work that is too dangerous for divers. For example, oil rigs that require repairs, such as those on Semi-Submersible Platforms, or large ships that cannot safely enter dry dock, can require emergency maintenance. With this device, I can perform that task. I just need to learn how... to do it... with finesse. Hah! I got the purple crab this time. I am getting quicker and more accurate," said Ellena.

"Practicing by playing video games. That's a fun way to learn," remarked Daryl as he opened a bottle of hard cider and put his feet up.

"Dude, you look exhausted," remarked Fernando.

"I am. Today's training just made me feel beat," he yawned. He looked at the hard cider and raised an eyebrow, "I probably should not be drinking this."

Daryl set the bottle down on the end table with a frown.

"You don't want it?" asked Janet.

"Nah, I just feel tired. I should not have opened it," he chided himself.

Janet got up, went to the upstairs lounge cabinet, and pulled out a glass. She walked over to the table, picked up the bottle, and started pouring it into a glass. "I'll drink it, and you won't have to feel bad about wasting a perfectly good cider."

Daryl halfheartedly laughed and said, "Thanks."

"So, hopefully…. You don't mind me saying this…. You look like a pretty buff, healthy guy. You don't look like the type that should be tired after doing the training," commented Fernando.

This caught Raven's attention, who was an EMT.

"You're tired? Not to be nosy, but do you have any medications or health conditions that would make you tired?" asked Raven.

"No. I have been feeling fine. I normally have plenty of energy. Ever since I recovered from the surgery… that was done by Cyberhawk Research and Development, I've been great," Daryl answered.

"Did they make you do follow-up visits every year?" asked Rafferty, who had also received repair surgery with implants to deal with paralysis.

"Uh, no…not recently. I was told that I should contact them if I had any pain in the injured section of my back or problems with numbness. I have not had any of those problems," replied Daryl. "Perhaps I am out of shape?"

"You do not look out of shape," said Ellena, pulling off the VR mask.

"I probably just need a good night's rest. So does anyone else think it is cool that the company has its own set of satellites and robotic animals?" Daryl asked, hoping to escape the spotlight.

"The satellites are going to be helpful along with all the high-tech communications equipment," remarked Chris thoughtfully.

"When I did disaster relief work, communication was critical and something that always went down when a hurricane or a tornado went through a community," added Fernando. "The loss of cell phone coverage scared people."

"Sometimes we would be at the mercy of cell phone coverage, and we would not be able to get the right people to come on site. We had our radios, but even those could malfunction. Having other options is nice," remarked Raven.

"Speaking of technology… no one is mentioning Jeremy. I can't believe none of you are freaking out about the robot stag that Kendra built. It's amazing!" said Janet.

"It is pretty cool," said Daryl. "I thought it was originally a surveillance statue. I was not expecting it to walk around."

"It looks very real," commented Ellena.

"I hate to admit it, but I nearly wanted to get my hunting rifle out and take it as a trophy!" laughed Rafferty.

"Oh yeah, but the stag is bulletproof or bullet resistant, right?" commented Janet.

"Yes. The robot stag is a great piece of tech, but I am unsure as to why she would want to construct something like that. We have no use for that. How about an eagle…. or better yet, a hawk flying about that works like a reconnaissance drone," suggested Chris.

"Well, if it doesn't fly, you are not interested in it, huh?" Ellena said to Chris.

"I'm just saying it is not something we need," said Chris.

Daryl frowned in thought and then said, "It would work for police work... like on a security detail. A location could be monitored without those involved knowing they are being watched. Especially for rural or park situations."

"That's not going to work in the city," replied Chris.

"But the stag robot is a prototype," said Janet. "Kendra has some terrific engineering skills that are just beyond my imagination."

"I wonder why the robot is named Jeremy," said Ellena.

"She said it was named after a close friend who passed away. It made her feel better to make something that would honor his memory," answered Janet.

"Oh. That's cool," replied Ellena. "If I die, I want a robot mermaid to be created in my honor. Something very feminine and pretty. She must be able to swim in the water."

"Does she lure sailors to their death?" asked Rafferty.

Ellena's eyes widened, "Of course not!! How awful. She would rescue them."

"Not gonna happen. It's not what people need. We need drones to fly in the sky," replied Chris.

Daryl sighed loudly and got up, "Hey guys, I am going to turn in early. Have fun."

Several weeks had passed since the team's discovery that they all had cybernetic implants. Everyone had become comfortable operating the newly named CyberSkeletons, and each had gained proficiency in the areas for which they were chosen. Chris Takahashi was now an expert in flying all three of the aircraft that comprised the Cyberhawk assets. He was now learning from Roy Ekstrand how to maintain each of the aircraft and their unique modifications. Ellena Schmidt, the mermaid, was skillful enough on the aquatic XTs that she had been loaned out to the Coast Guard to assist in an emergency rescue of a small fishing vessel during a rough storm off the coast of northern Washington. Dr. Hanni was settling into his role as doctor and adviser for the Emergency Services Team and had already been invited to assist with several procedures done by the LabCoat Crew's Cybernetics experts. He and Raven also planned out what was needed in the emergency medical kits, which were stowed away on the various vehicles used by the team. Diana Thomas needed no time to become Captain Justice's right-hand assistant, making sure that every management logistical problem was dealt with swiftly. This left seven individuals with law enforcement, fire, and rescue experience to train primarily with the CyberSkeletons. The seven had already completed all the basic training exercises and were now working on the mid-range skills. It was noon hour, and another exercise had been completed. The seven found themselves relaxing in the base dining hall when Lukas Knight showed up.

Seeing that Mr. Knight had come through the door, Captain Justice excused himself from the group and headed over to greet his boss.

"How are you doing on this fine spring day?" he asked.

"How ready is the team?" Knight asked, ignoring the niceties.

Captain Justice was a little surprised and replied, "Doing well. Everyone is settling into their jobs, and those who need to be experts with the enhanced equipment are becoming proficient. Chris Takahashi is now learning how to make field repairs on the aircraft he will be flying."

"Good. Do you think they are ready for some action?" asked Knight.

"I believe so. How serious is it?" asked the captain.

"A train incident. From what we have heard, it is a passenger train that has become trapped on a mountain bridge that is no longer stable. It is suspected that the past rough winter conditions may have damaged the hillside, rendering the footings on the bridge unstable. That is speculation. The terrain is rough in a forested area just southeast of Eugene. The Department of Lane County Sheriffs has contacted us to see if we have any heavy-duty equipment that could assist in the rescue operations. So, do we have at least two individuals ready to use the CyberSkeletons?" asked Knight.

Captain Justice wrinkled his brow a bit in contemplation and replied, "Currently, I have the highest level of expertise… with

Lewis, Sanchez, and Crane close behind. Crane has a law enforcement SWAT background, Lewis is from fire and rescue, and Sanchez is recently from FEMA and a former firefighter."

"Sounds like a good team to start with. I will let you manage your people while I speak with Miss Thomas about where you will be taking the team," said Knight.

"Diana, could you come over?" asked the captain from across the room.

Diana got up from the table with her tablet in hand. The woman, of English Indian heritage, came over with a smile and asked in her British accent, "How may I assist?"

Knight was pleased to see that she was adjusting well to her new life in the United States. Her uncle had apprised him of her situation approximately two years ago, and it was finally realized that she required a new start in life to move forward in a productive way. She seemed happy, but Knight knew that people who suffer intense trauma sometimes presented happy faces to the outside world while inside were suffering.

"We have a mission," Captain Justice said to Diana with a bit of a smile. He was excited about taking his team out in the field, even if it was only part of the group. "Please work with Mr. Knight to get the details of the mission, and I will gather who I need for this operation. I will be taking three team members with me."

"Yes, sir," said Diana with a twinkle in her brown eyes. She then turned to Knight, "What are the details that I need to plan for?"

The captain left Diana and Knight to deal with logistics while he strode back to the dining room table.

"Lewis, Sanchez, Crane! We have a mission to prepare for immediately. Get your CyberSkeleton gear on right away and meet me in the garage bay. We need to load up the equipment and get ready to go," said the captain.

The three men immediately got up, while the others looked excited and disappointed at the same time.

"What's the mission, Captain?" asked Chris.

"There is a passenger train that is trapped in a mountain pass on a bridge, and the Department of Lane County Sheriff's has requested some assistance, and we are going to provide it. Sorry, we don't need aircraft on this one. It is close by," replied Captain Justice.

"What about drone assistance for recon?!" asked Chris.

The captain paused for a moment, "You know, that is an excellent idea. Grab a drone and the equipment, and meet us all in the garage bay. And make sure you tell Diana you have been added to the mission."

"Aw, I was hoping to get to see some action soon," commented Janet.

"Sorry about that. Had to pick the people with the highest proficiency with the CyberSkeleton gear," replied the captain as he left to get ready.

Chris turned around to the others, grinning and said, "But I managed to find a way." He laughed and then ran off to get the drone equipment.

Janet rolled her eyes.

"Pilots. They are cocky bastards, aren't they?" commented Sandra with a grin.

"Well, the rest of us are not experts in fire and rescue operations," commented Ellena.

"Says the girl who has already gotten to work with people using the VR equipment," replied Janet.

Ellena just smiled and shrugged.

"I guess we detectives will have to find our own mission," said Sandra, with Morales nodding his head silently.

"We will all have action soon enough," said Dr. Hanni. "I just have that feeling."

"I hope so," said Raven. "But I understand why the captain took those three. They are further along in the training and have become very skilled with those machines. I need to spend more time on them."

Ten minutes later, the captain found Crane, Lewis, Sanchez, and Takahashi all assembled by the heavy-duty terrain truck with two CyberSkeletons already loaded onto the vehicle.

"Captain, do you want us to load four, which will make the vehicle heavier and drive slower, or have two sets in which we can take turns if needed?" asked Crane.

"Let's do two. This is our first time out with these bad boys, and I think we should have spotters. Crane, you will be my spotter, and Sanchez, you will be Lewis's spotter. And the pilot will fly his drones," said the captain, heading for the driver's seat of the big vehicle.

Diana Thomas came striding over with a navigation tablet ready with all the contact information of the parties involved in the rescue operation, including a few she thought might be needed. She handed the tablet to Crane, who was riding shotgun up front.

"Thanks, Diana," said Crane, taking the tablet. She nodded slightly with a smile. Crane thought she appeared friendly, but there was always a barrier or something between her and everyone else. She stayed close to the captain as if she were afraid of something.

The powerful engine of the Terrain Buster roared to life. It was a black, customized military-style land transport vehicle designed to handle heavy loads and rough roads. It was emblazoned with the bright blue and golden yellow Cyberhawk logo. They sped off, leaving Diana to watch them disappear out of the garage bay. Upon arrival at the scene at the Devil's Garden Trailhead, the Department of Lane County Sheriffs was there along with Pacific Northwest Rail Union engineers, and other local emergency personnel. The train route in question was the well-known Pengra Pass route that was riddled with tunnels, bridges, snow sheds, and a constant grade that required extra engines. A local officer immediately greeted the Cyberhawk Emergency Services Team.

"Glad you were able to make it. Let me get you up to speed about the current situation and the plan that has been devised between the fire and rescue team and Pacific Northwest Rail Union," the officer said to Captain Justice, leading him towards where they needed to be.

Chris jumped out immediately and started getting his drone equipment ready while Rafferty and Sanchez unloaded the CyberSkeletons. Crane tagged along with the captain and the officer to gather an idea of what was going on. The officer led Justice over to the sheriff's SUV, where a map was laid out on the hood, with other people discussing things around it. They quickly explained that the train was stopped approximately one mile up the tracks on a bridge with a support that had shifted enough to prevent the train from moving farther.

"We discussed separating the train using the support engines to guide the back portion down the tracks, but then there will not be enough power to move the front portion to a safe location," explained the engineer. "We can't repair the tracks or the bridge properly while there are cars upon the rails."

"And it also appears that there may be more than one support location that has locked the train in place," said one of the emergency personnel.

"Do you need help gathering information? I brought my drone and drone pilot with me," said Captain Justice.

"Oh, that would be perfect. Where is the pilot?" asked the fire and rescue officer.

"That guy over there," directed Captain Justice, pointing out Chris. Chris had just set the drone down on the ground.

"Thanks. I will talk with him about getting some eyes in the sky," replied the officer.

Captain Justice turned back to the engineer and the other officers, "So what is the plan? And how might we assist?"

"First, we need to assess the truth of the second damage point. That is key in knowing exactly how to proceed," replied the Pacific Northwest Rail Union engineer.

"So…... if there are two points of damage, what needs to happen to get people or cars off the track safely?" asked Justice.

"The best possible solution would be to shore up the damaged supports enough to make the rails fall back into place and allow the train to move off the bridge. Another solution would be the slow process of removing everyone and everything from the rails. Unfortunately, this was a special event train carrying additional passenger cars filled with senior citizens and veterans. We do these trains every couple of months to help people stay connected with family and friends," replied the engineer, making a frustrated expression. "You can guess the level of complexity of removing mobility-challenged people."

"Alright," nodded the captain, thinking it through. "What is required to secure the support structure enough to move the train safely up or down the tracks?"

The two railroad company experts exchanged a glance before answering. The second man answered Justice's question.

"We need to get some heavy equipment into the ravine where the bridge is located and make repairs. Once the temporary supports are secured and the rail sets back into the correct position, we can then move the train. We have already requested an additional engine from Eugene to assist in pulling the front section up through the rest of the mountain. That won't be available for another two hours," he answered.

Just then, a heavy-duty semi-truck came in loaded with metal beams and a forklift.

"There is no way that stuff can get to that location," commented one of the sheriffs.

"How do you normally repair tracks?" asked the captain.

"We use the rail lines themselves to haul things to various locations. We don't just let tracks get this bad," fumed one of the engineers. "This situation is the worst."

"How heavy are the beams?" inquired Captain Justice.

"Each metal beam is approximately seven hundred pounds. We have a welder ready to do the work, but we need a means for getting the beams to the location and holding them in place while the welder works," replied one of the engineers.

"Well, we can pick those beams up with the CyberSkeletons. Let's see how far up the way we can transport them with the forklift, and then we will take it from there," suggested the captain.

Several of the police officers and the two railroad experts looked surprised.

"Let's get on this before we lose more daylight," said the first sheriff who greeted them upon arrival.

Everyone agreed with this sentiment and got to work moving the beams as far as possible up the trail and along the train track easement using the sturdy forklift that came with the big rig truck. The welder, the engineer, the assistants, and the Cyberhawk team members gathered around to view the footage that Chris had captured using the drone. It was determined where the most effective temporary support adjustments would be placed, and that another rail was starting to shift out of place. These sections determined where the rail jacks and repairs would be required. It was twilight by the time Captain Justice and Rafferty Lewis made it through the tunnel and down to the area where the bridge supports needed repairs. The welder with climbing gear took a spray can to mark where the beams would have to go, with approval from an engineer watching the drone video feed. Sanchez and Crane added spotlights to the CyberSkeleton's framework to provide more illumination.

"That ravine is steep," Fernando commented to Rafferty as he adjusted the spotter light on the framework.

"Yeah, agreed," said Rafferty, taking a deep breath. "But I have had to do rappelling before on a rescue mission, so I should be able to do this."

"There are no safety cables," said Fernando. "You are not rappelling."

"Well, I am wearing this device. I did pass the falling training test where you roll up into a ball... and the machine acts as a protective barrier," explained Rafferty. "And I can hear the AI that is assisting us. Which is cool and reassuring."

Rafferty gave a boyish smile as if to say he wasn't as nervous as he should be using new equipment.

"That's Betty," said the captain, overhearing the conversation. He was ready to start the repair. He turned and looked at Rafferty and said, "You ready?"

"Yes, sir," replied Rafferty.

"After the engineering team installs the railroad jacks in the appropriate places, the engineer will want to install the extra support beam to make sure that railcar vibrations will not loosen the jack. He will climb over there, and I will need you to bring the first beam up; I will then hold it in place. Got that?" asked the captain.

Got it," replied Rafferty.

While the captain and Rafferty planned how they would safely lift the beams to the correct location, Crane and the welder double-checked their climbing gear. Crane was acting as an additional pair of eyes and hands. It was at this point that the engineer and his assistant came over. They were all suited up with safety gear.

"The jacks have been installed in the various positions, and... they seem to be lifting and pushing beams into place," said the engineer, sounding very stressed. He was scowling as he looked at the bridge structure. "I do not know how long this temporary fix will last. And that is why the added support beams that we are about to put in ......come into play. This is not a permanent fix. We just need to get that engine and those cars off the track so that proper repair can commence. Otherwise, we need to change this plan to remove all those people one by one... and then get heavy equipment in here to remove the cars and the engines."

"Not exactly a party, is it?" observed Rafferty.

"Nope," responded the assistant who was wearing a backpack and holding several equipment bags.

The captain could see how seriously the structural engineers were taking the situation. They looked worried.

"If it is required that we start removing the passengers one by one, then that is what we will do," said the captain, trying to assure the structural engineer and his team that efforts to resolve the situation would be dealt with regardless of which plan was needed.

The man nodded, still scowling at the bridge, "We wanted to avoid stressing out the passengers. Most of them are elderly and are disabled veterans. These train ride specials were designed to alleviate stress and... not make it worse."

By the time all the welds were done and the jacks were installed, it was very dark, with floodlights providing the only light. Chris flew the drone in close to examine the trouble spots, revealing that the repairs had brought the rails into a working position. It was time for the train engineer to attempt to move forward. With careful, slow, torque-filled acceleration, the train moved safely again at a crawl, allowing the entire set of cars to pass the danger area. There was a big cheer from everyone present, which also included the local press and passengers who had been stuck inside the railcars. The Cyberhawk team, plus the engineers, were all treated to cheers and congratulations when they arrived back at the trailhead area. Eager news reporters wanted details about the daring repair effort. The captain answered a few questions about the Cyberhawk team and their equipment while the others packed up the gear to head back to the base. The ride back home was filled with the retelling of the events and how amusing it was to see reporters there to interview the captain.

Once back at the base, the team members who lived on-site congratulated those who had taken part in the mission.

"What was it like to use the CyberSkeleton in the field?" Raven asked Rafferty.

"Exciting and stressful. I was extra nervous, but the gear held up as expected, and it made a big difference in getting those people safely out of that location," replied Rafferty as he sat at the big dining table drinking some juice.

"Are you hungry? We made lasagna tonight," said Raven.

"That sounds great," replied Rafferty. "You know the captain was as cool as a cucumber on site. He knows how to work the CyberSkeleton to its maximum potential."

"Hey, Captain," Fernando called out and looked around.

"The captain has already left to go home," said Dr Hanni.

"Oh. Well, he does have a wife and kid, and... they probably saw him on TV!" exclaimed Fernando.

"TV crews were out there?" asked Janet.

"Uh, yeah! And... I was interviewed about how the drone works and its usefulness in situations like the one we were working on. The reporter was hot. I think she liked me," said Chris.

"Naw, she was excited...when we showed up with the CyberSkeletons," laughed Rafferty as everyone sat back down at the table to visit while the others ate reheated lasagna.

"The reporters were very enthusiastic. I think Captain Justice was a bit surprised by all the attention. I got the impression he is used to doing his work without any fanfare," remarked Daryl.

"A lot of us are. No one gets excited about a bunch of guys arriving with trucks of food, water, and emergency blankets except those who need it," remarked Fernando as he worked his fork into a gooey layer of Italian food. "So, this was fun. At least for me."

"Cops don't get happy press either," sighed Daryl. "But I didn't sign up to be in the SWAT team for accolades."

"Says the guy that got a big policeman's award," remarked Janet with a smile.

"That could have been given to several other worthy people. I was just lucky they noticed me," said Daryl.

Dr. Hanni eyed Daryl.

"Were you very active on this mission?" Dr. Hanni asked Daryl.

"Not really. I was the captain's spotter. I did some climbing up the bridge trestles a bit, but it wasn't that bad. Not like running a marathon," replied Daryl, forcing a smile.

"You look tired. Have you been sleeping well?" asked Dr. Hanni.

"Pretty much. I think," answered Daryl.

"And you are eating reasonable food?" asked Dr. Hanni.

"For the most part."

"And you are feeling tired..." said Dr. Hanni.

"Yeah. Kinda."

"If you do not feel better tomorrow, I think we should do a blood test on you. Something does not seem right for such a healthy young man as yourself, feeling like an old man," replied Dr. Hanni firmly.

"Sure, doc," replied Daryl with resignation in his voice.

CHAPTER 6

Robert Justice halted just outside the front door of his home with a porchlight and some moonlight to guide his steps. Their garage was still full of boxes from the big move. The neighborhood was peaceful and quiet. It was nine o'clock in the evening, and he usually did not come home this late, at least not since he took this job. He felt bad about not briefing his wife about the mission he was going on. He didn't think he would have to. He had Diana call and let her know that he might be late getting back home. He wondered if they saw him on the local news. His mind briefly slipped back to his accident of over nine years ago, when he had been burned by an explosion, resulting in him having to replace both of his lower legs, which had been stressful for Jessica. He never wanted to put her through that agony again. They were a very close couple, and their bond of love was both their strength and weakness. She wasn't a fragile, clingy woman, but she counted on him and considered him her best friend. He took a deep breath. He thought about their boy, Ryan. She now had Ryan, and he was something special. A good kid with a lot of potential, and if something happened to Robert, she would have Ryan. He could not ask for a better son. He was so smart, too. They often wondered if such a brilliant child would fit into a regular school.

The captain put the key in and unlocked the front door, only to find that Jessica and Ryan were both still up, waiting for him to come home.

"Daddy, I saw you on TV!! You were wearing an awesome robot suit!" exclaimed Ryan, running up to Robert to hug him.

Jessica just stood in the hallway smiling with that knowing look of '*Oh my gosh, what are you doing now?*"

"Hey, buddy, you waited up for me!" said Robert to his son.

"Of course, Dad. We want to hear all about the train and the robot suit that you got to wear," said Ryan, who was seven years old.

"Well, the robot suit is called a CyberSkeleton, and it helps me be able to lift very heavy stuff, I can climb without getting tired, and it is less likely that I will get hurt while wearing it," Robert said to his son.

"Wow! That's great, Dad. Can I see it? Did you bring it home with you?" asked Ryan.

"No," said Robert, almost laughing, thinking about how it would probably flatten the tires on his truck from the sheer weight of the gear. "The CyberSkeleton belongs to Cyberhawk, where I work, so it does not belong to me. But maybe someday I will bring you and your mom to see it."

"That would be great," said Ryan, starting to yawn.

"I think it is someone's bedtime," remarked Jessica.

"Oh yeah, …....Mom, let me stay up to see you and tell you that I saw you on TV," replied Ryan.

"Come on, Ryan. Off to bed. That was the deal," said Jessica.

Ryan headed off without any complaint, so Jessica and Robert headed for the kitchen.

"Are you hungry?" asked Jessica.

"Not really," replied Robert.

"Is something bothering you?" asked Jessica, eyeing her husband.

"It's nothing," sighed Robert. "I just… was not expecting the attention. And to be honest, I should have been prepared for the hype. I am now working with a company that develops innovative products to help people, and we are the prototype team responsible for bringing these ideas to everyday life. So, it makes sense that we will catch the attention of the press. I guess…I am just not used to that kind of attention."

Jessica just looked at her husband, understanding his feelings of frustration.

"Are you sure you don't want something? Hot tea? Hot chocolate? A warm hug?" asked Jessica.

Robert smiled at Jessica and went over for that warm hug. She smelled so wonderful, and her soft brown hair felt good against his face.

"You know, …. maybe I do want that hot chocolate," said Robert as he gave her a bit of a squeeze before finally letting her go. "I should go take a shower and get the work dust off me."

"Sounds good. I will bring you some hot chocolate, and then you can tell me all about that CyberSkeleton and its amazing abilities," she said with a wink. Jessica then turned to make the hot chocolate.

Robert smiled, "I'll go take that… warm shower."

He headed off to their bedroom to get cleaned up. She was not upset, which was a relief. She even seemed to be happy for him about the new job. This was going to work out fine. Now all he had to do was get used to reporters.

The next morning, back at the base, Lukas Knight was there waiting for the Cyberhawk Team to assemble. Everyone appeared to be sharp and ready. The team was assembled around the large dining table. Lukas Knight seemed to be an alright guy, but he was the boss, and Captain Justice wanted to make sure everything was professional and ready. Mr. Knight stood as he addressed the group.

"Good morning, Cyberhawk team. We have some changes from yesterday's adventure. We are now receiving requests from various authorities seeking assistance. This means that we are no longer just on the training schedule but will be on an on-call schedule. We cannot answer every call, but only those where assistance is greatly needed, such as yesterday's train situation. This means some of you will have to be able to take missions that occur during typical night shift hours. We need everyone to bump up their efforts to learn how to use the gear more effectively. Chris, I would like you to participate in some IFR night training flights with Roy. You need to feel like the Cyberhawk group of aircraft is a part of you, understood?" asked Mr. Knight.

"Yes, Sir," replied Chris eagerly.

"Captain, I will need you to select two individuals that you think will make good lieutenants because we cannot expect you to be here at the base all the time," said Knight.

"I will start planning my selection today. I have several people in mind," replied the captain.

"As for the press, my media team at Cyberhawk Research and Development will handle press releases about the new technology and handle any requests for stories. None of you will have to deal with that. Stay focused on what you're good at. That is why you are here. You are all experts in your fields. Dealing with the press is what my media team does best," said Knight. He could see some of the faces before him look relieved, while others just nodded their heads. "Does anyone have any questions?"

"No, I think you took care of anything that was of concern," replied Sandra, looking around at the others.

"Good. Then I think I will steal the captain for some time," said Knight as he made a gesture to the captain, who already had Diana in tow with her tablet. "Let's get started on making some plans concerning possible future schedules. I have no idea if this media exposure will turn into something big or fizzle out as a special interest story."

Captain Justice chuckled and asked, "So, which do you want it to be?"

"It does not matter to me. We will deal with things accordingly, and the agencies that will have access to our assistance will be notified regardless of us being newsworthy or not," replied Knight as he and Justice disappeared into an office.

Dr. Hanni went over to Daryl Crane and eyed him.

"Let's see if the LabCoat Crew will let us in?" he said.

"Uh, sure. Why?" asked Daryl.

"The repetitive exhaustion," replied Dr. Hanni. "A simple blood test should reveal if something is not right."

"Okay," replied the tall, handsome former SWAT team officer.

Together, they left the base building and headed towards the secret entrance to the lab. Before they reached the building, they were stunned to find a stag standing amongst the trees and bushes.

"Wow, he is still here. He surprised me the other day when I went out for my morning run," remarked Daryl.

"He is an amazing piece of equipment," commented Dr. Hanni.

"Equipment?" inquired Daryl.

"Yes. That is Kendra's droid stag named Jeremy," replied Dr. Hanni.

The stag turned its head towards the two men as if now listening to them.

"You mean he is not a real deer?!" exclaimed Daryl.

"No. Jeremy, tell Kendra that Dr. Hanni and Daryl Crane are here to see Dr. Eirstone," Dr Hanni said to the deer.

There was a pause in the stag's movement, and then a male voice responded, "As you wish, Dr. Hanni. Kendra has notified Dr. Eirstone."

Dr Hanni continued into the garage bay while Daryl kept looking at the stag, whose gaze followed them.

"That just isn't right," said Daryl. "This whole time that deer has been spying on me."

"That is the purpose of the droid deer. Reconnaissance," replied Dr. Hanni as he used his card to access the secured elevator. "I thought everyone knew about it."

"Yeah. It sounds vaguely familiar. I feel stupid," replied Daryl.

"Don't. The purpose of Jeremy Stag is to gather as much information as possible about an area. It has multiple levels of applications, and he is being tested around the lab. It is required that the droid fool even the best-trained observers such as yourself," replied Dr. Hanni. "I saw the droid deer standing amongst several other deer the other morning. They didn't seem to mind him."

"Alright. I can tell you are trying to make me feel better about it," replied Daryl as he thought about several encounters he had with the stag on the running paths. One time, the stag ran away from him like a real deer would. Another time, he saw him appear to be eating something. Daryl shook his head in disbelief.

Which deer were real, and which were the droids he pondered to himself.

The elevator door opened into the central lab area, and all the worries about the robotic deer disappeared from Daryl's mind. There was so much to see and so much activity. The team rarely saw these introverted technicians, but they worked only a short walk away. Dr. Eirstone strode towards them. She was a striking vision, with her green hair and lavender-colored eyes; she seemed more like a comic con cosplayer than a Doctor of Medicine.

"Dr. Hanni and Mr. Crane, so pleased to see you both. Please follow me into the exam room, and let's get that blood sample taken," she greeted them in her always even tone of voice.

As they made their way, Kendra Boisen passed them in the hallway.

"Hello Daryl," she said with a flirty smile. "Thanks for participating in the Jeremy Stag project. You have been a great training test for him. Please don't be upset. I'd still like to track you on your morning runs if that is okay?"

"Yeah, I guess so," replied Daryl, feeling embarrassed.

"It does help. And now that you know, maybe you could try to evade him when you see him?" suggested Kendra.

"Alright. That could be fun," said Daryl. He then turned to follow Dr. Hanni and Dr. Eirstone into the examination room, where Dr. Hanni insisted that Daryl needed a blood test for safe measures. Dr. Eirstone agreed and proceeded to take samples for testing purposes.

Later in the week, Daryl and Dr. Hanni got the test results, which showed everything to be normal and healthy with only a few minor exceptions. None of those exceptions would lead to excessive tiredness.

"We will keep an eye on this," said Dr. Hanni as he walked alongside Daryl. "Since you have the monitoring implant, we might want to consider sending diagnostics to Dr. Cross and Dr. Eirstone regularly for troubleshooting purposes. Perhaps we can detect a pattern. I am not an expert on Cybernetics, but I am learning. That is why I disappear every afternoon. I am studying and doing some practical lessons with the LabCoat Crew. I hope to have full comprehension of the topic within a year."

"Wow, it must be… really nice to be so brilliant that you can learn this stuff so easily," commented Daryl.

"Being this smart isn't always so great. People tend to put you at arm's length because they find you…. strange. Sometimes threatening on an unconscious level. I am somewhat used to it," replied Dr. Hanni. "Perhaps a little jaded."

Together, they headed for the outdoor testing area. The LabCoat Crew had designed more refined appendages for the CyberSkeleton, proposing an entirely new design that was lighter and featured additional capabilities, including a bulletproof, fire-resistant, and cold-protective bodysuit. There was even a rumor that an aviation component was being considered.

Fernando had volunteered to be the first to try out the newly designed appendages. The CyberSkeleton to be tested had the original lower body support system, but the science team had changed both arm appendages, so it appeared almost lopsided.

"It does look weird," Sandra remarked to Janet.

"All I care about is if it works," replied Janet.

"We shall see. If Fernando falls over or goes into a fit of robotic boxing rage, I can run pretty fast," laughed Sandra.

"Well, let's hope that doesn't happen. I like the look of the new arms," said Janet as she watched Fernando go through all the test instructions.

"Hey girls," said Ellena, coming over to stand with Sandra and Janet. "Do we have a consensus on the family dinner party at the Cyberhawk clubhouse?"

"Everyone is in, and the captain is making sure that families can be welcomed at the base. This is not a normal protocol to have spouses and children on-site," replied Janet.

"I think my kids are gonna love it, especially my son, Michael," remarked Sandra.

"Your twins are twelve?" asked Ellena.

"Yes," replied Sandra, as she continued to watch Fernando work with Rafferty, who was handing him items.

"How old are Alejandro's children?" asked Ellena.

"Oh, they're young…...uh…I think two, five, …and eight? The captain's son is seven, so we need to make sure there is something fun for the children to do. We do have the video games upstairs and the big TV set." Janet paused and laughed as she watched Fernando and Rafferty. "We also have older family members that will need to be cleared… well… just Alejandro's father-in-law. He lives with them. Diana's great-uncle Richard was formerly part of Cyberhawk Research and Development and acts as a consultant from time to time. So, he will have no problems getting clearance. He is retired for the most part."

"You are a wealth of knowledge," commented Sandra, raising an eyebrow.

"There is a reason for the saying that *Mounties always get their man* because we do the necessary detective work to find them," replied Janet with a smile. "Nous sommes magnifiques."

Sandra just eyed Janet, and Ellena giggled.

"Of course we are," said Dr. Hanni, walking up at the end of the conversation.

"One of the few people that I can speak French with," said Janet, giving the doctor an arm squeeze.

"So, do the new arm appendages work?" asked the doctor.

"They appear to be great. I am hoping they will do that with the rest of the suit," commented Sandra.

"Oh, they will. I have seen the plans in the lab. The new CyberSkeleton will be lighter and easier to transport and require less energy," explained Dr. Hanni.

"So…. he must be a former Mountie as well?" said Ellena, gesturing to Dr. Hanni, who gave a knowing expression.

"He doesn't fit the profile of being in the RCMP," replied Janet, thinking about some of her male associates back home who were all models of physical masculine perfection.

The doctor looked at the women quizzically, then walked over to Daryl, who was helping monitor the equipment's responses along with Kendra Boisen.

"How are you doing?" asked Dr. Hanni.

"Fine. This software is easy to use," remarked Daryl.

"You can thank Renata and Trevor for that," added Kendra.

"Well, that is good, but I wanted to know how Daryl was feeling," Dr. Hanni re-stated.

"I am okay. I don't feel bad," replied Daryl, trying to reassure the doctor.

"So, I hear there is a group dinner being planned for the Emergency Services Team," commented Kendra.

"Yes, the team had been thinking it would be good for us all to know a bit more about each other, and well......we thought a dinner that included their family members would be nice," said Daryl while Dr. Hanni just stood and watched Fernando struggle to pick up a balloon.

"Oh," replied Kendra. "Are you bringing anyone?"

"No, I live at the base. My parents are in Seattle," replied Daryl.

Dr. Hanni raised an eyebrow but said nothing, as he was standing behind both of them while they were seated at the monitoring table. Fernando's heart rate was starting to speed up as he became annoyed with the fact that he could not pick up a balloon without popping it. The more Fernando got irritated, the more Rafferty had trouble keeping from laughing.

"Take a breath," said Rafferty in his cowboy drawl.

Fernando stopped and just fumed for a moment. Chris made a face.

"I could do it," he remarked.

Rafferty looked over at Chris and made a scowl at him, "That's not gonna help. He needs to calm down."

Chris rolled his eyes and folded his arms across his chest, "Just saying.... I have a light touch."

Just then, Elgin Cross came up and stood next to Dr. Hanni. He watched the scene for a few moments and looked at the screens that Daryl and Kendra were monitoring. The man made a sour face.

"We need to start using their cybernetic interfaces," he commented.

"What are you saying? Is there... something else that we have missed doing correctly?" asked Dr. Hanni.

"Oh yes. Doing stuff the hard way......the regular way. All of you are... essentially cyborgs," he replied in his matter-of-fact style. "We should be making use of that fact. Everyone will be able to use their equipment better if we stop dancing around the topic," replied Elgin Cross, adjusting his special glasses.

Dr. Hanni could see from the side that a display was being shown to Elgin Cross through the unusual glasses. They were augmented reality glasses. Daryl turned to look up at Dr. Cross and then at Kendra, and she made a face as if it were true, and she knew about it. Fernando made another attempt to pick up the balloon and failed. This annoyed Elgin Cross.

"Okay. This has got to stop. We are wasting time," he stated. He then reached over to the keyboard and typed something into the computer system that Kendra was monitoring. He then walked over to Fernando. "Stop! Stop what you are doing."

Fernando stopped and looked at Elgin Cross with a look of surprise. Rafferty and Chris stood silent along with Janet, Sandra, and Ellena. The rest of the team was working on something else and had not noticed Dr. Cross's arrival.

Elgin Cross looked Fernando square in the eye and asked, "Do you want to be able to do this better, faster, and more efficiently?"

"Well...yes," replied Fernando.

"Then we need to allow for the communication of your cybernetic implant with the piece of equipment you are using," said Cross, walking up to Fernando. He pushed a button on the back of the test machine that would turn it off. He then adjusted Fernando's gear to ensure it was correctly worn on his upper right arm and checked to confirm that the test CyberSkeleton was securely attached and touching his upper right arm. "Kendra, hit the CyberSkeleton's command to access the cybernetic implant."

"Yes, Dr. Cross," said Kendra, and then she did something on the computer.

"Is it successfully connecting?" asked Elgin Cross.

"Yes," replied Kendra.

"Alright, everyone, step back. Some people will make the exterior machinery twitch funny the first time," he directed as he switched the on button on the back of the test piece that Fernando was strapped into. Cross immediately stepped back to watch.

Nothing twitched, but Fernando felt something, "Hey, that felt funny. Not bad. It did not hurt but felt... different."

"Alright. Now pick up the balloon," directed Dr. Cross.

With everyone watching, Fernando reached down to grab the red balloon that was sitting on the ground with the mechanical arm of the CyberSkeleton. It was easy, like the suit was part of him.

"Hey, look! I did it!" exclaimed Fernando.

"Yes. I see that. Now we can stop wasting time. I want everyone to test their connections with the equipment," said Elgin Cross as he started to leave the testing area.

Dr. Hanni ran up to Elgin Cross and asked, "We all have Cybernetic implants that allow us to communicate with machines?"

Elgin rolled his eyes, made a slight face, and replied, "Not all equipment. You are not going to be one with the toaster. Just equipment designed for that purpose."

Dr. Hanni was somewhat surprised, as Dr. Cross had started to turn and leave, as if everything that needed to be said had been explained.

"Why didn't you tell us about this?" asked Dr. Hanni.

Dr. Cross turned about and let out a sigh.

"Oh, stupid politics about humans being weird about people being repaired, and it's not part of god's plan to have cybernetics. You know, the ignorant comment about not flying because we do not have wings. Well, gods…...evolution…. or whatever…. gave us brains, so we could think and be creative. Airplanes, cars, houses, guns, refrigerators… are all products of human creativity and thought. So is cybernetics. We repair people… just like a doctor gives a child an aspirin," replied Elgin Cross, and then he turned to go back to his laboratory.

Dr. Hanni found himself feeling somewhat flabbergasted. People generally did not leave him speechless or aghast from surprise. It was clear that Dr. Cross had been dealing with this problem for some time, and it vexed him. Dr. Hanni thought about the fact that he would be dead if they had not repaired or... possibly replaced his heart. He would not have been around to help the hundreds of people whom he and other doctors worked on. He turned and looked at the younger people he was working with. Most of them would be dead or stuck in wheelchairs, living marginalized lives. They were all productive members of society, giving back to the world by using their talents to help others. If that was not a gift from the Holy Spirit, then what was, he wondered, thinking back to his childhood church attendances with his family.

CHAPTER 7

Leonardo and Maria sat quietly with the group of immigrant workers in a small restaurant. The group had just finished a hard day's work outside, and tomorrow would be another one. The pair had been working with this group for a couple of months and had learned how to pick vegetables correctly and quickly. This group spoke very little English and relied on one person to arrange for jobs and pay. Leonardo and Maria knew this was a weak point that they could exploit. Work was already backbreaking, the pay was meager, and there were no benefits such as health insurance.

The pair had been given their instructions and were reasonably certain that by now they could influence the others into listening to them. The fact that the group could not speak, read, or write in English gave Leonardo and Maria power over them because they could understand English. The job was simple: sow seeds of distrust amongst the group. However, Maria had been informed that if they could get the group to travel to an isolated farm in northern California, she and Leonardo would be rewarded. Leonardo had been worried that the group would blame them for their misfortune and seek their rightful revenge. Maria had assured Leonardo that they would be sent to the East Coast to work on another project that was less backbreaking and more hate-stirring. He was a revolutionary and wanted to see America fall. This had been more covert than he wished for. He desired the thrill of the fight and told her that if their plans did not move forward faster, he would leave her and seek his fortune elsewhere. He had heard of other groups that he could join. Groups that shared his fanatical ideals.

Maria simply nodded to him, placating him. She was not worried. If he showed any signs of weakness or disobedience, she had a place for him to go. He would be an offering.

****

Alejandro Luis Morales pulled his new Ford Explorer into the parking lot behind the Cyberhawk aviation base. This evening was the big Cyberhawk dinner, planned for everyone to attend. His workmates had no idea about the amount of anxiety he felt about bringing his family to work. They also had no idea what he had been through or the dark fears he had kept secret from everyone. Only his wife had a vague idea of the dangers he faced back home in Mexico during his time with the Mexican NCB. His father-in-law, Pablo Mateo Garcia, who preferred to be called by his saint's name, was a quiet man who had worked as a master carpenter and never revealed that he had any opinions on the matter. Alejandro helped his children exit the new vehicle, which he hoped would make him appear more American. He was in the process of getting his American citizenship and had his wife enrolled in English classes to learn the new language. He was uncertain what Mateo would want to do. The Cyberhawk administrative team was helping him navigate through the bureaucracy of American paperwork and appointments. He still loved his homeland of Mexico, but it had become too dangerous for him to stay. He would do what was right for his family.

Ximena was holding their two-year-old son, Maximiliano, whom they referred to as Max for short, while Valentina, aged five, and Diego, aged eight, stayed close to their father. Mateo walked quietly behind as if taking in everything around him. He was not accustomed to the cool, wet climate and the type of vegetation found on Oregon's western side. Despite being semi-tropical, Mexico City was also an extensive, old, and crowded city with some design flaws and a bit of pollution. Mateo could breathe deeply in the fresh air of the Eugene, Oregon area. It was wonderful, he thought to himself. His beloved Isabella would have loved it. She always liked trying new things. He wished she could have been here with him. He knew he would barely understand anything that was being said at the dinner, but meeting new people and learning a new language was part of the adventure of moving with his daughter. He had his grandchildren to help look after, and Alejandro had set aside space in the new garage for him to have a woodworking shop, promising to build a true workshop for him later. Life would be good, and he had found a lovely Catholic church to attend.

When everyone entered the strange building, which resembled a warehouse, he was surprised by how fancy and homelike it was inside. There was a large table set for the adults to sit around, and little Max could sleep in his carrier next to his mother. The children were corralled upstairs by a lovely young woman with wavy blonde hair dressed in shades of aqua. Mateo watched as Diego took his little sister's hand and followed the young woman upstairs. Mateo wondered how much Diego understood. The boy was starting to learn the new language.

Introductions were made, and Mateo found himself sitting next to a short man with very refined behavior who was about ten years younger than he was. The man smiled at him and introduced himself in Castilian Spanish.

"My name is Dr. August Hanni. I am from Switzerland. And I am the only one here who speaks Spanish fluently, well, besides your family. I also understand that you are Roman Catholic as well," said Dr. Hanni, holding his hand out to shake Mateo's while speaking in Spanish.

Mateo smiled and took the hand. He knew this was going to be an enjoyable evening after all. He had someone to talk with, and they shared a connection.

Upstairs in the common TV gaming room, pizza, veggie, and fruit slices, along with drinks and other small snacks approved by the parents, were set out for the children to eat. Pillows were set out so the children could sit on the floor if they wished. Diego kept Valentina close by his side since she was the youngest of the children. Tessa sat on the couch with her feet curled under her, away from everyone else. Michael also sat on the couch, but leaned forward to talk with the other children.

"My name is Michael Ridgestone, and this is… my sister Tessa," Michael introduced himself, repressing the inclination to moniker his sister as a grumpy cat.

"I am Diego. I am just learning English. This is my little sister Valentina," replied Diego proudly, flashing his dark brown eyes.

"I am Ryan Justice. My dad is the captain of the team. He gets to wear a robot suit!" said Ryan happily. "I also like space stuff."

"Oh, hey, Michael, you can hang out with him if you don't make any geeky friends your age," commented Tessa as she sneered at her brother behind her newly trimmed and dyed hair. It was a short straight bob with the bottom two inches dyed dark red to contrast with her blonde hair.

Michael made a face regarding his sister's comment, but said nothing.

"That's your sister. She's mean," remarked Ryan as he helped himself to a slice of pizza.

Tessa just scrunched up her face and acted like everyone in the room was beneath her.

"Yeah, she gets that way now," replied Michael, getting a slice of pizza and something to drink. He turned to Diego and asked, "Do you and your sister like pizza? Or how about something to drink?"

"This pizza is different from what my mami makes, but I have had this before. And I like it very much. I like it… with…," said Diego, starting to gesture, trying to find the right word.

"Lots of yummy stuff on top?" asked Ryan enthusiastically. He pointed at all the toppings on the non-plain cheese section of the pizza.

Diego got the idea and nodded with a smile. "Si," he exclaimed as he got a slice of the loaded pizza onto his plate and then turned to his sister and asked her something in Spanish. She responded, and then he gave her a slice of cheese pizza.

The children sat in silence for a few moments while they ate. Tessa got a slice of cheese pizza and some of the fruit, but insisted on sitting away from everyone. Michael felt embarrassed. He thought she was being rude, but she had been acting odd for a while now, and he had no idea why. The new hairdo and makeup were a recent interest of hers, which was not surprising, considering all the girls around them were starting to experiment with makeup choices.

"So, your dad is Captain Justice. He was a fireman, right?" Michael asked Ryan.

"Yes, he was. We lived back in Carson City, and it was very different there. It rains a lot here, and there are more plants," remarked Ryan.

"That's because Eugene, Oregon, has a different climate from Carson City, Nevada," replied Michael.

"Is Eugene the capital of Oregon?" asked Ryan.

"Uh, no. Why do you ask?" inquired Michael.

"Oh, because we used to live in the state capital," Ryan replied with a frown. "I guess we got downgraded."

"Why would you think that?" asked Tessa unexpectedly.

"Because Carson City is the capital of Nevada, where all the important government stuff happens, so now we no longer live where the important stuff happens," replied Ryan.

"Well, that is a simplistic point of view," chided Tessa, rolling her eyes.

"Hey, he is only seven. I think the fact that he understands and has opinions about stuff says a lot about him," replied Michael to his sister.

"I told you she was mean," remarked Ryan. "She called me stupid."

"Well, I don't… think that is exactly… what she meant," said Michael, looking at his twin sister, who gave him a look. It was what she meant. "Okay, well, you do not have to live in the state capital to be important."

"What about the capital of the country?" asked Diego.

"Now, that's really impressive," said Ryan.

"My sister and I lived in Mexico City," said Diego. "Mexico City is the capital of Mexico."

"Wow, that must have been a really important place," responded Ryan with admiration.

"I guess so. It was a big place," replied Diego. He then turned to Michael and asked, "Where is your family from?"

"We lived in a suburb of Los Angeles," replied Michael. "Our Mom is a detective. She got hurt at work, and I think it made her worried. It scared me. She was in the hospital for quite a few days. Now, she is always saying that people are so violent these days. Her injury changed her, along with .... dad being gone."

"I don't want to hear about that," grumped Tessa.

"Policía?" asked Diego.

"Yeah, she was a policeman," replied Michael.

"You mean a police officer. She is female, and you have to say and make everything perfect, or people will scream at you and call you bad names," Tessa snarled.

"Sorry. It's just the name of a job. I don't see why that stuff matters," replied Michael. He then turned back to Diego, "Anyway, Mom is a great detective."

"Papá... is a police officer. I heard .... him cry at night. He has ...... La pesadilla," replied Diego, making a worried face. He looked down at his sister, who was blissfully eating her cheese pizza and drinking fruit juice.

Michael and Ryan frowned, looking at each other.

"Use your phone, stupid," said Tessa as she typed in the word Diego said. "It means... nightmare."

Ryan made a face.

"I don't like those," declared Ryan sympathetically to Diego. He then turned to Michael and asked, "So what does your dad do?"

"Not sure anymore. He was in the military. He and Mom got divorced several years ago, but I am hoping he will come back. I used to think Mom felt that way too," said Michael.

"Michael, Dad is not coming back," said Tessa.

"You don't know that," retorted Michael.

"Yeah, I do," said Tessa.

"What do you mean?" asked Michael.

"I mean that something weird happened a while ago. Mom started getting special checks from the military. I found them on her desk, and they were death benefits. Then they suddenly went away like someone had claimed that *we* were not his beneficiary family. He probably got married to some other woman and has a new family. He is not coming back," Tessa said irritably.

"But…... Mom still loves Dad. I know she does. He still loves her. He would not forget about us. And I don't believe he is dead. Did Mom say to you that he was dead?" Michael asked his sister.

"No. But he's not coming back. You are such a baby. You need to grow up. Mom is taking care of us by herself," replied Tessa, looking angry, as if at any moment she might get up and run off to be alone.

"My parents are still together," whispered Ryan to Diego. "They both like each other. I feel sorry for them." He then made a gesture towards the twins.

Diego nodded, understanding the idea that something was not right and upsetting the twins.

Down below on the main floor, dinner was proceeding smoothly, and everyone was getting to know one another better. Captain Justice made a toast to the progress the Cyberhawk Emergency Services Team had made and for an inspirational future of many missions where hope would be restored to those they assisted. Team members and family all agreed and clinked glasses together with that goal in mind. Dinner was a shared preparation with Dr. Hanni preparing and baking his homemade rolls while Raven assisted Janet and Ellena with the main courses. Jessica Justice and the Thomases brought the desserts.

"So, what's your part in the dinner?" Sandra asked Rafferty, who was sitting next to her.

"I'm part of the cleanup crew with my pals Chris, Daryl, and Fernando," he answered with a smile.

"Well, I could help. No one asked me to bring anything," said Sandra, feeling guilty.

"You have children. You and Ximena are exempt," said Ellena.

"What about Jessica? She brought a homemade key lime pie, one of my favorites," retorted Sandra.

"She is an overachiever," said Janet.

"I'm a what?" asked Jessica, only hearing the last part.

"They said that you..." The captain paused to look at his watch, which was showing incoming messages from his phone. "Are an...overachiever." He stopped and pulled out his phone. "Excuse me, everyone, I need to take this call."

Captain Justice moved away from the dining table into the dark and empty area near the roll-up door.

"I wonder what that is about," pondered the elderly Prof. Richard Thomas.

Diana and Jessica both replied at the same time, "It's an important phone call from someone he cannot ignore."

Jessica and Diana looked at each other and laughed.

"But seriously," said Diana in her heavy British accent. "He was not planning to take anyone's calls tonight unless it was someone like......Lukas Knight."

Jessica could not ignore the pacing form of her husband in the darkened area of the Cyberhawk base. He didn't look upset but was very focused on the conversation. After ten minutes, he came back to the table.

"Well, I hope everyone wants to have dessert now. We have an early morning planned for a large portion of the team. That means everyone going will have to be dressed, packed, and standing by the airfield at five hundred hours," said the captain.

"Who is going and what is the mission?" asked Daryl Crane.

"There is a big wildfire in Northern California, and they are asking for all the help they can get. I will be going with Lewis and Sanchez as part of the fire and rescue team. Thomas and Hallman will act as logistics for our team. Dr. Hanni and Smith to assist with medical. Takahashi, you will be flying the M-28. Make sure she is fully fueled and loaded for takeoff at five thirty," said the captain.

"Please schedule your flight tonight. Diana will have the details in about an hour."

Chris nodded, "Yes, sir."

"So, the rest of us are staying home?" asked Sandra.

"Yes. You, Morales, Crane, and Schmidt will continue your training. Mr. Knight might come by tomorrow morning, so please be ready to work with him on anything he needs," replied the captain.

"Captain, who is in charge while you are away? In case we need to make a decision about something… important," asked Ellena.

The captain paused for a moment. He appeared to be working through a decision while everyone watched silently.

"I was planning to have more preparation for this…," he said as he turned to Janet. "You are staying here. The Mountie is in second command; you are to handle matters while I am away. Diana, your job just got more hectic."

"I can handle it," replied Diana confidently.

Across the table, still seated, Dr. Richard Thomas felt a sense of pride and relief for his great niece. This was the place where she could feel at home and be herself again. Her transition to America was the right decision.

The next morning, the bulk of the team boarded the M-28 turboprop and headed for Northern California. Janet watched as the plane roared to life and took off into the cool, clear morning sky. She had wanted to go, but taking care of things back at the base was alright too. She was in a place where she could rebuild her life. She put her left hand to her upper right arm and wondered about the piece of technology that had been implanted into her arm. She wondered what it looked like. Did it ever need repairs? She knew that Lukas Knight would show up during the day. She was going to ask him some questions that she and the others had. Ever since Dr. Elgin Cross had something turned on for Fernando and the rest of them, something seemed different. Everyone felt it. She was going to get answers for her teammates.

It was seven in the morning when Janet found herself sitting with her fellow Cyberhawks: Sandra, Alejandro, Daryl, and Ellena. They were all drinking coffee.

"So did your children have a good time last night?" Sandra asked the ever-so-quiet Alejandro.

"Si, very much. Diego found the other children very interesting and hopes to see them again. Valentina was only concerned about the strange cheese pizza that she enjoyed," replied Alejandro with a slight smile.

"Good. Because my kids came home arguing and grumpy with each other last night, and I could not get out of them ....what could have made them so irritated with each other," remarked Sandra, momentarily taking off her sunglasses to clean the lenses.

"Children are beyond my understanding. I suppose that when I get older and have a spouse, I will figure it out," said Daryl.

"That's if I ever find anyone who wants to be married to a person like me."

"Are you kidding? You are kind, smart, and *handsome*. There is a woman out there for you," remarked Ellena, thinking to herself how much she found him to be attractive.

"I'm a cop... or I used to be a cop. With all the unpleasant stuff happening around the country, people just view us as the enemy. I've had people become instantly uncomfortable around me when they find out that I work in law enforcement. They always want to know about guns and killing people," Daryl rolled his eyes in frustration. "I just get tired of it."

"There will always be that stigma of people being nervous around someone who is seen as an authority figure," remarked Janet. Just then, the Cyberhawk base door opened, and Lukas Knight walked in. "Speaking of authority figures."

Lukas Knight walked over to the large, mostly empty dining table where everyone was sitting and drinking their morning coffee.

"Good morning," he said, placing his cell phone down on the table. Ellena had already gotten up and brought him a cup of hot coffee. "Thank you, Miss Schmidt. This is a nice way to start our morning together while our team is in the air heading to their mission destination. So, do any of you have questions that you would like to have answered? Projects that need clarification?"

Janet straightened up, knowing this was her opportunity.

"I want to know......as well as all the other Cyberhawk members......what are these hidden electronics under our skin?" Janet asked, gesturing to her upper right arm. "Dr. Cross changed something while Fernando was practicing with the CyberSkeleton, and......Fernando said it made using the equipment instantly easier, as if he could talk to the machine."

"Yes, Elgin does get impatient at times," remarked Knight, taking a deep breath as if thinking over what to say next. "That was supposed to be the next step in training, but things have pushed us forward to requiring a more accelerated approach. Those devices are designed to help individuals gain better control over their implants. Imagine trying to walk without enough control over where you place your foot, lift your leg, or simply remain standing. This is what this device is for. But we have discovered over the past few years that they have other applications. We have been concerned that civilians would be uncomfortable about the idea of having electronic attributes modifying the performance of the physical self. Some might say it is unnatural and counter to their religious beliefs."

Daryl set down his coffee cup.

"It is certainly better than being paralyzed for the rest of your life," remarked Daryl. "I see no reason to complain."

"I am not complaining either. I have felt so much better since the implant. I had no idea how much it could change my life," said Janet.

"First of all, not all of you have the same amount of repairs and conditions, and you all knew going into this that these implants were part of an experimental process and what the researchers have found with your help, has enabled us to help a lot of wounded soldiers, victims of natural disasters, those afflicted with horrible illnesses, civilians caught in the crossfire of military exchanges.....the list goes on. You all have one thing in common, and that is the communication implant located in your right arm. It is comprised of a series of computer parts that fit into a flexible pad. This device helps us update the artificial hearing system used by Ellena, as well as the repaired sections of Daryl's spine. Sandra's eye, ear, and nerve damage to her left arm, and .... it monitors several of Alejandro's internal organs, and for you, Janet, the ability to regulate systems in your body correctly. The technology is amazing. No more weird drugs with strange side effects. It is corrective," Knight explained.

"What does it look like? I never got to see this stuff," said Sandra. "When I was shot, they brought me into the emergency room... and I don't clearly remember what exactly happened. I had this dream that my ex-husband was there...... and he gave them permission to......help me. I had not seen him in about two years and....... I even thought that he might have been killed while on one of his missions. I still miss him."

Lukas Knight and everyone at the table just eyed Sandra, who appeared to be repressing tears. Ellena then wrapped her arm around her and said, "Hey, you have us now. We are kind of like a family."

Sandra gave a half smile and looked a bit lost for a moment.

"Family is everything," Alejandro murmured in Spanish.

"I can certainly show all of you what the implants look like. After all, they are now a part of you. I have one too," said Knight, getting up from the table. "I am a beneficiary of this technology. That is why I want to see it further developed, and…... I feel like this Cyberhawk… thing…has become perhaps better than a family. We all have chosen to be people who participate in making the world around us better, safer, and hopefully…more peaceful in the future."

"I lost both of my parents four years ago in a car accident. I feel like an orphan. I miss them as well," Janet added. "I like the idea of becoming a part of a new family. I loved my Mountie brothers and sisters back home, but…. I needed a change. And there is something about this group of people."

"I feel that way, too. I lost my wife of thirty years of blissful marriage some twenty years ago. She was everything to me," said Knight as he led them out the door towards the entrance to the underground lab.

"That… must have been awful. My parents would be devastated if they lost each other," said Daryl, thinking about his own family. "I have been fortunate so far and have not lost anyone close to me. My grandparents are still alive.   My family is very close to each other."

"Good family is a treasure," said Knight as they proceeded towards the secured garage. "My siblings couldn't even be bothered to send me a card or show up to... do anything kind when my wife unexpectedly passed away. We even lived within driving distance of each other. It was as if my beloved wife never existed, and neither of us mattered to them. And she was always kind to them. It was not as if she were a stranger whom they rarely saw."

"I can't imagine," said Ellena as she closed the security door behind her. "What kind of family does that?"

"One that does not care," replied Knight bitterly. "Our Cyberhawk is different. Some of us may be assholes, but we care about each other."

The elevator door opened, and Elgin Cross was yelling at several interns and then turned to look to see who had arrived, "Oh. Did I forget a meeting?"

"No," replied Knight. "The members of the Emergency Services Team want to see what a communications implant looks like."

"I see. Go ask Dalen. He is currently not as busy," replied Dr. Cross, who abruptly turned away to chide someone about some technical issue. He then yelled to Knight, "Major Bluster is coming to see that new device. He'll probably want to speak with you."

Knight nodded and then turned back to his little group. "Government project. We will need to be quick. He is not always too fond of civilians."

"Why is that?" asked Sandra.

Knight paused contemplatively and then said, "He feels that civilians will make foolish choices. I am sure that all of you have experienced, through work moments, when you wonder what people are thinking and if they are thinking at all."

"Oh yeah," agreed Sandra.

Ellena made an uncharacteristic expression of irritation.

"Two guys on the homemade boat made of liter-sized soda bottles, which got pulled too far offshore by currents," sighed Ellena, thinking back to past events. "I had to jump into the water and rescue one of them because he did not know how to swim......and he was wearing a child's life jacket."

Alejandro covered his mouth in a chuckle.

"And I thought the hidden distilleries in the forest were a problem," replied Janet as she shook her head in disgust.

Lukas Knight led his group to Dalen Hughes's office. He knocked on the open door and said, "Dr. Cross said you had time to show the Emergency Services Team what a communications implant looks like."

"Oh, he did? Not like I am working on anything important for," he paused and eyed the people standing behind Knight, "..........Major Bluster and his team."

Dalen Hughes's office was filled with pictures and diagrams of airplanes, rockets, a race car's engine bisected, pictures of the Rocketeer, Mandalorians wearing jetpacks and flying, and other versions of historical attempts and designs of working jet packs. He set down what he was reading and got up from his desk to assist the company's president. The engineer managed a cheery and professional attitude despite being pulled away from his work.

"Everyone, follow me. We are going to the Installation Med Room......wait," Dalen backtracked. "Uhm, I don't normally do that kind of work. And none of you are dressed appropriately to be in that room. We store cybernetic parts, do installations, and do repairs in that room. It is a clean room environment. And if I messed up Dr. Cross's room, ...he would be livid with me. And rightly so. We are going into this exam room, and I will get a damaged Communications Implant that I can show you," said Dalen, leading them into a small exam room. "Hold on while I ask Dr. Eirstone for a sample to show you all."

Dalen was gone only for a few moments when he came back with Dr. Eirstone.

"Good morning," said Dr. Eirstone in her calm, soothing, serene manner of speech. "In this container is a damaged Communications Implant that we keep for training purposes. It may not look broken, but these are finely crafted items that must meet the strictest standards. After all, this is put into the Human body to help someone walk, pump blood, or monitor chemical imbalances. We do not want to open the body up to make numerous repairs that could have been avoided in the first place. These items must be perfect. Our goal is to retain a good quality of life. Dalen, I will leave you with the sample," said Dr. Eirstone, who nodded to everyone and then left.

"Thanks, doctor. I owe you one," replied Dalen, watching her leave the room.

"Sushi," she said as she disappeared down the hallway.

Dalen smiled and said, "I can deal with that. I like Sushi." He paused and then turned his attention to the visiting group, "The seafood in this region is excellent. How many of you are new to the Pacific Northwest?"

"I am. I am from Quebec," said Janet.

"Oh, wow, an east coaster, but you probably got good seafood over there, too. We are fortunate to have a lot of fresh food here," said Dalen as he opened the plastic box to reveal a supple jelly-like material that was also strong like tissue. The material was reasonably thin and semi-clear. He held it over a light so that its semi-translucent form could reveal some of the tiny items that were held within its fabric. "From what I was told, this one was too thick, so it could not be used, but this would be placed under the outer skin layer where the fatty tissue is located."

"So do I have something like that....... in my arm to help me regulate how my hearing implant works?" asked Ellena.

"Yes," replied Dalen.

Lukas Knight looked closely at the item Dalen held. He had seen how things had changed rapidly in the past decade. So many new things were available to help people. Years ago, the device was larger and strapped to the person's arm to send signals to the implants. It was remarkable strides in advancement with dedicated people working hard to make that happen. Throughout the years, they built networks of sharing across the globe. Lukas looked at his artificial arm, which did not seem artificial at all. His arm was encased in the prototype see-through material that was just like Human flesh. It was clear, but it worked and felt very much the same. He had been the original recipient of this material. It could now be dyed various shades to match the recipient's skin tone, along with delicate hair implanted to make it look and feel more real.

"The advances are hope-inspiring and.........the more recent repairs have been done with a more lifelike artificial flesh material, but I have kept my arm this way to help people understand how this stuff works," said Knight, drawing his hand and lower arm to their attention. "I am very proud of this technology. I want people to realize there is hope and that they can live a normal life after suffering a life-changing injury."

Ellena held the implant in her hand and examined it.

"This stuff seems so strange, but when you think about the body being like a machine the soul uses to... drive like a car, then it seems to make more sense. Cars need to be repaired, maintained, and so does a person," said Ellena.

"I am just happy they saved my life, and I can still work. My kids need me," commented Sandra.

"Si, my family needs me to be there for them," said Alejandro in a somber tone.

"So, Janet, does this explain what you needed to know?" asked Knight.

"Sorta. But…. why was it easier for Fernando to use the CyberSkeleton after Dr. Cross made that change on the computer?" asked Janet.

"Ah, that's a good question," said Dalen, starting to look more enthusiastic about their conversation.

"You want to answer this?" asked Knight.

"Sure. These are used by the body to send signals to the implants. As time went on, we began to realize that the Human brain could also send signals to other items if we provided that it was in close proximity to the communication implant. I work with stuff outside of the body," said Dalen. "Think of it like Wi-Fi or Bluetooth. Follow me to my lab."

The small group followed the short black man dressed in a lab coat through the maze of offices and workstations. They halted at a workstation that had several mechanical-looking projects strewn about, most of which appeared to be under construction. Dalen went to the shelving unit, where he pulled out a basket labeled *test devices*. He set the basket down and pulled out an object that had a panel of LED lights, along with a wiring harness attached to a semi-flexible, curved disk.

"I have a piece of equipment that we use for testing implants. Do I have a volunteer?" asked Dalen.

"I'll do it," said Sandra.

"Okay, I want you to take this piece and hold it firmly against the upper part of your right arm. It needs to have firm contact, but you don't have to squeeze it like a blood pressure cuff," instructed Dalen.

"Okay. How's that?" asked Sandra.

"Looks good. Have you ever communicated with a device outside of your body?" asked Dalen.

"No," answered Sandra, wondering if talking to an Alexa device counted.

"Alright. I want you to close your eyes while the others watch this piece here," Dalen directed the others to look at the light panel. "Now, I want you to imagine or to think... lights on."

"Uh, is this like some Jedi test? Will I get hit by a laser beam if I don't deflect the lights?" laughed Sandra, keeping her eyes closed.

"She did it!" exclaimed Ellena.

"I did what?" asked Sandra, opening her eyes.

"You turned on the lights," said Daryl. "Can she do anything more complicated? Like turn on only the green lights."

"Are there different colors of lights? Okay... and you want only green ones," said Sandra, and before she finished her sentence, only the green lights remained on.

"Wonderful. Now make the pink ones flash on and off," suggested Ellena.

And before anyone could say anything, the pink lights were flashing on and off.

"Sandra, are you sure you have never controlled a device outside of your body before?" asked Dalen.

"Yeah," Sandra replied emphatically.

"Well then, you are a natural. We need to test you on more items," said Dalen, starting to sound a little excited.

"Okay," agreed Sandra. "Go for it. What's next?"

"Hmm," said Dalen, looking about the room, wondering what a challenging test could be. "Ah, this won't get us all killed…. or damage the lab." Dalen went to another box on the shelf and pulled it down.

"What do you mean, won't get us killed?" asked Ellena.

"Oh, well… some of the devices I work on… can be somewhat hazardous," said Dalen, glancing at Lukas Knight, who just gave him a knowing look. "This item will not get us into any trouble but will offer an excellent test of Detective Ridgestone's skill level."

Dalen then pulled out another communications patch and a small toy car.

"Ellena, will you take the light panel testing set and put them into their box? And I will give this… to Sandra," he said, handing Sandra the communications patch that went to the toy car. This item did not have any wires attached. "Hold this up to your arm. And I will put this on the floor."

Before Dalen could set the car down, the wheels of the vehicle were already racing.

"Oops, I am sorry," said Sandra. "I got a little carried away."

"That is perfectly fine," chuckled Dalen. "I am excited to see how you will perform this task."

"Okay. I am not making the wheels turn. What do you need me to try?" asked Sandra, getting herself composed.

"Move the car forward and then backward," Dalen directed.

The car moved forward and then backward.

"Now, make the car drive in a circle," said Dalen. The car started to drive in a circle. "Make the circle tighter." The toy started moving in a smaller circle. "Good. Now, a figure eight pattern." The toy drove in a figure eight pattern. "You are talented at this. How about something more challenging like... navigate the car under the lab table and chairs around the boxes and stop at Mr. Knight's feet."

"Okay. This is just like a car chase through traffic," said Sandra as she moved the car, not as fast but skillfully, between the table legs without hitting anything, to rest at Lukas Knight's feet finally. "So, was that good?"

"That was excellent. Only the military pilots have gotten through that test the first time," remarked Dalen, glancing at Lukas Knight.

There was silence for a moment as Dalen picked up the toy car and then pulled the light panel back out.

"Are you thinking what I am thinking?" Knight asked Dalen. "We need to test them all. Some of you might be ready to work with more sophisticated equipment."

"Let's do it! And later, ...we will need to schedule testing for those that have left to deal with the California forest fires," said Dalen, feeling excited about the prospect that the new Emergency Services Team was going to be ready to use more sophisticated equipment sooner than expected.

CHAPTER 8

The smoke should have been choking him, but the helmet, which was part of the Cyberhawk gear, was incredible. He could breathe clean, filtered air and not feel the tremendous heat coming from the fire. Captain Justice was thankful for the new technology. He was skeptical at first, worried that he and his team would get burned, but the equipment was truly fire-resistant and seemed to have some barrier interwoven into the special jumpsuit he was wearing with the CyberSkeleton.

In a different section of the conflagration, a two-hundred-plus-year-old foxtail pine tree had fallen across the only roadway up the canyon, where equipment and personnel needed to go. He, along with Lewis and Sanchez, was going to push the tree off the road. There was not enough time for the tree to be cut out of the way. If the ridge above was to be saved, they had to reach the area now. The upper region was also crucial in preventing the fire from spreading further down the canyon on the other side, where a small community was nestled at the canyon's bottom.

The three of them took specific positions along the giant old tree and began moving in unison. The captain could hear clearly and speak with them through the HUD system, which made everything easier. How many times had he wished their communication system were better during challenging rescue missions and wildfire abatement? The Cyberhawk equipment had real-world applications that came through. This was the next test. Could the three of them remove this tree from blocking the road so that heavy equipment and firefighters could gain access to the area they needed? As the tree started to budge, Captain Justice got an answer to his question. Together, they could move this enormous tree out of the way. It rolled slightly and then got wedged on a branch.

"Hold on," ordered the captain. He backed away from the tree and surveyed the space. "Okay, it is stuck on that branch as we thought it might. It's not gonna roll anymore. So, since that is in the middle, ……. we can pivot forth on that side to allow for enough space for the trucks to travel through."

"So, you want me to move down next to Rafferty and help him push?" asked Fernando.

"Correct," replied the captain.

Fernando walked over to where Rafferty was waiting. When they were both in position, the captain gave them the order to start moving slowly. Within ten minutes, there was enough space for the big firefighting equipment to drive up the hill safely. The crews in the trucks waved to them as they went on by. One of the fire captains in a pickup truck stopped to chat with Justice.

"Captain Justice, I love your Cyberhawk crew. You saved us two hours of hard work with this big old fallen lady. Too bad, she came down. We are seeing fewer of these foxtail pines growing these days. Thanks again," he said.

"You are welcome. So glad we could be here to assist," replied the captain. "Stay safe."

"Will do," said the other man in the truck as he headed up to follow his team.

The captain turned to Rafferty and Fernando and said, "Let's head back down for a break. Recharge the CyberSkeletons and find out if we are needed anywhere else."

"I feel like Superman," said Rafferty.

"Perhaps a little like the Incredible Hulk…although I have not yet gotten a chance to smash anything," commented Fernando.

"And you will not be smashing anything, Sanchez," said the captain as the three of them proceeded down the rough dirt road.

The dirt road had a steep incline and was covered in loose soil and rocks.

"I am so glad we have cleats that pop out of the bottom of the feet," remarked Rafferty as he slowly made his way down the loose gravel. Occasionally, sliding a little. "Trudgin' up and down roads like this with a full pack of gear makes you feel tired… and this machine…. does it all for us. I love it!"

"Did either of you notice how much easier it is to do stuff with the communications implant turned on for outside devices?" asked Fernando as he looked up to see a drone buzzing above them. "Hey, it's our drone!"

"It certainly is on both accounts," remarked the captain as he eyed the gold and blue-marked drone making its way through the smoky sky.

Fernando waved to the drone and said, "Hi, Chris!"

The drone circled them once, as if in response, and then headed up towards the ridge area where the next tactical staging was to occur. The three of them arrived at the upper base camp to get some rest and prepare for their next project. Nobody saw Dr. Hanni or Raven Smith since they were both very busy at the first aid station. A rescued camper went into labor that morning, so word was out about the happy arrival that was safely birthed at the first aid station and was later taken away on the medical helicopter. Diana was waiting at the upper base camp, where all the necessary supplies, including food, water, towels, charging cables, and generators, were set up for her team. She also had their next assignment, which would require them to load up the truck they were given to use and head down the road forty miles. The equipment was performing well, and so were the team members.

"So good to see you, Miss Thomas. Any word on the status of the fire in general?" asked the captain as he stepped out of his CyberSkeleton and started to hook it up to the generator for charging.

"I was told that they thought they would get the fire under control in a week. That is assuming the winds do not come up. A storm is expected tonight, and if there is rainfall, they could do mop-up work in three days. It just depends upon the weather," she replied.

"Then everyone should pray to their deities for help," suggested Sanchez.

"That would be Indra for me," said Diana.

"Raven said something about the Rain Maiden earlier," commented Rafferty.

"I don't care who we ask as long as we get some rain to put out that fire," commented the captain as he sat down and chugged his bottle of water. "Heck, I will sit down with Roy Ekstrand and offer mead to Loki if necessary."

****

Back at the Cyberhawk airbase, Lukas Knight was working with the five team members who had been left behind. The LabCoat Crew had brought out their latest invention to show Major Bluster and the Emergency Services Team, who just happened to be present, to see it.

"Why are the civilians here?" Major Bluster asked Lukas Knight.

"Because eventually, they will need to use this equipment as well. That has always been part of the plan," replied Knight.

"Can I assume they all have clearance, including the two foreign nationals?" Major Bluster asked through gritted teeth.

Lukas Knight gave Major Bluster an enigmatic look.

"Staff Sergeant Janet Hallman of the Royal Canadian Mounted Police has a special diplomatic privilege, along with passing our strict clearance procedure. She is the selected representative for Canada in the Cyberhawk Program," replied Knight.

"And what about the Mexican policeman?" Bluster asked.

"Alejandro Luis Morales of the Mexican NCB is part of the AIC and also has been selected by his government to be the official representative for the Cyberhawk Program. He is also under a certain amount of protection since he and his family are in grave danger from one of the drug cartels. There is some consideration of granting him citizenship for himself and his family. From what I have read, it would be unwise for him to return to his homeland," replied Knight.

"I see," replied Major Bluster, appearing uninfluenced by the additional information.

Dalen Hughes came out with Kendra Boisen and Dr. Cross, introducing a new version of the CyberSkeleton that also featured an attachment installed at the back. He and Kendra rolled the device out on a special heavy-duty cart not far from the tarmac of the runway. Dalen looked a little nervous, but also excited.

"Oh boy," Dalen said under his breath.

"It will be fine," Kendra encouraged him with a positive whisper, with her back turned to those he was about to present to.

Dalen straightened his lab coat and proceeded, "This is the version of the CyberSkeleton with the requested modifications from Major Bluster. We have also been able to streamline the jetpack attribute to a more manageable size and fuel consumption. The level of communication between the Communication Implant and the exterior device has been solid with no errors over the past ten months of testing. We are still in the process of implementing the AI as an additional resource for the pilot. We have Trevor Vermeulen and Renata Washington working on those coding parameters."

"So, we still do not have the Mechanical AI emergency copilot ready in case of pilot failure?" asked Major Bluster as he walked up to the device. His uniform medals flashed in the sunlight.

"No, sir, but we are making progress," replied Dalen.

"What is the problem?" asked Major Bluster.

"The level of communication required needs to be perfected. There are…. problems with so much noise in the frequency ranges, and…. the pilot's life may rely on this ability to communicate," replied Dalen.

"We already lost one pilot. And those who fly now know they are on their own. We need to test this now, with Betty being allowed to communicate and assist the pilot, when necessary, just like in other aircraft. I want it to be AI-enabled," said Major Bluster.

"Alright, Sir," said Dalen, looking over at Dr. Cross.

Major Bluster followed the look that led to the lead scientist of the LabCoat Crew.

"Well, Cross, any objections?" asked Major Bluster.

"No. I think the baby bird needs to take flight. We have tested it extensively and require field usage to understand what needs to be adjusted and upgraded. The fuel cell already lasts for three to six hours of flight, depending upon the weather conditions and what the pilot is doing," replied Cross. "We have so many fail-safes that a novice should be able to fly it without any problem...as long as the AI is there to assist."

"I take it... You are recommending a test with a novice," said Major Bluster, eyeing Cross critically. "As proof that the CyberSkeleton with jet pack is ready." He turned and looked around, and his sight landed upon the Emergency Services Team members. "How about one of them?"

"Oh well, they have not been trained on this model at all," Kendra piped in.

"And I just tested them this morning to find out how well they can use the Communications Implant with an external device," added Dalen.

"And how did the civilians do?" asked Bluster.

"Well, actually.... fairly well. Detective Ridgestone is extremely talented. One would think she had been using a device like it for years," replied Dalen. "The others also performed well, but not to the degree that the detective did."

"Well, then, here is the answer. We have Detective Ridgestone test the device right now... unless the civilians are not up to it," suggested Major Bluster, then turning an eye to Lukas Knight.

"That is an unfair challenge," said Knight. "She should go through training before testing a device like this."

"No. I can do it. As a detective, an investigator, … and as law enforcement, we are often thrust into unexpected situations. We must adjust to each situation using the training and experience we have. Now, I would like to clarify… that I am just seeing if I can make this version of the CyberSkeleton work, right?" said Sandra.

"That would be correct," said Dr. Cross, then turning to everyone else, "We will need her put into one of the body suits. Her street clothes will not protect her from the heat from the jets, or if she falls over. Kendra, take the Detective to put on a jumpsuit."

"Yes, Dr. Cross," said Kendra, inviting Sandra to follow her.

As the two women left, Major Bluster walked over to Lukas Knight.

"Well, I guess we shall see if the civilians have what it takes. She already shows signs of courage, but that could also be foolhardy arrogance," Major Bluster remarked to Knight as he folded his arms across his chest in defiance.

"I think she will do fine," replied Knight, thinking Bluster would know all about foolhardy arrogance.

"We shall see," said Bluster.

Fifteen minutes later, Detective Sandra Ridgestone found herself encased in a robotic suit reminiscent of a Star Wars armor and helmet, slowly hovering above the ground. Sandra thought to herself that her son would love this. It was fun, and it seemed easy. She felt like a cross between Iron Man and a Mandalorian. To think that she was hovering above the ground like some techno hummingbird.

"What do I do now?" Sandra asked the AI through the helmet's HUD system.

"How about flying a low maneuver above the paved ground. A circular pattern. Make sure you keep plenty of space between you and the others on the surface," suggested the AI.

"How come I can't fly towards the trees and back?" asked Sandra.

"Because the exhaust from the jets could start a fire," replied the AI.

"Oh. I understand. Don't want to do that. We sent all the firemen off to California," commented Sandra with a chuckle as she started the circular maneuver.

"Just follow the AI instructions," a voice that sounded like Dr. Cross suddenly came through the HUD system. "I don't need Major Bluster giving me more grief about allowing the ......*civilian* to use the equipment."

"Agreed. Do you require me to perform any other task to prove that the new CyberSkeleton is working as planned?" asked Sandra.

"Hover for a minute while I make a request to the airfield management," said Dr. Cross.

Sandra was high enough up that she could see the top of the Cyberhawk Base building. She could see the large mechanical doors mounted into the roof and realized that she could probably land inside the building if she needed to. She now wondered if that was what the doors were for. Or perhaps the drones? The hawk's view was incredible, and she began to feel a childlike excitement about being part of the Cyberhawk program. Learning how to fly a device like this was a life-changing experience.

"Sandra," she heard Dalen's voice come through the HUD system.

"Yes."

"We got clearance for you to fly across the runway and up to five hundred feet and then circle back around into the flight path to land. Betty will help you by bringing up the aviation flight path through the HUD display and guide you through the process since you have not yet started any aviation training courses," said Dalen. "Are you willing to do this?"

"Oh, heck yes! But.... wait.... who is Betty?" asked Sandra.

She heard a chuckle from Dalen, and then he said, "That is the name of our AI. Her name is Betty."

"Okay. Good to know. Hello, Betty," said Sandra.

"Hello, Detective Ridgestone. You are doing well, but your heart rate is slightly elevated. Are you feeling alright?" asked Betty.

"Oh yeah. I am just excited….and a little nervous," replied Sandra.

"Good to know. Please move towards the north end of the airstrip and hover about thirty feet," instructed Betty. "We will wait there for our permission to take off. We have been granted permission to enter the strip for takeoff."

Sandra followed Betty's instructions and made her way safely to the end of the airstrip. She hovered at thirty feet and could see a variety of data streaming on the HUD screen in her helmet. She saw how much fuel she had left, her current elevation, the GPS location, and the time of day.

"You have been granted permission to take off. I want you to fly forward with the idea that you want enough speed to obtain a body position that is more horizontal than vertical. Do you understand?" asked Betty.

"Yes. I think so. I am to pretend to be an airplane or… a really fast bird," replied Sandra.

"That idea works. You may proceed when ready," said Betty.

Sandra took a calming breath to clear her mind and focused on what she was to do next. The runway lay before her. Then she decided to go. She moved forward, picking up speed rapidly. She could see the speedometer readout climbing up to thirty-five mph, fifty mph, and then seventy mph, and she realized that she was now in a more horizontal position. With Betty's help, she was climbing in elevation. She followed the designated flight path that Betty had planned and displayed through the AR setup in the HUD. The view from above was fantastic. Sandra felt like a bird. It did not feel like she was flying in an airplane. She had a sense of the wind rushing across her and could see half of a 360° spherical view with no obstructions. The trees below were starting to bud in various locations, streams were flowing, cars on roads, birds fluttering below, small aircraft off in the distance near the Eugene airport, and the valley opened up before her with numerous rolling hills covered in vegetation and houses nestled about with the city structures off in the not-so-far distance. Then Betty showed her where her next turning maneuver was and that it would line her up with the traditional aviation landing pattern. Sandra did not want to return to the ground. This was too wonderful to end.

"Do I need to have a landing strip like an airplane?" Sandra asked.

"No. However, we agreed with the control tower that we would follow a traditional aviation takeoff and landing procedure, allowing them to plan for incoming traffic. The Cyberhawk is more akin to a helicopter or an Osprey in terms of its landing capabilities. This test was unscheduled, so we are being considerate to our control tower, who was kind enough to grant us testing time on the airstrip," answered Betty.

Once on the ground, Sandra was bombarded with questions from everyone. It was determined that the LabCoat

Crew required debriefing time with her. Lukas Knight turned to Major Bluster as they stood twenty feet away from the others.

"She did well. You have to admit that," said Knight.

"I do not have to admit anything. But she has potential. If all the civilians you have selected have the focus, courage, and understanding of how to follow instructions, then the Emergency Services Team might be a success," replied Major Bluster. "The equipment looked good, too. I look forward to hearing the results from Dr. Cross. If all is well, how long do you think it will take to get the upgraded Cyberhawks into service?"

"I would speculate a month for a full team to be ready. These are not mass-produced like an automobile assembly line. I am having trouble finding reliable people to work on technical projects. There are not enough properly educated personnel, and...HR has been battling with some strange social behaviors within the average population," replied Knight.

"Well, if this team is as good as you say they are, then they are gonna be priceless. I'd like to know; what problem specifically is HR dealing with?" asked the Major.

"Lack of dedication to do a project correctly, lack of focus, not willing to show up on time, and the worst of all is......a bizarre......type of anger or temper," replied Knight with a bit of frustration. "We have let ten people go just because they went nuts. Things like politics and religion can stir the hornet's nest, but other topics can also set them off. The lower management team is extremely frustrated because they have great jobs to offer with good benefits and a nice work environment, but we cannot find reasonable people."

"We've seen evidence of this strange behavior in other sectors of the military and some government service locations. And it is not just confined to our country. Intelligence sources say it is happening all over the world. Originally, it was thought to be a side effect of the global pandemic. However, historical sociological researchers argue that this behavior has occurred in waves throughout history and has peaked at times, even causing events such as world wars, extreme religious persecutions, and mass disasters. Something odd is happening," commented Major Bluster with a sour expression. "And I don't like it."

CHAPTER 9

Several days have passed since the team arrived in California to help bring the large wildfire under control. The group made some good friends during the process, and when it was finally time to do the basic mop-up operations, it was no longer necessary for the Cyberhawk crew to remain. It was time to pack up the gear, say goodbye, and head for the airport, where their transport was waiting for them. Everyone was tired, but it had been a meaningful experience. The firefighters already had some ideas for improvements. The small community located down the ravine had been saved, but a significant amount of acreage had suffered, and wildlife had been displaced. The drone proved especially useful, as it was designed to withstand extreme temperatures and high winds. Chris knew that his efforts to provide the best intel on the fire had turned out to be useful, including saving the lives of ten firefighters.

"I am exhausted. I can't wait to curl up in my own bed," said Fernando.

"I am right there," yawned Rafferty as he slowly moved the big truck out onto the freeway to head towards the airport, where the M-28 was waiting for them. "Looks like Chris is already taking a quick nap before the flight."

"He was asleep the minute he hit the seat," replied Fernando, taking another glance at the always eager pilot.

"I wonder what the others have been doing," pondered Raven as he made himself comfortable in the front seat of the truck. He pulled out his cell phone to check for messages from family.

"Don't know, but Diana might know," suggested Rafferty, somewhat distracted by the traffic that he had to merge the big truck into.

"She's in the other vehicle," said Raven.

"Yeah, she's the captain's assistant. That is her job to be by his side," replied Rafferty.

"The others have probably been hanging out, eating great food, sleeping in soft beds, watching movies, and playing video games at night. Ellena has probably surpassed me in our little gaming competition," said Fernando. He was fidgeting in his seat, desperately trying to get comfortable.

"You mean that training game that she's been playin'?" asked Rafferty.

"No. We have been playing Beat Saber from time to time," replied Fernando with another big yawn.

"Oh yeah, I like that one," said Raven, adjusting the seatbelt to be more comfortable. "Makes me feel like a disco Jedi, but … what I really miss is good coffee. What have you guys missed while out on this trip?"

"My bed," replied Fernando.

"Hmm," Rafferty pondered. "Nothing. I'm pretty much happy no matter where I go or what I do. I do miss the others. I have grown fond of you all."

Raven chuckled, "That's nice to hear. I like hanging out with you guys, too."

"Really? You guys are going mushy on me?! Good thing Chris is asleep," said Fernando. "He would be teasing us."

"Why?" asked Raven.

"Because being mushy is not his hotshot pilot persona. And I don't..." Fernando started to yawn in mid-sentence. "Damn, I'm exhausted."

"Go to sleep. We'll be on the road for an hour. Raven will keep me company," said Rafferty.

"Yeah, you are probably right," he yawned again as he pulled his jacket over him like a blanket. "The others are probably sitting around having a beer and playing video games."

****

Back at the Cyberhawk Airbase, Janet reviewed the details of the requested mission while Roy Ekstrand flew northward with the heavy-duty Cyberhawk helicopter. Embracing her new responsibilities while the captain was away, she had just sent Sandra, Daryl, and Alejandro off to assist Portland Metro Police in finding teens that had disappeared into a large, abandoned mall. The London Center was once a thriving commercial supermall that drew thousands of shoppers daily. However, as the years passed and online shopping gained popularity, the shoppers and stores began to disappear, leaving one section of the mall desperately trying to hold on while the other half was closed off to conserve power. According to the information provided by the Portland Metro Police Department, a group of teenagers wanted to go exploring in the closed-off section in an attempt to be paranormal researchers hunting for ghosts. The closed-off section had developed a creepy reputation over the past five years, one that was only getting worse. Janet was not worried about sending three highly trained law enforcement professionals to a haunted location, but was concerned about a dilapidated location. Sandra and Daryl were using the new prototype Cyberhawk suits since the local police were concerned about the poor condition of the dark part of the mall. Alejandro was going to act as the handler. The teens had been missing for three hours and were not responding to cell phone calls or messages. The parents of the teens and the friends who alerted the authorities had assured that the teens in question were not the type to run away or do drugs. The fire and rescue team of Portland Metro had complained to the city and the mall owners that the dark section had become too hazardous to enter due to contaminants such as black mold and structural problems. They had been advising that the dark section be demolished. There had already been problems with homeless people trying to find shelter within that section of the mall, and there had been five deaths in the closed-off wing and numerous reported missing people in the area.

One of the big, burly, uniformed officers came over to brief the Cyberhawk team on the details concerning the location and the kids. Sandra felt sorry for the worried parents. Her twins were only a couple of years younger than these kids. It could be Tessa and Michael off in that derelict structure.

"Here are the pictures of the kids that you are looking for. These were taken today. This was supposed to be some big fun adventure," said the Portland Metro officer, showing images on a tablet.

It was two boys and a girl who had entered, while the two remaining friends had refused to go. Daryl and Sandra took note of what the kids were wearing. Alejandro also looked at the image closely, as he stayed behind and monitored the exterior-facing cameras mounted on the outside of the helmets. He could assist in looking for any signs of the kids or danger.

"Do any of the children have health conditions that could cause them problems in such a toxic environment?" Alejandro asked the local officer.

"None that we know of. But with the ceiling rotting and collapsing in some sections, who knows what kind of chemicals and molds are festering in there?" The officer shook his head with frustration. "The kids might develop an illness from just being in there."

The group nodded sympathetically.

"Well, our Cyberhawk equipment is designed with filters and breathers so that we can enter the environment safely. Is there any place in particular that the kids wanted to explore?" asked Sandra.

The uniformed cop wrinkled his brow in thought.

"No. But I would stay out of the three-story Ford & Stone department store. It has been unoccupied for over ten years and ....is probably in the worst condition of all the locations within that section," suggested the officer. "The location where the kids gained entrance is currently being monitored, and the mall is in the process of getting materials to seal that off better."

"Good to know," said Daryl, closing his helmet to get ready to enter the restricted section of the mall.

The mall security janitorial tech stood waiting by the locked entrance. He looked spooked. Daryl eyed the man behind the special protective glass of his helmet and thought that it was a sad state when the janitor also had to be the mall security. The funds to run this place were obviously slipping away. Daryl turned back to the uniformed officer and asked, "Is the heat and power both turned off in this section?"

The Portland Metro Officer looked at the janitor holding the set of keys. The uncomfortable-looking man made a face and answered Daryl's question for the officer.

"Nothing is running over there. No water, no electricity, no heat, no Wi-Fi ...nothing," he replied, looking nervous as if debating whether to say anything more.

The man looked down at the ground. Daryl took that as a sign that he should proceed through the open doorway with some caution. Sandra followed close behind him. Her prototype Cyberhawk gear made her feel strong and safe. She wondered if that was wise. The LabCoat Crew were talented engineers and could do all sorts of amazing things, but she and Daryl were the first people to take these devices out in the field.

"Daryl," said Sandra. "I got the impression that the janitor had more to say… but he was afraid to do so."

"Yes, I got that impression as well. He was probably afraid of losing his job. Companies are always worried about being sued," replied Daryl.

"I get that," said Sandra as they both exited through the boarded-up hallway and into the open section of the closed-off wing of the London Center Mall.

"Wow," said Daryl. "This place… was once incredible. Those high ceilings, the open structures, natural light coming through the above windows…"

"It makes me feel sad. I grew up with malls being a fun place to go with my parents and friends. This place feels… weird," remarked Sandra as she looked about, scanning for any signs of the missing teens.

The location's space was huge, with the Ford & Stone department store looming at the end as a retail anchor. It was all dark inside, even on the upper-floor entrances that they could see from the ground level looking up.

"Where should we go first?" Daryl asked, looking around.

"We should start in the location where they snuck in. Perhaps we shall see or hear something that will give us some idea of where they went," said Sandra, leading Daryl out of the main open section and to a small side wing. There, they found a closed Hank's Homecookin' that had an exterior entrance as well as a mall entrance. It was unlocked and open. The restaurant had an open courtyard with a roof for patrons to sit outside, and the remaining teens explained that the door was no longer secured. The kids climbed into the courtyard and went inside. The two friends who had exited the mall explained that they had seen something in the central area that made them uncomfortable, while the others wanted to investigate further and set up equipment. The remaining kids promised that they would only stay inside for an hour longer. Daryl and Sandra went into the restaurant just in case the kids returned there for some reason and had not exited.

"Hello! Anybody in here? Your friends and family are worried about you," Daryl said in his best friendly voice. "We are here to help you."

He and Sandra stood still, listening for any voices or movement. Then Alejandro's voice came through the HUD system, stating that he was not seeing anything either.

"I can monitor the thermal readout here on the big screen. I don't see any heat signatures. I will let you know if anything shows up," said Alejandro. "I would suggest heading back out into the main section."

"Agreed. Perhaps you will see some heat signatures," suggested Sandra.

"There is also a chance that homeless people are living inside there," said Alejandro.

"Copy that. We will keep an open eye for homeless individuals. We have already seen evidence of drug use and some graffiti," replied Daryl.

"Si," said Alejandro, keeping focused on the screen in front of him.

Sandra and Daryl made their way back out of Hank's Homecookin' restaurant and back towards the central open area of the mall. They walked slowly, peering into the closed stores, some of which still had shelves and items strewn about, while others were completely void of any improvements. Sections of the place had a chaotic, utterly destroyed, and decayed feel, while other stores looked like they just needed the lights turned back on and they would be ready for business.

"Does this place feel creepy to you?" Daryl asked his more experienced female partner.

"Yeah," she replied somberly.

"Did you hear what scared the two kids that refused to stay?" asked Daryl.

"Yeah," replied Sandra as she continued to scan the mall. The HUD AR system displayed a wide range of data, with a focus on toxins and chemicals in the air. Curious mold counts were showing up in one of the store fronts. Luckily, it was gated off securely, so the kids could not have gone inside.

"What scared them?" asked Daryl.

"They saw several shadow figures down by the Ford & Stone department store," replied Sandra.

"Oh," said Daryl, pausing for a moment. "Are you seeing the mold counts over there?"

"Yup. It's gnarly toxic. I don't see how any of the homeless would survive living here," said Sandra, walking over to the sunken mall couch area where she saw signs that people had been sleeping in this section. Old, dirty blankets, rags, and food containers were strewn about. "We need to find those kids soon."

"This is just the ground floor," remarked Daryl. "We need a bigger team with hazmat suits."

"Apparently, the city could not afford such a luxury. Currently, they are experiencing a financial crisis, having lost vital experts, and their equipment has aged, necessitating replacement. This is one of the reasons why they reached out to us for help. If it were not for the missing kids, we would not be here," replied Sandra. "We both know that these Cyberhawk suits are prototypes. They assured me that the breathers and filters have been effectively tested along with the other components."

"So, it is just the flying part that is new?" asked Daryl.

"Basically. This version of the flying part is new, along with the more streamlined body design. The CyberSkeletons that the captain and others took down to California are bulkier than these. I love this suit," said Sandra. "It makes me feel...... awesome."

"Agreed. Awesome is a good feeling," said Daryl, noticing something up on the third floor catching his attention. "Did you see that up there?"

"No. Where?" asked Sandra.

"Up to our left, just past Claire's, where the sunlight is hitting from the windows on the right," directed Daryl.

"Hmm. Don't see anything," replied Sandra.

"Well, I did. And I want to investigate," said Daryl. He looked around for the stairs.

"The stairs will take too long... and I have not practiced walking upstairs in this gear," remarked Sandra.

"We could fly," suggested Daryl.

"They said we should not fly inside a building," replied Sandra. "It would take a great deal of careful concentration because we could set this place on fire or land too hard."

"I know you can do it. And I can do it as well," replied Daryl.

Sandra sighed a little, and then they both heard a loud noise that echoed throughout the empty mall section.

"What ......was .... that?" asked Daryl, scanning around him.

"Let's go look," said Sandra. "Betty, I need an assist in making a very light touchdown on that upper level."

"Understood. You know that it is advised not to fly within the confines of a structure," said Betty through the HUD.

"I know, but we gotta find those kids, and the longer they stay in here, the more likely they will die from exposure to toxins," replied Sandra. "Daryl will need assistance as well."

"Understood. I am ready when needed," replied Betty.

Sandra moved to a spot where no flammable materials were lying on the floor and took off slowly, gently landing on the third floor of the mall near the empty Clare's store. The floor felt stable and secure. Daryl flew up after with Betty's assistance as well. The upper section was well-lit from the sunlight coming in from all the upstairs windows. It almost felt cheery, except that a strong, oppressive feeling emanated from the Ford & Stone entrance, which was completely open. It was jet black in there, but wide open.

"Wow, that looks awful in there. If I were ghost hunting and wanting to find paranormal evidence… that place would be top on my list," said Sandra as they both walked towards the entrance area of Ford & Stone.

They stood at the threshold of the store entrance, which was like an open maw waiting to ingest something. They both thought they saw something moving about in there, along with a strange greenish light source.

"The power is supposed to be off in this entire section, right?" asked Daryl.

"Yeah," replied Sandra soberly with a scowl on her face as she tried to discern what she was seeing. The only way to find out the light source's origin would be to go inside and investigate. She took a couple of steps towards the entrance when another loud bang happened. It came from one of the upper stores on the other side of the Ford & Stone entrance. She and Daryl both looked over in that direction.

"The sound came from there," said Daryl, pointing to the old toy store that had a happy facade that seemed like an oxymoron for this tense, serious situation.

Daryl started walking towards the direction from which he had heard the noise. Sandra paused and looked back into the Ford & Stone department store, wondering if she had really seen anything in there. A chill ran up her spine. She thought she heard a whisper or a hissing noise.

"Sandra," Daryl called out. "I found a K2 meter and a cell phone."

Sandra left the Ford & Stone entrance and went to see what Daryl had found in front of the closed toy store. Daryl showed her the cell phone with the cracked screen and the K2 meter.

"I think we are on the right track," said Daryl, suddenly bending over as if in pain.

"You both need to get out of there, now," said Alejandro through the HUD system. His accent grew thicker with each word.

"But we have a lead on the kids. We found a cell phone and a K2 meter," said Sandra. She walked into the entrance of the toy store and peered into the colorfully painted space. "Are you picking up on any heat signatures in the store?"

"Uh, yes," said Alejandro, sounding agitated.

"I am going to investigate. Daryl, are you coming along?" Sandra asked.

"I don't ……. feel right," he replied.

"He is showing serious signs of fatigue. He appears as if he might pass out," said Betty, who had been monitoring their vital signs. "I think he needs to leave immediately."

"Okay. Daryl? Can you fly down?" Sandra asked as she turned towards her younger and usually much stronger partner.

"What?" he said vaguely.

"Ah, shit. Betty, are you capable of taking control of his suit and getting him out of this place?" asked Sandra, realizing the gravity of Daryl's situation.

"Yes. I am perfectly capable of managing operations. I will safely take him outside the toxic mall area. I will request that Alejandro get emergency medical services to look him over," replied Betty.

Then, suddenly, the jets on Daryl's Cyberhawk suit activated, lifted off, and headed downward. Sandra stared after him for a moment, watching him land and walking directly towards the entrance through the boarded hallway.

"You need to get out of there right now!" Alejandro said, his Mexican accent coming in heavier than usual. He was agitated.

"The kids. I have kids, ...and I would not want someone to give up on my twins if they were in danger," replied Sandra as she turned towards the empty toy store and headed inside. "Hello, I am not here to hurt you," she said through the exterior mic of the Cyberhawk helmet.

There was rustling and a repetitive banging sound coming from the back of the store. Then she saw a pair of sneakers attached to legs and slowly walked around the cashier's counter to find three teens lying on the floor. Two were unconscious, and the third was unable to speak and was coughing up some blood. She had a metal part in her left hand that she had been using to hit against a metal fixture. The girl looked terrified and was shaking. Sandra had to repress the urge to pop open her helmet mask.

"I am here to help you. My name is Detective Ridgestone. You can call me Sandra. Can you speak at all?" asked Sandra.

The girl shook her head.

"Alright, I need to know, did the others get hurt?" she asked.

The girl nodded and shook her head, and then finally held up one finger and pointed it at the black teen who appeared to have blood on his pant leg. The boy looked pale. Betty popped in and said through the HUD system that he needed medical attention immediately or else he could die.

"Alright, what about the other boy?" Sandra asked, looking at the boy with long red hair.

The girl shrugged her shoulders, but Betty responded that he also needed medical attention, as he was experiencing shallow breathing. Sandra turned to the girl.

"Okay, I need to get him out of here right away. I will have to come back for you and the red-haired guy. Do you understand?"

The girl looked as if she were about to cry, but nodded her head.

"Stay awake and keep an eye on him," said Sandra, trying to give the girl a sense of purpose. The detective then carefully maneuvered into a position where she could lift the unconscious boy. He did not respond at all to being lifted. "I'll be back," she said as she trotted out of the store and into the open space where she used the jetpack to lower herself down to the ground floor. She then trotted towards the boarded hallway to be greeted by paramedics who had been apprised of the teenager's condition.

"Where is Daryl?" Sandra asked Alejandro.

Alejandro looked extremely uncomfortable and replied, "Mr. Ekstrand landed our helicopter in the parking lot and took Daryl back to Cyberhawk base to be tended to. He is seriously ill. You should not go back in there. It is more dangerous than you realize."

"I can't leave those kids, and I am wearing the Cyberhawk gear. I promised the girl I would return. And I am protected from the toxins," said Sandra as she headed back, hoping she reassured Alejandro's concerns. "There are no hazmat suits for the police. I'm their only hope."

Alejandro shook his head and said worriedly, "It's not the chemicals you should be worried about."

Sandra went down the boarded hallway back into the mall and flew directly up to the third floor again, landing just outside the toy store with Betty assisting to ensure an extra gentle landing on the third-story structure. Sandra glanced over at the Ford & Stone department store and thought she saw more greenish light glowing in the darkness. She paused at the doorway of the toy store, her focus drawn to the large anchor structure. She thought she saw something dark moving about, and then nothing. She felt that shiver go up her spine again and realized she needed to be focused on the two kids in the store. She made her way back to pick up the teenager with long, red hair. The girl still looked scared, but she also appeared relieved that help was a reality, not just wishful thinking.

"It is gonna be alright. Paramedics are now looking over your friend, and they will take him to the hospital," said Sandra.

The girl nodded and then began to make a gesture when, suddenly, a loud roaring sound filled the toy store. Sandra stood up to see what was happening to find another Cyberhawk that she had never seen before. It sparkled deep, dark blue with a slick paint job and the Cyberhawk logo painted upon it. This machine was larger and older, but more powerful than the prototype she was wearing.

Sandra stood up and asked, "Who are you?"

"Civilian, the cavalry's here! Or in my case, the Air Force. I am here to assist you in getting these two young adults out of harm's way," said the voice that was vaguely familiar to Sandra. Familiar and somehow annoying.

He walked over to the cashier's counter and pulled away the heavy furniture so that they could both have easy access to pick up the kids. He reached down and gently lifted the unconscious male.

"Pick up the girl. We need to leave this location now," he instructed firmly.

Sandra did not hesitate.

The teen girl in her arms said in a whisper, "Are you a real Mandalorian?"

The question seemed silly until Sandra saw her reflection in one of the storefront glass display windows. She did look like a Star Wars character, or perhaps some version of Iron Man or a Halo figure. Either way, she felt like a superhero and was proud that she could help.

CHAPTER 10

Caleb walked home alone because he wanted to think about what he had just heard from the others at the African culture meeting. The meeting was exciting and very pro-African American, and he enjoyed learning more about his heritage. The people were so glamorous and successful. His heart skipped a beat as he momentarily thought about the lovely black woman with the sexy, curvy figure wearing a traditional head wrap. She wore an unusual piece of jewelry that seemed to glow a greenish hue. It sorta reminded him of Kryptonite. She seemed to be attracted to him. Her lovely smile and figure seemed to haunt him. Everyone was so pumped up about the powerful words that had been spoken, but there was something that did not seem right to him. It wasn't focused on African culture, which was why he was interested in attending. It was more about the suffering of Africans once they arrived on the North American continent. Sure, his parents and grandparents suffered from the effects of antiquated, stupid, racist ideas, and he wanted to do something about it. Other young people like him were hurt and angry about the things they heard, and some had experienced it personally. Caleb wanted to be a part of positive change. The presenters repeatedly emphasized that it was time to stick it to the 'man' and put people of color in the front instead of behind. The speakers were very persuasive and impassioned about the cause. They dressed impressively in expensive clothing and wore diamond and gold jewelry. Even their hair, shoes, and eyewear were top-notch. Nothing second-hand about these people. They were successful. And they wanted to share their success. They wanted everyone to join their group like a family. It was suggested that members should only support black-owned businesses and black artists. Keep dollars within the black community.

It all sounded like a peaceful and reasonable way to stand up for the rights of Black Americans. But Caleb kept feeling like something was gnawing at him.

Then there was the discussion that more aggressive tactics needed to be employed, like protests. They wanted to organize large demonstrations where the public could see their numbers and the power they wielded. The speaker emphasized that they had a lot of power in numbers and in consumer dollars. It was as if everyone was entranced in a foggy frenzy. It was like being in the room right next to famous rappers or athletes who exuded prestige and respect. They had it all. Money, respect, power, connections... But still, ...something just didn't feel right, and Caleb could not fathom what that was.

Another speaker drew upon historical events where murder and rape happened, and there was no justice. The speaker called for justice. He demanded justice. This got the crowd going, and everyone agreed that justice should be for everyone. The speaker noted how many innocent black men had served time in jail because justice was not served to the black community. Some of the others suggested that they make more violent stands because they were not being listened to. And they were tired of being stereotyped. Then they circled back to the idea of a massive demonstration, but the provision was added that everyone should be prepared not to receive justice and be ready to fight. They should come armed. They would need to. Sign-up sheets and phone apps were encouraged to help start growing participation and ensure everyone was connected.

Caleb heard many things from the speakers. It made him feel angry at white people. His heart was pounding hard as he thought about the events that had been explained to him. It was like a pocket full of rage exploded in his body. Every muscle in his body felt tense by the time he reached his apartment building and went inside. He checked his mail and found nothing of interest. He then proceeded to go upstairs to his floor, still feeling the residual anger that the people at the meeting had felt. It was so real and intense. And then, …………he saw Howard stepping out of his apartment across from his. Howard was an overweight white man with a beard and short brown hair. He always wore t-shirts with dragons and knights emblazoned on the front. The guy was a nerd. He did not convey a sense of success or prestige.

"Oh, hi, Caleb! Hey, the mailman put several of your letters in my box," said Howard, reopening his apartment door. He stepped in and quickly came out with a couple of letters in his hand. "I thought instead of putting it back into the mailbox that I would just hand them to you." Howard handed the letters to Caleb and looked up at the taller man. "So, do you want to join us on Friday night for gaming? We'd love to have an additional player. And the game always runs better when you are part of the adventure crew."

"Uh," Caleb paused. His mind was spinning. An intangible emotion hit him deep inside. He loved to play role-playing games, and Howard was a pretty good dungeon master. "Let me think about it. I was supposed to do something that night, but ……... I might cancel those plans."

"Sure thing. Just let me know, and even if it is last-minute, that's okay too," said Howard cheerfully, heading down the hallway to the elevator. "We are planning on having pizza. I am ordering two different kinds."

Caleb went into his apartment. He was alone again with his thoughts. Howard was a nice person. He always treated him as an equal. He had even asked Caleb for advice on certain things. Howard thought of him as a friend, and if Caleb was honest with himself, he thought of Howard as a friend. The man never made him feel like he was being taken advantage of or manipulated. His friendship was rock solid.

It hit him again. Something did not seem right. This was not years ago. Caleb did not hate or judge people because they were different from him. Caleb struggled to think of anything bad happening in his neighborhood based on prejudice. He could not think of anything. People here liked each other. He would feel very hurt if he saw Howard marching down the streets with signs saying negative things about Black Americans. Suffering hate had not been allowed, like back when his parents were kids. He and his white classmates in the past stood up for a Latino boy who was being picked on by a rival school sports team. This was his generation and time. It was getting better and not worse. The apartment felt very silent. He looked up at the photo of his grandparents, who were both now passed away. His grandma used to say that love was the greatest gift anyone could share. Friendship was a form of love, reasoned Caleb. He realized there was no love in that so-called African culture meeting. There was no discussion of distant traditions and their connections. Those people back there did not care about him. Suddenly, the room seemed to get lighter, and Caleb felt like he could think clearly again. Something had lifted. He could hear the noise in the streets and the birds that were nesting in the tree near his window. He was going to play RPG with his pals on Friday night and not join that weird group that seemed to have unclear motives. Grandma was right………. *a heart filled with love would stay on the right path.*

****

A week later, the Emergency Services Team was assembled in one of the presentation rooms in the underground laboratory. They were going to be issued a new piece of equipment and given an update on Daryl Crane's condition.

"I wonder when they will let us visit him?" Ellena asked Janet, who was sitting next to her.

Janet eyed Ellena a little and then responded, "Probably when they think he can handle having guests ask him all sorts of silly questions." Janet was starting to think that Ellena was sweet on the handsome young former SWAT officer.

"Hmm. I suppose so," said Ellena, not taking any offense at Janet's comment.

Janet decided to let it go. Ellena was a kind soul and did not deserve any browbeating for being a person with light in her heart. Janet looked over at Fernando, who was sitting on the other side of Ellena. He heard the conversation.

He shrugged his shoulders at Janet and then said, "Ellena, I miss the tall guy too."

Ellena smiled and said softly, "Yeah."

Dr. Elgin Cross came into the room with Captain Justice, who took a seat in the front row. Dr. Cross approached the front of the room, holding a pair of strange-looking glasses. He wore a set all the time. They went well with his striking dark hair, mustache, and goatee, as well as his fancy lab coat and a wristwatch that would probably rival any smartphone.

"I have been wearing these glasses for years and have been perfecting them. No, my eyesight is not poor. It is enhanced with the latest technology that Cyberhawk Research and Development can offer. I am the inventor. It appears that the Emergency Services Team has progressed faster than expected, and it is time to get all of you fitted for a pair of these. They will assist you. They will assist you both while you are working and when you are not. They are the best visual enhancement just short of getting cybernetic eyeballs," said Elgin Cross with great conviction.

"So, what do they do?" asked Rafferty, shifting his weight in the chair that seemed uncomfortable. "And when do we get word about Daryl?"

Elgin Cross looked at Rafferty and then at Captain Justice. "Do you want to give an update on Mr. Crane?" Dr. Cross asked the captain.

"Yes, I might as well. They are chomping at the bit to know how he is doing," replied the captain, standing up. He turned to face his team and said, "Daryl's surgery went well. The medical team had to put him into a short coma-like stasis while the LabCoat Crew created the parts they needed. As most of you know, he had a cybernetic implant surgery after being shot in the line of duty. Unfortunately, an implanted part had a hairline fracture that was causing him to lose energy and feel tired, and when he ran the Cyberhawk suit, it overwhelmed him. They have created a new part."

"With no imperfections," added Dr. Cross emphatically.

"Can we visit him?" asked Ellena.

"I don't see why not. You all have clearance, but only one at a time. Perhaps spread it out over the day," said Dr. Cross, waving his arm about, revealing some of his frustration at not being able to focus on his presentation fully.

"He did seem restless, and......I think Sandra and Alejandro need to see him first. He is upset about not being able to assist with the rescue of the kids from that toxic mall," said the captain.

"I can stop by," said Sandra with a smile.

While Alejandro nodded quietly in agreement.

"The rest of the team will need to get a visit time from Dr. Eirstone," said Captain Justice.

"Any more questions?" Dr. Cross asked as he prepared to begin his presentation and training on the new eyewear.

"Yes, I have one," said Sandra.

"Okay. What is it?" asked Cross, tightening his lips a bit.

"Who was the other Cyberhawk that helped with the rescue at the mall?" she asked.

Elgin Cross made a face and then replied, "You need to ask....... Mr. Knight."

"Alright," Sandra responded, feeling like she was getting the brush-off. Alejandro was the only other person on the team who had seen the other Cyberhawk, and he began feigning not to understand English so clearly whenever she brought up the subject. It was evident that he was uncomfortable about something. And he didn't wish to discuss it. Sandra resolved herself to be patient and wait for the answers she wanted when she could speak with Mr. Knight.

Finally, Dr. Cross managed to get the team back on track with the new technology. The HUD system installed on the eyewear made having a cell phone somewhat useless unless you wanted to play the little app games or watch videos. The glasses did everything else, plus a lot more. After receiving step-by-step instructions, proper care for the glasses, and even the option to program them, the team was instructed to spend the rest of the day shopping or doing enjoyable activities while wearing the tiny HUD systems. Dr. Cross wanted everyone to get practice using them.

"Hey, detective hotshot flier! You wanna come with us to see the Oregon Air and Space Museum?" asked Chris and Fernando as they were getting into Chris's car.

Sandra wrinkled her brow momentarily from the strange moniker and then replied, "Thanks for the invite, but a group of us is heading to the Museum of Natural and Cultural History to test out the new glasses."

"Aw, a bunch of old bones and dusty woven baskets cannot compare to the fuel-injected wonderfulness of things that fly," replied Chris with a grin.

"Thanks, guys, but I already told Dr. Hanni that I would go with him. We promised the captain that we would take Diana with us so that she would try out the equipment and enjoy herself for a few hours," replied Sandra.

Fernando nodded his head in contemplation and then asked, "Hey, do you know what the captain is doing?"

"He already knows how to use the new HUD glasses and has a meeting with Mr. Knight," said Sandra as she got into her car with Dr. Hanni, Diana, Raven, and Ellena squished in the back seat.

"Maybe we can get Rafferty, Alejandro, and Janet to go with us?" suggested Chris.

"Alejandro went home to take his wife shopping," said Rafferty as he got into his truck. "Janet and I are following them. Sorry guys. You could come with us?"

Chris gave Rafferty an incredulous look.

"Okay. Have fun," said Rafferty.

"Raven looks squished in the back seat of Sandra's car. Maybe he will want to come with us?" suggested Fernando as he made an invitation to Raven.

Raven rolled down the window and said, "I am in the back seat with two lovely girls. I consider myself lucky."

Ellena laughed and patted Raven on the knee.

"Diana and I are beautiful ladies, and he would be a fool to leave our company," said Ellena.

Diana looked embarrassed and remained quiet.

Chris shook his head and turned to Fernando, "They have their hearts set on seeing a bunch of dusty old stuff that has been sitting in the ground for hundreds of years. Let's go."

As the Cyberhawk Emergency Services Team members dispersed in different directions to follow their prescribed homework assignment from Dr. Cross, Mr. Knight pulled his car into the Airbase parking lot to be greeted by Captain Justice.

"I am under the impression that we have some important matters to discuss concerning the mission at the London Center Mall in Portland," said Mr. Knight after getting out.

"Yes, we do," replied Captain Justice as he invited Mr. Knight to come into the building.

In the back seat of Sandra's car, Diana looked back at the Captain and Mr. Knight with the heavy thought that she should be there to assist. Raven noticed Diana's preoccupation.

"Diana, it is healthy to spend a little time learning something new in a fun way. You, of us all, work so very hard; you need time for fun," he said.

Diana remained silent, looking almost guilty.

"He is correct," added Ellena. "I did not want to leave Daryl by himself, but he insisted that I go out with you all."

Diana smiled softly. The others had no idea what she hid within herself. The terror, the shame, the fear, the remorse, the uncomfortableness….and there was no way she could verbalize it to any of them. It made her feel so bad. Her great-uncle would say that spending time with people her own age and doing everyday things was essential and healthy. It would help her move forward.

"Come on, Diana. I won't bite. I might put fingernail polish and makeup on you, but I won't hurt you," said Ellena with that warm, cheery smile of hers.

Diana cracked a genuine smile, shook her head a little, and said, "Alright. I will attempt to relax and have fun with you all."

****

Back inside the Cyberhawk Airbase, the captain turned to Lukas Knight.

"What's this story about another Cyberhawk? Sandra had help the other day, and then this person disappeared. I thought this was the prototype team," the captain confronted Lukas Knight.

Lukas Knight looked down reflectively and then up directly at Robert Justice and said, "Did you think that we would not test this equipment prior to handing it off to your team? And yes, you are the prototype Cyberhawk Emergency Services Team. What you do here will help to establish a civilian-based usage of our technology, allowing more people to benefit from what we have developed."

The captain eyed Knight and strode about thinking, and finally turned, "But who was that? Detective Ridgestone will not drop this until she receives satisfactory answers. That is the nature of her personality. She's a detective. She said this other Cyberhawk looked like a completely perfected suit, like a product off the shelf. He was bigger and bulkier and... looked like he had armaments..."

The captain stopped and then stared at Knight.

"Oh. You are starting to get it," commented Knight.

"He was a military version?" he finally asked.

"Yes. They conducted all the early testing, so they have items that work and are ready, but the gear can always be improved. Your Cyberhawk suits will not be supplied with weapons. Don't worry about that, but they will still have the bulletproofing that was required for the military design," replied Lukas Knight.

"Geez, I feel effing stupid. It is all quite self-evident, now," said Captain Justice.

"Your job is to train those people and work them into a cohesive team. You seem to be making progress with them. We did not expect them to pull together so quickly. They are an extremely diverse group of people, but they are somehow willing to come together and make this all work. Elgin Cross is impressed......and he is normally only impressed by himself," said Knight as he strode around the room, looking about at the vast open three-story space above. "They have also managed to keep this space neat without you having to *get chain of command* on them."

"Yeah. They are an unusual group of people. I was expecting them to be more difficult. I thought Doctor Hanni was going to be complaining all the time about the young guys, and I thought the young guys were going to be overly flirty with the gals on the team. Everyone is respectful of each other. I hate to say it, but that is odd. Maybe my dad and grandfather would have had polite people in their day, but...now......"

"But now people seem easily offended and quick to anger," said Knight.

"Yes," agreed Justice.

"Since I am older than you, I have had more time to see stuff happen around me. I have seen protests and wars. But the day-to-day life was never quite this abrasive. This abrasion appears to have increased over the past fifteen years or so. Something is happening, and it is not good," commented Knight.

"I thought maybe it was the new technology or the influence of various types of media on people. I thought perhaps it was a ......humanity...... growing pain? Are you saying it is something else?" asked Justice.

"There are those of us who suspect something is influencing Human behavior. But we are not certain as to what that is," replied Knight. "But whatever it is.... It is a problem not to be ignored. Studies are being done to determine where this behavior is seen the most and where it is seen the least."

"Really? Where is it seen the most?" asked Justice.

"Highly populated areas for the most part. However, in isolated areas of South America, the northern polar regions, the Himalayan areas, certain island locations, parts of New Zealand, and a few remote African communities, we have observed none of this behavior. Those individuals are happy, rational, and respond appropriately to life's events. So, it appears that technology or modern life may be the culprit. But historians have noted that similar behaviors have been described before both World Wars, the Napoleonic Wars, the Russian Revolution, the Chinese Revolution, the American Civil War, and some battle stories that have occurred between the Native American tribes, Feudal Japan, and are in some descriptions during the religious upheavals in Europe. Now, we have to realize that we, as Humans, have probably lost thousands and thousands of stories and histories due to natural disasters and wars, so this cycle of disharmony may have been going on for a very long time," said Knight.

"Are Humans just violent assholes?" speculated Justice sadly.

"Eh…. maybe. But recently, some of our engineers have discovered an energy signature that they have started to track, and it shows up in violent confrontations like those big anti-police riots that happened a couple of years ago," said Knight as he paced about the room. "Think about some of the road rage incidents that have occurred."

Robert Justice's shoulders dropped in defeat.

"This is all above my pay grade. I am just a fireman. I want to help people. I can't save the world," said Justice.

"We don't expect you to. But if you want to contribute to making someone's life better or saving one person from a circumstance they cannot handle, then maybe you are saving the world. Less hate," commented Knight somewhat reflectively.

His mood seemed downcast. They both stood quietly in the ample open space of the Cyberhawk airbase living quarters.

Robert started to chuckle and said, "You are going to think this is stupid. But…. what you are describing reminds me of that old Star Trek episode where Scotty is accused of murdering several women and it turns out to be some life form that feeds on fear, violence, and hate…. or something like that."

Lukas Knight turned to Justice and nodded while pondering Justice's observation.

"Robert, we don't know what exists out there," Knight turned to the younger man. "We don't have answers to all of Earth's mysteries, and we certainly do not know much about what is beyond our little planet. But you have…. we have a great team that is coming together, and those people are going to help a lot of people."

CHAPTER 11

August Hanni had visited museums all over the world, and regardless of their age, complexity, or content, he always enjoyed looking at old things and wondering what life was like when those items were still in use. Why did this particular item survive? Was it exceptionally well-made? Or was it loved by its owner and well cared for? Was it just dumb luck that researchers found it? The strange glasses added to the experience, even though he would have enjoyed it just as much without them. He could access any programmed Augmented Reality components that had been added to the display, as well as identify the types and quantities of dust and pollutants in the hallways. The chemical compounds of someone's super-strong-smelling perfume, if someone had a fever, or if their heart rate was not healthy, were just a few of the monitoring options available to him in the usage of the HUD glasses. He had insisted that one of the guests sit down and asked for a curator to get a portable blood pressure monitor. He had to explain that he was a medical doctor and thought that the guest could be about to have a serious medical problem. The guest reported feeling very tired and unfocused, to the point of feeling dizzy. Their heart rate, according to the glasses, was dangerously low. Raven made sure the museum staff called for paramedics, and it was not too soon before the guest then slipped into unconsciousness while speaking with them.

Within minutes, the paramedics arrived and were informed about the situation while attending to the patient. The man was taken away to the hospital. The glasses had probably saved the guest's life because the device caught the symptoms sooner than normal. Dr. Hanni usually did not get excited about fancy, fun tech devices, but the glasses were undeniably useful. He and Raven had both developed a stronger appreciation for their new toys that afternoon.

"I heard you were at the center of all that ruckus with the ambulances," Sandra said to Dr. Hanni as they stood together by the indigenous woven basket display.

"Yes, I was," the man replied with a strong European accent. He smiled broadly. "I think I am going to like these glasses."

"Good," replied Sandra.

"What about you?" asked the doctor as he eyed an intricate woven basket from the Washoe by Dat so la lee.

"I wish they were more like my normal sunglasses," replied Sandra sullenly.

The doctor turned and looked at her. He could now clearly see the differences between her eyes.

"That's right. You wear sunglasses to hide the variant eye color. I've seen people who naturally have two different-colored eyes. There's no need to be embarrassed about it. And you have a special situation as well," said the doctor.

"It doesn't help. I still think I look weird," replied Sandra, making a slight scowl.

"Really. I think you are a beautiful woman. You should not feel bad at all," said Dr. Hanni.

"You sound like my ex-husband," replied Sandra.

"You say that like…... you miss him," remarked Dr. Hanni.

"I do. I thought our separation should not have been. Then he disappeared," she said. Sandra made a contorted expression, fighting off more intense feelings of remorse and regret.

"What is wrong?" asked the doctor, suddenly realizing she was not happy.

"I think he might be dead. I have not talked to him for a couple of years, and I got a strange letter from the government stating that the children and I were to receive death benefits, and then when I called about it, the people on the phone backtracked it all. It was extremely odd. And I miss him," Sandra replied, looking away to hide her tears. "The twins miss him, too."

Doctor Hanni put an arm around her and said, "Let's go outside and get some fresh, cool air. It will make you feel better. Losing someone is hard."

As they exited the museum to go outside, Sandra asked, "Have you lost someone?"

They took a seat on a bench near a lovely garden display.

"Yes and no. I have lost the normal people like aging grandparents who have lived a full life, my parents are still alive, I still have my siblings, not many friends due to the way I grew up," replied Dr. Hanni.

"What about a wife?" asked Sandra.

August Hanni made a sad face and said, "Ah, that is the one I lost. I never got to marry her. She did not die. She married someone else. And that was my fault. I never told her how much I cared about her. You are fortunate to have had someone in your life whom you cared about and shared life experiences with. You have two beautiful children."

"The twins are special, but I don't know if I will survive their teenage years. Tessa has developed a strange attitude that even her brother cannot fathom," replied Sandra reflectively. "They are both brilliant, and I hope bringing them up here was the right decision. They need an environment where adults take their intellect seriously. Michael had some interesting ideas, and one of his teachers back in LA just dismissed him as if he were a silly child. How is he supposed to develop his own ideas and creations if subpar educators are beating him down?"

"Ah, you are singing to the choir. I think that is the saying. I had the same situation as a child, and that was why my parents sent me off to university early," replied Dr. Hanni. "I am glad they did. I would be dead if I had not been at the symposium."

Rafferty, Diana, and Ellena emerged from the museum all excited.

"Hey, you have got to turn on the feature for looking for germs on surfaces!" said Rafferty.

Daina was shaking her head in disgust.

"Why?" asked Sandra.

"Just do it," said Rafferty.

"Just do what?" asked Janet and Raven, coming from the garden area.

"Turn on the microbial app for looking at germs on surfaces," suggested Rafferty.

"Okay," said Janet. Janet seemed unimpressed.

"Go look at a door handle or some other object that people touch a lot," suggested Rafferty.

Janet walked over to one of the museum doors.

"Oh yuck!" exclaimed Janet.

Doctor Hanni got up from the bench as he turned on the app and then looked at the door handle.

"Ah, that is normal. It does not look like anything harmful is festering there," said the doctor. "But like with healthy daily life, we should wash our hands after being out and about."

"That is normal?" asked Rafferty, gesturing to the door handle.

"Yes," replied Dr. Hanni.

"Huh, I think I will leave that app turned off," said Rafferty, stuffing his hands deep into his jean pockets.

"You *really* want to leave it off when you eat food," said Ellena.

Rafferty scrunched up his face from his generally jovial expression. "Alright, I think I should just stick to fightin' fires, drinkin' beer, and dancing. This expanding…my knowledge base is making me queasy."

"Good idea, buddy," said Janet, patting him on his muscular shoulder.

"We should be heading back to the base. We have been gone for three hours," said Diana.

There was a group sigh and agreement amongst them. Today had been fun, but that was not the purpose of going out; it was to learn how to use the glasses. Dr. Cross and the LabCoat Crew would want to know if anyone had suggestions or problems working with the smaller versions of the HUD. Later that evening, back at the Cyberhawk airbase quarters, the group that stayed on base, minus Daryl, who was still recovering, were all hanging about watching TV. Ellena had just come back from visiting Daryl.

"So how is he doing?" asked Fernando.

"He is much better. In fact, they think he can return tomorrow to sleep and continue his recovery here. They gave him his HUD glasses," said Ellena as she pulled her blonde hair back into a ponytail. "So, what are you all up to?"

"Just watching the news," replied Janet.

"The captain said that next week, we will start to be assigned our Cyberhawk gear. The testing proved that the smaller, sleeker design is still as effective as the previous version," said Chris.

"I'm excited," said Fernando with a big grin. "They all will have jetpacks attached to them."

"Yes, but not everyone will get theirs next week," said Janet. "Remember, he said they would be issued in phases."

"Oh, hey! Look at the TV! Sandra and the mystery Cyberhawk are on the TV," exclaimed Raven.

"Turn it up so we can all hear it," requested Janet.

"...... There has been considerable speculation about these two heroes, who rescued the teens from the abandoned section of the London Center Mall. Everyone wants to know where these two came from and if they belong to any special organization. Sam Tredwall is out on location in the downtown area, asking people on the streets what their thoughts are concerning the jetpack armored warriors," said the TV broadcaster.

"Thanks, Susie. I spent the day visiting with the downtown community to gauge what the people on the street think of those armor-clad heroes. This is Bob Burnside. Bob, we were chatting earlier about the incident at the London Center Mall. What are your thoughts?"

"Well, Sam, I think they were amazing. I am so happy they saved those kids. We need more people like that. They were people, right? And not some kind of AI robot thing?" wondered Bob.

"That is a good point, Bob. We do not know what or who they were exactly," replied Sam Tredwall.

A young woman came up to the reporter and Bob Burnside and said, "I think they are aliens here to help us. And I love them! Love you wherever you are!!"

She then dashed off, giggling.

"Well, that is an interesting take," said Sam Tredwall, making a slight face. "Anyone else in the crowd have some ideas about who these heroes were?"

Two young men wearing pop culture clothing and accessories came over and said, "I think they are part of an elite military jetpack armored warrior team called JAW. And they are here to protect us from the aliens. Just like Superman."

"Naw, they are more like Batman because they are using technology to fight crime, not Superman," whined the friend standing next to him. "And Superman was an alien."

The reporter stepped past the two friends who were about to get into an argument and spotted another person to interview.

"Hello! It's the mayor of Progressville, Ms. Joan Malapert. Would you care to comment about the jetpack armored warriors that heroically saved those teens from that dangerous section of the London Center Mall?" Sam Tredwall approached the older woman, who appeared to be still dressing for the 1960s and 1970s eras.

The slender older woman with long grey straight hair approached the reporter seriously and said, "I think it is fine that the teens were successfully rescued, but couldn't that have been done by our fine fire and rescue persons. There is a serious unhoused persons issue happening right here, right now, and funding is being wasted on silly toys for childish men. Where is this money coming from? Our schools need better funding, and there are many single parents who are struggling to feed their children. I want to call for an investigation into how our community funds are being spent on unnecessary weaponized devices, such as armored persons wearing jetpacks. Think of the pollution this is causing!"

"Indeed. You have made some very valid points, Mayor Malapert. I think our viewers would appreciate hearing more about your thoughts on the matter. Perhaps we can plan for a conversation with other community leaders about this topic," said Sam Tredwall.

"Yes, I would be interested in dialoging about these issues," replied Mayor Malapert.

"Who was that ol' mare?" asked Rafferty, scrunching his nose.

"That was the mayor of Progressville, which is a small community outside of the Portland area," replied Chris, taking a sip of his soda. "Roy told me about her. He had a run-in with her a couple of years ago concerning a language program that he was trying to start to help immigrants learn English. She was against it. She said he was the 'oppressive white man stealing their heritage' from them. Roy is a first-generation American, and he understands the importance of learning the language. He thinks she is a crazy man-hater."

Ellena was still staring at the TV with a curious look upon her face as if something was puzzling her.

"Her clothing was rather odd," said Ellena lowly. "More like a costume party attire…. unless she's trying to stay young by dressing like people used to. She seems out of touch."

"Yes, but she is the mayor of a town. People voted for her, right?" questioned Janet. "She can't be horrible."

"Not the way Roy explains it. You should talk to him. I can't do justice to the story as he tells it," replied Chris.

"Alright," said Janet.

"That interview she gave was rather intense and…...like she was spoilin' for a fight," remarked Rafferty, leaning back on the couch and looking at his teammates. "And this all goes with what the captain was saying about the team being in the press. We need to be mindful of our actions when wearin' Cyberhawk gear and thoughtful about what we say to the media. We could easily end up speaking for everyone, which is not what any of us were trained for, right? I know I am not."

Almost everyone in the room was shaking their heads. None of them was PR trained. The mood dropped.

"That woman was just one person. We have already helped dozens of people, and that was the goal of our team: to help others. I pray that we can continue to do so for many years to come. I am not going to let one bad person keep me from being a good doctor and training Raven to aspire for more. All of you are incredibly talented, and as each day passes, I learn more about each of you. I didn't think this would be a place for me to follow my path, but these glasses helped me save a person's life today. I called the hospital. The man was having a stroke, and we caught it in time for it to be treated properly. These glasses help. I am not losing sight of my goals, I am starting a new path using better tools," said Dr. Hanni. Dr. Hanni looked back at the large flat-screen TV, which had been paused with the image of the hate-filled politician. "I am not letting someone like that stop me from helping others."

Ellena smiled and said, "The doctor is right. We can't let some crazy person get in the way of our goals and dreams."

"To Dr. Hanni and his positive outlook!" said Fernando, holding his iced tea aloft like a toasting glass.

"To Doctor Hanni!" cheered the group with glasses and containers raised.

Dr. Hanni looked surprised and pleased.

Next week could not come quickly enough for the team. The first four Cyberhawk Emergency Services Team suites were ready for assignment. The four gleaming, golden-yellow sets had been set up by the LabCoat Crew, who had already run through the quality control system checks. The bodysuits were black and made of a strange form-fitting material that would protect the pilot from all weather conditions, plus fire, and were bulletproof. The bulletproof helmets had activated UV visors that were full HUD systems, complete with pressurized breathing for upper-altitude flights, which filtered out toxins. It was as if the pilot was becoming part of the airplane, with attachable jetpacks and folding wings that provided lift and sustained fuel for long flights. The CyberSkeleton was still heavily reinforced and could lift hundreds of pounds, but it was now a leaner design that was both aesthetically pleasing and fuel-efficient. Additional armor plates had been added to the gear for safety, which made the group look like a clan of Mandalorians dipped in gold. The first four to receive their Cyberhawk armored suits were Captain Justice, Rafferty Lewis, Fernando Sanchez, and Sandra Ridgestone.

Daryl stood with the others and inspected his teammates' new equipment. Captain Justice was all geared up and preparing to take the newly outfitted Cyberhawks out on a training run. He noticed Daryl amongst the group.

"How are you doing?" he asked.

"I am feeling much better now. The whole feeling of being tired early in the evening is going away, and my body is adjusting to the repairs," he replied.

"Daryl, you would have been one of the first to get your gear. Don't worry, we will have you suited up in no time," said the captain.

"Oh yeah, I know. Dr. Eirstone said I am cleared to use the regular CyberSkeleton gear and... actually, she wants me to practice with it today to make sure everything is good. They had me do so many tests. I am pleased to be sleeping in my own bed now," added Daryl.

"Glad to hear it," said Justice.

"The Cyberhawk armor and jetpack system looks amazing. It looks like an expensive car paint finish," commented Daryl as he eyed the captain's gear. "And the logo is emblazoned on all the right areas. You must feel like a million miles per hour."

"Well, …. probably not that fast …. but yes, I do," laughed the captain. The captain then turned to everyone standing in the downstairs area of the airbase quarters.

Everyone, geared up, felt just a little taller in their suits. They stood ready to begin their day of training.

"Alright, team! Janet and Diana have your assignments for the day. Those of you suited up will follow me out the roll-up door and off to the tarmac. We are doing flight training. Ground rules. Air rules. Getting used to Betty. And I will be showing you some designated landing sites where we can refuel if necessary. Some will be private, and others will be military locations where we must follow specific protocols. Betty can assist until you can do it yourself. It takes time to learn how to use the exterior Communications Implant seamlessly. Once you get used to it, it will feel like all of this is just part of your natural body."

Sanchez, Ridgestone, and Lewis all followed the captain outside. It was going to be an exciting day. Sandra already had more experience than her teammates in using the jetpacks, except for Captain Justice. He spent hours with the LabCoat Crew testing the equipment before the assignment. After the team spent an hour on various procedures to make sure everyone felt confident in performing basic maneuvers, it was finally time to take a short flight. Once in the air, they learned how to maintain safe spacing, correct landing speeds, and understand beacon warning systems since they were not the only ones using the sky.

"Most planes have an Emergency Locator Transmitter installed, and all airports and airfields have virtual spaces around them that require rules of conduct. The bigger the airport, the more complicated the airspace becomes. This is all done for safety. Does anyone see that bright pink line and grid in your HUD's field of vision?" the captain asked through their comm system.

"Oh yeah. It looks like a corral around the airfield," remarked Rafferty. "There are even arrows pointing."

"I see something flashing," commented Sandra.

"That is a plane heading this way to land at the airfield. We are required to keep a certain distance. All of this will eventually become a normal routine, just like when you drive a car," said the captain as he led the others further away from the airfield to give space for the small incoming aircraft.

"What about parking lots? These suits are not restricted to taking off only from an airfield," commented Sandra.

"Good observation. We can take off and land with a lot more flexibility than an airplane or even a helicopter. This is why these suits are so crucial for enhancing rescue operations and tracking down criminals. We can go places where other aircraft cannot. Currently, Cyberhawk Research and Development is working with the FAA to develop flight rules and regulations for our flight suits. We know that eventually the general population will take an interest in having suits like these, so getting rules set up now to prevent problems is important," replied the captain. "And to answer your question, yes, we can land in parking lots when necessary."

"Captain, what about privacy? I could fly over people's backyards during the summer to look at sunbathers," remarked Sanchez.

Rafferty started to laugh, losing his concentration during the flight, and began to dash and wobble.

"Stay focused, Lewis," ordered Justice.

"Yes, Captain," replied Rafferty, regaining control.

"And Sanchez... no spying on sunbathers," added the captain. "People more informed than I are working on rules concerning airspace."

CHAPTER 12

Sandra hugged Karl Ridgestone tightly. She was so happy to see him again. He looked to be in good shape. He had been a member of the US Navy SEALs and had finally retired. She was grateful for that, and now he could spend time with her and the twins. They missed him, too. They were sitting on the beach at Sand Harbor on the shores of Lake Tahoe, and the twins were playing in the cool, clear water. This was one of their favorite places to go. The twins were playing with an inflatable pink flamingo and having a good time. Tessa was no longer dark and moody. She was back to being her usual self. This made Michael happy, too. He had been worried and genuinely hurt by his sister's change in attitude.

Sandra turned to Karl and said, "I always felt like some negative force orchestrated our breakup. We got along so well. You were my best friend. Did you feel like things were *that* bad that we had to be apart? And then I got those weird letters that made me think you had died."

Karl Ridgestone turned to Sandra and looked lovingly into her eyes, "I had to leave you and the twins for your safety. There was......"

The phone rang super loud, waking Sandra out of the blissful dream. She sat up and reached for the phone, feeling torn apart inside, realizing it all had been just a dream. She wished she could return to the dream and see his face again. It was one o'clock in the morning. Who on earth could be calling, she wondered. Was there something wrong with the family back in Los Angeles? She looked at the smartphone's screen and saw CYBERHAWK as the identifying ID.

"Hello?" she answered.

"Sorry to wake you," said Diana. "There is a big car pile-up on the I-5, and we have been requested to assist. We need everyone to come in right away."

"Yeah......okay. Uh......I don't have anyone to watch the kids," said Sandra.

"Bring them here to the Cyberhawk base. They can sleep in one of the unoccupied quarters. Ellena and I will be staying at the base," replied Diana. "Come right away. I gotta call Alejandro."

Diana hung up, and Sandra felt a wave of panic for a moment before regaining her focus. She had been called into work for nighttime investigations, but never an emergency. This was a different job. She quickly grabbed some basic clothing and combed her hair back as she walked into the twins' bedrooms and woke them both up. Sandra pulled her hair back into a simple ponytail.

"Tessa. Michael. I need both of you to wake up right away. I have to go to work, and I need to bring you both with me," Sandra ordered firmly. "Just put your robes on over your PJs."

"Can't I stay here? We are old enough to take care of ourselves, Mom," complained Tessa.

"Not yet. Get up and grab what you want to wear tomorrow and your backpacks. We need to leave now. You can sleep at the Cyberhawk base," said Sandra as she quickly put her jacket on and hunted for her keys and purse.

"We get to stay at the Cyberhawk base?!? Oh, that's cool!" said Michael, suddenly waking up and moving a lot faster. "Come on, Tessa! We get to sleep at the base."

"Whatever," grumbled Tessa.

After some help from Michael to get all of Tessa's stuff together, they all piled into the car and headed for the old airfield. The fog was extremely dense, much to Sandra's surprise. Upon arrival at the base, the Cyberhawk Team, along with some of the LabCoat Crew, were busy getting equipment ready for their departure to the scene of the accident. Ellena came over to Sandra and the twins.

"I'll take care of getting Tessa and Michael situated in one of the spare quarters. You had better go and get suited up. They want all of you who can fly to take off right away," said Ellena as she helped the twins with their bags.

"Okay, thanks, Ellena," replied Sandra as she headed for her locker, where she could store her personal belongings and get into the protective jumpsuit that went under the armor and enhanced CyberSkeleton framework that held the jetpacks and wing structures. As she rushed out the door to get the rest of her gear on, she braided her hair back as she strode out onto the foggy airfield. She was disturbed by the lack of visibility. Captain Justice was waiting with Fernando and Rafferty. They were ready. Daryl and Chris helped Sandra get suited up while the captain went over the situation.

"Just about forty-five minutes ago, a multiple vehicle pile-up occurred on the I-5 due to the weather conditions. Apparently, along with the dense fog, there is a vapor of condensation that has made the road surface slippery. The size of the affected area is currently unknown, as visibility is so poor that aviation by normal means is prohibited. This means no care flight for the injured," said Captain Justice as Sandra finished getting suited up.

"What have the ground emergency crews reported?" asked Rafferty.

"From what they can see, the northbound lanes are completely clogged up, and the police are trying to divert traffic into other directions. Luckily, this time of night is less busy, and there are road condition signs in both directions instructing drivers to turn around or to exit at a rest stop or town. The additional problem is that part of the southbound lanes appear to be affected, and this may stretch out over a two-mile area with several independent pile-ups," the captain continued.

"Holy shit. How are we gonna help?" asked Fernando. "Can we fly in this fog?"

"We will fly using IFR with Betty's help. She can track us in multiple ways to make sure that we do not run into each other.

And our suits have a form of proximity radar... that helps us know if we are getting too close to objects like trees, power poles, structures like bridges and towers, so this will be our first serious mission with Betty and these suits," replied the captain. "Diana and Ellena are doing research concerning that stretch of road, looking for hazards that might affect our flight. How are you all feeling?"

"Let's go," said Rafferty.

"A little nervous, but I am up for this," replied Sandra.

"A Sanchez is always ready for action," replied Fernando.

"I am ready whenever you are, Captain Justice," said Betty through their HUD systems.

"Alright. Everyone, fall into diamond formation with me on point. We are headed to an area where Little Muddy Creek is located, which is the farthest south of the accident zone, and then we shall move further north, reporting back to the emergency ground crews on what we discover. Takahashi is going to send out one of the drones to assist in surveying the situation once he arrives with our ground crew," said the captain through the HUD system.

Chris and Daryl waved goodbye and headed back to where the Terrain Buster was waiting for them with Alejandro, Janet, Raven, and Dr. Hanni inside.

Captain Justice lifted off, surveying the ground to see if the others were ready down below, but visibility was already gone. He was flying in a sea of white moisture, like an ant exploring a wad of cotton candy. It was an unnerving feeling.

"Betty, please show assisted navigation on the HUD," Captain Justice requested.

"As you wish," replied Betty. "I have taken the liberty of applying the assistance to all your team's HUDs. All communication levels are strong. I would advise that if communication were lost, all Cyberhawks land and wait 'til VFR conditions return."

"Understood," replied the captain.

Within five minutes, the team was flying over the accident site, and the glow from the emergency vehicle lights was visible through the fog. As the group slowly lowered in elevation, they could see the various vehicles that had crashed into each other, some of which were tipped over. Captain Justice found a safe spot for the Cyberhawks to land, allowing him to speak with the officials on the ground.

The police officer in charge of the scene on the south end of the northbound lane came over right away. Rows of cars were stopped on the freeway for an unknown distance, waiting behind barricades.

"Glad you could make it! I heard there was a chance you could come and assist," said the officer.

Captain Justice flipped up his helmet's faceplate so that he could have eye contact with the officer.

"Glad to be of service. That fog is extremely dense. I am Captain Robert Justice of the Emergency Services Cyberhawk Team. Our ground crew should arrive in ten minutes in the Terrain Buster, if they can get past the traffic jam. How can we help?" asked the captain.

"I am Reserve Officer Campbell of the Coburg City Police. We are a small town, and currently, all our reserve officers are on duty, helping the Chief. This is...the largest freeway accident I have ever seen. Our Coburg City Fire and Rescue department is overwhelmed. We have crews from Eugene and Springfield en route. We have already removed ten injured individuals, so we currently have no ambulances. One of the accident victims said he saw a vehicle go rolling violently out into the fields to the right here," said Officer Campbell, gesturing in the direction of foggy darkness.

"What's over there?" asked Captain Justice.

"Uh, I believe there is a field... and possibly a small grove of trees. The problem is that we do not have a practical method for searching those areas for missing cars, and sometimes people are thrown from vehicles. Can your team search along the freeway for vehicles that could have been tossed into the fields, irrigation ditches, and streams? And there are a few ponds along this route as well."

"We are here to help, and if that is what you need, we are on it. My ground crew will arrive with special equipment that can lift. We also have medical people who can help stabilize the injured for transport," replied Captain Justice.

"Well, that's certainly a blessing. Thanks for the help," said Officer Campbell.

"If you need to get a hold of me, call this number and my assistant will call me through my HUD," said the captain, handing a card to the officer and then flipping his faceplate back down.

The captain then turned to his team and relayed their objective, and they all took off. Janet Hallman could see the Cyberhawks disappear into the foggy darkness as Daryl slowed the Terrain Buster down, not far away from Officer Campbell's police car. Officer Campbell walked toward the vehicle with the word 'Cyberhawk' emblazoned upon it. The blue hawk with white data circuit traces and a gold solder point for the eye logo was just beneath the text. Daryl rolled down the window.

"Is it all right to park here to unload our gear?" asked Daryl.

"I take it you are the other half of the Cyberhawk team. You are welcome to park there. What kind of gear do you have?" asked Officer Campbell.

"It's a CyberSkeleton that is… basically like a suit that helps us lift very heavy objects without getting hurt. We figured that the wreckage might be bad, and we would need these," replied Daryl, hopping out of the Terrain Buster.

"Could you lift a rolled-over car?" asked the officer.

"Easily," replied Daryl. "Or at least roll it onto its wheels."

"Great. I will radio the guys ahead in the wreckage area to figure out where they want help first," replied the Coburg reserve officer.

Dr. Hanni and Raven grabbed their med kits and headed towards the areas being worked on by emergency crews. Daryl, Janet, and Alejandro started to unload their gear, while Chris began setting up the laptop, reserve battery, table, and the drone. He sat down on the drone box as he prepped the device for flight. He turned on the infrared thermal camera and looked at the results on the laptop. Everything looked good. The communication between the computer and the drone was excellent. Chris put his HUD glasses on so that he could communicate with the others.

"Captain, this is Takahashi. I have set up the drone for infrared thermal imaging scans. Shall I deploy the drone?" Chris asked.

The captain heard Chris through the HUD comm system and replied, "That is an affirmative. We are currently flying a pattern on the east side of the freeway. Could you fly a pattern down the center to make sure emergency crews have not missed anyone? We will need GPS if you find someone not being assisted."

"I am on it, Captain. Who do I report the information to?" asked Chris.

"Is Officer Campbell still there?" asked the captain as he was flying his search pattern across a field where he discovered several horses standing about.

"Yes, he is," replied Chris.

"Ask him if he is acting as the coordinator for logistical information," said Captain Justice.

"Copy that. Will do. And good luck on your search," said Chris.

"You too," replied the captain.

Chris got up and went over to Officer Campbell and confirmed that he was acting as the south end of the accident zone's information checkpoint. He informed the officer of the orders he had received from Captain Justice. Officer Campbell found the prospect of flying a drone to be fascinating. Chris showed him the drone's camera view that the laptop was receiving from the infrared thermal imager.

"That's impressive. Let's hope we find everyone," replied the officer, keeping a sharp eye on the area around him. Every once in a while, calls would come through his radio, and he would walk away to focus on the call, while Chris prepared the drone for its mission through the fog.

The drone took off, sending back its flight image along with GPS location and elevation information. Chris started his scan through the center section of the large interstate freeway. He flew about half a mile when he spotted something giving off a heat signature. It was small. He lowered the drone to get a better reading of what the image was. As the drone drew closer to the heat signature, it became evident that it was a pet inside a carrier.

"Officer Campbell, I have found something," Chris called out.

The Coburg police officer came over to see what it was.

"Look. It appears to be some sort of small animal in a… pet carrier?" said Chris. "I think it is still alive."

"Get the GPS location of that. And then start a radial search pattern for an automobile. Perhaps the pet was flung from a car rolling over," suggested Officer Campbell.

"Okay," said Chris as his fingers flew across the keyboard, programming a basic search pattern of the area at a low elevation.

Officer Campbell grabbed his radio and asked if any of the rescue crews were in the area of the GPS location that Chris got from the drone. Voices came back that no one was in that area and would not be able to go there anytime soon. Campbell made a face.

"Are you able to speak with your captain in real time?" asked the officer.

"Sure. Why?" asked Chris.

"I have a gut feeling about that pet carrier," said the cop.

"I bet the captain could send one of the Cyberhawks up there to investigate," said Chris, pulling his jacket closer to ward off the foggy chill in the air.

"Please do," requested the Coburg officer.

"Captain. This is Takahashi," said Chris.

"Yes, Takahashi," replied the captain.

"The drone found a life form trapped in a pet carrier up the center of the freeway about a half mile away from the start point," said Chris.

"Do you have GPS and visuals?" asked the captain.

"Yes. I do. I am sending them to you now through Betty," replied Chris.

"Thank you. Received the data, Takahashi. I will personally investigate. The other Cyberhawks will continue their directive of scanning the east side of the freeway for accident victims," replied Captain Justice.

"I have your flight planned now," said Betty.

"Thanks, Betty. Ridgestone, Lewis, Sanchez continue to scan the eastside until you have reached the two-mile mark and then start on the westside from the north portion of the affected area," said Captain Justice.

"Will do, Captain," said Rafferty.

Robert Justice then followed the flight path planned for him by Betty to take him to the location of the pet carrier. It was less than a minute before he located the area and landed. He spotted the heat signature using his sensor system. He carefully strode over with a helmet light showing the way. He flipped up his faceplate to discover a pet carrier holding a very frightened calico cat. She looked terrified.

"Wow, little lady, you are lucky to be alive," said the captain as the cat complained and cried. "Sorry, sweetheart, I don't dare let you out of that cage. You would just go running off."

He picked up the carrier gently and then looked about the area and listened. He thought he heard something breathing or gasping for air. He quickly flipped his face plate back down so he could scan the area with his HUD system.

"Betty, I thought I heard something. Can you assist me in scanning the area for life signs?" Robert asked the AI.

"Certainly. Please make a slow rotation of 360 degrees. I am also detecting the sound of a life form nearby... it sounds like a cat," said Betty.

"I am holding the cat carrier, and I did find a calico alive, but I heard something else in the fog," replied Robert. Using the night vision scanner, they both slowly examined the foggy darkness. It felt oppressive and somewhat lonely in the moist, dark atmosphere.

"Move forward two meters," directed Betty.

"Okay," said Robert as he complied with Betty's request. A heat signature started to appear. It was small. "It appears to be another small heat signature. Perhaps another pet," said Robert as he slowly made his way through the tall grass into the down-sloping area. "Oh shit, it's a child's car seat."

As he strode towards the car seat and flipped his faceplate up, he discovered that the car seat was lying on its side with a child, who appeared to be about one or two years old, strapped into the device. He gently righted the car seat and eyed the child, who had a few scratches on its face. It was wearing sturdy clothing that probably protected it from more extensive scratches, but he had no idea if there were any broken bones or internal injuries. He needed the child to be transported to a medical facility. He started to reach for the child to check for a pulse when he realized that his hands were gloved.

"Betty, do I have the ability to read for a pulse without taking my gear off?" he asked.

"Yes, flip your faceplate back down, and I will pull up the right sensor and application," she directed. The captain did as Betty requested and then continued to look over the child. He then watched a display on his HUD, which showed various readings. He looked at the child, and a number appeared, and then he looked at the cat, and a different set of numbers appeared. "I think the cat is stressed," he commented and then turned back to the child.

"The child's heart rate could be better. I am also noticing that the child's body temperature is lower than it should be. Do you have any blankets available?" asked Betty.

"No, I have nothing like that with me," said the captain, looking about, hoping to find a blanket that may have been on the child originally. "I need an emergency crew to get here. There has to be a car somewhere in this fog."

"Sensors are also detecting chemicals. Gasoline," stated Betty.

"This is the captain. I need all Cyberhawks to come here immediately… and one should bring emergency blankets. I'm also detecting a possible gasoline spill near my position. I need the removal of accident victims that may be injured, and one is an infant showing signs of hypothermia."

"We got yah, Captain. Sanchez and Ridgestone are headin' back to the Terrain Buster to retrieve a container with first aid materials for coordinated flight. I'll be there in a jiffy," replied Rafferty. "The ground crew using CyberSkeleton only gear is busy assisting emergency crews already. Do you want me to request that they be redeployed?

"Only if they can be spared," replied the captain.

Within seconds, the captain heard the roar of another Cyberhawk landing in the area where the cat had been found. Rafferty came striding out of the gloom with his head beacon shining.

"Hey, Captain!" exclaimed Rafferty with his cheerful cowboy drawl.

"Glad to see you, Lewis. I think the gas odor is coming from that direction, so it may be safe to assume that taking the baby and the cat back to where you landed might be safer for them until we can evacuate them properly. Please take the child and the cat back and wait for the others to arrive with the blankets," directed the captain.

Rafferty picked up the child's car seat, waking the infant up. The child made a complaintive sound as Rafferty headed back to his landing spot. He knelt down to look at the child. The child cried and shivered. Then the cat started complaining as well.

"Okay. Okay," said Rafferty, flipping up his faceplate. "It's just me. I am not a scary robot guy. We're gonna get you a blanket real soon. It's gonna be *alright*. Both of you."

The sound of more Cyberhawks arriving could be heard through the misty gloom. Sandra and Fernando were carrying a sealed container between them. They both landed in an unsteady fashion.

"Damn, that's hard to do," said Sandra.

Fernando nodded, saying a few swear words under his breath, and started to open the container right away. He pulled out the blankets for Rafferty to use on the child and cat while searching for other items to assist the child.

"You two go help the captain. I have a lot of experience dealing with people and children in shock," said Fernando, still pulling out items from the container. "I have thermal packs that I can wrap up so it does not burn the baby, but will give him some warmth. I will take care of the cat as well."

Sandra and Rafferty nodded and headed off to help the captain find the rest of the wreckage. They found Captain Justice examining a turned-over vehicle with all its glass broken out. The driver was unconscious but appeared to show signs of life. This was the vehicle that was leaking gasoline.

"We need to remove her from the vehicle without causing any sparks," said the captain.

"We could tear open the door and remove it, so we have better access to the driver. She looks like she is still securely strapped into the driver's seat," commented Rafferty as the woman started to show signs of becoming conscious. "Ma'am, can you hear me?"

The woman opened her eyes and seemed to slowly take in her surroundings.

"Oh, my god, I've been in a car accident!" she exclaimed and then looked around. "Where is my baby?! My little boy.... Christopher! And Sparkles...where is Sparkles?"

"We found a baby in a car seat. He is in safe hands and appears to be okay. Just a few scratches. Who is Sparkles?" asked Rafferty as he did his best to kneel down in his Cyberhawk gear.

"Sparkles is my cat," replied the woman, then appearing to be terrified. "What are you?!?"

"I am part of a special rescue crew. We found the cat, too. Can you feel your arms and legs? Do you have any pain?" asked Rafferty.

"My head hurts, but I can feel my arms and legs," she replied.

"Okay. We need to get you out of the vehicle, but there is a lot of broken glass. First, we are going to remove the door and then place a blanket upon the ground area," said Rafferty. "Which is... actually the roof of your car."

"I think I can climb out on my own," said the woman.

"Well, we want to wait until we can place something on the ground for you to land on because... gravity is going to drop you. You understand?"

"Yes," she replied, finally comprehending and not allowing her fear to take control.

Sandra brought one of the emergency blankets while the captain kept an eye on the gasoline situation and looked for other wreckage nearby. Sandra then stepped out of her CyberSkeleton to get closer to the car's driver. They placed the blanket between the door and the driver, and then Rafferty peeled the door away from the frame, as if it were part of a banana. After the door was removed, Sandra knelt down to make sure the blanket would provide the woman a safe place to fall into once she was free of her seatbelt. This all went well with the woman having only a minor head injury from the accident. Rafferty escorted her back to where Fernando was working with the child and the cat. The woman was pleased to see her baby and her kitty, as Fernando insisted that she accept a blanket wrapped around her. It was about this time that the hum of several vehicles could be heard, along with the footsteps of one of the CyberSkeletons on the roadway. It was Daryl with an ambulance and a small fire truck. He strode alongside the vehicles.

"Hey, Fernando!" Daryl called out. "The area back there is now under control, and we are starting to move vehicles deeper into the accident zone. What do you have for us? I heard there was spilled gasoline from an overturned vehicle that needed to be managed."

"Yeah. Great to see you all. I have an infant that requires care along with the child's mother, and a cat," replied Fernando. "The overturned vehicle is that way, and I suspect more vehicles are hidden in the fog nearby. The driver of the overturned car said she swerved to avoid a collision with several vehicles that had already crashed into each other. That's when she lost control and went into the center zone."

"One was a big truck!" said the woman listening to the conversation.

"Do you recall what kind? Was it a tanker or cargo?" Fernando asked the woman.

"Not a tanker. It was hauling big stuff on a long flatbed. It was flying all over the place," she replied with a shiver. "Really scary."

"Alright, I will pass that along," said Fernando, then using his HUD comm system to relay the information to the whole group.

Daryl turned to the firemen in the truck as the Ambulance paramedics started to get ready to assist Fernando with the first victims.

"It sounds like we have an overturned semi with materials spilled on the road. The driver does not describe it as being a tanker, thank goodness," said Daryl.

"Good to know," said the fire truck driver. "Shall we go in together?"

"Sure, I can do that," said Daryl as he flipped his face plate back down and turned on his front flood light to assist him through the gloom.

Fernando watched as Daryl and the slow-moving fire truck disappeared into the fog. Once the paramedics had taken over the situation with the woman and her family, Fernando closed the emergency box and pulled it behind him to find the others. Just up ahead, they discovered fourteen more vehicles in various states of damage and distress, one of which was an overturned semi loaded with steel pipes that had been thrust off the flatbed that they had been secured to. The Cyberhawk team, along with those wearing the CyberSkeletons, worked through the rest of the morning hours, helping to remove wreckage and assist victims from their automobiles. It had been a long, arduous task, but it was fulfilling to know that the Cyberhawk gear was doing what it was supposed to. It was making it easier for emergency crews to do their jobs. Once the fog had lifted a little, the Cyberhawks took to the air over the accident zone to search for any potentially missed victims. From above, they could see the long lines of cars that had built up on the freeway system. The need to get traffic flowing again was imperative. Captain Justice was finishing up one last recon of the area before rejoining his team, which was still assisting ground crews in moving debris from the road to start a single lane of traffic.

The captain's proximity sensors went off, and he quickly scanned the area for any emergency aircraft. He hovered in place for a moment and slowly circled to discover that a camera drone with a TV news logo painted on its side was filming him and buzzing over the accident area.

"Diana, this is the captain. Did the Coburg City Police or the county sheriffs give permission to the news crews to fly over the accident site?"

"Hold on, Captain. I will check," replied Diana through the private comm system. There was a momentary pause while the drone continued to get dangerously close to the captain during his flight. Diana came back, "Sir, no one in law enforcement or fire and rescue has given permission for camera crews to fly drones over the accident zone. It is currently a no-fly zone unless it is a designated emergency craft."

"Thank you," replied the captain, feeling a bit irritated by the drone's insistence on getting too close to him. He took a quick turn to the left away from the drone, causing jet wake turbulence to rush in the drone's direction. The obnoxious insect-like flight device spun wildly, then took a nosedive downward and disappeared. The captain smiled with gratification. He then landed near the law enforcement command area and strode over to talk to the county sheriff, who was in charge of the north side of the accident.

"I am Captain Justice of the Cyberhawk Emergency Services Team. The news crews are violating the airspace over the accident. I just had an aggressive encounter with a drone. The logo had a number three on it," said the captain.

The sheriff sighed and made a face, "Okay. I am not surprised. That crew has a reputation for getting in the way. I will send an officer to go over and speak with them."

"Thank you," said the captain.

"So, was it as bad as it sounds over the radio? Down there?" asked the sheriff.

"Yeah. The semi that turned over with the steel pipes… really made a mess. One of the pipes landed on a motorcyclist and broke his neck. It was… bad," replied the captain.

"Closed casket," said the sheriff.

"That would be the only way," replied the captain.

It had been a long morning, and he was sure that the rest of the Cyberhawk Team needed some well-earned rest. It was time to go. Crews were cleaning up spilled chemicals and had begun allowing a single lane of traffic to resume.

CHAPTER 13

It was afternoon when everyone had reassembled for the debriefing of the morning's operation on Interstate 5. The crew slept, washed, and ate. It was now three in the afternoon. The captain looked at his team with a certain amount of pride and satisfaction. They had all done a good job. There were no problems with egos or lack of knowledge. This was a good group of people, and to his amazement, they all got along with each other, despite coming from different backgrounds and countries. Morales was a good trooper, and he worked diligently to learn the new language. It must have been challenging to step into a new environment that did not share the same language and culture. Hallman and Hanni had similar situations, but they both spoke English fluently before they arrived. Their situation was not as challenging as Morale's.

"Alright, that was our first mission where our entire team took on duties to make sure jobs got done. I know Diana and Ellena stayed behind at the base, but they were performing behind-the-scenes coordination that helped make things run more smoothly while the rest of us were out in the field. I want to say to all of you, …good job! I am pleased with how things went. I have spoken with the Coburg law enforcement, the county sheriff's department, and the emergency crews that were assigned to the incident. We got good feedback. Our help was effective, and the other agencies are looking forward to working with us again if the need arises," said the captain, looking at the faces of his team. Some still looked tired, but they all looked pleased.

"I'd like to hear from all of you on how you feel it went and what we could do better. Hanni and Smith, you assisted the emergency ground crews. How did that go?" asked the captain.

"I thought it went fine, but Raven has more experience with this kind of operation. I was just there to lend a helping hand," replied Dr. Hanni.

Raven sorta chuckled and then replied, pushing his long black hair back, "Dr. Hanni was a bonus to have. Most of the time, we do not have a doctor on site to consult with. He was able to observe symptoms and suggest precautionary procedures to protect the injured. I would like to have more supplies available so that we do not have to wait for the traditional crews to arrive."

"Sounds good. Diana, please take note of that," said the captain. "So, how did our CyberSkeleton crew feel about this morning's operation?" The captain turned to Janet, Daryl, and Alejandro.

"The suits work great for dealing with wreckage," replied Janet. "When we finally got to the location where the semi-truck with the steel pipes had turned over, we saw the tremendous power that we have with the CyberSkeletons."

"Sure, it took two of us to lift and coordinate a safe removal of each pipe, but us being there... reduced the wait time for traditional equipment to arrive. We saved lives and helped get the freeway back to being operational," added Daryl.

"And Alejandro's knowledge of Spanish helped him to keep a trapped driver calm while we worked to free him from the vehicle," said Janet, getting the idea that Alejandro would not say anything. The man was so quiet.

"All of this is new to us. All three of us are cops, so lifting heavy objects like the Incredible Hulk is... amazing and very different. Wouldn't you say?' asked Daryl, turning to Janet and Alejandro.

Alejandro managed a grin, and Janet nodded in agreement.

"Any suggestions for improvements?" asked the captain.

"Does the gear that flies have the same strength?" asked Daryl.

"Yes. So, eventually, all of you who will don the Cyberhawk gear will have flight abilities as well as the extra strength. I want everyone to learn how to operate as a Cyberhawk, but I do not expect everyone to use it on a regular basis," replied Captain Justice.

This met with understanding nods.

"I love flying planes and drones, but learning how to use the other tech is a bonus in my opinion," commented Chris.

"And that is why you are our pilot," replied the captain. "So, how did the drone perform? And are you happy with the software and readouts?"

"Funny that you mention that. I do have some ideas for improvements. I need to be able to set up better monitors that are at least 4 K resolution. And there are some problems with signal strength. I was viewing an area with Officer Campbell, and we had to wait several times for the screen to stop pixelating. I am concerned that we could miss important data if the signal strength is not strong enough to transmit detailed imagery," commented Chris.

"I will set up a time for you to voice your concerns with the LabCoat Crew. If you can explain what exactly is happening in the field and your needs, they should be able to come up with a solution," replied the captain as he walked back and forth, listening to his team's ideas.

"I would welcome that," said Chris. "Oh......hey, there is one other thing. I almost ran into another drone flying in the fog. Was there another authorized drone pilot in the area? Because I was not informed."

"No. You were the only authorized flight craft besides the Cyberhawks," Diana said firmly.

"Oh, well......some jerk was flying his drone around in the fog," replied Chris.

The captain made a face and then responded, "You are not the only one who almost ran into a drone. There was a drone from a... news agency? I think. Could you search your footage to see if you can identify that drone?"

"Easily. I will get on that right away," replied Chris, enjoying the idea of getting a little revenge on the unauthorized drone.

"So that leaves us to hear from our Cyberhawks. What do you three think of the mission?" asked Captain Justice.

"I loved being out there. I can't wait to do more training and more missions," Fernando piped up right away. "And I agree with Raven and Dr. Hanni. We need to have our own set of supplies readily available."

"Yup, I was mighty stressed about gettin' that infant warm. I was almost to the point of stepping out of my gear so that I could put the child next to my body, but we did not know if the child had any broken bones. I was trained to leave that sort of thing to the experts because removing him from the car seat could have been... life-threatening. He was alive and breathing in the seat," remarked Rafferty. "But with a low body temperature."

"Hmm, what about adding some kind of scanning technology into our glasses.... or HUDS to allow for more comprehensive analysis of the patient's well-being?" suggested Dr. Hanni. "Is that possible?"

"Like something that would tell me if the bones were broken," added Rafferty in agreement.

"These are all good suggestions to bring up to the LabCoat Crew. They are seeking ideas on how to improve these devices for use in the field. And suggestions based on real-life experiences are the most useful inspiration for proper improvement," said the captain.

"While we are at it," paused Sandra, looking about. "Hauling that crate between us in coordinated flight was… not exactly practical. We need containers that can … follow us like… R2-D2 follows Anakin and Luke around. I see this stuff in science fiction all the time. Captain Kirk's communicator looks an awful lot like a flip phone. Perhaps we could have a droid that follows us with the necessary equipment. We can't take the Terrain Buster everywhere."

"Yeah, I agree. That is a good point. It was very awkward trying to fly with that container between us," added Fernando.

"Okay, so let's plan some meetings between the LabCoat Crew and us. Diana, can you set up appointments with the various experts with our Cyberhawk Team members who have ideas?" asked the captain.

"I will get to work on that as soon as this meeting is over," replied Diana.

"Anything else that someone wants to add?" Robert turned to his team.

"Yes," said Sandra. "I would like to thank Ellena and Diana for looking after the twins. I don't have anyone to leave them with. It was nice to have them stay here. Is that going to be a problem in the future?"

Robert Justice paused for a moment in thought and then replied, "You know...... I don't know. Currently, we have extra rooms available for people to stay at the base. This is a new type of service being offered, so we are unsure how often we will be asked to come and assist others. If we become overwhelmed, we may need to add more personnel and adopt a day shift and night shift scenario. Until that time, we can offer space here at the base as long as someone is here to keep an eye on the twins."

"They were both well behaved," commented Ellena. "I had no trouble with them." She then turned to Diana, who was also at the Cyberhawk base during the mission.

"In the morning, they were both ready for school, but we had no one to take them, so I called the school and advised them of the situation. They were allowed to arrive late since I called for a car to take them. You may need to advise the school of your work situation and see if they can work out something concerning emergency calls," suggested Diana.

"And I can call the school as well as your employer. If they don't want to play ball... we could find a private school for them if you like," said the captain.

"They are both exceptionally brilliant," remarked Ellena. "Have you noticed that?"

"I know they are smart, but I had not noticed anything unusual about them. Their old school never said anything," replied Sandra. "And nothing has been mentioned here either."

"Your kids...are probably both geniuses," commented Ellena.

"Oh," said Sandra, feeling a bit stupid for not realizing how smart the twins could be. Work and the loss of Karl had consumed her thoughts to some extent for the past couple of years.

"We could have them tested formally if you like," suggested the captain.

"Well, ...I guess that might be good. I have heard that brilliant children can find traditional school boring, and Tessa has been acting odd lately. Michael naturally gravitates towards intellectual and creative pursuits. He seems to manage himself most of the time. I would not want to neglect their education, especially if they will not get what they need in a regular school. Who would I need to bring them to for testing? Do you know?" asked Sandra.

"Bring them here. Several people in the LabCoat Crew love to run tests," said Diana. "I will see about making arrangements for that as well."

"Thank you," replied Sandra, feeling relieved.

"Does anyone have anything to add?" asked Captain Justice.

The team members looked around at each other, and no one appeared to have anything additional to say.

"Well, since we are done with our meeting, in about thirty minutes, Lukas Knight and some of the LabCoat Crew will be joining us for a pizza celebration dinner of our first full team mission," said the captain with a big smile.

"Oh, pizza! That's exactly what I want tonight! Cold beer?" asked Rafferty.

"Cold beer if you like," replied the captain. He then turned to Sandra and said, "And I had my wife, Jessica, and our son head over to your home with pizza and sodas for the twins. So, you could celebrate with us."

"Dang……. you think of everything," said Sandra, almost getting emotional.

"Hey, the news is on. Maybe I will see that drone logo that I saw early this morning," commented Chris as Rafferty handed him a cold soda.

As some headed over to eye the news, Ferdinand turned to the captain.

"That's kind of cool that the big guy is coming to celebrate with us, right?" he said to the captain.

"Oh, you mean Mr. Knight, yes," replied Justice, who pondered the thought that Knight was not very tall.

"Well, it is his celebration too. He… put this all together, didn't he?" commented Janet.

"Yes. For the most part, if I understand correctly. He was assigned a team of people, and he was the original organizer who made all this work," said the captain.

After the fast-food commercial ended, the screen flashed a new setting with a high-end news broadcasting stage, featuring a well-groomed man of mixed ancestry dressed in a tailored suit and sporting a fashionable haircut. The man looked physically fit and was considered handsome until he opened his mouth. His sonorous voice greeted the viewers in a friendly manner. It was easy to see why he had been chosen for the job as lead reporter and evening anchor.

"And now Sam Tredwall and the KPIE evening news," said an unseen announcer amongst a flourish of music and bright colors that matched the Channel 3 KPIE logo.

"Good evening, greater Portland metropolitan area...... KPIE, your sweet source for all your news. We have several major stories to cover this evening, starting with the big I-5 crash and the hazardous fog that shut down the freeway in both directions for five hours this morning. And then another win for the Portland Timbers, continuing their big winning streak. How far will it go?" Sam Tredwall paused for a moment and then turned to an up-close camera shot of himself at his desk. "Our first story is the big crash and Interstate closure. Live on-site is Debbie Kale. Debbie, what is the status down there?"

The screen turned to a brunette with heavy eyebrows, thick eyelashes, and dark lipstick.

"Hi Sam! The cleanup is progressing well here, and traffic is now moving in both directions, although it is limited to one lane in a section where a semi-truck loaded with steel pipes overturned. Crews have been waiting for a crane and a new truck to remove that debris. Earlier today, the county sheriff's department gave a briefing to the public," said Debbie, and then the screen turned to film footage of the actual County Sheriff speaking before news crews.

"That's the logo I saw," remarked Captain Justice as he watched the TV.

"And it is the one that our drone footage caught this morning as well," replied Chris, messing around with a large touch-screen tablet.

"Captain Justice, do you want me to send a confirmation with the FAA and local authorities that the drone came from this news agency?" asked Diana.

"Yes," replied the captain, making a face.

"I will send you a shortened version of the footage captured by our drone. It's vital that airspace above restricted zones is not violated. Not just a legal thing, a drone can easily compromise an aircraft performing emergency services, causing damage to the craft and, in some cases, there have been deaths," added Chris.

"Whoa, get a load of her," remarked Rafferty, looking at the TV screen. A slender, older woman was now being shown dressed in 1960s fashion, with long, straight grey hair. "She looks like she stepped out of a time portal or…..."

"A Halloween party?" Janet finished Rafferty's thought.

"Yup. People do not dress like that in Wyoming. Is that normal here?" asked Rafferty.

"Uh… you do see some strange stuff in Portland, but…. generally, not. She's the mayor of Progressville. Remember," replied Raven. "We saw her a week or so ago on the news. She's.... known around a bit....as a...wackadoodle."

"A wack a doodle?" questioned Dr. Hanni. He felt like he had seen her visage before on TV.

"Kinda weird...fanatical?" Raven tried to explain.

"We saw stuff like that in LA all the time. She's pretty tame," remarked Sandra to no one in particular.

"......so, Mayor Malapert, are you saying that you do not think that such specialized emergency services like Cyberhawk should be allowed?" asked Sam Tredwall.

"Well, no. This is just some ego-driven men playing with expensive toys that taxpayers are paying for with their hard-earned funds. They get to play superheroes while the average citizen goes hungry or cannot afford rent or utilities. We have unhomed persons here, right now, who could have used this money spent on that testosterone-driven equipment. We have children who are cold and face food insecurity in the streets, Sam. So, no, I am against this kind of useless spending of taxpayers' hard-earned money. Besides, what is dispositive about our wonderful firefighters? Why are they being disenfranchised? Why doesn't this money go to them for new equipment? I am calling on all voters to stand up and ask for an accounting!" replied Mayor Malapert.

"I thought we were funded through a private company," Sandra side-commented to Daryl, who was standing next to her.

Robert Justice heard Sandra's comment.

"We are. This bitch doesn't know what she is talking about," replied Captain Justice, gritting his teeth a bit.

"......so, there you have it, folks. Sounds like Cyberhawk is just a bunch of tech jockeys playing superhero with taxpayers' dollars. Now let's hear about those Portland Timbers," said Sam Tredwall with a smug smile on his face.

"This.......is normal...... to have wackadoodles in charge of whole villages?" asked Dr. Hanni, trying to figure out what he just watched.

CHAPTER 14

Two weeks had passed since the big I-5 foggy car pile-up and the strange drama that erupted in the news. The Cyberhawk team's joy over a highly successful rescue mission turned to gloom. All the enthusiasm had been drained like a thief in the night siphoning gas out of a car's fuel tank. Robert Justice pondered his morning coffee with Jessica. It was Saturday morning, and he planned to mow the lawn quickly and then take Jessica and Ryan to the Heceta Head Lighthouse. Ryan had not yet seen the ocean, and it was only a short drive away. Robert needed a little family fun time to recoup and put his mind back into a better state. The strange, hate-filled news stories surrounding Cyberhawk made him feel like a failure. He kept wondering what he could have done better.

Robert took another sip of his hot coffee and eyed Jessica. She was still the beautiful woman he fell in love with when they were younger.

"So....you like the idea of going to see Heceta Head Lighthouse?"

"I love it," replied Jessica. "Ryan has been asking when we could go and see the ocean."

"It won't be like our normal going to the beach trip... at least I don't think so. This area is very different from Lake Tahoe or Donner Lake, but I figure it would be a good way to start exploring the area," replied Robert.

"He'll be thrilled. He's never seen a lighthouse either," she replied. "And I think you need a little break from the worries of work."

"I know," he nodded and then abruptly got up and set his empty coffee cup down. "Gotta get the lawn mowed. Then I will take a shower, and we will head out."

"I'll be ready. And I will make sure Ryan has showered and dressed. Do you want to take a picnic lunch with us?" asked Jessica.

Robert paused for a moment in thought and then said, "Yeah. How about we get some of those sub sandwiches we like, bring some snacks, and something to drink? Perhaps pack the beach blanket to sit on, and the camp chairs just in case. It will be fun."

Jessica smiled broadly with a twinkle in her eye as she sipped her coffee and eyed Robert. The love was still there, Robert reflected. He then headed for the garage to fire up the lawn mower and get that task out of the way. Stepping out into the cool garage, he wondered if the others would have a relaxing Saturday or if something would come up. He hoped everyone would have a peaceful day.

Back at Cyberhawk base, Rafferty gazed lazily out the bedroom window. A car had pulled into the lot. It was Sandra's. She had the twins with her.

"Oh dang, Sandra's here with the twins. Did we not hear an alarm?" Rafferty asked Raven, who was still lounging in his bunk.

"Uh, no. I didn't hear anything," Raven pushed his long black hair away from his face and grabbed his phone to check messages. "Dude, I don't see any messages. The only message I am getting is that I am hungry."

"Alright. She's headed off to the lab entrance anyway......and she is bringing the twins with her. I wonder if that is allowed," said Rafferty, yawning.

"We'll find out when people start yelling at us," replied Raven, stepping into the bathroom and then closing the door.

"Yup, I can see that, if it's a problem. Hey, I'm gonna head downstairs to see if anyone is making anything. You want anything special?" Rafferty said loudly at the bathroom door.

"Yeah. Hash browns. I want crispy hash browns... and some bacon. Eggs would be nice too," Raven yelled back through the closed door.

"Sure thing," replied Rafferty, stepping out of their quarters to head downstairs to see if anyone was awake yet.

Meanwhile, Sandra had to convince Michael that going to the strange, corrugated steel barn-like structure was the correct place to go for testing. She put in her code to open the outside door.

"Mom, I think this is a garage," said Michael, looking about at the obvious parking spaces within the enclosed structure.

Tessa said nothing but looked annoyed and bored at the same time.

"Mom, maybe you got the instructions incorrect, and we should be going inside the cool Cyberhawk clubhouse," said Michael.

"It's not a clubhouse. It's a base of operations where the team members live and work," replied Sandra, using her new HUD sunglasses to find the hidden keypad.

"So why are we doing this again? I am losing a Saturday that I could have spent hanging out with friends," remarked Tessa.

"Yeah, your friends are sooo…. much fun," grumbled Michael.

This caught Sandra's attention. Michael rarely ever complained about people.

"Why…. uh…. don't you like her friends?" Sandra asked Michael.

"Not really. They are mean," said Michael.

"You act like a dork," replied Tessa.

"I didn't do anything to them. I don't know why you hang out with them," retorted Michael.

"What happened?" asked Sandra, now curious.

Both twins clammed up.

Sandra wrinkled her brow as she tapped the command to call for someone down in the lab to respond. She had no idea what was going on with the twins, and she found that perplexing. Was she supposed to be a nosy mom or give the kids some space to figure out their problems? When did she become an outsider, she wondered?

The door to the elevator to the lab suddenly opened, catching the twins by surprise, and for a moment, they dropped their irritation with each other.

"Where ....does this go?" asked Tessa, wide-eyed.

"Yeah, this is a single-story building," said Michael, looking at the open steel-beamed ceiling.

"It goes to the lab where you will be tested," said Sandra, observing their expressions. "This is just a placement test... no needles or anything scary."

"Are you sure? This looks like mad scientist stuff," commented Michael as he followed his sister into the lift.

As the door closed, the image of Dr. Elgin Cross came to Sandra's mind: "There could be a little mad scientist stuff going on here. But it's all for a good cause."

"Uh huh. Mom, that's what the victims in scary movies are often told just before a horrible thing is done to them," replied Tessa.

"I'll be there with you the whole time," said Sandra, rolling her eyes a bit.

"This is going down.... below ground," commented Michael.

The elevator door opened, revealing the high-tech foyer of the Cyberhawk lab. The grumbling suddenly stopped; both twins seemed to be mesmerized by the lab entrance, where they saw people in lab coats walking around, one of whom was accompanied by a robot that resembled a six-legged spider. The technician walked alongside the robot while monitoring something on a tablet. A woman in a lab coat was walking with another robot that resembled a deer; she was heading towards the elevator.

"Good morning! Gotta take Jeremy Stag out for his morning patrol. We are tracking Daryl on his morning run today," said the short blonde woman cheerfully.

"Good morning, Dr. Boisen. We are here to see Dr. Eirstone," replied Sandra.

"She's on her way to meet you. Just wait here," replied Kendra Boisen as she and the robotic deer got into the elevator.

"Did she call that deer robot.... Jeremy?" asked Tessa.

"What did you expect? Bambi?" Michael quipped to his sister, still feeling annoyed about her new friends.

"Guys, knock it off. I want you two to be on your best behavior. I work with these people, and they are... on top of their professions. Experts," said Sandra.

"And you don't want them to think you are a loser with cruddy kids?" asked Tessa.

Sandra tilted her head to the side and rubbed her hand across her forehead. "I did not say that. And I don't think you two are cruddy. You are both acting... obstinate, and I am not used to that. Everyone here thinks you two are gifted and perhaps deserve special educational opportunities. I don't want to screw that up. I love you both... and I want the best for you."

The twins could tell their mother was stressed and suddenly dropped the pre-teen angst.

"We love you, too," said Michael.

"Sorry, Mom. I didn't know you were concerned," replied Tessa. "This is a very different place. And I miss Grandma and Grandpa. And then there is dad…...who…seems to be dead."

Tessa looked like she was about to cry. Sandra wrapped an arm around her daughter and pulled her close for a hug and said, "I miss them too. And your dad."

"Whoa, who is that?" asked Michael in a whisper.

Tessa and Sandra looked up to see Dr. Idunna Eirstone walk into the foyer wearing her typical long white lab coat. The woman had very pale skin, yet she looked healthy, with lavender-colored eyes, and long, light green hair that she had tastefully pulled back into a soft, braided structure.

"That is Dr. Eirstone," replied Sandra, pausing as the woman walked towards them. "So pleased you could make time for us," Sandra said to the doctor.

"I can always make time for members of the Cyberhawk team and their exceptional offspring," replied Dr. Eirstone. "Come with me."

The doctor turned and led them through a doorway and down a hallway that had a series of doors.

"This is one of our training areas," she said as they walked along and gestured to various equipment. She stopped at a door and put a code into the security system. "And this is one of our testing rooms."

The kids, including Sandra, were expecting a dull white room with a sterilized feeling. This room was wonderfully colorful, with walls and ceiling covered in realistic depictions of the night sky, featuring stars, planets, and galaxies.

"This is cool!" exclaimed Michael. "It would be even better if it lit up when you turned the lights off."

"Really," said Dr. Eirstone, reaching for the light switch. The room went dark, and within seconds, their eyes had adjusted to reveal an incredible starlit sky scene that seemed very realistic. "I use this to relax patients and test subjects that need a more meditative atmosphere. There are two viewing chairs located at the far end of the room, which are ideal for this purpose. Not all tests are about calculating numbers or answering questions."

The four of them stood in the semi-darkness for several minutes, and then Dr. Eirstone turned the lights back on.

"Detective Ridgestone, please take a seat in one of the viewing chairs," requested Dr. Eirstone, gesturing towards two leather reclining chairs.

Sandra complied with the request with a smile. She could use a little rest.

"Tessa, please take a seat here. And Michael, please take that one," instructed Dr. Eirstone.

The twins each sat down in comfortable chairs that were set up with a computer display, a mouse, a keyboard, and headphones. The computers were set up so that the twins could not see each other's screens, thereby avoiding any feelings of competition.

"Once you have the headphones on and you are comfortable with the volume settings, click the proceed button and simply answer the questions honestly. Just do the best you can, and there is no rush," instructed Dr. Eirstone. "If you have any problems, just let me know. I will be sitting with your mother."

Both twins settled in, put on their headphones, and focused on the screens before them. Dr. Eirstone came over to Sandra and sat down in the other viewing chair.

"I would like to ask you a few questions," said Dr. Eirstone.

"Sure. What do you need to know?" asked Sandra.

"I was able to get certain test scores from their previous school in Los Angeles. This test is mostly a problem-solving exam, and they are wearing noise-canceling headphones, so they will not be distracted by us talking," said Dr. Eirstone. "Now, according to the records I have, their father is Karl Ridgestone, a former Navy SEAL."

"Yes," replied Sandra. "He re-enlisted into something… that he was not allowed to speak about."

"I see. He has an excellent record. And I am under the impression that you are now divorced and no longer have communication with him?" asked Dr. Eirstone.

"Yes," replied Sandra, feeling a bit uncomfortable. "I am… not even sure he is still alive. There was some strange correspondence from the government that... made no sense."

"Interesting. This is important information, thank you," said Dr. Eirstone, tapping something into her tablet. "I will leave you here to relax while your children work on the test."

Up outside on the grounds surrounding the Cyberhawk base, Daryl finished his morning run with the robotic deer keeping pace with him. When he finally reached the entrance to the base quarters, he found Kendra Boisen standing outside, wearing a big smile on her face.

"Jeremy Stag found you," she said.

"Yes, he did. I still feel strange running with a robot stag through the woods. What if…if people see me? Isn't this deer supposed to be top secret or something?" asked Daryl.

"You have a point, but I need to have Jeremy Stag fully tested before we send him off to do work. Besides, most people would think you were running away from the deer and not with it."

"Oh, great. So, I look like an idiot being chased by a stag through the woods," said Daryl, putting his hands on his hips. "Hey, it's breakfast time. Have you had anything to eat yet?"

"No….I haven't," replied Kendra, somewhat surprised.

"Well, come on in and have some coffee and whatever they are making this morning," Daryl invited Kendra in.

"That sounds terrific," replied Kendra, almost blushing with enthusiasm that Daryl missed. "Could you open the roll-up door so I can bring him in. The building is close to the airfield, and I don't want the civilian pilots to get too curious."

"Sure thing," said Daryl, opening the door and then tapping in the code to open the roll-up door so Kendra could bring the robot inside.

The other Cyberhawks turned, eyeing the robotic deer.

"I have to admit, at this distance, he looks like a real deer," commented Raven.

"Thank you," replied Kendra, making sure the robot was safely in standby mode inside.

"Shouldn't you be worried that some hunter will shoot him? I mean…. I know plenty of guys who'd be extremely excited to see a stag like that trollin' about with that set of antlers. They would think of lunch and the trophy wall," remarked Rafferty, who was wearing an apron and holding a spatula.

"The robot has a skin underneath the fur covering that is bulletproof. It is a special lightweight experimental material. After all, he is an expensive piece of technology that needs to be protected," answered Kendra.

"Ah, heck, that makes perfect sense," said Rafferty, nodding and then quickly walking back to the stove to deal with breakfast. "Hey Daryl, you want somethin' to eat?"

"Yes. And can you make some for Kendra, too? She's gonna have coffee with us, and I don't feel comfortable eating in front of someone," said Daryl, gesturing for Kendra to take a seat at the large dining table. "I'll get us some coffee."

Kendra smiled as she sat down next to Raven, who was already drinking his morning coffee.

"No, problem. I hope everyone likes scrambled eggs, crispy hash browns as requested by my roomie, and bacon," said Rafferty.

"Hey!" said female voices from above. "I hope you have enough for us, too. My stomach is grumbling."

Janet and Ellena came down the stairs wearing casual morning attire. Ellena was in her typical stylish shades of pink sportswear. She looked like she had already showered, while Janet looked like she needed to run a brush through her hair. They made quite the contrast. The two women sat down at the table and took seats near Daryl.

Kendra looked at everyone seated and asked, "Where are Dr. Hanni and Mr. Takahashi?"

Fernando, who had his head resting on his folded arms on the table, lifted his head and yawned, "Chris went out around three this morning to go on some kind of flight with Roy Ekstrand." He yawned again, "Excuse me. I didn't get back to sleep after he left for some reason."

"Here. Have some coffee," said Rafferty, bringing over a cup with the coffee carafe in his hand. "Does anyone else want some?"

"I could use some," said Janet.

"Well," said Rafferty, looking at the nearly empty container. "I think we need to make some more. Can you do that?"

"Not a problem," said Janet, getting up and taking the carafe from the lanky cowboy fireman.

"So that leaves Dr. Hanni missing," said Kendra, as she poured a little creamer into her coffee.

"Oh, he got a request from a physician in Bend that wanted a second opinion on something, and he agreed to go visit today," replied Janet. "He probably left early this morning. I guess it's a two-and-a-half-hour drive there."

"Are all of you getting requests for help from other agencies and institutions?" asked Kendra. "That's good, right?"

"It is...... although I am a little uncomfortable with the crazy press lately. I don't understand this strange attitude," commented Raven. "You would think that since we are helping people, they would like that."

Rafferty set a big pile of plates down on the table along with a handful of silverware and napkins. The group, without instructions, naturally started sorting the dishware. Then Rafferty came back with a plate full of bacon and another plate of crispy, golden, steaming hash browns, which everyone slowly circulated about the table. Then he came back with the scrambled eggs and sat down.

"Y'all better leave some bacon and hash browns," he said, taking a spoonful of eggs and passing the container off.

"I have not been watching the news. So, what is being said?" asked Kendra.

"It's more like implied," said Raven as he contemplated a piece of bacon.

"Yeah. We are all men… and the government is wasting money on us so we can play… or pretend to be superheroes," added Ellena with a frown. "I have used the VR system to control the aquatic robots several times already, and I have saved lives and property. This is a very worthwhile endeavor, and I hate being called a phony. I am now being asked to assist in oceanic research to determine the extent to which pollution is affecting aquatic life. I'm going to be assisting a child-genius inventor who created a device that removes microplastics from water! This is what I wanted to do in college. So, these jerks are saying… that what I am doing is a waste of time."

Daryl put an arm around Ellena and said, "Hey, we all know that you are contributing to the team. You work in a different field. And you might be the spearhead of a new kind of team that works especially in water situations. Don't let the so-called news people get under your skin."

"They are just assholes," commented Fernando.

"But they are getting under the skin of the general public," remarked Rafferty with a mouthful of food.

"How do you know that for sure?" asked Kendra.

"Here's a story, for example… a small town not far from here requested to have some of the CyberSkeletons show up and help with an overturned semi-truck loaded with heavy equipment. The truck owner did not have insurance coverage to deal with the situation, and the town lacked the resources to remove the truck. It would have blocked off the entrance to the school. They contacted us, even though they were nervous about what was said on the news about what we do, and we came to help them," replied Rafferty.

"And when I went to speak with the police chief, who was also the town mayor, he was surprised that I was female. He said he was under the impression that only men were part of this militaristic club," said Janet. "I was surprised by the fact that he was surprised. And asked him where he got that idea."

"What did he say?" asked Kendra.

"Social media and the news," replied Janet.

"Oh. I don't have time for that kind of thing. Is social media important?" asked Kendra.

"It's hard to evaluate the stuff," said Fernando. "It has so many great aspects like chatting with friends and family…making new friends."

"You make friends on social media?!" commented Rafferty.

Fernando shrugged.

"I have never made any friends on social media. I just have followers that like my artwork," remarked Raven.

"The school kids seem to like us," Rafferty commented to no one in particular.

"Alejandro has forbidden his children and his wife from having any social media. Something has got that man spooked," said Fernando.

"I have noticed that. Dr. Hanni can connect with him a little because they are both Catholic and well......the doc can speak Spanish fluently," added Raven. "I think he made friends with the older gentleman they brought with them for the evening get-together."

"The old guy was his father-in-law," answered Fernando.

"Oh," nodded Raven. "That's nice. He cares about his elders."

"You know, Captain Justice had some woman come up to him in the grocery store. She yelled at him for taking money away from the homeless and the fire departments so that he could run around and play with electronics. She told him he was going to burn in hell," said Rafferty. He then turned to Kendra and said, "The media is getting under the skin of the general population."

Kendra frowned.

"Well......where is all this...... coming from?!?" asked Kendra, feeling much more concerned about what was going on in public opinion. Dr. Cross had just dismissed it as being nonsense of ignorant buffoons, but too much ignorance was a problem. A problem that could not be ignored. Especially if the stupid gained control over government agencies and critical educational institutions.

"Not sure," said Fernando.

"It could be the wackadoodle mayor of Progressville. She likes to hear herself speak. She says a lot of strange things," said Raven, finishing his breakfast. "She is bad... medicine. Toxic."

"Yup, she is a weird one, isn't she?" added Rafferty.

"I don't like her. I don't trust her," Janet said firmly. "People like that have hidden agendas with dark purposes, and when they get into power, they seek only to make things worse. We, the RCMP, had to deal with someone like that a couple of years ago. This individual was a personality of a religious cult type, and he was elected mayor. He began taking measures to restrict the town's population from having any freedom. He passed laws that enabled him to prevent people from leaving the town without incurring fines, and if individuals disagreed with him and his followers, then well… people started disappearing. He also put restrictions on businesses. Finally, someone had the courage to reach out to us. The web of legal craziness that was established within that town was disturbing. The people felt trapped and frightened. She reminds me of that kind of personality."

Janet pushed her empty breakfast plate away from her with a certain amount of defiance, expressing her sincere feelings about the matter.

CHAPTER 15

It was going to be a beautiful early summer day. The sky was clear, and it was the perfect time to train the additional Cyberhawks, now that more gear was available for the team. It was determined over a year ago that each team member should have their own Cyberhawk suit of equipment, as each user would ultimately personalize settings to make them more comfortable. Simple things, such as height and weight, were essential for calibrating the equipment. Betty could monitor the mechanical AI that was part of each personalized set of Cyberhawk suits. This mechanical AI would learn and customize the suit to the individual's specific needs. The more time spent flying or running the suit meant a smoother, more integrated experience. The mechanical AI would work in conjunction with the commands received from the individual's communication implant. Captain Justice was pleased to see that the team members assigned to regular flight duties all had their training gear. His experienced pilots, Ridgestone, Lewis, and Sanchez, were all eager to assist Crane, Hallmann, and Smith. No one seemed to be burdened by selfish jealousies or insecurities that would make them act negatively. At times, he felt like they did not need a leader. He felt blessed for having such wonderful people to work with. Perhaps in the future, they would no longer need him to be captain, and his duties would be to serve as the contact point for other agencies.

"We have a light mission today. The goal is to train our teammates who have just received their Cyberhawk gear and to do a little fun PR trip to an elementary school. The teachers at the school are hosting a Science and Technology Month, and we are part of that lesson plan. We will land at a safe distance from the students in the playground area, then answer their questions. If you don't know the answer to a question, it is okay to say you don't know... or you can ask Betty. She is our special AI who helps keep an eye on us. Any questions?" Captain Justice asked his team, who were neatly assembled on the edge of the airfield.

"What happens if a bird flies in front of me? I don't want to hurt them," said Raven.

"Well," Justice paused for a moment, thinking of what to say. "Sometimes things cannot be avoided. Betty and the mechanical AI are designed to look out for that kind of hazard... and collisions can be avoided,... but there are moments when the backwash from the jets can hurt the birds. We can't control what the birds choose to do. All you can do is be mindful and aware of your surroundings. I suspect that as the technology gets more refined, we will be better at avoiding objects that do not carry beacons or transmitters."

Raven frowned a little and nodded his head and said, "Okay. I understand. We do not live in a perfect world, but I can try."

Sandra turned to Raven and said, "The last time we were up, I spotted some geese flying, and I was able to log that into our flight path awareness system, and everything was fine."

"Nobody wants to have that stuff happen," added Daryl.

"So, we are nothing like the guys in the videos where birds rest on their hang gliders," commented Raven.

"No, we fly much faster. More like airplanes," replied the captain, looking at Raven closely.

"His heart rate is higher than normal," said Betty through the HUD system.

"Smith……. Raven……are you okay?" asked the captain.

"Yeah. I think I am nervous. I have never done something like this before," replied Raven. "I paint images about flying creatures and think about what it would be like, but this…….is very different and……exciting."

"Well, heck, like your namesake…. There comes a time when the baby bird must jump out of the nest and fly," remarked Rafferty, looking at his roommate, trying to give him some encouragement. "You trust me, right?"

"Yes," said Raven with a chuckle, thinking his silly roommate was a good guy.

"I would not steer you wrong. I can fly this contraption, and I am not Chris, but I can do it. And so can you," said Rafferty.

"It's actually…...pretty fun," added Sandra. "Almost addictive."

"Okay," said Raven, still feeling his nerves and heart pounding a bit. He looked over at the captain, who acknowledged his readiness.

"We are going to start with something simple. First, we notify the airfield that we are taking off, and we have already been assigned an airspace for our training today. I am going to assign partners for this exercise, so none of our new fliers will feel alone. Ridgestone and Smith. Sanchez and Hallmann. Lewis and Crane," said the captain as he started up his Cyberhawk suit and hovered for a moment.

The captain smiled. He knew it was going to be a great morning.

****

Thomas Strand frowned a little as he pressed the button on his Hyundai IONIQ 6 and locked the door. He was pleasantly surprised by how much he liked the car. His parents had pitched in to help him buy the vehicle. He had initially felt forced into buying an environmentally friendly car, as his employer could be aggressive about her opinions. Today was no exception, and it was not going to be a great morning. Carol Fairling, who was the other assistant, was already on her way to the office. They both had been called in to arrive early. No extra pay was offered, but refusal was not an option in the town of Progressville, Oregon, especially when it came to the mayor, who owned at least half of the property in town and the surrounding region.

Thomas momentarily caught sight of his tall, slender self and appraised that his attire was neat and appropriate for work. He did his best to wear nothing that would draw any attention to him. Carol did the same thing. They were both the same age, but Carol had the advantage of being Native American. Their boss often used Native Americans as examples of how certain people abused other people. Carol served a special purpose, and… she was female. The short, curvy young woman was also kindhearted. Despite being only twenty-three years old, she had a certain amount of confidence and wisdom that enabled her to steer the volatile older woman's tantrums away from herself and Thomas. He was grateful for Carol's skill since the mayor did seem to hate men. Joan Malapert often claimed to have Native American ancestry, but Thomas and Carol both believed that was a lie. Neither of them would confront the woman about the claims because that kind of drama could cause problems for their families and friends.

Thomas turned on the lights in the office and set about getting the place ready for the day's work. Carol arrived a minute later.

"Good morning, Thomas," said Carol.

Thomas looked up from his desk to see that Carol had her jet-black hair neatly combed into a new hairdo of a short, straight, jawline-length bob. She looked adorable. She wore business casual attire and had nice makeup.

"Wow, I like the new haircut. It looks good on you," said Thomas.

"Why, thank you," said Carol. "She's not here yet, right?"

"No," answered Thomas.

"I am going to start the coffee and check the water machine to make sure it is functioning correctly. Yesterday, she wanted tea, and the machine was not working right," said Carol, putting her purse away into her desk and turning on her computer.

"Oh......that must have been bad," commented Thomas.

"It was. And I am going to make sure that everything is working properly. I also threw out the non-organic stuff that upset her. She also made a memorandum that all office food items must be organic, locally sustainably sourced, or ethically grown outside products. So now, I must do some research on the coffee and the tea......," Carol sighed.

"I could help with that," offered Thomas.

"That would be brilliant. Here is the list of items that must follow the new guidelines. If you can at least take care of finding half of them, it would really help. She has a meeting this morning with the town chamber group, and I might have to be present to take notes," said Carol, handing Thomas a memo.

"You know the video conferences are recorded. She could keep the recording. I could assist with that," said Thomas.

"Oh no. She insisted that the lead chamber members attend a meeting this morning in person, which is why I am in a panic to ensure the coffee and tea are prepared correctly. Dang!! I don't have the morning pastries," said Carol, starting to feel her blood pressure rise.

Thomas got up from his desk.

"Look, I am just doing the monthly correspondence. This takes me the whole day, but... this is obviously more important. I can walk over to the bakery and get what is needed so you can have everything ready," Thomas offered.

Carol paused. She looked up at the tall, pale-skinned man with kind eyes.

"You are a sweetie. Thank you. That would remove an extra task," said Carol, trying to calm her breathing.

"Do you have a list?" asked Thomas.

"Yes," replied Carol, grabbing her phone. "I will text it to you. It is very specific. No substitutions."

"I got this," replied Thomas. "Hey......we are here for a reason. Sure, we are young and... very affordable assistants, but... we care about the town. And someday, things won't be this way."

"I hope you are correct," said Carol, fiddling with one of the baubles on her bracelet.

Thomas headed out the door. It was a lovely day for a walk down the street to get the pastries for the meeting. Progressville now had a population of around ten thousand residents. They no longer had a police department, so the county sheriff was responsible for all law enforcement. Mayor Malapert had defunded the town police. Luckily, she kept the fire department. The town used to be called by another name, but it was not acceptable to mention that name. It had been the same family name as the closed paper mill, which loomed ominously at the edge of town. It was once the center of life in the modest rural community. Over half of the residents earned a living from the factory. The elementary and middle schools received extra funding from the paper mill, and community events were also supported by the plant, which occasionally filled the air with unpleasant odors. It was bittersweet having the paper mill close down. The air was better, but so many people lost their jobs. This was how Joan Malapert was able to obtain so much property in and around the town. Families that had been homesteaders back in the pioneer days were forced to sell their homes and small farms. It was a mystery how Malapert managed to obtain the funds. She had shown up during the seventies, a time when hippies were losing their social prominence. Many boomers who had followed that path abandoned their old, trendy habits and redirected their efforts toward their own families and businesses. Joan Malapert did not appear to have any family. She arrived and bought an unwanted piece of property in the woods where an old cabin had been erected, and worked odd jobs in town. She continued to wear the styles of clothing popular in the 1960s and 1970s.

Thomas Strand's family had lived in the area for several generations. His grandfather had worked at the paper mill, and his father went to college, became a CPA, and started his own business. The Strands were well-known in the community, and Thomas had several cousins whom he saw frequently. A certain part of him felt guilty that he would not help continue the family name, but he had no desire to be something he was not. He was still not sure if his family knew that he was different. And he wanted a life on a different path as a result. He hoped that when the time came, his family would still love him.

He opened the door to the bakery and was assailed by the wonderful smell of freshly baked bread and pastries. The clerk behind the counter looked up and smiled.

"Hi Thomas! Kinda early for you to be here," said the young man who was a few years older than him.

"Hi, Kip. I am here early because the mayor is having a meeting this morning with the chamber of commerce leaders, so we need to have the right kind of baked goods," replied Thomas.

"Oh. I know exactly what you need... unless the mayor has changed her mind," said Kip, looking somewhat concerned.

"I have a list," said Thomas, looking at his phone and bringing up the text message from Carol. Thomas showed the list to Kip.

"Yep, that is the standard list. I hope I have the right amount for each item. One time, I didn't have the organic vegan whole wheat non-GMO scones with cranberries, and she came over here… and really… yelled at me. It was unpleasant," said Kip, looking around to make sure no one else was within earshot.

Thomas nodded adamantly but looked uncomfortable. Kip folded a pastry box and then started counting out the items from the list that Carol provided.

"What do I owe you?" Thomas asked, reaching for his wallet.

"Don't. We have a special account just for the mayor's office," said Kip, closing the box and forcing a smile and sense of cheerfulness. "Hey, I will talk at yah later when you come by in the afternoon."

"Sure thing," said Thomas as he carefully picked up the box of baked goods and left the bakery. Kip seemed stressed.

The special scones looked great, but Thomas had tried one and found them to be lacking in flavor. He knew the bakery made those specially for the mayor, along with a few other vegan people in the town. Thomas thought the lack of butter and eggs made the bread and cookies taste weird. But he figured everyone had the right to like different stuff. He felt sorry for the Chamber of Commerce members who would be expected to eat this with a smile, regardless of their preferences.

When Thomas arrived with the baked goods, the chamber of commerce members had already arrived, and Mayor Malapert was in full fury. Carol was repressing tears as she tried to make it appear that nothing was missing. She quickly took the box of baked goods from Thomas and brought it into the meeting room, where everyone was already ready. Carol came into the room to hear one of the chamber members make a bold request.

"The chamber members would like to… encourage some …...improvements concerning the city. You know…to help businesses and encourage economic growth. We…...would like to see…. the old paper plant be torn down. Perhaps the materials could be recycled?" said the female chamber member, trying her best to be professional.

Mayor Malapert picked up her coffee and sipped it as she eyed the chamber members who sat before her at the big meeting table. She sat at the far end, and they huddled like mice on the other end. There was an uncomfortable silence as she eyed them. They all looked frightened. That was good.

She finally set down the coffee mug and coldly replied, "The paper mill is too expensive to be torn down. Do you think the mayor's office is made of money?"

"Uh, oh no. We... were... hoping to fix things up a bit... and well... the paper plant does seem to be a bit... of... an unpleasant looking place," replied the female chamber member.

"Well, it is too expensive. Keep the dialogue concerning issues of city economics to what is *actually* achievable prosperity goals," replied Malapert.

"We appreciate your... willingness to dialogue concerning this issue. Uh," the balding male chamber member stammered for words. "Would you be agreeable to …...dialogue with us on any improvements that you wish to see concerning......the wellness of our town?"

Carol had heard enough. She had to leave the room. She knew that she needed to prepare the post-meeting data for the mayor.

The mayor had not answered the man, so Carol dared to speak.

"Mayor Malapert, do you require me to stay?" asked Carol.

The mayor flashed an irritated glance in her direction, then covered it up like a wave dissipating into the ocean, and said, "You may leave."

Carol obediently left and gently closed the meeting room door behind her. The tension in the room was intense. The topic of the paper mill had been raised before, which ultimately led to the defunding of the police department during a period of intense political unrest concerning law enforcement. Carol was a teenager at that time, but she remembered it well. Several teens were believed to have entered the paper plant property and were presumed to have become lost or injured. She knew of these older kids by rumor as being adventurous, exploratory types who took videos of themselves visiting places all over the region. They posted their exploits on a shared YouTube account and had started to gain some followers. Their ultimate goal was to become like Josh Gates, Ghost Adventures, or a modern land-based Jacques Cousteau. They would explore the local beaches, historical sites like Fort Vancouver, and journey down trails, sharing their discoveries. Then they discovered a trend of exploring forgotten and abandoned places, so they decided the paper mill was their next big adventure. Carol, like most of the local kids, looked up to these three as courageous role models. One of them had landed a scholarship at a Portland art school, with plans to become a film director.

"Carol," she heard whispered to her, and felt a hand guiding her to her desk chair. It was Thomas.

Something must have happened.

"Are you alright?" he asked in a whisper.

"Yes....I think so," she replied quietly. "What happened?"

"You were just standing there and had a very faraway look on your face. I was worried," replied Thomas.

She took a deep breath and tried to refocus herself.

"I was just thinking about stuff that happened......back when those three teenagers disappeared. You know... the paper mill," she whispered to him.

"Yes. I remember that. One of those teenagers was my cousin," Thomas replied.

"The chamber of commerce members asked about tearing down the paper mill," said Carol.

"Oh. I see," said Thomas. "Better get that post-meeting paperwork ready. She will want that information right away."

Carol turned to her computer and began compiling names, addresses, phone numbers, photos, websites, blogs, social media profiles, businesses, and any other information associated with the people who attended the meeting. She often wondered what Mayor Malapert did with the information that was gathered. She shuddered to think of the possibilities.

CHAPTER 16

The Cyberhawks had a successful morning of flight training, and the three newly equipped members excelled under the instruction of the more experienced fliers. The school kids loved seeing the team land in the playground and were excited with so many questions. The teachers were also enthusiastic once they realized that the team members were nothing like what was being said on some of the local TV stations. Once back at the base, Captain Justice sat at his computer in his office. He had just emailed Lukas Knight about the day's progress. The phone rang, and it was Lukas Knight.

"Hello?" Robert Justice answered the phone.

"Hey, it's me, Knight," said the familiar voice.

"Hello, Mr. Knight. I just sent you an email," said the captain.

"Yes, I saw that, and it reminded me that I had wanted to call you," said Knight. "I wanted to congratulate you on the news of Ridgestone's twins. Elgin Cross told me that they are both geniuses!"

"Oh wow! I had not heard this," replied Robert, leaning back in his chair. "Did someone tell Detective Ridgestone?"

"You know, I have no idea. You'd better get her down to the lab to chat with the LabCoat Crew. I was told both twins have

IQs around two hundred and twenty, which is phenomenal," replied Knight.

I didn't know IQ levels were that high," responded the captain. "I had better make sure Sandra Ridgestone knows before someone says something to her."

"Good idea. I will talk to you later," said Knight, hanging up.

The captain paused, feeling the enormity of the discovery. The twins were super smart. Geniuses. He wondered if that would create changes in their lives. He reflected upon how intelligent Ryan was and wondered if he needed to have his son tested as well. Work often consumed his time, and Robert wondered if he was paying enough attention to Ryan. Jessica would marvel at some of the things Ryan would observe and do. He had straight A's in all his classes. But then again, he was only seven years old, on the verge of being eight in a couple of months. Robert got up, realizing that he would be annoyed if such news were not brought to his attention right away as a parent. Robert tapped his HUD glasses and said, "Hello, Ridgestone."

"Yes, Captain. What is it?" answered Sandra.

"I think we need to make a quick visit to the lab and chat with the LabCoat Crew. I heard a rumor that they have some test results for you," said Captain Justice.

"Great. I will meet you outside by the garage entrance," replied Sandra.

It was a comfortable sunny afternoon, and the temperatures were starting to warm up in Eugene as Summer arrived. The sunlight felt good on Robert's head and shoulders, and he revelled in the idea that it should not be as hot as it was in Carson City, NV. While he missed some of his friends and associates there, he did not miss the idea of the nineties and hundred-degree temperatures. Sandra was waiting by the door, watching some of the small aircraft take off from the airfield.

"You know, I never thought I would find watching planes take off and land to be interesting.... but for some reason, I do," Sandra laughed at herself.

"Well, you'll have something more interesting to contemplate after we chat with Dr. Eirstone and Dr. Cross," said the captain, leading the way into the cooler, dark garage area. They headed down the special elevator for their meeting. Down below, they came across Dr. Cross.

"I was just going to call you to come here," said Elgin Cross. "Dr. Eirstone has completed her test results on the twins, and she has some fascinating news about Tessa and Michael."

The four of them went into Dr. Eirstone's office, where she made Sandra sit down while Dr. Cross and the captain remained standing.

"What is the news, Dr. Eirstone?" Sandra asked, unsure of what to expect. She figured that the kids were probably a bit above average.

"I have gone over the results several times and looked into other fascinating data that I will explain in a moment, but both of your children are extremely gifted with IQ levels well above two hundred," said Dr. Eirstone in her calm and serene manner.

Sandra felt her eyes widen, her jaw drop slightly, and then she said, "What? Did I hear you correctly that... their IQs are over... two hundred?!"

"Yes," said Dr. Eirstone. "Both of your children are extremely gifted, and that being so, you should consider alternative educational routes for them. I will need you to bring the twins back for a serious conversation about this. The reason why this is so important is that individuals like them being stuck in a traditional educational path can be detrimental. I am not trying to scare you; I want to make you aware of the situation. There have been cases with brilliant individuals languishing in basic schooling, to end up doing drugs, and sometimes take their own lives. Some gifted students will be so bored that they will be labeled as being autistic and thus never be given the challenges and guidance that will make them thrive."

"Oh. I had no idea. I feel terrible that I didn't know," said Sandra.

"Don't feel bad. Parents often are so busy with work responsibilities, and you being a single parent now, along with a demanding occupation, would have your attention divided," replied Dr. Eirstone.

"Should I quit Cyberhawk?" asked Sandra.

"No," responded Captain Justice, not thinking.

Everyone turned and looked at him.

Captain Justice shrugged his shoulders and said, "She's very good at being a Cyberhawk. She flies well and has taken to the technology as if it were second nature. Her detective skills... being analytical and observant are a bonus ... she is a great team member."

Sandra chuckled with embarrassment, "Oh, thanks, Captain. I'm glad to hear that I'm doing well. So, how do we make this work?"

"Let's bring Tessa and Michael in for a meeting and brainstorm with them about what their hopes for the future are. We may need to remove them from school or supplement their activities with outside pursuits that are better suited to their intellectual level. They could also be candidates for early admission into college. If you are worried about them needing to socialize with other children their age, they could be enrolled in activities like after-school sports teams, dance, martial arts, just to name a few ideas," suggested Dr. Eirstone.

"You don't want to allow them to suffer the.... irritation of being stuck with....people that have no clue and treat you like you are stupid," remarked Dr. Cross.

His words came out with a touch of pain laced into them. Robert looked at Cross, who always seemed arrogant, brilliant, and untouchable.

"Did you have a rough time in school?" the captain asked.

Elgin Cross turned to Robert Justice with a cold stare and replied, "I was always smarter than the teachers. And eighty percent of them did not like that."

Robert nodded and then turned to Dr. Eirstone, "I am...hoping that you would also be willing to test Ryan, my son. He often seems more mature than his age."

"I would be delighted to do so," said Dr. Eirstone, kindly sensing that the parents were now worried, and Dr. Cross had unfinished emotional trauma.

When the captain and Sandra returned to the Cyberhawk base, Diana came up to the captain with her tablet in her hand, ready to update him on the latest news.

"Captain, we have just received a request from the Sheriff's Department of Marion County. There are some missing children from a summer youth group that wandered off from a field trip near Silver Falls State Park. They are hoping we could assist them with some aerial reconnaissance," said Diana.

"Well, certainly. Find out where they want us to focus our search, and I will get the Cyberhawks and Chris going," replied the captain.

Sandra already ran off to get her gear on while the captain tapped his HUD glasses to make an announcement to the team that they would be doing a mission. Chris and Alejandro gathered the drone equipment and hopped into the Terrain Buster, heading north before the Cyberhawks had finished putting on their gear. Ellena accompanied them to get some field experience. Luckily, it was still daylight, and with the summer months, it would be several hours before sunset. The goal was to find the missing children before nightfall.

Alejandro took the driver's seat while Ellena acted as navigator. Chris sat in the back seat and requested a flight plan for deploying the drones in the Silver Falls area. Flight plans had to be filed with the authorities to ensure safe conditions.

"So, how are you doing back there?" Ellena asked Chris.

"Just fine. I made some modifications to the drone's systems to increase its speed and improve its aerodynamics. It will use less battery and allow for more hours in the air, which, for a search and rescue operation like this, is vital," said Chris.

Ellena admired his confidence.

"I brought two drones with me this time, and one uses the VR headset which you are used to using," said Chris.

"Oh, really. I get to use one. That should be exciting," replied Ellena, glancing over at Alejandro, who kept his eyes on the road. The Terrain Buster was blazing down the road smoothly, but at a speed that she hoped would not attract the highway patrol. Although the vehicle did have the Cyberhawk logo emblazoned all over it. It was not certain that law enforcement would recognize their status as an emergency services team and that they were en route to a call. "So, which one do I get to fly?"

"The little blue and gold one. It is one of the standard models that Ekstrand and I worked on to allow for the VR control system. You have the most VR experience, so it makes sense to have you be the test pilot. You will be flying low along the creeks," said Chris.

"Okay. I have never flown that device before, so I am unfamiliar with the interface," commented Ellena, feeling a little concerned.

"Don't worry. It has the same interface as the underwater modules. We got one of the LabCoat guys to fix that up," replied Chris.

"Great. Sounds like an adventure. Do we have a description of the kids yet?" asked Ellena.

"Don't know," said Chris. He tapped on his HUD glasses and said, "Hello, Diana. This is Chris."

"Chris, this is Diana. What can I do for you?" asked the voice through the HUD system.

"Do we have a description of the lost kids yet?" asked Chris.

"Yes. I have sent the descriptions and photos through the HUD system, so when you are ready, you can view the descriptions and most recent photos," replied Diana.

"Thanks," replied Chris.

Chris tapped his glasses to send the data to his tablet, where he pulled up the images. There were five teenagers. Four girls and one boy were dressed in outdoor clothing. He eyed the pictures first and then showed them to Ellena.

"These kids are big teenagers. They should be able to take care of themselves until we find them," commented Ellena.

"I would hope so, but one can never assume," said Chris.

Shortly thereafter, they arrived in a small town not far from the state park and set up their gear in a local middle school parking lot on the advice of the sheriff's department. Chris and Alejandro pulled out the small generator along with the table and chairs. Ellena helped set up the new monitors that Chris and Alejandro would use to watch the main drone. And then they got Ellena ready to fly the small drone. In a matter of minutes, Ellena was busy in the VR world, heading off to the park that was just a few miles away. Ellena was safely inside the Terrain Buster while the guys made sure their monitors wouldn't be hit by sunlight.

"You should have a... small tent for this," suggested Alejandro to Chris.

"That's a great idea. Especially if it is raining, or... perhaps we should have a vehicle that is just designed to house this equipment like a tech van," said Chris.

"That's a good idea too," replied Alejandro, watching closely what Chris was doing.

The highly modified drone took off at an incredible speed and disappeared into the sky.

"Whoa! That was much faster than I expected," said Chris, moving his hands across the keyboard in a flurry of clicks.

"What happened?' asked Alejandro, eyeing the monitor footage that was blurry and unviewable.

"The drone is going faster than the camera can process correctly. Ekstrand was not joking when he said the modification that he made would make the drone fly super-fast." Chris finished typing in a few commands and made a few flight adjustments.

The video footage stopped pixelating, and finally, they could see something clearly on the screen.

"Where is that?" asked Chris, scrunching up his face.

They both looked at the GPS readout on the software. Chris copied the data and entered it into a mapping system, while Alejandro continued to view the drone video footage. There was a small town situated on one side of a forested area, and the other side was open farmland. The drone was slowly making its way towards a large industrial-looking structure. The place appeared to be three to four stories tall and was very much abandoned or no longer in use.

Chris focused his attention on the video coming back and said, "Wow, look at that old, creepy-looking place. The GPS says we are flying over a town called Progressville." Chris laughed, "Hey, it doesn't look like they are making much progress .... anymore!"

Alejandro said nothing but remained riveted to the video. Chris piloted the drone to do a respectful flight around the structure and then hovered near an open section of one of the taller buildings. Alejandro leaned in closer, thinking that he saw movement or a shadow of some kind.

"Can you zoom in? I thought I saw someone," said Alejandro.

"Where?!? I doubt anyone would be inside that place," replied Chris.

Alejandro pointed to the area where he thought he saw something. Chris zoomed the camera to focus on an opening that looked dark and grimy. For a moment, they both thought they had seen a shadowy figure along with a strange greenish light.

"This looks like ghost hunting stuff," commented Chris. "Did you see that weird shadow-looking thing?"

Alejandro felt a chill go up his spine, and his mouth went suddenly dry.

"We should move away. Get back to work on finding those kids," Alejandro said with his Mexican accent coming in thicker than usual.

"Sure thing," said Chris. "Are you okay?"

"We should leave this place. It is probably trespassing," said Alejandro sternly.

Chris's fingers tapped rapidly across his keyboard, and the drone spun around and headed for Silver Falls. Chris glanced up at Alejandro. The normally healthy, tanned-skinned man looked pale, and he had goose bumps all over his arms. Chris decided not to say anything. The guy seemed upset and was usually very reserved and private, so Chris did not want to impede his comfort by bugging him.

"Hey guys! Did you hear? Daryl and the captain found the missing teenagers," said Ellena. "I am bringing the little drone back here asap, okay?"

"Sure thing, Ellena," replied Chris, sending a return home base request to his drone.

Within minutes, the small drone could be heard landing nearby, so Chris got up and helped Ellena start packing her gear. The experimental drone was scheduled to return in five minutes.

Alejandro excused himself to get something from his bag in the Terrain Buster.

"Is Alejandro okay?" Ellena asked as she walked over to Chris, holding the VR headset. "He looked upset."

"Not sure. We should probably give him some space," suggested Chris.

"Maybe, we should get some food on the way back," suggested Ellena.

"That's a good idea. I'll ask him," said Chris.

"Perhaps it is low blood sugar, and good food always seems to brighten people up," remarked Ellena, giving a concerned look towards Alejandro.

When the big drone came back and safely shut down, they finished packing up and were ready to head back to Eugene. Alejandro seemed to have regained his usual demeanor and agreed to stop by a hamburger joint to get some snacks. Chris and Ellena said nothing to him about his odd behavior, and he offered no explanation. When they arrived at the burger place, Alejandro said he wanted to make a quick call to his wife, letting her know that he was getting food with workmates. Chris and Ellena said they would meet him inside.

Alejandro quickly sent a text message to his wife. Then he went through his phone and selected a saved number to call. He waited for the call to go through and for the answering machine to pick up.

"This is Morales. I have seen something again. Small town in Oregon just south of Portland. There is a video of it."

****

Later, Alejandro Morales found himself back home with his family. They all appeared to be safe, which made him feel more comfortable. Family was everything. His family was his primary concern. That evening, he watched television in bed while his wife slept. He looked down at her. She was beautiful and kind. The world seemed to be in chaos as he watched the news. He watched the news from the US and then the news from back home in Mexico. He had always been proud of his Aztec ancestry, a proud people renowned for their warrior spirit and the construction of great things. He felt like a coward hiding in the US, but he had a duty to protect his family. He absently scratched at the scar tissue throughout his chest where he had been stabbed several times. It felt odd to him. He lifted his t-shirt to inspect the scar tissue. The tissue looked red and swollen, which was unusual since it had healed a year ago. He looked down at the scar on the right side of his chest. It looked like it was opening, and green mist was coming out of it. His breathing started to accelerate with fear. He needed to call for help right away. His wife needed to get away. He looked for his cell phone. It was gone.

"Ximena! Ximena! Ximena! Wake up. Please. Wake up, dear," cried Alejandro as he started to shake his wife, who remained unconscious. She didn't even move from being shaken. What was wrong with her, he wondered. More and more green mist started to escape from the scar that was opening. "Ximena?"

She was not responding. He had to get up and find his phone to get help. The Cyberhawk people would come. The people in black suits would come. He turned to get out of bed to see a shadowy thing with green mist evaporating around it, staring at him, and then it began speaking to him in a hissing language. It had a maw full of sharp black teeth. Alejandro wanted to scream, but he couldn't. He felt like he was choking and could not breathe to make a sound to warn anyone.

"ALEJANDRO! Wake up!!" cried Ximena.

Alejandro woke up covered with sweat, and every muscle in his body was tense and painful. His heart was racing as he desperately tried to focus on Ximena, who was standing over him in the living room. She looked frightened and concerned.

"You were having a nightmare," said Ximena.

Alejandro quickly glanced down at his chest and touched the scar. Everything was fine. He tried to slow his breathing and nodded to Ximena.

"I was… having a bad dream," he replied slowly. "Are you okay?"

"Si. Stay right there. I am going to make you some manzanilla tea," she said, immediately walking off to the kitchen.

Alejandro peered around the room. The dream seemed so real. The television was still running. He must have fallen asleep while watching the news. He gingerly tried to ease his body into a more upright position. Every muscle ached. The dream still haunted him with images. He wanted to shake it off. It was only nine in the evening. It wasn't even late. He wondered where the children were.

"Ximena," he called out. "Where are the children?"

Ximena came back into the room with the hot tea, "Max and Valentina are both asleep in bed. It is their bedtime. And Diego is probably finishing up his homework." Ximena handed Alejandro the cup of tea, which he gratefully accepted. She sat down next to him and asked, "Do you want to talk about it?"

"No. It was just a stupid dream. I'd rather sit here with you and sip this tea," replied Alejandro, hoping that he would not have any more nightmares like that.

CHAPTER 17

The next morning, the news was awash with conflicting stories. The entire team sat in the upstairs lounge area and just watched what was being said.

On KGIU, the broadcast showed the previous night's interview with a law enforcement official of Marion County.

"Cindy, I am so pleased that our interaction with the Cyberhawk Team turned out to be such a success. They came through for us, and we were able to find the lost campers before nightfall," said the officer.

"Were the parents happy? We have heard so many negative stories lately about the Cyberhawk Team," Cindy of KGIU asked the officer.

"Nothing happened that validates or hints at those weird stories about the team. They are here to assist us in our job. And our job is to protect and serve the public. As for the parents, they were happy, and the teens themselves were also happy to have been found so quickly," replied the officer.

"Do you feel like the Cyberhawk team is taking funding away from the sheriff's department? Are they stepping on your... toes?" the reporter asked.

"No. It is nothing like that. They are a privately funded group comprised of professional individuals like me. I am grateful to have them as a resource when we need them," replied the officer conclusively.

"Well, there you have it. Cyberhawk is a hit with law enforcement as well as the public who need their help," said Cindy, the reporter.

The TV switched to a commercial showing a guy running around on his front lawn in his bathrobe, yelling about coverage.

"So that's not bad at all," commented Rafferty thickly with his cowboy drawl. "They like us!"

"Yeah, ...but you need to see what they are saying on this other news station," replied Janet, taking the remote and switching the channels. "Look at what they are saying here."

The screen switched to an image of Sam Tredwall on Channel 3 KPIE.

"....and that sounds like a great weather forecast, Jim. But not everything is sunny in the state of Oregon. A dark cloud has moved in, and it is called ......*Cyberhawk*. Where do these men get their funding? Why are they showing up now? Why do they wear masks? We have Progressville's mayor, Joan Malapert, here to give her insightful opinion about all this strangeness that is happening all over our fair state of Oregon," said Sam Tredwall, turning to Mayor Malapert. "So, who are these Cyberhawk individuals?"

Sam Tredwall appeared, his perfect hair, stylish clothing, and gleaming smile complementing his invitation to the mayor to expound upon her ideas.

"Men wanting to play superhero and interfering with the emergency services that are already in place. And you asked why they wear masks? Sam, isn't it obvious? These men wish to hide their identity to circumvent the laws already put in place to create community wellness. I am concerned that they may have a hidden agenda that could cause dispositive issues within our communities. They are not part of the public dialogue. They are a hidden group that is doing intelligence gathering on the general public with their sophisticated equipment," said Mayor Malapert, expecting a response from Sam Tredwall.

"Intelligence gathering? Spying?! Do you have any proof of this?" asked Tredwall.

"Yes, I do. I have sent you the footage regarding the invasion of our town's privacy. It's a HIPAA violation for certain. The wellness of Progressville has been violated by their data-collecting technology," replied Malapert, still attired in her peasant blouse and simple hairdo, appearing to be a thoughtful grandmother type. "These Cyberhawks do not have good intentions. The public needs to be aware of this," said the mayor.

Then, film footage from a camera located on the outer fence of the Progressville paper mill property showed a drone flying around the upper part of the plant. It was there long enough for the camera to zoom in on the object and capture footage that showed Chris and Ekstrand's experimental fast drone, featuring the Cyberhawk logo.

"Oh shit," said Captain Justice.

"Sorry, Captain, the drone took off more quickly than we expected, and the video went crazy on us as well. I was just happy we were able to get the drone to fly normally and come back home," said Chris. "I had no idea they had surveillance cameras on the property. Honestly, I didn't even know this place existed until the drone came across it."

Robert Justice ran his hand through his hair and down the back of his neck in contemplation. He sighed and said, "This was probably the worst possible place that this could happen. This mayor has been gunning for us since the first day we were seen in public."

"We should ignore the bitch. She has hate in her heart," said Ekstrand, who was also in the lounge drinking coffee with the team. "I am sorry, Chris. This is partially my fault. I should not have let you take it out without going through full, extensive testing."

"Well, placing blame is not of importance here. We need to figure out how to deal with people like her. That reporter is not helping either. We need to let the PR team deal with matters such as this," replied the captain, thinking all he would want to do is punch Tredwall in the face. The guy was encouraging the old biddy to harp on her pet peeves in a public venue.

"But this stuff, ...it hurts. We do amazing things, help people, and get slapped in the face for doing it. At least... that is how I feel," replied Fernando, tapping his hands against his chest.

"Heck, she doesn't even acknowledge that I am a woman. She thinks we are all guys," commented Janet.

"Oh, I think she knows. I think she is trying to stir hatred in every direction she can," remarked Sandra with a scowl. "You know…. get the whole feminist thinking groups hating us because we discriminate against women…...you know the tactics. I've seen this in LA. It's ugly."

"Are you sure? She misused the term HIPAA," commented Dr. Hanni. "Perhaps she is just some… old hippie that used too many drugs during her youth and can no longer discern reality from ideological propaganda."

Sandra shook her head and said, "I just don't think so."

"Whatever she is… it is not good," remarked Alejandro.

Later in the afternoon, Captain Justice called the team together for a quick meeting just after their lunch break. Everyone gathered in the main training room downstairs.

"Alright, before everyone disperses off to do their training and other projects, I've got some news from the head office. We have a PR team that is working on improving relations with the general public, as well as with local law enforcement, search and rescue, and fire departments throughout the state. The emergency services organizations are completely on board with us. A protocol has been established so that they may call for assistance when needed, and we can report to local jurisdictions in case we discover something that should be brought to their attention. We need to make this work well in the state of Oregon.

I have been told that the goal is to make this eventually a national organization, and Oregon is the test state," said the captain.

"Wow. Really?! That is exciting. We are pioneers of...a sort, right?" said Fernando with a big smile.

"Yes," the captain chuckled. "I don't plan to get a coonskin cap, though, or carry a long rifle."

"Soooo, ...how does this solve our problem with people like Malapert and that stupid news guy?" asked Janet.

"The PR department has come up with several ideas, one of which may seem... odd, but they want us to wear Cyberhawk jackets, t-shirts, and other apparel that will affiliate us with the program to instigate conversations... hopefully pleasant ones... with the public. They want first to get the girls to wear this stuff to prove that we do have women as a part of the team." The captain then looked at Janet, Sandra, Ellena, and Diana. Diana made a face.

"Yes, Diana......you are a part of this team just as much as the others. Being a logistics assistant does not make you less of a Cyberhawk member," said the captain.

Diana rolled her eyes and made an uncomfortable expression.

"Which reminds me, have you completed your CyberSkeleton training?" he asked Diana.

"No, I have not," she replied.

"We need to remedy that today. Dr. Hanni, how is your training going on the CyberSkeleton?" the captain asked.

"I think I am close to completion. I have one last test to pass," replied the doctor.

"This afternoon will be the three of us getting your training finished and yours further along," the captain said to Dr. Hanni and Diana.

"Sounds delightful," said the Swiss man with his eyes twinkling. "I am finding these new challenges most entertaining and engaging. It is giving me a broader understanding of how I can be an effective part of the cybernetics group in the future. We need to make this into something that the common man can obtain after suffering a great loss. It will restore hope for the future."

"I agree," Robert Justice said, nodding his head. "Come on, let's start those exercises now."

A couple of days later, a shipment from the home office in Wilsonville arrived. The boxes contained various kinds of sportswear, all of which had the Cyberhawk logo emblazoned upon them. Stylish t-shirts, polos, lightweight jackets with embroidery, hats, and even a few scarves, even though it was too warm to wear them. The Emergency Services Team members were asked to wear and test the items for comfort, durability, and style. A note was also attached, stating that the PR department wanted the female members to make an effort to be seen in public wearing sportswear with the logo. The four women stood around the table selecting their choices and sizes.

"Too bad they don't have anything in pink or aqua," commented Ellena.

"Those colors would look terrible with the logo," frowned Sandra. "Take one of the white ones. Or.... actually, ... the black one would look good with those pink leggings you are wearing." Sandra held a t-shirt up to Ellena.

"I guess so," said Ellena, making a face as if trying to decide if the colors were suitable together.

"You would look pretty in anything," said Janet, grabbing a shirt, looking for tags that would need to be removed. "When I was with the Mounties, we had uniforms. That made life so much easier. No worries about what to wear in the morning. I like having these."

"Did you always wear those red jackets?" asked Ellena.

"It depended upon the office you were in and the position you were assigned to. But no, we wore other clothing during regular duties," replied Janet.

"Oh," said Ellena in a disappointed voice. "I thought those were romantic-looking. Almost sexy."

Janet grinned.

"Yup, nothing like a handsome guy...or in your case, a lovely lady dressed in a sharp uniform," commented Sandra wistfully. "My Karl was pretty hot in his fancy dress uniform."

Everyone snickered except Diana.

"I do not want to wear this... out in public," she declared.

"Why not?" asked Janet incredulously.

"I don't... know how to fly. And.... I am not interested in dealing with aggressive people who will confront me," replied the woman with the caramel complexion who rarely exhibited any emotional outbursts. "I don't want to let everyone down by not doing what is needed."

The other three women exchanged glances with each other. None of them knew Diana that well, even though they had been working with her for almost half a year.

"Why don't we do a girls' day out? We can all wear our Cyberhawk gear, and then Diana will be with us in case anything strange happens," suggested Ellena.

"Okay. Like what? I am not into having my nails done or any of that stuff," said Sandra, looking over a black polo shirt. "And I have kids. Can we do this on a Saturday and have it be a family-friendly outing?"

"Geez, that is a good question. It needs to be something where other people see us.... otherwise, it won't do what the PR team was hoping," added Janet.

"How about a concert?" suggested Ellena.

"Sounds fun," added Janet.

"I have kids. Too expensive," Sandra dashed the idea away.

"Sometimes there are outdoor concerts in the parks," suggested Diana. "My great uncle likes to do those when they are offering the right kind of music. People bring picnic dinners."

"That does sound nice, but are we going to agree on the music? And then I have fussy kids...... okay, I have one fussy daughter. She is starting that teenage angst thing early," said Sandra.

"How about a farmer's market? They usually have all kinds of food, music, shopping, and lots of people casually wandering about," suggested Janet. "Raven was just telling me about one time when he set up a booth and tried to sell some of his artwork. It sounded like fun. The shopping part, ... not the selling."

All four women looked at each other as if they had struck a consensus.

"Then this Saturday is our day to parade the Cyberhawk gear and do some shopping," declared Janet.

"I will send out the invites with time and location," said Diana.

Farmers' markets had become regular outings for many people throughout the western states, and the Pacific Northwest excelled at it. So many wonderful vendors brought in food in various stages of preparation, allowing buyers to purchase raw ingredients to fully baked cookies and wrapped candies. Many artists and crafters also brought their wares, and shoppers could stroll along with friends, family, and their pets. Local performers often supplied live music. There was an incredible energy to community activities like this. It created an atmosphere of wonderment and hope, akin to the feeling vacationers exude as they explore new places and discover interesting and exciting experiences.

Some thought that the energy generated by life was something to be harvested and consumed. Intention had a lot to do with such paraphysical matters, and rarely did there exist people with the skills to discern the dark, the light, and the grey from each other. Modern society had a way of labeling esoteric experiences as nonsense, making it easier for those who wished to conceive darker plans to blend in with the masses. Sandra got out of her old car and locked the doors after the kids were out. There was a strange feeling in the air. Standing still, she looked around, and nothing seemed amiss. Everyone looked happy. No one was acting suspiciously. But her detective *'spidey senses,'* as her son called them, were giving off a vague warning. By no means was she as talented as the legendary Spider-Man that Michael loved to read about, but she had learned to listen to them like a Jedi was mindful of their surroundings.

"What's up, Mom?" asked Michael.

"Not sure. Both of you, be careful. Watch out for pickpockets or …predators," was the word that rang out to Sandra.

"Mom, we are almost thirteen. We aren't babies anymore," remarked Tessa.

"I know you are not a baby anymore, but you can still be fooled by bad people and taken advantage of," said Sandra, feeling overprotective as the words came out of her mouth. "Just stay close to us, but still have fun looking at things. You both have money with you, right?"

"Yeah," said Michael with a smile. He looked at the closed-off street with pop-up tents lining the road in a park-like setting. The tall trees provided ample shade to rest under from the sun, which would grow warmer as the day progressed. "It smells great here. It makes me feel hungry."

"That's what the vendors do, silly. They make food that has a great aroma so that it attracts buyers," said Tessa.

"Cell phones?" Sandra asked the twins.

Both twins pulled out their phones and showed them to their mom.

"Great. Let's go find the others, and we can start this little adventure of showing off our Cyberhawk clothes," said Sandra.

"I like the shirt. When do I get one?" asked Michael. Tessa ignored Michael's appreciation for his mom's new sportswear.

"So, your work wants you to wear the clothing with their logo on it like some kind of walking billboard?" Tessa asked her mom.

"No. That is not the point at all. We are not acting as salesmen. Those stupid news people are making it sound like only men are a part of Cyberhawk," replied Sandra.

"Oh. I didn't know that," said Tessa, making a sad face and dialing back her attitude.

Janet, Ellena, and Diana came over from a different section of the parking area. They were all wearing their Cyberhawk gear, and, of course, Ellena made it look stylish with her aqua yoga pants, black Cyberhawk t-shirt, and a black baseball-style cap.

She twirled around and said, "What do you think?"

"Great!" said Sandra.

"You look very pretty, Ellena," said Michael with a touch of boyish awe in his eyes.

"Why, thank you, Michael," said Ellena.

"So where do we want to start first?" asked Janet, eyeing a vendor close by that sold artisan candles, lotions, bath bombs, oils, and lip balms.

"At one of the end points," suggested Sandra. "What are the bags for?"

"Shopping for produce. We are required to bring our own bags, and I asked if we could make purchases for the Cyberhawk base kitchen," said Diana, handing bags out to each of the women.

"Okay. We then support local farmers while enjoying a great time outdoors. More good relations," said Janet. "Besides, I don't think we interact with enough people who live here in Eugene. Speaking of Eugene......I heard that there are two new bright stars about to start college studies next Fall." Janet turned to Michael and Tessa.

"Only if we pass certain entrance exams," replied Michael. "We are scheduled to tackle that next week. Regular school is over now... and Mom doesn't know what to do with us."

Sandra just shook her head and smiled.

"Just beware that when football season comes, I am a big Beavers fan," said Ellena.

Janet laughed.

"They have not yet been admitted," said Janet, laughing some more.

"Well, I have to support my old team," said Ellena with a smile. "Seriously, that was no threat, but I'm a supporter of my old school."

"So, what do you wish to study?" asked Diana, bringing the focus back to education.

"Guys, we need to pass the tests first before we can go running off planning what classes and teams to support. Chill out," said Tessa.

"I'm conflicted between mathematics and computer science, architecture, and or… perhaps comics and cartoon studies," said Michael.

"Don't get too excited. What if this doesn't turn out?" Tessa said in a low tone to Michael.

Michael turned to his sister and said to her privately, "I think it will. You've got to have a little faith. I have always felt like I was different from the other kids. You were the only one who seemed like my equal. You can do this."

Tessa sighed a little but did not dismiss her brother's honesty and belief that they could attend college at the age of thirteen. She had some ideas about what she wanted to learn.

She enjoyed dancing but also possessed a talent for languages. Perhaps she could study both interests, she pondered.

"Let's do this thing," said Janet, walking towards where the pop-up tents started. Music could be heard in the distance. It sounded like a cover band playing rock songs from the 1980s and 1990s.

The group headed towards the first section, which featured several produce sellers with displays of local fruits and vegetables. The group wandered through picking various items for some planned meals that would serve the whole group. The twins moved closer to the vendors who had t-shirts, action figures, and cool artistic items.

A man walking with a beer in his hand stopped Ellena, noticing her shirt, "Hey, are you a cheerleader for that group or something?"

"No," she responded, thinking the man probably had too much to drink.

"Oh. You know what I mean. That Cyberhawk group with all the guys flying around. You are wearing their brand," said the man.

"I am aware that I am wearing a Cyberhawk t-shirt," she replied coldly, starting to move away.

"Well, are you one of their wives or something?" asked the guy.

"No, she is part of the team. Just like me," said Sandra, gesturing to herself with her thumb towards her chest. "And I fly."

The women walked away from the man, who seemed to ponder the idea and then continued on his befuddled way.

"He was a rude jerk," said Ellena.

"He just had too many beers," replied Sandra.

"Hey, I overheard that you are one of the Cyberhawk fliers. I think that is cool," said a young guy with his arms full of pool noodles. "I'd ask for an autograph, but my hands are full." He started to chuckle.

Sandra smiled and nodded to the guy, "Maybe next time."

The guy nodded and then made his way through the crowd with his awkward armful.

"See, not everyone is a jerk," Sandra said to Ellena.

"Hey, Mom," said Tessa, coming up to her mother from a different part of the market area. "I found a super cool cat wall hanging, but I don't have enough money to buy it. Could you look at it?"

"Sure," said Sandra. "Lead the way."

"Where are they going?" asked Janet.

"To investigate a cool cat wall hanging," said Ellena. "I want to see it as well."

"Alright. Come on, Diana," said Janet, lugging her bag of spring vegetables. "I should have bought the vegetables at the end of the day.

"We could walk them back to the car," suggested Diana.

"Hmm, maybe, but it'll be warm soon, and they will cook in the trunk," replied Janet.

"You could get yourself a little red wagon like those people," Ellena pointed out, an elderly couple who had their dog riding in a fold-up wagon.

Janet frowned and decided she was not that old to need a wagon. After all, she had been a Royal Canadian Mountie, and they were known for being strong and in good shape. She also did not want Rafferty, Fernando, and Chris to tease her. She could carry a few vegetables.

They arrived at the vendor, who had the cool cat wall hanging and all sorts of borderline occult-lite items such as candles, incense, crystals, and dark, moody-colored, flowy clothing. It almost looked like pre-Halloween. Skull-themed items, along with numerous cat and raven pictures and tiny sculptures, were abundant. The woman manning the booth looked like she was ready for Halloween as well. At least that was Janet's impression. The cool cat wall hanging was a screen-printed material, similar to a flag, that could be hung on a wall, flagpole, or even in a window. It was a charming-looking black kitty sitting in the moonlight next to a pumpkin with an owl perched in the trees, all under a starry sky. The colors were reminiscent of van Gogh's *The Starry Night*. Tessa was only a few dollars short of buying the flag-like picture. Sandra agreed to get it for her.

Ellena looked at the clothing in the booth and found nothing she desired. It was just not the color or style that she liked. She walked out and waited with Diana, who seemed not to be enjoying herself. Ellena felt bad that Diana did not appear to be having fun.

"You were very brave with that strange man," Diana commented unexpectedly.

"Oh. I guess so. He was just drunk. And sometimes being drunk enhances idiotic behavior," replied Ellena.

"I am glad that you all are here with me," said Diana. "I could never do this alone."

The two of them stood watching people walk by. It was a diverse group of people who attended the Farmer's Market. All kinds of ages, shapes, sizes, colors, and languages. They all had one thing in common, for the most part, and that was they were dressed for the warm afternoon that was coming.

Sandra paid the vendor in cash, making the vendor happy since she did not have to incur credit card fees. Tessa seemed very happy with her purchase. The dark-haired vendor, who had a slight accent that was probably Italian, eyed Sandra as if wanting to say something.

"It is so nice to see a mother taking an interest in her daughter," said the vendor, finally. "So often these days parents neglect their children, and they are forced to find other role models."

"Yes, well…it's up to me now to make sure they have what they need," Sandra replied offhandedly, not really thinking about what the woman was saying.

"Oh, a single mother," said the female vendor, raising her arms with the long, drapey sleeves catching the air. "You poor dear." The woman reached out and hugged Sandra, saying, "Such love and dedication."

Sandra was surprised by the unexpected hug. The woman pulled back and looked her in the eye firmly and said, "You are a good one, aren't you?" There was a strangeness about the way she said the phrase.

Sandra just nodded and stepped back, ushered Tessa out of the booth, and left with the others. They walked quickly through the booths and wound around a few corners.

"Sandra, what is the matter?" Janet asked, grabbing her arm.

Sandra made a strange face.

"Tell me," Janet almost demanded.

"I just had a very odd experience," said Sandra.

"What? Back at that booth?" asked Janet.

"Uh, yeah. That woman said something strange to me and… the way she said it… made me feel very uncomfortable," replied Sandra.

"Did she threaten you?" asked Ellena.

"No. She hugged me for some reason, and after hugging me, she acted like my very being revolted her… and she said, 'You are a good one, aren't you?' like that was something awful and repulsive to her," Sandra answered.

"Weird," said Janet.

"Let's get something to eat. Michael is hungry, and… maybe you are too," suggested Ellena. "Let's head over there."

"Okay," Sandra nodded, feeling ill at ease. She had seen many strange things and met a lot of odd people while being a detective, but she had never had an encounter with someone like that. It was so unexpected. She felt like she had goosebumps all over her body. She was not cold. It was warm outside. Then the thought of the children came to mind. Michael was walking alongside Ellena. "Where is Tessa?"

"I'm right here, Mom," replied Tessa, grabbing hold of her mother's arm and squeezing it affectionately. "Are you going to be okay? You don't look right."

"She's just hungry. Probably blood sugar is low," said Janet.

Tessa tipped her head to the side and said, "Hey, remember I am the kid with an IQ of 223. Something strange has happened."

Janet made a face.

"It makes me feel better thinking it is low blood sugar and not some… sort of weird who do voodoo," replied Janet.

"Alright," said Tessa. "Mom likes burgers with cheese, bacon, tomato, lettuce, mayo, brown mustard…"

"And that's what we will get her," said Janet.

The group settled under a large, covered pavilion that had been set up for the food vendors, complete with tables and chairs.

Janet and Ellena went to get burgers while Sandra sat with the twins and Diana.

"I am going to use the bathroom quickly. I will be back. Stay with your mother," said Diana, getting up to leave.

A few minutes later, Ellena came over and asked, "Where's Diana?"

"She went to the bathroom," replied Sandra.

"Oh. I was going to ask her if she wanted a vegan burger or if she wanted the turkey patty," explained Ellena.

"Probably should go with the vegan burger just in case," suggested Michael. "Do you need help carrying the food?"

"No. Stay with your mom," replied Ellena, looking around. "I think I will tell Janet to get the vegan burger for her."

Ellena went off again. It was ten minutes before everyone returned, including Diana. The group eagerly started on the good-smelling food and shared a large plate of French fries. Conversation had stopped while everyone ate. It wasn't until the burgers were half finished that conversation resumed.

"Do you feel any better?" asked Janet.

"Yes, ...and no. I was hungry, but I still have... an uncomfortable feeling," replied Sandra. "It was like I just had an unexpected encounter with something extremely malevolent. When we did investigations back home in LA, there were some places where you knew that you were going to find ugly situations." Sandra glanced over at Tessa and Michael, pausing. She did not want to describe anything that would upset the kids.

As a detective, sometimes she saw things that stayed with her and would not go away. She was left with questions that made her ask how a human could do something like that to another human. "The whole Hollywood scene had some dark undercurrents that were... let's just say unpleasant... and weird. That made the idea of taking this job a no-brainer. To be further away from that dark element that bred hate and distrust is like a breath of fresh air."

"I wish we knew more about what happened. Was it just a fluke, or was that woman something bad?" commented Janet, trying to rationalize what had occurred.

"Oh, we can do research now," said Diana. "I went back to the area where her booth was, and I took pictures of her and her booth. She has some rather interesting tattoos."

"You went back and did surveillance on her?" asked Sandra with a smirk of surprise.

"Oh yeah. My job involves logistics, and I need to know certain things so that the Cyberhawk Team can work effectively. This seemed like something we needed to know more about. Besides, she gave me an uneasy feeling as well. That is why I did not go into her booth. I thought I was just being discriminatory because I am Hindu, and what she was selling was something I am not. But after what happened to you, it seemed like I should investigate and learn whether I was being judgmental or if there was something else going on. I think there is something else going on. She is not just a vendor selling witchy Halloween stuff, but perhaps an actual witch," replied Diana.

"But I thought witches were generally good, like in Harry Potter. You know, just people with special talents," said Tessa.

"Mm, no. Historically, witches are individuals who negatively utilize magical talents with selfish intentions. Pop culture has tried to make them into underdogs and victims like the poor people who were murdered in Salem, Massachusetts. Just because a person is labeled a witch or erroneously calls themself a witch does not mean they are actually what a witch really is. The Harry Potter stories are good fictional fun, but the real stuff is nasty," replied Sandra, making a face.

"You have experience with this?" asked Ellena.

Sandra nodded and replied, "Back in LA... law enforcement saw things and heard things that would make your skin crawl. Most officers tried to act like they were only noticing facts and taking down hard data, but frightened people would tell you strange things, and they had no reason to lie unless they were high on something. We even had an expert on the force who knew all about the occult. Everyone considered him to be a bit broken because he seemed odd." Sandra paused, taking a few long French fries. She let out a mirthless chuckle and said, "And I felt bad about not inviting the LabCoat gals on our outing.... but this has turned out to be ......not so fun."

"Hey, I enjoyed being with you all, and I learned more about my teammates," said Ellena. "So, this has been a good adventure. And Tessa got a cool cat wall hanging."

Tessa looked at the folded cloth in the bag and frowned.

"Mom, I had no idea that your job was so hard. I am sorry that I have been such a jerk lately," said Tessa, looking at the bag some more. "Do you think something bad is attached to this?"

The four adult women exchanged glances. They had no idea about such things.

"Dr. Hanni would suggest that you take it to a church and have it blessed," said Diana.

"Would that make you feel better?" asked Sandra, seeing that Tessa and Michael looked ill at ease.

"Yes," Michael answered.

Tessa nodded her head in agreement with her brother.

"Okay, let's find a church," said Janet. "Do any of you go to one?"

"Let's ask if Dr. Hanni will take it to church with him tomorrow to have it blessed. He's more likely to get a better response from the priest than we would," said Sandra. "Is that okay with you, Tessa?"

"Yeah," said Tessa.

"Should we go somewhere else? I feel like we need some fun," suggested Janet.

"How about bowling at the mall?" suggested Michael.

"I'd like that," agreed Janet.

"I am up for it... If we can, we give the girls from the LabCoat Crew a call and see if they want to join us," suggested Sandra.

"I can make that happen," said Diana, pulling out her smartphone.

CHAPTER 18

It was eleven at night, and Hank Dawson was doing his rounds at the building that he was paid to protect. Portland had always been a curious city with a rough past, yet a deep love for the arts. The people who lived in Portland seemed to love it, but lately, keeping it weird had become worrisome. Weird had morphed into violent and destructive. Buildings were being vandalized, so extra security was required for those who wished to sail the rough seas of Portland's changeable population. The structure was five stories tall and made of light-colored brick. The downstairs entrance door was alarmed and locked for the night. No one should be in the building except employees working late into the night. This was Hank's last round for the night since Joseph arrived at midnight. The elderly black man claimed he liked the very late hours because it was peaceful. Hank just nodded with the old man. He, personally, thought that the building was rather creepy at night, and by the time midnight came around, he was ready to leave. He spotted a light on in the gem dealer's office. It had two sets of double-locked doors to pass through to enter. One could get trapped in the middle area, especially if no one was in the office to let you out. The glass doors were bulletproof.

He stopped at the glass door and flashed his light in. He spotted a woman dressed in business attire beyond the double set of doors. She waved to him as she looked like she had just gathered her purse and keys to be ready to leave. She was wearing tennis shoes with her skirt and carried a pair of dress shoes in her other hand. It all looked cumbersome. Hank was glad he did not have to mess with all that fashion nonsense. He watched as she packed everything into a backpack, keeping her keys in her hand. She entered the first door and made sure it locked behind her. Then she turned and exited through the second door, making sure it was locked.

"Oh my," she sighed tiredly. "It's been a long night."

Hank eyed the woman and then asked, "I hope you do not have to go far. Is your car close?"

"I have to walk a couple of blocks to get to the garage," she replied.

"I hope they pay you well to take such risks," he commented. The neighborhood turned rough at night. It was like a completely different place.

"Well, it's a job. I gotta pay rent. The work is okay. Just the hours can be stressful sometimes," she replied sensibly.

"I understand. You know…. I get off work in ten minutes. I could walk with you to the garage to make sure you get there okay. There has been some unrest with protesters several blocks away. They can get pretty crazy at times."

The woman looked at him appraisingly and then said, "That would be very kind of you. I would like that."

"We'll go as soon as Joseph arrives," said Hank. "I need to make one more stop... at the precious metals dealer downstairs. You want to come along?"

"Sure. That sounds fine," said the woman.

****

Captain Justice was up early. Strange things were happening in Portland again, and he received a call that the team might be asked to come and assist. The state's largest city could be problematic. Robert turned on the small TV in the kitchen while he made himself a cup of coffee. Jessica had offered to get up and make him breakfast, but she needed her rest too, and today was a big day for Ryan. Robert had managed to schedule a test for Ryan with the LabCoat Crew. When Robert told his seven-year-old son, the boy was all excited. Robert had not expected that response.

The coffee smelled good as he sat down for a moment to collect his thoughts and have a light breakfast.

The TV volume was set low, "......there has been some growing concern amongst local environmentalists about the pollutants created from new technology. One such example is the new Cyberhawk jetpacks. I have Dr. Haines from the University, who has had his students bring up concerns about the new technology. Dr. Haines, what exactly are your students worried about?" asked the TV reporter.

"Well, as you know, jet fuel can be highly volatile and does cause air pollution. Some of my students are concerned that as the Cyberhawk people grow in numbers, they will begin to pollute our precious environment. This kind of technology could become very popular, and I can easily envision it becoming available to the general public in a matter of years. Then the sky would be filled with these personalized single-person air-polluting vehicles. This could be worse than automobiles," replied Dr. Haines to the early morning reporter.

"Oh wow, I hadn't even thought about the idea of a sky filled with noisy jetpack fliers that were each filling the air with noxious gases," exclaimed the reporter, making a face.

"It is a daunting concept that could be another problem for our Mother Earth to deal with. It seems like we are heading towards making the traditional fossil fuel vehicle more efficient and less toxic, but now... we could be introducing a whole new problem that could be boosted by how much fun it looks," said Dr. Haines.

"I see your point. I think our viewers would love to hear more about this. Are you going to continue to monitor the situation?" she asked the college professor.

"Well, yes. I think it is my duty as a citizen of Mother Earth," replied the man.

"Then we will want an update from you sometime in the future. Thank you, Dr. Haines, for being on the Super Early

News," the reporter concluded, and then the meteorologist came on to explain the weather.

Robert watched the forecast and then turned off the TV. He sighed to himself. Another thing people are complaining about or worrying about. He wondered what they would come up with next. It was perplexing to him. The Cyberhawk team was specifically designed to help the general population, and it was like the news was going out of its way to discourage that.

When Robert arrived at the Cyberhawk base, it was four in the morning. He assumed that the team members who lived there were probably still asleep. He went directly to his office and closed the door. He needed to speak with the authorities in Portland to determine the situation and assess the likelihood of being requested. The online web conversation lasted about fifteen minutes, and he could tell that everyone involved was seriously concerned. The Portland mayor was considering closing sections of the city to prevent the problem from worsening. Fire and rescue departments were on alert, and the police were already on the streets trying to deal with the situation. No one seemed sure about how things got out of hand and what the original causes were for the protests, now turning into riots in some sections. The guesses were something to do with the homeless problem, intermixed with drug addiction, but it was not clear. Speculation about politics and outside foreign governments' involvement was also put on the table as potential influences, but it seemed as if no one had any solid evidence to support any of these claims. It was as if people had just gone nuts. Captain Justice explained to them that the team's mission was not about enforcing the law or dealing with protestors. He was not sure exactly how his group could be helpful. The big concern seemed to be around the fact that the protestors, turned rioters, were starting to set things on fire. It was determined that Cyberhawk could assist in rescuing people who could be trapped in any buildings that could come under the control of the violent offenders.

"So, are you saying that sections of the city are no longer under the control of local authorities?" asked Captain Justice.

"Yes," replied the police officer on the video conference.

"And we are concerned that people will get hurt and property damaged," added the mayor, who was relatively new in the position. "We just recently did a lot of refurbishing of areas that had been damaged years ago. I hate seeing everyone's hard work thrown away."

"I understand that. But Cyberhawk is about assisting agencies that are already in place, doing their job, and finding that they may be understaffed or lack the right equipment to be successful. We are not generally first-line responders. We do not take the place of your established agencies," replied the captain. "We are to assist those agencies when needed and requested by them."

This reply received positive responses from the police and fire department officials who attended the meeting. There had been some wild speculation on the news about Cyberhawk replacing these people.

Mayor Lawrence Jones nodded his head as if finally understanding the purpose of Cyberhawk.

"So, I guess what I should be asking......is .... will your team be available to help if our local agencies require it?" asked Mayor Jones.

"Yes," replied Captain Justice.

"Okay. Thank you. I will let you get back to your day, and we will keep in touch concerning how things progress here," said the mayor.

"Sounds good. My logistics assistant, Diana Thomas, will be in at eight o'clock. I will provide her contact information to you, and if something happens before then, I am here," said Robert Justice.

"Thank you so much," said the mayor of Portland.

****

"Anybody know what is going on?" asked Sandra.

"We are waiting for a request from the officials in Portland. We are on standby," replied Diana.

"Nothing may happen," said Raven, sitting down on the lounge chair not far from the large TV. "It's been my experience to be ready but not waiting."

"We used to go through standby mode when doing the big summer fires in California. We could be called to assist any moment, but often there was a lot of waiting," said Fernando.

Janet and Ellena came into the upstairs lounge room to hang out with the others.

"So, Diana, did you ever get any dirt on that weird woman we met at the Farmers' Market?" Janet asked.

"Actually, I did," replied Diana with a look of self-satisfaction.

"Oh, I want to hear this," said Janet, taking a seat. Ellena joined her on the couch.

"I did some careful research and discovered a few interesting things," said Diana. "The tattoo she has links her to a group called the Witches of Grüner Nebel, which also had ties to another group from World War Two called Ahnenerbe."

Dr Hanni came into the room and made a face upon hearing what Diana said.

"What is Ahnenerbe?" asked Raven.

Diana was about to answer when Dr. Hanni spoke up and said, "The Ahnenerbe was a pseudo-scientific branch of the SS founded by Himmler. A twisted group of people....and I have heard stories about the Witches of the Green Mist. They were part of fairy tales told to children to warn them about strangers with evil intentions."

"So......this is a Nazi thing?" asked Fernando.

"No, it is older than that. Dr. Hanni mentioned fairy tales, which are European stories that have been around for hundreds of years before World War II. They originated around the 1600s, but stories have been passed around for a very long time in many cultures around the world. I keep thinking there was a story that my mother told me that was from India about evil magicians that came with a fog of toxic green mist about them," replied Diana. "I have also found, with Betty's help, two more stories referring to people or things with green mist around them from World War One and the French Revolution."

"And what were those stories?' asked Dr. Hanni, now having his curiosity piqued.

"The French Revolution example was a description made by one of the tradesmen who lived in Paris. He described one of the executioners as having a strange aura around him, which was a foul, green fog. He also mentioned that the executioner seemed to enjoy his job a bit too much. I am paraphrasing since this was written in French," said Diana.

"I would love to read that for myself," said Janet.

"I can have Betty send you the document," replied Diana. "And the World War One example was a bit more extensive. It was written in German by a pilot of the famed Jagdgeschwader I, also known as the Flying Circus. The pilot described his effort to claim proof for a shot-down plane."

"I would like to read that," said Dr. Hanni.

"It's right here," said Diana, showing Dr. Hanni her tablet.

Dr. Hanni took the tablet and began reading it aloud, translating the document loosely so that everyone could understand and hear.

"It says………. I made my way into No Man's Land to find the pilot, or at least gain proof of the kill. The Commander feels that bringing the airman back with us is better than leaving him to the ground troops. He believes we are all like knights and should be treated with respect, that is, we pilots take great risks each time we take off in our machines. I was lucky this time and did not have to wade too deeply through the muck and mire. Everything is dead out here. It has a very somber and sad feeling to it. Nothing lives. No plants or animals. Sometimes I feel my boot crunch onto something….and there have been times, it was the bone of some unfortunate life form. The smell can be horrendous. This time, I had a cover of fog to keep the enemy from seeing me. I made my way to the downed aircraft, and the pilot had not survived the crash. I put my hand against his face to see if I could feel any sign of life. It was one of the British pilots. They were brilliant adversaries. I took out my knife and took a part of his aircraft as proof. I looked at him and wondered if I should take some of his personal effects to send back to his loved ones. After all, this could be me sitting dead in my own plane…… then I saw it. Something was moving in the fog. I ducked down behind the plane, wondering if it was enemy troops. I felt the hair on the back of my neck rise, and a coldness seep into my bones. The form did not walk like a soldier, and it had the silhouette of a woman with long hair, partially put up and somewhat tattered garments."

Dr. Hanni paused, looking up at everyone. He had a strange look in his eyes.

"Don't stop," said Chris, who had entered the room and was fascinated by the pilot's tale.

Everyone else in the room nodded, so he continued reading and translating.

"She walked as if she were a force to be reckoned with, and I kept thinking I was seeing a pale green mist about her. This made me worry that there had been another mustard gas attack, and I wanted to warn her, but something deep down inside said that she would not be affected by such poison. My gut instincts told me to leave as soon as possible. I had my proof of kill, and if I did not leave immediately, I would be the next dead to lie in No Man's Land. Once I safely made it back to the wooded area, I stopped to look back. She was now near the recently crashed plane. She walked towards the cockpit and paused there. I could not see what she was doing because I was terrified that she might see me. This was no normal woman. She seemed to look around as if she had lost something. Then, as if overcome by some primal desire, she looked upwards into the sky and made a terrifying sound that chilled me to the bone. This was some kind of demon. I hid behind the tree that I had been peering around, and then I saw the ghost of the man who had been the British pilot. He beckoned me to follow him away from the battlefield back to the safety of the airbase. He looked just as scared as I was. Both of us made our way back to the airbase behind the lines. He seemed relieved and smiled at me, then vanished before my eyes. I will never forget the demon woman with the green mist about her."

The lounge room was quiet for several minutes.

"Well, that was sufficiently creepy," remarked Sandra, making a frown.

"We should have saved that for Halloween night," said Fernando.

The sound of footsteps coming up the stairs echoed as Captain Justice approached the group.

"Hey! I just found out that my son Ryan is also a genius, just like your twins!" he proclaimed proudly.

"Congratulations!" said Dr. Hanni to the captain after handing Diana's tablet back to her. "That is wonderful news."

"Wow, I guess we are going to have a little group of geniuses to raise," smiled Sandra.

"Yup. He was so excited to take the test," laughed the captain. "But I'm happy to know so that we can plan appropriately for his educational needs. I also have some learning to do as a parent. I guess adults have a habit of not... taking children as seriously as they should, and that could be harmful to children like him."

"How is Jessica taking this?" asked Janet.

"Like she knew all along," replied the captain.

"Any word on the concerns in Portland?" asked Ellena.

"No. I'm not sure what's going on there. We need to be ready if we are called to help," replied the captain.

"Well, I am famished. Anyone want to help me get lunch ready?" asked Fernando.

Ellena, Raven, Dr. Hanni, Janet, and Sandra offered to help.

"Where are the others? Crane, Morales, and Lewis," asked the captain.

"They are off doing something with the Terrain Buster and one of the other vehicles. I was going to join them when I heard the intriguing story that Dr. Hanni was reading," said Chris.

"You were reading an intriguing story?" the captain asked Dr. Hanni.

"Yes. It was a letter or a journal entry from a Great War pilot," replied Dr. Hanni.

"And it was spooky...," said Raven, getting up to go downstairs.

"A Halloween page turner," commented Janet, also getting up with the others to follow Fernando downstairs.

"Where did you get this Halloween page-turner?" asked Captain Justice.

"Diana," answered the Doctor, also heading off downstairs. "You should join us for lunch."

Robert Justice looked at his assistant quizzically. Diana locked eyes with him, knowing he was about to ask her what all this was about.

Diana sighed and said, "I was doing research after the girls, and I had a strange experience while at the Farmers' Market."

"Really," said the captain.

"It yielded some strange stories and curious leads to dark people. A woman at the market had a booth there and… it looks like she may be… some sort of witch," replied Diana.

The captain frowned.

"Oh, I knew you would have that reaction," replied Diana, heading towards the stairway.

"Wait a minute. You are serious," said the captain.

"Yes, I am serious. There are occult groups that claim to use paraphysical means to manipulate the wills of others," said Diana. "The woman in the booth had a tattoo that linked her to a rather nefarious group called the Witches of the Green Mist. I was doing research and came across some rather interesting historical tales connected people and this green mist or fog that some claim to see."

"You said it was green?" asked the captain, wanting to make sure he heard correctly.

"Yes, why?" she asked.

"I… think you should share your findings with Dr. Elgin Cross," said the captain.

"Oh great, so he can ridicule me as being an unscientific moron," Diana said, feeling flustered by the suggestion.

"No. That's not it at all. In truth, I do not know what the deal is. I was just told that if we came across anything odd concerning a green light, mist, fog, or gas, that I was supposed to share it with Dr. Cross," said Robert Justice.

"Alright, then I need to take Chris with me as well. His drone camera picked up on something to do with the color green as well," said Diana.

"Uh, that's already been dealt with. Takahashi showed the video to Ekstrand, and he got Cross involved right away," replied the captain.

"Oh, I see," she paused in contemplation. "Captain, what is going on?"

"I don't know," he replied.

"I didn't even get to the part about who that woman in the booth was. She has no family background here in the United States. I did find another woman by the same name from Italy in the nineteen twenties.......and that was only because I used a photo recognition software that pulled up her portrait. The woman in the old photo looks just like the woman at the Farmers' Market. That shouldn't be possible, right?" said Diana.

"Diana, I didn't think flying a jetpack or having robotic ankles were possible. And here we are. Let's go downstairs and help the others. I will let Dr. Cross know that you have some interesting data for him," said the captain, heading down the steps.

CHAPTER 19

The Justice family had an eventful day. Ryan had been tested and was discovered to be exceptionally gifted, like the twins, validating all of Jessica's suspicions about her son's abilities. Now she had to decide with Robert how to proceed. She was not comfortable homeschooling Ryan, thinking that he needed the company of other children. Robert and Jessica thought that a half-day at a traditional school with an afternoon course in an advanced program might be the best for him until he was a little older. Ryan liked the other children and was very outgoing. He had developed a friendship with Diego, and the year-older boy seemed to enjoy his company as well. Jessica did not want to ruin that. Both needed new friends since they had both moved. Ximena seemed to find Ryan agreeable when the boys hung out to play.

The Justice family gathered in the kitchen to prepare for dinner.

"How about I fire up the BBQ and we do hamburgers tonight?" suggested Robert.

"I like that idea," replied Jessica. "I didn't know you were going to be home tonight."

"I didn't either. You know, search and rescue had been the same way. The need to be ready at a moment's notice is required for this job. I figure we should enjoy whatever time we have free to be together," said Robert.

"Agreed," said Jessica, pulling items from the refrigerator.

"Mom, can I help?" asked Ryan.

"You certainly can. How about setting the table?" said Jessica.

"I was hoping for something more important, but that will do," replied Ryan, heading for the silverware drawer.

Jessica smiled and then looked over at Robert, "See, he says things that…...are just…. not his age."

Robert nodded, "I'll get the BBQ cleaned off and started."

Ryan set the table and then turned on the small kitchen television set. The evening news was on. There was a story that a security guard had been found dead not far from a parking garage in Portland. The authorities were not sure if the murder was connected to the protestors or just an isolated incident. Ryan got up to get the condiments and set them on the table for his mom.

Jessica smiled, thinking how kind her son was …and intelligent too. She was a lucky mom. Robert was ready for the hamburger patties. Jessica handed the plate to him and asked, "So if he has a special program to go to in the afternoon, then maybe I should look for a job or take classes? What do you think?"

"Well," said Robert. "I think we first need to figure out what the schedule will be and then see what you want to do. I get paid enough to support us, but I understand if you need some time away from home to broaden your horizons."

"Hmm. Sounds like I should learn how to fly one of those Cyberhawk jet thingies," replied Jessica.

"Yeah," replied Robert with less enthusiasm.

"What's the matter? You don't think I could learn how to fly those?" asked Jessica.

"No. That's not the case," Robert frowned. "You would probably need specialized equipment to be able to fly. You know…. like the stuff that came with my ankles and lower legs."

"Oh," said Jessica sadly. "That's too bad. I thought your flying around helping people sounded like fun."

"Well, I do find it fun when I am not concerned about something. Let me get the burgers started," he said, stepping out the door to the patio.

When the burgers were ready and the cheese had melted to perfection, Robert placed them on the plate and brought them inside. He sat down at the table.

"That smells great, Dad," said Ryan as he pointed to which side of the bun he wanted the patty placed upon.

Everything was good except for the TV. A special report stopped the show they had been watching, showing unrest in downtown Portland. The footage showed the police forming a shielded line of officers trying to keep the protesters away from one of the museum buildings. There was screaming and yelling of profanities at the police. Protesters threw objects and then dashed away. The line of officers just stood their ground.

"Dad, why are they doing that?" asked Ryan.

Robert Justice paused for a moment to listen to what the reporter was saying about the situation and then turned back to his son, "I… guess those people have no better way of saying they are upset about something."

"But they want to destroy the museum. Why would they do something like that?" asked Ryan.

"Honey, they are upset, and they want people to listen to them," replied Jessica.

"What are they upset about?" asked Ryan, turning back to the TV with a frown.

Jessica and Robert exchanged glances. Neither of them was sure what the protesters were upset about. Nothing egregious occurred that could have upset people. They did not know what to tell their son.

"If I acted like that in school, I would get in trouble," commented Ryan. "And the teacher would not give me what I wanted. This doesn't make sense."

"Better eat your dinner while it is still hot," said Robert.

"Okay, ……but changing the subject isn't going to make that make more sense to me," replied Ryan, picking up his burger to take another bite out of it.

Robert shook his head and shrugged his shoulders at Jessica and then leaned into her ear and said, "I don't know what to tell him. I think he is right. They don't make any sense. This isn't like the nineteen-sixties civil rights movement. It's like chaos for the sake of chaos."

****

That night, sometime after midnight, the crowds seemed to disappear into the darkness of the streets. The police officers were hopeful, yet had a bad feeling that they had not seen the end of the weird behavior and violence. They no longer had to hold their shields up to guard the museum building. Some were sent home to rest while others stayed on duty. The fire departments sent their people back home to rest and answer calls for help. An eerie silence fell over the city. Nobody was working late. Nobody wanted to be out in that area of town.

Underneath a freeway bridge structure, a man moved himself back further into the poorly growing shrub that had leaves and garbage underneath it. The plant was growing right next to the concrete of the bridge support. It was late in the evening, and he wanted to rest. The lights had gone out in the big buildings across the river. It was often hard to find a safe place to sleep, especially now that so many people were living on the streets. The newcomers had cell phones and tents, and they stayed together as powerful, cohesive groups. The newcomers did not seem to be truly homeless and unwanted. They had money for food. They had special boxes that could recharge their cell phones and other small devices they had with them. He did not understand them. Many of them appeared healthy and able-bodied, with a good understanding of the new technology. They could get jobs. People would hire them. Employers would want them. Unlike himself. He was now old and broken, with no knowledge of how things worked. He smelled bad, and his teeth were ruined. He had been told once or twice that he would be better off dead. And he wondered if that was true. Portland was becoming rough like the old days when people were shanghaied. There were stories amongst the homeless of strange things that took people in the night, never to be seen again. He had chalked that up to heavy drug use.

As he settled down on the ground, trying to push a few pebbles out from under key resting points, he spotted an unusual group walking along the isolated pathway near the river. He felt a cold shiver go up his spine like a bad omen. A warning from the street spirits to hide. Dark people approach with ill intentions. It was too late to get up and amble away, so hiding was the best strategy. These people did not appear to be homeless; they seemed to be several women and perhaps a man or two. They walked with purpose and strength. So often, people assumed that the homeless were crazy or high on something; perhaps, he could just close his eyes and appear to be unconscious. He pulled a few leaves and bits of trash over himself.

The feeling of fear intensified, and he wished that he had run away before they had gotten this close. It was much too late for that. The outlines of these people were not clear, as if an extra shroud of darkness hovered around them. He tried to calm his breathing. Voices told him to play dead. You must play dead, he heard. He closed his eyes and obeyed the voices.

"When will the plan start?" asked a voice.

"It has already started many years ago, but we have a new way to intensify this era's event…. the bloodshed and fear will be ripe with hatred and panic," said a powerful female voice that had a duplicate quality of sound, like two voices speaking in unison.

"Social media has been a powerful tool," said a young-sounding female. "Humans seem to be easily manipulated into believing anything. They are nothing…but prey."

He felt another chill run through his body, making all his joints ache and burn as if he were being tortured. But he had to remain still or else they would notice him. Must endure the pain, he thought to himself. The footsteps drew closer and were now just nearby on the pavement.

"They are tired of waiting. They will want more ……soon …...if we cannot make this happen faster," said a male voice in an agitated state. He then continued to speak, but in a different language that sounded ancient with a hissing quality to it. Parts of the words seemed as if they were being spoken on a different frequency than what Humans heard.

"Calm yourself," said the powerful female voice. "We shall find food for you regardless of when we can start the next major war. The Humans are a primitive race that can be easily trained into destroying each other."

"It has been done many times. This is not the first world to serve as our place of feeding," said a strange raspy female voice.

"He is new to the campaign. He will learn," replied a different male. "He and I have set everything up for our associates, and the building will come down as planned. The assets have been procured and will sustain our earthly organizations' funding for a few more months. The new recruits are also following orders. The plan will work."

The group moved on, and then finally, the footsteps could no longer be heard. Or their disturbing conversation. The homeless man felt relieved, although he still felt terrified. He would find a different place to sleep. Perhaps it was time to ask for help from one of the church types. He did not care for their judgmental attitudes, but he did not want to stay on the streets any longer. He felt like he wanted to warn someone, but who would believe a homeless man of ten years? He finally dared to open his eyes.

Only a foot away from his face was some shadowy, gnarled-looking lifeform that was staring at him with all black eyes. A greenish mist seemed to emanate from the creature's body. It drew closer to him and opened its mouth, broadly revealing sharp, spikey teeth. The man was so frightened he couldn't scream.

****

It was a beautiful summer morning with no sign of rain. It was a tranquil morning, thought Officer Richards, as he expected the early morning commuters to start arriving at any moment. There was no sign of the rioters or protesters. He took that as a blessing. Soon, he would be relieved from duty and get to go home, kiss his wife, shower, and sleep for a couple of hours. It had been a weird night, he thought.

As he stood wishing for his replacement next to his squad car, he started to hear a rumble and felt a vibration under his feet. It continued to grow. He looked around, reaching for his radio, and asked if anyone else was experiencing the strange phenomenon. A voice came through the radio, difficult to hear, saying something about the sidewalks caving in. There was panic in the officer's voice. He heard concern about a building that the other officer was standing near, which was losing its foundational strength. Then nothing. Officer Richards looked around, not sure where this was happening. He tried calling for help over the radio.

"Officer needs assistance. Does anyone hear me?"

Then he spotted a cloud of dust coming towards him between the tall buildings, with the rumbling continuing and the concrete cracking.

"Oh shit, we must be having some kind of earthquake," he said, hopping into his car to drive away from the cloud of dust and the cracking pavement. "This is gonna be bad. Luckily, no one is around to get hurt."

He tried his radio again, "This is Officer Richards leaving Flanders and Fourth…. the sidewalks are collapsing in and…… I am attempting to head to a safe location, going northbound…. Oh Jesus!!! The road is buckling… and caving in!!"

"Officer Richards? Officer Richards?!!" The radio in the squad car squawked until it was crushed into silence underneath the rubble.

****

An alarm bell sounded in the Cyberhawk base house, waking everyone up. It was six in the morning. Dr. Hanni bumped his head, being shaken out of a profound slumber, while Rafferty literally fell out of his bunk. Luckily, for Rafferty, instincts kicked in, and he partially woke up to slow his fall to the floor.

"Dude! Are you alright?!" exclaimed Raven, experiencing the shock of the alarm.

"Shit, is the place on fire? Have you heard that alarm before?" asked Rafferty with his cowboy drawl sounding thicker.

"No, I have not," replied Raven, swinging his feet out of bed to get up.

Rafferty regained his balance, opened the door to their quarters, and peeked out. Lights were flashing, and the alarm was even louder because it was echoing throughout the structure. Janet and Fernando were also standing in the hallway. Dr. Hanni came around the corner from his section of the suite, rubbing his head.

"What is the alarm for? I do not smell any smoke or see any?" asked Dr. Hanni, trying to yell over the alarm.

Daryl came around from his room holding his phone up and then said loudly, "We have to acknowledge that we heard the alarm... before we can turn it off. Go check your devices!"

Everyone dashed off, except for those wearing smartwatches. Within a minute, the alarm sound went silent, and the lights were reduced to gold instead of red. Janet's phone rang, which she answered right away. She did a lot of nodding and saying 'yes,' and then asked when and where. Everyone stood around her patiently waiting to hear what was going on.

When the phone call was over, she turned to everyone and said, "We need to respond to some kind of disaster in Portland. It seems like an earthquake...caused the streets to collapse and a building to topple to one side? I need everyone dressed and ready to deploy in fifteen minutes. Diana will stay here and monitor things from a distance. Ellena, you will oversee the submersible drone to assist in searching the river. That means the submersible must be packed to come with us on the aircraft. Cyberhawks will fly to the emergency location as soon as the captain arrives and is suited up."

Everyone nodded and scrambled off to be ready within fifteen minutes. By the time Captain Justice arrived, the entire team was up and loading the aircraft, and Morales, Ridgestone, and Thomas had arrived and were already doing their jobs. Robert Justice had no idea precisely what they were heading into. It seemed like a strange coincidence that there had been rioting the day before, and now sections of the city's streets in the state's largest city were collapsing. Diana, wearing her HUD glasses, approached him with her tablet in hand.

"Captain, I just got word that the USGS is having difficulty confirming that an earthquake happened in the Portland Metro area. Seismology is not consistent with earthquake activity," Diana reported.

The captain frowned, thinking about all the volcanoes in the area and the potential for ground-shaking events. "So... what do they think happened?"

"Right now, they are considering it a possible seismic swarm because there were lots of small center points," replied Diana.

"Perhaps gas lines erupted?" speculated the captain.

"They are discussing that as well. And there is a problem with several fires due to gas line ruptures, but the gas company was quick to react and shut down systems feeding the affected and nearby areas," she replied.

"Okay, keep me informed. I am going to head out with the others to Portland. Please ensure that they bring additional fuel cells with them. I think we'll need those," said the captain as he walked over to his locker to get suited up.

"I will make sure that those are included in the cargo right now," said Diana, heading out the door.

"Oh! ....and Diana," said the captain, making sure he got her attention before she left. "Dalen Hughes is also coming along. Don't let them take off without him, or else I will get an earful from Dr. Cross."

"Yes, Captain," replied Diana as she went out the door.

CHAPTER 20

The team of seven emergency services Cyberhawks, clad in protective dark blue foundation suits and featuring golden CyberSkeleton and jetpack exterior armoring, hovered over the section of the city ravaged by the devastation of the odd tremors. The rest of the team would have to land at PDX airport and unload to secondary vehicles. Not an ideal situation that had not been planned for. Robert was not happy thinking about how long it would take for the rest of the team to arrive on site to assist quickly, but at least the flight team was ready. From up high, it seemed like the cave-ins happened along routes within the city. Betty was currently examining the pattern.

"Captain Justice, I have analyzed the pattern. It appears to be following along the historical underground tunnels from the late 1800s, which would explain why some of the buildings are listing, and sections have collapsed," said Betty over the HUD system.

"Okay, that makes sense, but that would not follow the fault lines. This seems to have a man-made origin," pondered Captain Justice.

Just then, an enormous billow of smoke rose from a structure fire that the ground crews were working on to control. The captain's attention was drawn to the building, and then, through the smoke, he noticed that several people were on top of the building.

"Betty, patch me into the local search and rescue communications," the captain requested.

"You are patched in," said Betty.

"This is Captain Justice of Cyberhawk. I have eyes on a structure fire where five people are stranded on top of the building. Crews are down below working on containment," said the captain.

"Cyberhawk Captain, which building are you looking at? We have two structural fires right now," replied a voice.

"Copy that. Not sure of the address, but it is a red brick of approximately five stories," answered the captain.

"Hold on while I confirm with ground crews." There was a pause, and then the voice came back. "Cyberhawk Captain, the ground crew was unaware that anyone was left in the building. Can you assist in removal?"

"Yes, we can. Do you have a designated drop-off point?" asked the captain.

"Northwest Hoyt is where we have a first aid station set up," replied the voice.

"Understood," replied the captain as he directed his Cyberhawk team to land on the building in question.

The stranded people looked relieved and excited to see them.

"Oh my God!! It's the Cyberhawks that they keep talking about on TV!!" yelled a guy with a joyous expression on his face.

"Yup, that's us," replied Rafferty, who had to land not too far from the excited man carefully.

"We can't get down. We came up top to get away from the heavy smoke in the stairway, and then the door locked behind us," said a young woman in a bathrobe.

"I don't think we can go down that way even if we could get the door open," said the older man. "We could not breathe."

"We will get you down," said Janet, trying to reassure the elderly man. "Captain, can we call in a helicopter?"

"No, the updraft from the smoke and heat is getting worse, and I am not sure if there are any copters available. We are going to have to carry them out," said Captain Justice.

"How do we do that?" asked Sanchez.

"We each take one person and strap them to us and fly to the drop zone immediately," replied the captain, reaching for a compartment on his CyberSkeleton. He pulled out a set of harnesses. "You each have one. I have done this in training with dummies; it does work. You need to instruct your passenger to stay still; otherwise, the flight can be difficult. Your gear will fly with a sluggish quality, so be aware of that."

"I am terrified of heights," said the young woman in the bathrobe.

"Don't you worry. I am a good pilot, and I will keep you safe," replied Rafferty while he eyed the image flashed on his HUD on how to take a passenger safely with his system. The passenger would first step into the safety harness, like the one a rock climber would wear. Then the passenger would stand upon the pilot's foot stirrups and would face inwards like a hug, tucking their head down. The heavy-duty straps of the harnesses would then be attached to the CyberSkeleton frame. It was not an activity that should happen for much more than a few minutes. The passenger would not have all the protective safety gear, so the flight would have to be slow and short.

While the Captain made sure that each passenger had a rescuer, he ordered Crane and Ridgestone to search for others in need in the surrounding area. He also instructed them to keep an eye out for anything odd.

"Odd, like suspicious?" Crane asked, looking at the captain. The captain nodded his head. "Okay, I will make sure I document carefully... anything I find suspicious."

"Come on, Daryl," said Sandra, moving to a position away from the others to prepare for flight.

Justice watched as Ridgestone and Crane took off, then returned to ensure everyone had their passengers secured. This was a first for the team. Even the captain had never taken an actual person for a flight using his suit. The smoke was getting thicker and more toxic. The passengers were starting to cough more.

"Make sure your passenger knows to stay as still as possible. You should instruct them to close their eyes since we do not have any protective goggles for them to wear," said the captain to his team.

The group of four acknowledged their instructions and had their passengers secured. Captain Justice ordered a gentle takeoff and directed the team to follow him to the drop-off location on Northwest Hoyt. Everyone successfully took off with their precious cargo and flew towards the first aid station set up in a parking lot.

****

"So, Sandra……what do you think the captain meant by that?" Daryl asked through the HUD system.

Sandra paused as she thought about her response and what was going on around her, "I think this all looks wrong. We experienced earthquakes in California, and the results did not resemble this. This seems too isolated to one area."

"Oh, I see," said Daryl. "What do you think is happening?"

"I am not certain….," said Sandra, hovering for a moment to scan the area for people seeking assistance.

Then came a series of strange, concussive waves that hit her and Daryl in mid-air. They both turned to see a sequence of explosions triggered all around a large, pale brick building. The building began to implode and crumble inward. The shockwave came as a surprise and threw both Cyberhawks out of normal flight operation. Daryl was further away from the structure, but Sandra was hit full force and thrust backward in uncontrolled flight.

That was when two bulkier blue Cyberhawks appeared out of nowhere.

They both heard through the private comm systems, "The cavalry has arrived, civilians!!"

The voice was familiar to Sandra, but she had no time to be concerned about who it was, as she was headed for a collision with another high-rise building. Then she felt a hard jolt on her left and right sides, and then felt herself being pulled upwards. She could see Daryl off in the distance, in his golden-yellow gear, and he was okay. Dust was flying everywhere as the plume erupted outwards down the city streets as if they were canyons filled with rushing water. She and the other mystery Cyberhawks had landed upon a tall building further away. She was relieved that she did not crash into the other structure.

"Oh, my goodness! Thanks for the save. That would have hurt...or possibly killed me. I am not sure," said Sandra, opening her faceplate to breathe in some cool air to calm herself.

"Anytime, civilian," said one of the bulky, deep blue Cyberhawks with golden tracer paths decorating the armor along with the Cyberhawk logo emblazoned upon the helmets and chest plate. The gear had weapons as well. This Cyberhawk had gold oak leaves on each pauldron of his armor.

"Who are you guys?" asked Sandra.

"Well," said the blue Cyberhawk with oak leaves. "Detective Ridgestone, we're the cavalry." He then popped open his faceplate.

"Oh geez, you're the obnoxious military guy that I met at the base," Sandra half-laughed in exasperation. "And you were the one who assisted me in the abandoned part of that mall."

"She's a sharp one, isn't she?" said Major Bluster to the other military Cyberhawk, who did not open his face plate.

"Yes, she is," he replied. He had gold captain's bars and a white unicorn on his pauldrons.

The voice sounded familiar. It gave her a shiver up her spine and a strange emotional feeling. She just stared at the other Cyberhawk.

"Well, we had better let your Captain, and I use that term loosely, know that you are alright," said Major Bluster, then addressing his HUD system. "Betty, better let the leader of the civilian group know that his detective, Cyberhawk, is alright. The military team saved her from crashing into a building."

"Yes, Major Bluster," replied Betty.

"So, there is another team. Some of us had wondered about that since the applications for such a device seemed practical for the military," said Sandra. "What do you think is happening here?" Sandra gestured to the destruction going on below.

"What do you think it is?" Major Bluster answered with a question.

"I don't think it is a geological occurrence. And those systematic concussive explosions looked like demolition," Sandra replied.

"That would be an accurate appraisal," said Major Bluster.

"Terrorism?" asked Sandra.

"Not certain. There is not enough intel to say so in any regard," replied Major Bluster.

Daryl finally spotted Sandra with the two military Cyberhawks and flew over to join them.

"Ah, this must be the other mystery team," said Daryl as he landed.

"They are military," replied Sandra.

Two more blue military Cyberhawks landed on the building and headed for the Major.

"Major Bluster, Captain Washington wanted you to be personally informed that he has found evidence that the subversive group known as the Action Men is tied to this incident," said a female voice.

"Lieutenant, where did he find this evidence?" asked Bluster.

"In the tunnels, Sir," replied the female military Cyberhawk. "Captain Washington and Master Sergeant Rogers engaged five combatants, resulting in two escaping and three being terminated."

"So why didn't he inform me over the secure system?" asked Major Bluster, looking a little irritated.

"During the engagement, his helmet suffered damage, resulting in his HUD no longer working properly. He was also concerned that the suspects may have technology to intercept our communications. He was hearing additional chatter, which," the female paused, looking at the two blue and golden armored Cyberhawks. "Was probably the Gold Team."

"That would be affirmative, Lt. Buckshot," replied Major Bluster. He then turned to the two golden Cyberhawks, "So, how did your team get pulled into this engagement?"

"I'm not exactly sure, but you could ask the captain," said Sandra, gesturing to the group of golden yellow Cyberhawks that were flying towards them.

Captain Justice landed on top of the building and headed towards the group of unfamiliar Cyberhawks.

"Who the hell are you?!" Captain Justice asked Bluster, since his faceplate was open and he had been talking with Detective Ridgestone.

"That would be, who the hell are you, Sir?" replied Major Bluster.

"Captain, this is the military officer who had me test the equipment a couple of months ago. His name is Major Bluster," Sandra stepped in to make introductions.

"Geez, no wonder why the general public thinks we are a bunch of boys playing with toys," commented the captain, taking a serious look at the military Cyberhawks that had all sorts of armament attached to their gear. "Have you been out playing superhero, freaking them out?!?" said the captain, turning to address Bluster.

"No, that would be your team playing with the local press. We keep a low profile, unlike your team," replied Major Bluster.

"Major, Washington, and Rogers have discovered more Action Men and require backup if they are to take any for questioning," said Lt. Kelli Buckshot.

"What is going on here? And who are the Action Men? This whole situation looks like arson...or something worse," declared Captain Justice.

"It is," replied Major Bluster. "You want answers, come with us."

Captain Justice paused for a moment, quickly thinking about the offer and the people who required help. He did want answers. He turned to Janet.

"Hallman, you take Lewis, Sanchez, Smith, and Crane. Continue to assist the search and rescue teams. I am taking Ridgestone with me, and we are going to see what the other Cyberhawk team does."

"You can count on us," said Janet. "Come on, boys, let's head back to the first aid station and find out where we are needed next."

Janet then took a step or two and then took off with the rest of the team following her. The golden Emergency Services Team disappeared into the smoky sky, leaving Justice and Ridgestone with the military team.

"As our guest, you will follow orders from us. This is our mission, and you do not have weapons. You are observers, and if we tell you to evacuate, it means leave immediately. Do you understand that?" Major Bluster asked the captain, looking him directly in the eye.

"Yes," replied Captain Justice, keeping eye contact.

"And you?" Major Bluster turned to Sandra.

"I understand," replied Sandra.

Suddenly, Sandra was getting mapping and flight coordinates on her HUD. This group of military Cyberhawks was about to reinforce the others that had found the group called Action Men. The curious name meant nothing to Sandra. The military Cyberhawk with the unicorn painted on his pauldron came alongside her.

"Stick close to me. I will watch out for you," he said.

Sandra nodded, feeling like she could trust this guy for some reason. His voice sounded familiar.

Major Bluster led his team, plus his additional civilian recruits, off towards the coordinates that Betty had received from Captain Terence Washington. Terence had been part of Bluster's team almost from the beginning. Washington and Sokolov were the first two top-notch pilots to be brought into the Cyberhawk Military Team. Sokolov had presumably died in a mission in the Mediterranean region. The three of them had been requested by the United Nations to conduct a reconnaissance mission concerning an apparent natural disaster that had some not-so-natural attributes. It was during that mission that Sokolov was presumed to be killed in action. They never found his body and only bits and pieces of his Cyberhawk gear. Bluster and Washington took the loss hard. Washington had proven to be a top-notch second-in-command.

The GPS coordinates led them to a tall office-type structure along Alder Street that appeared to be in some state of disrepair, possibly due to foreclosure. Evidence of slow neglect had started to erode at the building's once-nice facade. Tagging had marked some of the windows, and boarding had been put up around the lower section to prevent break-ins. The once vibrant city had become strangely desolate and empty. The nine Cyberhawks landed just a building away to minimize the noise.

"Rogers, we are here to assist. What is your position?" Bluster asked through the secured comm system.

"Inside the structure, below the street level. Approximately twelve individuals disappeared down a tunnel heading towards the river. Do you want us to track them?" asked Rogers.

"Is the tunnel passage large enough to accommodate your suit?" Bluster asked.

"I believe so. The entrance is located on the lower level of the garage building. It may have been used to transport small amounts of cargo to the building unseen by the public. The structure and lighting appear relatively modern and have been well-maintained. We are uncertain if it is under surveillance," replied Rogers.

"Send a small drone to investigate," Captain Rossi suggested.

"Good idea," agreed Bluster. "Rogers, did you copy that drone suggestion?"

"Yes, I did. And Captain Washington agrees," replied Rogers.

"Make sure you have the drone set to relay back as much detailed GPS information as possible," said Rossi, who had been recruited from NASA.

"Are you thinking what I am thinking? That tunnel... could be a planned escape route. We need to determine their exit strategy before they can execute it," said Major Bluster, pondering a strategy for catching the Action Men.

"The drone is off, Major," said Rogers through the comm.

"We have a setup for drone recon and surveillance output if your drones use a compatible system," suggested Captain Justice.

"They do. A code will be required to access the data feed," replied Rossi. "I will need to do it in person. Major, I can have their system give us detailed maps through our HUD."

"Make it so. Justice, Captain Rossi will need the location of your ground team," said Major Bluster.

Captain Justice reached Diana through the HUD system to discover they were set up, which was not far from the search and rescue team's first aid station on NW Hoyt. Captain Justice relayed the information to Captain Rossi, who then took off. Captain Justice also instructed Diana to be helpful to Captain Rossi, who was part of a different Cyberhawk team.

"So, who are these so-called Action Men?" asked Sandra.

"They are a foreign-based terrorist group under the guise of being an American patriotic activist group. There are several of these types of groups with the same modus operandi throughout the country... actually......... throughout the world," replied the military Cyberhawk with the unicorn.

Sandra shook her head, "But why? What is their goal?"

Major Bluster turned to Sandra and replied, "Their goal is to sow disharmony amongst the general population of the world, create uprisings, and encourage disinformation that makes the civilians want to hate each other."

"They are anarchists?" asked Sandra.

"That has been considered, but there seems to be a direction with their actions. We have not discovered exactly what that is. Until then, our job is to detain them, stop them, or end them," replied Bluster.

"Okay. Then what is the direction that is being observed?" asked Sandra.

"That's on a need-to-know basis. And you don't have that clearance," replied Bluster.

Sandra just made a face and said nothing. She understood, but she didn't like it.

CHAPTER 21

Chris was impressed with Captain Anthony Rossi's ability to patch into other systems with ease. The man's military Cyberhawk suit was also impressive. He had the same design of body suit as the other Cyberhawks, but his CyberSkeleton, armor plates, and jetpack equipment were a deep sparkly blue with gold data trace lines running throughout the gear. It had the appearance of being like computer circuitry in the night sky. On his pauldrons were the NASA logo and captain's bars. The man also had various pieces of extra equipment that Chris wanted to ask him about, but the need to focus on the situation took precedence.

Chris designated one of the flat-screen monitors to show just the feed from the military group's spy drone as it made its way down the long, concrete corridor. The special drone could roll on the ground or take flight if needed. Alejandro was keeping an eye on the other drones that were gathering helpful information for the rescue and fire suppression crews. So far, the drones had spotted three people in need of assistance, and considering the damage that had occurred, that was pretty good. The dust lingered in the air, making it hard to breathe, and the crew without Cyberhawk gear had taken out full-breather masks to be able to work outside. Most of the disaster victims were having trouble breathing due to the high levels of particulates in the air. Dr. Hanni and Raven, who was still wearing his gear, were working with other paramedics to get the injured off to safety as soon as possible.

Dalen Hughes stood aside, wearing a small backpack filled with electronics repair parts, just in case they were needed. He stayed respectfully out of the way, as this was not his area of expertise, and observed. He wore a set of HUD glasses as well as a respirator mask. He took mental notes of how the equipment was performing and what kind of improvements might be needed. Turning his attention to watch the monitors that Chris had set up for the drones, he was thrilled to see his designs in action, but a little scared to see the destruction that was happening before his eyes. The small, specialized military drone moved quickly and efficiently through the passageway. It had already gone a quarter of a mile with a few turns, and the GPS was mapping a trail towards the Willamette River.

"Major, it looks like the drone is leading us towards the Hawthorne Bridge area. Perhaps there is an exit point," suggested Rossi through the HUD comm system.

"Copy that," said Major Bluster over the comm. "Stay with the drone surveillance equipment and keep us informed."

"Understood," said Rossi, continuing to watch the video and the GPS coordinates coming in that were building a map superimposed upon a digital version of a street map.

****

Major Bluster turned to his team and said, "It appears that the bad actors are heading towards the river. Rossi is speculating that there is an egress point somewhere near the Hawthorne Bridge. Buckshot, Bondarenko, and Meyers, you three will head down the tunnel to give support to Washington and Rogers. I am going to take the remaining members of the team, plus our observers, out towards the Hawthorne Bridge to see if we can catch them making a getaway."

Three 'yes sirs' were heard through the HUD before the three Cyberhawks headed down the tunnel where the drone had gone. Bluster knew the one major fault with his team's equipment was the lack of stealth. That was typically Shadow Team's job. At least they had the intel from the drone to make sure they were not walking into a trap. Washington and Rogers would wait until the backup arrived before moving in.

"Let's head out," said Bluster, turning to the remaining members of his team and the two gold ones. "I'm on point."

The two military Cyberhawks followed, with Justice and Ridgestone, both looking at each other and then falling into step behind.

"Betty," Sandra spoke to the AI. "Where am I supposed to fly?"

"I will put you and Captain Justice into a modified diamond pattern," replied Betty, putting up a diagram for Sandra to follow. She would fly next to Robert Justice, as they were accustomed to flying in a less organized manner. "Your job is to be aware of your surroundings and report to the flight leader of any dangers. Stay in formation unless he tells you to engage, ...which you and Captain Justice are not prepared for. Neither of you is to engage in combat. You have no weapons."

"Okay. Thank you, Betty. I think I would be scared to death if it were not for you. I feel like you are here in the suit with me," replied Sandra as she eyed the city, looking for any additional problems.

"To a certain degree, I am with you in the suit. Being a lifeform without biological boundaries does give me some special attributes that allow me to be more helpful and engaging," replied Betty. "And don't forget the Mechanical AI in your suit will learn as you use it more, and it will help you develop a better experience using the Cyberhawk suit."

"So, you are not like a normal AI, are you?" said Sandra, starting to fully realize that Betty was something special.

"I am not sure the term normal would be accurate. I am not a Mechanical AI. I am something different," replied Betty.

"Well....different...normal...I like you. And I am glad that you are with us. This situation is scary," replied Sandra as the flight group did a slow curving maneuver and then hovered above the Hawthorne Bridge.

"I am pleased that you like me, Detective Ridgestone. I like you too. We are all part of the Cyberhawk Team," replied Betty. "I do question Major Bluster's decision to bring you along on this part of the mission. Please be aware that the Action Men do use weapons, and they will not think twice about killing people."

"Alright. I have dealt with a few situations like that back on the force in LA. Perhaps keep an eye on the captain. I don't think many firemen get shot at while doing their job," said Sandra.

"I am watching out for both of you, but I am not perfect, so you must do your part too," replied Betty.

Sandra took that advice to heart and made another active search for anything out of the ordinary. Just then, Major Bluster's voice came over loud and clear on the HUD.

"Gold team, we are engaging the bad actors. You two are to search the Hawthorne Bridge for explosives. We have intel that the Action Men are in possession of explosive devices!"

The three military Cyberhawks then suddenly jetted off down toward the area underneath the Hawthorne Bridge. Sandra turned to Robert Justice.

"Looks like we start looking for bombs," said Captain Justice through the Emergency Services comm frequency. "I'm going to request Crane and Sanchez to join us in the search."

"Good idea. More eyes on the job will give us a better chance at success," added Sandra, looking at the steel and concrete structure. "Captain, where should I start first? And......what about under the water?"

"Let's start with the lifting section of the bridge," the captain paused. Then Sandra could hear him speaking over the comm system, "Diana, is Ellena equipped with the submersible drone?"

"I can check, Captain. She is currently using the VR headset to fly a drone. Where do you need the submersible?" she asked.

"The Hawthorne Bridge. We need to inspect the pilings," replied the captain.

"I will speak with her immediately," replied Diana.

Sandra flew up to the top section of the west lift area and realized that cars were still driving on the bridge, although very few.

"Captain, if they suspect a bomb on the bridge, shouldn't traffic be diverted elsewhere just in case?" commented Sandra.

"Diana, did you hear that?" asked the captain.

"Yes, I did. And I am informing law enforcement right now about the concern of the bridge's safety," replied Diana.

The hover mode on the Cyberhawk system took more fuel, and Sandra was already down to fifty percent. She needed to keep an eye on that. The captain took the other lift tower and started to investigate. Crane and Sanchez arrived and were asked to inspect the underside of the bridge first. The fact that the HUD system had a scanner capable of detecting explosive compounds assisted in the process. After scanning the upper towers and finding nothing, Sandra landed on the bridge surface to walk the road and inspect the side rails. The captain was already doing the south set of side rail structures. From this vantage point, Sandra could see the smoke from one of the fires slowly diminishing. Then a golden Cyberhawk appeared out of the smoke heading their way, carrying something oddly shaped. It sorta looked like a giant banana, Sandra thought.

"Oh my god! It is hard to fly with this weird thing!" exclaimed Janet through the HUD comm.

As Janet got closer to the river area, she started to descend as if she were going to crash. Her flight looked wobbly as she fought with the awkwardly shaped object. Then, when she was about ten feet above the surface of the water, she dropped it. There was a big splash as the object tossed about for a few seconds and then started to move, gaining speed, before dipping under the surface and heading towards the bridge.

"Successful deployment!!" exclaimed Ellena through the HUD system. "I am now making my way to inspect the pilings."

"Captain, I found something," said Sanchez through the HUD.

"Does it look like an explosive device?" asked the captain.

"Oh yeah. We need an expert right away," replied Sanchez, using his HUD to record and transmit the details of what he had found under a section of the bridge.

"Diana, are you receiving this data?" Captain Justice inquired.

"Yes, we are. The details are obvious. Morales is going to talk with the local law enforcement to discover if they have a bomb squad and if the expert is available," replied Diana.

"Don't touch anything," said Captain Rossi to the Gold Team. "I am informing the Blue Team of your discovery."

Diana, Chris, and Captain Rossi all eyed the flat screens that were displaying all the action going on around them. Morales came back and reported that the local team was already engaged in dealing with a problem in Troutdale, where an explosive device was found in a bank early in the morning.

"They only have one team?" exclaimed Chris while he was giving his drone some more flight instructions.

"The officer said it was due to budget cuts," replied Morales. "What do we do about this?"

"Major Bluster has called for a specialist to come in," replied Captain Rossi.

Morales shook his head in disbelief, "The streets are completely … gridlocked. No one can travel here fast now."

"Remember how you thought you all were the only Cyberhawks," Rossi said, turning to the three members of the Emergency Services Team. "Well, our team has been around a lot longer, and we have more members. And……" Rossi paused for a moment, looking at something displayed on his HUD. Diana seemed to be seeing the data as well on her HUD glasses. "We have help arriving."

Rossi and Diana both looked up to see two more blue team Cyberhawks arrive and land five meters away from them. One Cyberhawk landed a bit more roughly than the other, and the other one reached out to steady the other. Then they both walked over to the group sitting by the monitors. Both flipped open their faceplates. One revealed a black woman in her mid-fifties, who appeared a bit agitated. She had been the one to make the rough landing. The other Cyberhawk was Lukas Knight, with a slight smirk on his face, as he eyed Captain Brenda Davis, a semi-retired weapons expert who now only conducted training.

She turned to Knight and said, "I know you think my flying is funny, but I told you I did not want to fly."

"It was the quickest way to get here," replied Knight. "And don't give me that *'I'm too old spiel'* because I am older than you."

"Oh, holy mother of god!" exclaimed Brenda, walking toward the monitor. "That's what is under the bridge?!"

"Yes, ma'am," replied Captain Rossi, knowing who Captain Davis was and how she had been a pivotal part of developing the Cyberhawk program.

She stared at the screen for a few minutes and then said, "I am going to need some specific tools and a safe way to get under there...." She paused to turn and look at Knight, "That does not involve me flying this contraption."

"Let me know what you need. I have access to First Lt. Archstone's gear," replied Captain Rossi.

"Why isn't she taking this on? I could use an extra set of eyes," replied Davis, frowning and still looking at the video of what Sanchez discovered.

"She is currently engaged in active combat in the tunnels below the city," replied Captain Rossi.

"I'm going to need her," replied Davis. "This specific device looks like it is designed to work with others. It appears to have a failsafe device that, if one is deactivated, the others go off, so rest assured, there are more. This is a cluster bomb, and one that has some specialized components. You tell Major Bluster that I need Archstone out here right now."

"Yes, ma'am," replied Captain Rossi.

"So, you know First Lt. Archstone?" Knight asked Davis.

"Oh yeah. I trained her. She was one of my best students," replied Davis. She kept her eyes focused on the video. "Can you get the guy who did this video to do more? But he must not touch anything. It is a very sensitive and dangerous design."

"I can do that," replied Diana. "Sanchez, our expert Captain Davis, wishes to see more details of the device, but she warns that you must not touch it. It could......... go off if you do so." Diana added as she watched Captain Davis's reaction. "She also thinks that there should be another device. Crane, can you please continue to search for another device?"

"I will do that. Any idea where the devices would most likely be?" asked Daryl.

Diana turned to Davis and asked, "Captain Davis, are there any locations where such a device would most likely be located?"

"Anywhere on a structure that would cause the most damage. It would also need to be within a quarter of a mile. That design sends signals to other locations. Generally, cluster bombs are closer together, but this design has been seen before.

Everything within that range must be gone over. There should also be an evacuation of all civilians within that area," replied Captain Davis, thinking about what she recalled from the previous interaction with that type of cluster bomb.

"I will speak with the commander of the local law enforcement and let him know your recommendations," said Diana, heading off.

Sanchez had already flown back to get additional views of the explosive device. Captain Rossi patched the Gold Team in so that they could speak directly with the Blue Team, allowing Davis to request that Sanchez adjust the video angles in real-time. Meanwhile, Lukas Knight studied the areas damaged in the tunnel cave-in and noticed the building that had imploded.

"Chris, is this the address of the building that was imploded?" asked Knight.

"Yes, Mr. Knight. Why?" Chris asked, hearing concern in the man's voice.

"There was a physicist who had a private office in that building... Dr. Pierre Arnaud. Have you heard of him?" asked Knight.

"No, I can't say I have, but I really don't walk in those circles. I am not a scientist," replied Chris, sending a message to his drone to come back to base. "Did you know him? Do you think he was in his office?"

"Yes, I do know him, and I have no idea if he was in his office. I have a really bad feeling about this. There is something curiously wrong… going on here," pondered Knight. "Situations are not what they seem to be."

Just as Chris had canceled his drone's flight video feed, Ellena requested the HUD.

"Chris, can you put my VR video feed up on the monitor and get Captain Rossi to tell me what he thinks?" she asked.

"Sure," replied Chris, working his fingers across the keyboard and pulling up Ellena's submersible drone video.

The water appeared murky and had very little clarity, making it difficult for light to travel through. The submersible had made it to the bridge and was positioned next to one of the pilings located in the more eastern part of the bridge. A foreign device appeared to be attached to the concrete piling. It was encased in a modified airtight lock bag, and another portion appeared to be sealed in black plastic. This video caught Captain Davis's attention.

"This is the last piling that I have inspected. I hope I did not miss anything. The water is so turbid today. The Secchi depth is shallow. There is a lot of suspended sediments… probably due to the cave-ins that happened just up shore," speculated Ellena. "Well, regardless of the reasons, it is hard to see. Are the images coming in clear enough?"

Chris looked up at Captain Davis, who nodded her head as she continued to study the images.

"Yes, Ellena," replied Chris.

"What do you think, Brenda?" Knight asked Captain Davis.

"I think we have a dire situation on our hands. That does look like a companion bomb to the first one found. And it may be that their goal was to destroy the bridge. But there could be more bombs. It would be nice to have more information. Hopefully, Bluster can obtain a person of interest with something to say. This whole thing stinks of planned sabotage," replied Brenda Davis, sounding concerned.

"And then......what is the goal and motive? Was it to destroy the bridge? Cause chaos within the city? Were they after something? Why did the building that housed the jewel and precious mineral offices implode? And... I think Dr. Pierre Arnaud's secret office was located in that building because of the extra security from the gem and precious mineral dealers. I need to check my contact information for him... and it is on paper because I promised not to put it in digital format. After all, he was worried. I am wondering if he had a good reason to be worried," said Lukas Knight.

"I am surprised he did not ask you to memorize it and swallow the paper," Davis murmured.

Frowning a bit, Knight requested Betty to send a message to his personal assistant, Trevor, to find the address of Pierre Arnaud's secret office in Portland.

"We have good reason to be worried right now. We have two bombs on that bridge that need to be removed, and there is a danger that there could be more," said Brenda. "I will need First Lt. Archstone to help in unison to deactivate the bombs, and there could be three of them. I will need a third expert if that is the case. You had better start calling people. I also think we should have some detailed maps of the city. We need to see if there is anything else in that area that would have been targeted."

Chris Takahashi turned around from his screens and said, "Diana has already made a call to the city government for those kinds of materials."

CHAPTER 22

The evacuation process had already begun for a one-mile radius around the Hawthorne Bridge. News agencies had started to cluster around the outer edges, trying to gather information for the public, hoping to catch a pivotal moment of action. Local law enforcement and fire department heads were answering questions and requesting that the public not travel to the affected region. Rumors had already started to swirl about it being a terrorist attack. Schools within the area were also canceled, and students were turned away and sent back home. The fires had been contained, and the known injured and dead had been removed. The first aid station was closed up, and everyone was moving further away. The Cyberhawk Emergency Services Team had gathered at the new command area, where Chris had set up the flat-screen monitors. Chris sent out a new batch of freshly charged drones to search for the homeless and other individuals who were unaware that the area had become dangerous. Ellena had finished scanning as much of the river area as she could and did not find any additional explosive devices.

Janet and Rafferty flew together, carrying a special net device to retrieve the submersible drone from the river. Both came back, regaling the others with their dramatic scooping and flying the device in coordination back to where their loaner vehicle was parked. Dr. Hanni and Raven had taken Dale Hughes with them to assist the injured, since his engineering services were not needed.

"Your jobs are so difficult. I am amazed at how you can make people feel safe and calm after having such a frightening experience," Dalen said to Raven and Dr. Hanni.

"A lot of it is good training... and a certain amount is patience with others. People react differently. Some want to cope using humor, while others just cry or become stoic," replied Raven.

"Well, I think being here and seeing what you do will give me, and essentially the rest of the LabCoat Crew, some ideas on how we can make the Cyberhawk design for your team better. Perhaps some useful accessories," said Dalen.

"I have been pleased with the HUD glasses," remarked Dr. Hanni. "They have proven time and time again that these are a useful tool in helping to diagnose a variety of situations."

"Dr. Cross would be gratified to hear you say that. He was the main designer and proponent of the HUD glasses," replied Dalen Hughes, adjusting his own HUD with a smile. "I am pleased that none of the items I have designed have had any problems. The idea has always been that we want these tools to be both sturdy and remarkable in expanding everyone's ability to respond to unexpected situations. So many of our designs seemed to have only military applications. It is, to a certain degree,... exciting to see some now being used to assist the general population."

Dalen smiled broadly, feeling satisfied with his work. He felt like he was making a positive difference with his design projects. He had a vision of an advancing Human community and not one regressing to tribal squabbles.

****

"Archstone, Captain Davis needs you for a special mission," said Major Bluster through the Blue Team comm system.

"Major! We are in the middle of an engagement!! I can't leave now," replied Archstone.

"I appreciate your loyalty, but topside is a different, dangerous situation where your expertise is required. You go now," replied Major Bluster.

"Yes, Sir," replied Archstone, disengaging from the action and heading off to report to Captain Davis.

"Major, I suspect these individuals are just trying to hold us here so we cannot deal with what is occurring topside," said the Cyberhawk with the unicorn on his pauldron. "Have you noticed that this group seems to be subpar from previous encounters?"

Jack Bluster quickly contemplated his previous encounters and how intense and tricky the Action Men had been. This group of Action Men seemed to be spraying a lot of bullets wildly and lacked the cunning they had displayed in previous engagements.

"Captain, I think you are correct. Let's change this up. Take 'em out and regroup. Use Gas Number Seven since I think the city officials would be perturbed if we set off explosives and made another building fall," said Major Bluster with a sly smile. He sent the command through to everyone's HUD, and Rogers made sure that Washington understood.

The Action Men noticed a sudden cessation of gunfire. They all looked at each other, nodding their heads as if they had achieved a great victory.

"They ran off!! We won the day. Let's head out," said one of the Action Men triumphantly.

"We showed them who's boss!" hooted another, waving his weapon in the air. "Those bastards couldn't take us out. They will bow down to us all."

"It's now time to find their women and take them," said another wearing a black baseball cap backwards.

"I thought one of them looked female," said the guy who had been waving his weapon in the air.

"Shit, no, you dumb ass. No woman could take us on. Besides, they were wearing a man's battle suit. Women, they're for submitting for our pleasure," replied the guy in the backwards baseball cap.

"And cleaning the house," muttered another one.

"I don't think we killed any of them," said the first guy who started looking around. "Doesn't that seem odd?"

Then came the clank of metal canisters rapidly spewing yellowish-white smoke, filling the tunnels with a noxious gas. The Action Men were wearing masks to protect their identities, but not to protect themselves from any biochemical harm. Panic set in as they scattered in two different directions, some dropping their weapons in the confusion. This group had never received any training and had been recruited off the streets of Portland. They were promised money, fame, and power over others. None of that was going to happen for any of them today and perhaps ever. This group was cannon fodder, also known as expendable assets.

The blue military team regrouped at the new command area. Captain Archstone was already getting briefed by Captain Davis about the explosive device. Captain Washington pulled off his helmet in frustration as he started to examine the piece of vital equipment. This caught Dale Hughes's attention.

"Captain Washington, are you having trouble with your Cyberhawk helmet?" asked Dalen.

"Yes, I got hit in the head with something forceful, and now the HUD is acting strange," replied the tall black man, who appeared to be in his late thirties or early forties. He spoke like a career military man who had seen a bit of action. "Looks like a large caliber bullet grazed or hit the helmet."

"Well, that's why I am here. Come with me, and I shall run some diagnostics on your helmet," replied the short black man as he tapped a few commands on his HUD glasses to bring up special apps to scan for fractures. "Oh yes, I see some damage already."

Captain Washington went off with Dalen Hughes to get his helmet looked at. Major Bluster was in good spirits as he removed his helmet and turned to Lukas Knight, who was standing by a table under a pop-up awning, examining some maps.

"Retrieval of the Action Men in that underground section was not a good use of our time," said Major Bluster. "I deployed Gas Number Seven. The local authorities will find approximately ten or twelve of them down there. The area should remain off limits until a bomb squad can go in there to retrieve the explosive devices that Washington and Rogers reported being in their possession."

"Alright. I will notify the authorities. So, were they a threat?" asked Knight.

"Not really. Just a waste of our time. The amount of firepower and *how* it was used led us to determine that these were low-level assets and unlikely to have been the instigators of the explosive devices. I am under the impression that Captain Davis thinks there could be a third device," replied Major Bluster.

"Both she and Archstone are of that opinion. The water area has been thoroughly investigated, but this area here," Knight said, directing Bluster's attention to a map of the city around the Hawthorne Bridge. "These sections have not been scanned."

"What about satellite data?" asked the Major.

"Solar flares are making the technology less than accurate," replied Knight.

"Okay, so we need to do a visual inspection," concluded Bluster as Captain Justice came up to join them.

Knight and Bluster both looked up at Justice.

"My team has recharged their fuel cells and is ready to go out as directed," said Captain Justice. "I have seven Cyberhawks at your service."

"Good. Major, is your team refueled and ready?" asked Knight.

"Everyone except Washington, Archstone, who is busy with Davis, and… me. I still need to get a new fuel cell," replied Bluster. "So does the civilian HUD system have the same scanning abilities as ours?"

"Yes. That attribute was important for the emergency services activities that they would normally provide," replied Knight.

"We should send out Cyberhawks to search in pairs. One Blue Team and one Gold Team," said Major Bluster.

"Why can't my team work together? Don't you trust us to do the job right?" asked Captain Justice.

"Oh, I trust you as far as one can trust any civilian operator. It's the fact that you don't have any weapons and can't fire back at the bad guys that worries me," replied Major Bluster, getting ready to have another fuel disk installed into his suit. "You should be worried about that."

Captain Justice felt annoyed with Bluster, but the man had a valid point that he hadn't considered. His "gold team" had never been prepared for a situation like this, except for the three cops he had on his team. Robert watched as the military personnel charged up the military man's Cyberhawk gear and quickly inspected it. Robert privately hoped he would not get stuck flying with the Major.

"Who will decide the teams?" Robert turned to Knight.

"Oh, I will. I know everyone… at least a little bit. I don't know your team as well, but I have been keeping a close eye on their progress. They are a good group of people. You can be proud of them. They will do fine with the military team. Don't worry," said Knight, taking an appraisal of Robert Justice's state of mind. "And I won't pair you up with Bluster." The older man added with a wink and smirk on his face.

Robert worked hard to hide his surprise from his face, but Lukas Knight sometimes had a way of reading the room very well. As soon as Major Bluster had his new fuel cell installed, the groups were ready to take off. The two teams assembled for instruction.

Lukas Knight had stepped out of the CyberSkeleton of his gear to be able to move about and interact with the numerous people coming and going. He wished he were younger and could go out with the team to see the action. But that time was over, and now he had a different vital role to fill. He looked at the young men and women assembled before him. He was proud of them.

"As you already know, this is not a simple disaster… as we were first led to believe. This is a man-made disaster constructed by or with the assistance of the subversive group known as the Action Men. There is a set of bombs designed to work together; if one is deactivated without the others being deactivated simultaneously, they detonate. The concern is that just two bombs for this design… is a lot of work for only two devices. Our experts, Captain Davis and First Lieutenant Archstone, both believe that there will be at least one additional bomb. We need to find that other bomb. We need to have this area here scanned and searched." Knight had Betty put the mapped area of concern into the HUD systems of both teams.

Everyone's HUD flashed an AR image of the city, showing the locations of the two current bombs, the radius of the area that could have another bomb within range of the special transmitters, and the color-coded regions where each of the teams was expected to fly and inspect. Bluster and Lewis had an area that was highlighted in blue, while Buckshot and Hallman had a section colorized in green.

"Does everyone see the mapping system with the colorized zones for inspection?" asked Knight. He looked up to see heads nodding, and a few 'yes, sir' came through the auditory system. "Pair up with your partner, work together, learn from each other. The local groups have explosive detection canines, also known as bomb dogs, that are preparing to go out now, along with the FBI and ATF, which have specialized dog units that have already started searching. They are aware of the Cyberhawk teams and will not consider you a threat. If you see someone suspicious, call it in to verify. We don't want to make mistakes. Don't be afraid to ask questions. Alright, let's head out!"

Lukas Knight tried to end the briefing on a positive note. It was difficult to conceal his concern. He watched them all pair up and start to make plans with each other, which was a good sign. He turned towards where Davis and Archstone were standing, getting their equipment ready and discussing how to deal with the explosive devices.

Just then, a man in a suit arrived and headed straight for him. "Are you Lukas Knight, Commander of the Cyberhawk program?" the man asked, extending his hand for a shake.

"Yes, I am," said Knight, shaking the man's hand. "And you are?"

"I am Agent Leonard Phan from the Federal Bureau of Investigation. I am here to assist in the bomb deactivation process," he said.

"Oh great! Let me introduce you to Captain Davis and First Lt. Archstone," said Lukas, directing the FBI agent to follow him to meet the other experts.

****

"Hello, I'm Rafferty Lewis," said Rafferty, extending his enhanced Cyberhawk grip out to the blue military team Cyberhawk.

"Major Bluster. You are the nephew of Dr. Benjamin Lewis," replied Major Bluster, sizing up his search partner and shaking hands.

"Yes, I am, Major," replied Rafferty. "Are you an expert at finding explosive devices?"

"I'm an expert in everything. Come on, let's be the first to start searching our zone," said Bluster, popping closed his face plate and taking a few steps away to lift off.

Rafferty closed his face plate and immediately followed the Blue Team leader. Rafferty caught up to the military man and flew alongside him.

"I have never had to search for bombs," Rafferty remarked to Major Bluster. "Do you have any advice?"

"Don't get blown up," replied the Major, then realizing that Lewis genuinely wanted advice. "Use the scanning application on your HUD. The bomber's motive is important, but we currently do not know it. The Action Men like to cause disruption, chaos, panic, and fear amongst the civilian population. And since we know they are somehow involved, I would recommend searching areas that are particularly vulnerable to causing great distress and destruction for the people who live here. That's why they want to destroy the bridge; the loss of it will cause frustration, anger, and perhaps civil disharmony that they can use for their plans."

"Wow, they sound like a bunch of assholes," Rafferty remarked as they started to scan the OMSI building, which was on the farthest edge of their perimeter.

Both Bluster and Lewis scanned the entire exterior of the OMSI facility, including the surrounding parking lot, which took time because it was a large place with a complex structure design. They found nothing. Lewis had heard good things about the museum and wished he had been part of the group to inspect the inside. Looking around the area, there were warehouses and railroad tracks nearby. Then he spotted the tall freeway ramps and recalled what the Major had said.

"Major, should we check the freeway structures next? That would fall into the motive parameter that you described. Traffic is always hectic in this city, and I can imagine that if somethin' got closed like that freeway ramp, ... well heck, I think people would be pretty irritable about that," suggested Rafferty.

The major eyed the freeway ramp structure.

"Good call, Lewis. Let's go inspect that next," agreed Major Bluster.

The enormous concrete pillars were nearby, and it was easy for the two Cyberhawks to fly around the posts, scan them, and then up and underneath to the freeway platform, where usually thousands of cars traveled across every hour. The area below was an open natural area along a concrete pathway. A few trees and shrubs were growing near the shoreline of the large river. Sometimes people abandoned their trash, and a box caught Bluster's attention. He noted to himself that he would scan that after the bridge was done.

"Good call, rookie! I found one on the upper part of this outer pillar," Major Bluster reported and then flew in close to get detailed scans and video of the device to show to Captain Davis.

Chris Takahashi immediately brought the new video to Captain Davis's attention. She was followed closely by Archstone and Agent Phan, who stood next to her. The three bomb disposal experts studied the video sent by Major Bluster.

"We need to create another radius for inspection," commented Captain Davis.

Diana, who was standing by Chris, took that as a request for action. "Captain Davis, do you want me to inform the local authorities of the latest discovery and the need for a greater ground inspection?"

"Yes, but let's first get the radius mapped before we inform them. Less confusion is better, and the teams we have will need to finish searching the areas they are assigned," replied Captain Davis.

"I have a full Cyberhawk suit. I can help," said Lukas Knight, standing aside, feeling a little bit useless.

Just then, Captain Washington and Dalen Hughes came over to join those looking at the newly affected area.

"I think I have Captain Washington's helmet repaired. Just needed a little resoldering. He could return to duty," said Dalen. "And Captain, this should work for this mission, but we may have to construct you a whole new helmet."

The tall, serious-looking man nodded to the smaller man.

"I am fine with that. As long as I can get back up in the air and be able to function properly," replied Washington.

Then, through the HUD system, Betty's voice could be heard, "I have received Major Bluster's GPS coordinates for the third explosive device. I have incorporated the third radius into the search area zone. It should be reflected in the mapping system now."

"I see it, Betty. Thank you," replied Captain Davis.

Knight stood looking at the maps and the various screens, studying them for a few moments.

"It looks like they want to take out that entire area of travel. That whole section of the town will become permanently gridlocked. I want to take Captain Washington with me and search the other side of the freeway," said Lukas Knight, stepping back into his CyberSkeleton to complete his Cyberhawk gear.

"I think he is correct," Agent Phan observed. "I have lived in this area for many years and the loss of these two vital traffic paths ......will cause...... if I were an insane terrorist, this is what I would do to disrupt this city."

Knight looked over at the FBI agent and gave him a look of agreement. It was a practical yet nasty plan that would result in years of gridlock, potential civil unrest, and economic stagnation.

"Come on, Washington," said Knight as he flipped his face plate closed, took a few steps away from the others, and lifted off. Captain Washington was only seconds behind him.

****

Sandra worked hard to keep up with the mysterious *Captain Unicorn*, who flew precision maneuvers around the large brick building that was part of their assigned area to scan. They had just completed scanning the outside of another red brick building that was not as tall, and Sandra felt almost exhausted keeping up with the military team member.

"Geez, can you really scan the building that fast and do a good job?" she finally exclaimed to her partner.

He stopped and hovered in midair and replied, "Yes. I have developed a pattern for scanning the most footage while maintaining search quality. Are you having trouble?"

"Yeah. I am not as good as you are at this," she replied somewhat sadly.

"Detective Ridgestone, you have not been doing this kind of work as long as I have, so it is reasonable that I will be better at it than you. You will improve. I believe in you," he replied.

Sandra found herself smiling inside her helmet. It was nice to hear the words 'I believe in you' again. She used to hear that from Karl every time she tackled something new or challenging.

"So, what is this special pattern you use?" she asked him as they both started to fly and run scans around the building again.

There was a long pause before he replied, "I... don't think I could explain it. It is a complex mathematical formula. It's not the way I used to think about things, so it is tough to explain in terms that... are easily understood. I am under the impression that you are aware of your fellow team members' repairs. Some of the modifications made certain features better than they were before,... like your eye."

"You know about my eye?" she replied, half laughing and half concerned.

"Yes. Your eye has special features that I do not think they have trained you fully about how to use," he replied.

"Well, I can see. Isn't that enough?" remarked Sandra as she landed on a flat patio-type portion of the building to inspect some areas that could be accessed easily by people.

"Well, of course, sight is the most important thing the cybernetic eye can offer, but you can also record images like a camera and send them off to another digital device like the HUD system, and you can scan your environment for toxins. They wanted it to do more than toxins, but that seemed to be the most important for survival requirements," he replied.

"Do you have that ability?" she asked as she finished checking the patio area.

"Yes. Now I do," he said.

"Can you show me how to make that work?" she asked.

"Yes, I can," he replied. "But we need to focus on scanning for potential explosives first."

"Agreed," she said, feeling a little embarrassed that she had lost focus while doing a job. It was hard not to feel a little excited about the new skills she might have with her cybernetic eye. She did not realize the potential for her to expand her life skills. Be a better police officer, be a better mom, contribute more to the community.......... Being a Cyberhawk was a great new experience.

Together, they scanned the lower portion of the building and started to move to the upper section. The further up they went, the more uncomfortable Sandra started to feel. It was a strange sensation, as if she were being watched, which, considering what she was doing and how she was doing it, seemed pretty obvious. People were watching her and all the other Cyberhawks. The building had a unique shape that was not just a giant rectangle standing on its side like some skyscrapers. It was eye-catching with lots of structural features that made it attractive to the eye and sorta Art Deco-esque. At the very top was a pyramidal shape that was constructed of metal. She knew the building was of importance to the city, so it was reasonable to think that people should be watching them fly around this iconic structure.

She tried to shrug off the disturbing feeling and did not want to say anything to her partner. She didn't want him to think she was being silly. But the feeling intensified as they got closer to the top. Now she felt like she was in danger. She had felt that feeling before in LA while on the force. She knew not to ignore it. She paused her scanning and looked around to see if she could spot a threat or something out of place.

"Are you alright?" asked the Cyberhawk with the unicorn on his pauldron. He flew up next to her and hovered with her as she scanned the area with her HUD.

"I have a bad feeling. I cannot explain it. I have felt this before and……in the past it has been valid," she paused. "Do you feel… like… something is about to happen?"

The military Captain paused to check his systems. He had more sensory devices on his gear than the civilian Emergency Services Team.

"I am currently not picking up any anomalies," he replied. "But I will make sure that I keep an active awareness of anything threatening."

"Okay, thanks," replied Sandra. "I guess we need to get back to finishing the inspection of this building."

Sandra returned her attention to the scans, and so did her partner. They finally reached the top where the red brick stopped, and the exterior turned to steel. The feeling intensified. Sandra felt unnerved and tried to push it aside. There was nobody up on the building, and no one was to be seen on the nearby buildings either. The smoke from the fires was starting to reduce as the firefighters below were having success putting out the conflagration. It looked like the city drama was beginning to calm down. They headed towards the very top of the building and inspected the opposite sides to make good use of the flight time. Then the dizziness hit her again with an unnerving intensity. The world seemed to spin and flicker out into spots of darkness.

"Betty……Captain Unicorn……," she barely called out as she sank into darkness, and all went black.

CHAPTER 23

The news trucks were required to stay behind the boundaries set up by law enforcement. Crowds had started to develop in locations where people could see the Hawthorne Bridge and the downtown Portland area. Several news stations had parked their vans in a location that provided a reasonable view of the situation from the top of a parking garage. The team from KGIU had just finished their follow-up broadcast for the live morning news feed. Greta Schmidt handed her microphone to the technician and took a deep breath. She was trying to stay professional as she watched the city she loved succumb to this bizarre and horrendous disaster. Rumors were swirling that a swarm of earthquakes may have caused the historic tunnels to collapse beneath the streets and buildings, resulting in broken gas lines and fires. But the sight of the building imploding upon itself reminded her of the events of September 11th in New York City. Could this be another tragic event, she wondered. The news crew was holding itself together, but everyone was worried.

Greta was a local with family and friends throughout the city and in surrounding communities beyond the city limits. Despite her age and youthful appearance, she had proven herself to be a top-notch journalist and had the support of her fellow professionals.

"Oh great, look at who has decided to join us up here," moaned the cameraman.

Greta turned to see the KPIE news van pull into a space not far away.

"We don't have to interact with them," said Greta.

"It's hard when they thrust their attitudes upon you like an angry pit bull that's been poked by a stick," said the cameraman.

"Try an angry, *rabid* pit bull poked by a stick. They make no sense and jump to wild conclusions. I have no idea why anyone watches them or pays to have commercials on their station," grumbled the sound tech. "I hate being anywhere near them."

"I don't like it either, but hopefully it is too early in the morning for their anchor monster to get up," said Greta, glancing over at the KPIE truck. "OH, crud, that bastard is here."

"He is like a curse that you can't get rid of," said the cameraman.

"Shhhhh, he's coming over," said Greta, quickly hopping into the van to drink her coffee.

"Coward," grumbled the sound tech.

The dreaded man sauntered over to their location.

"I hope you don't mind us setting up nearby. It's time for the grown-up newsman to start reporting on these events," said the man dressed in fashionable outdoors attire. His hair was perfect, his multiracial skin was perfect, his smile looked like it had been plucked from a teen magazine, and even his wristwatch was perfect.

"Mr. Tredwall, we have already reported on this story and are keeping our viewers happy with quality journalism. We are not worried about you and your phony Beverly Hills appearance," retorted the sound tech, flexing his shoulders a bit and jutting out his jaw.

"Go back across the border, peasant," replied Tredwall as he turned and left.

The cameraman quickly grabbed the sound tech's arm, "José, don't listen to that piece of trash. We need to do another report in ten minutes. He's just trying to get under our skin. Greta needs us. She's been dealing with that jerk ever since she got this reporting position."

"It just pisses me off. A guy like that deserves a good punch in the face... that snotty, arrogant face," replied José.

Greta Schmidt suddenly hopped out of the van.

"Guys, do you see that? It looks like two of those Cyberhawk guys are flying around the I-5 Freeway!?" exclaimed Greta.

José and the cameraman both looked out towards the cityscape to the west. Together, the three of them spotted more Cyberhawks flying around the buildings and bridges.

"They look like they have blue ones now. I thought they were only a gold color," remarked the cameraman.

"Can you zoom the camera in to film them?" asked Greta.

"Sure thing," replied the cameraman, grabbing his gear.

José reached for the microphone, "You are going to need this, Greta. This will be a great update!"

****

Lukas Knight and Captain Washington headed for the I-5 freeway ramp that crossed over the river just south of the Hawthorne Bridge.

"Commander, where do you want to start first?" asked Captain Washington.

"My gut is telling me… the section where the two sets of ramps meet together," replied Knight.

"Okay, let's start there. Do you have the scanning software installed on your HUD?" asked Washington.

"I have everything on my system. Remember, I was one of the first testers for this stuff," replied Knight.

"I do recall that. And those crazy stories about those people dressed in black suits with no sense of humor," said Washington as he started scanning the freeway pylons.

"You haven't met any of them?" asked Knight as he scanned alongside Washington.

"No, I never did. At times, I thought Bluster was full of it," replied Washington.

"Oh, Bluster is full of it, but the Black Suits are real. And I have a feeling that everyone is going to meet them after this mission," said Knight, noticing something odd higher up. "I see something curious about two o'clock and up from my position.

"Oh yeah, that doesn't look right," agreed Washington. Together, they flew upwards to the object that caught Knight's attention. "And it is another bomb. It took a lot of effort to get this up here."

"Scan it and send the images to Captain Davis," said Knight, looking about, wondering if the malefactors were watching them. Knight was familiar with such matters, having worked for some time as a highly successful contractor for a PMC. If he had placed a device like this, he would have eyes on the situation. He scanned the area looking for people, drones, or something that could be used for surveillance. He switched his HUD scan from chemical to electrical readouts. Down below, he saw jogging paths, a few trees, streetlights, a fenced-in area underneath the freeway pylons, and a parking area with a vehicle.

The scan alerted when he went over the automobile. Anyone with half a brain knew to put security on their cars in Portland. It was probably just a car monitoring device.

"Washington, I am going to investigate the car below," said Knight.

"Sure thing, Commander. I am almost finished with Captain Davis's required video," replied Washington.

Knight landed on the scenic view platform, where visitors could look at the river. He didn't want to set off the car alarm by landing too close. The electrical scan was showing activity from the vehicle. A camera device was monitoring the car, which was a very common economy model. He spotted the camera on the dashboard, but it was not pointed forward; instead, it was pointed upward. That seemed curious and, for some reason, unsettling. Was it a coincidence? Possibly. Was it worth investigating further? Yes.

He switched his HUD scanning back to the chemical HAZMAT setting and began scanning the car. Nothing odd about the front or passenger area… but the scan was showing warnings about the trunk.

"Captain Washington, I think we may have an additional problem," Knight informed his search partner. "It appears that the car parked below also has explosive materials in the trunk."

"Copy that. I will come down once I am finished with Captain Davis," replied Washington.

"No, don't. I am heading up as if I found nothing to be concerned about," replied Knight. "The vehicle has a camera that appears to be active and watching us."

****

Hallman and Buckshot had completed scanning the small marina area and lodging location. A park-like setting surrounded them, and they were zipping between the trees to conduct scans. Hallman was having a hard time keeping up with her military partner.

"Dang! You fly like a badass fighter jet pilot," commented Janet as she attempted to follow Lt Kelli Buckshot through the bright green vegetation.

"That's because I am a badass fighter pilot," replied Lt. Buckshot. "So, what are you? A fireman? A cop? You have an accent."

"I am from Quebec, and I was a Royal Canadian Mounted Police Officer," replied Janet.

"So......a female version of Dudley Do-Right," replied Lt. Buckshot.

"Well......yes and no. I hope you don't think I am stupid," replied Janet.

"No, of course not. He's just a fun, silly cartoon character," replied Buckshot, pausing to land in an open intersection. "Did you wear the red coat and the hat?"

"Why does everyone ask me that?" retorted Janet as she landed not far from the Lieutenant.

"Because the coat is cool and iconic. So, which building do you want to inspect next?" asked Lt. Buckshot.

"And bright red like a giant target," mumbled Janet under her breath, still thinking about the iconic coat.

Janet looked up the street and at the various tall structures that required outside scanning. She spotted a ground team going into one of the buildings. What a job! So much to look over and inspect. At least they had their dog's keen nose to help. She consulted the HUD for the boundaries of their assigned section. They were right next to the Ridgestone assignment.

"Let's start with this one here since it is right next to the Ridgestone team. That way, we can make sure we do not neglect any areas and can work our way deeper into our assignment," replied Janet.

"Sounds good to me. Let's get this done," replied Lt. Buckshot, lifting off.

Janet followed, looking around, having thought she saw the two Cyberhawks from the Ridgestone team working on the top section of a decorative-looking building. She followed Buckshot around the white structure, which was not as tall as the fancy red brick building. At the very top, she spotted Detective Sandra Ridgestone with her military partner. They were probably doing their final scans up there. Her thoughts turned to her teammates and the new friends she had made over the past months. She was happy now and felt she had a direction to go in. The sorrows with her old girlfriend and health concerns seemed trivial now. She would find someone new when the time was right. But she was happy with these new people. She was proud to be the second-in-command of the Emergency Services Team, and now, seeing all the military Cyberhawks, that definition made perfect sense. There were two types of Cyberhawks, each with different responsibilities. Her parents would have been proud of her.

She rounded the corner of the light-colored building and tried to catch up with Lt Buckshot, who flew like she was born in the Cyberhawk suit. As she reached the top of the building, she scanned the HVAC system that was installed on the roof. It looked fine, and nothing odd appeared on the data feed. Janet looked over at the building where she had seen Sandra and the other military Cyberhawk. They had reached the top, but Sandra had stopped moving and was hovering near the apex. Suddenly, her Cyberhawk suit seemed to move strangely, like someone having a seizure. Janet thought she saw a green beam of something sparkly. She blinked her eyes, trying to refocus since what she saw made no sense. Then Sandra stopped convulsing, and the golden Cyberhawk started to plummet to the ground.

****

"Code Red!! We have a Cyberhawk down!! Detective Ridgestone is in a free fall. Betty, take control of her suit!" said an urgent voice over the HUD comm system.

"Roger that, Captain Unicorn. I am in control of her Cyberhawk suit, but it is damaged. I will need assistance in reducing landing speed," replied Betty.

"I have a lockdown grip on her gear, but the unexpected weight is making me lose control," replied Captain Unicorn. "I need… assistance."

Major Bluster and Rafferty Lewis had completed their section and were on their way to start a new one, and were nearby. Immediately, they swooped towards the endangered team and assisted Captain Unicorn and Sandra Ridgestone. The three of them were able to land Sandra's gear safely on the ground.

"What happened?" demanded Major Bluster.

"We were scanning the last section of the building when she stated something about ...having a bad feeling. I searched for any anomalies, and we found nothing. But she has these gut instincts that are pretty spot on," replied Captain Unicorn. "Betty, can you open Sandra's face plate?"

"It seems to be malfunctioning," replied Betty. "I am working with the Mechanical AI to diagnose the problem. The Mechanical AI states that they had been hit with an unusual form of energy. It scrambled some of the applications."

"Is Sandra okay?" demanded Captain Unicorn with a worried tone in his voice.

"Hold on. I am receiving biological diagnostics right now. She is breathing. Heart rate is fair. She is unconscious. Brain activity is curious. The Mechanical AI is directly accessing her cybernetic eye data," replied Betty.

Another Cyberhawk team landed nearby and came to investigate the situation. It was Hallman and Buckshot.

"I saw her drop! Is she okay?" asked Janet, who had popped open her face plate immediately.

"She's alive, civilian," replied Major Bluster, followed by a strange sound on his microphone.

"Why haven't you opened her face plate?" asked Janet.

"It seemed to be locked somehow. Betty is working with the mechanical AI to resolve that. Her vital signs seem to be alright, but she is unconscious," answered Captain Unicorn.

"Take her back to base. Dalen Hughes is there. He should be able to figure it out," Bluster ordered.

"Major," Betty said privately through the comm system to him. "You should take her back and remove the passenger from your helmet."

"Oh, you know," retorted Bluster.

"I know everything," replied Betty firmly. "You cannot fly safely with that in your helmet. While I understand your compassion, it could cause problems."

"Understood," replied the Major. He knew Betty was correct. He then turned to the others, "I will assist the Unicorn in taking her back to be looked over. Lewis, team up with Hallman and Buckshot. You three will have to take over the Ridgestone search section as well as your own. Buckshot, take point on this."

"Yes, sir," replied Lt. Buckshot. "Come on, we have some work to do," she said to Hallman and Lewis. With a turn and a few steps away, the three of them resumed their designated scanning mission.

"Betty, can you control Sandra's Cyberhawk suit?" asked Captain Unicorn.

"I can, but on a lesser level of control. I can power up the jetpack system, but I have little control over steering or speed. To move her back safely, it will require the assistance of both of you," replied Betty.

"Understood," replied Captain Unicorn, sounding a bit upset.

"These things happen on a mission," remarked Bluster as they both took a locked grip on Sandra's Cyberhawk suit. "We train for every possible danger, but there are actions we have no way to plan for. These suits still have unknown factors about them."

"I understand, Major, I just… have a personal connection with this situation," replied Captain Unicorn.

"We all know that. Why do you think that we agreed to call you by your nickname instead of your real one? We understand. We are a team. She's a strong one, and we'll get Dalen Hughes to open the suit up.... and the Emergency Services team has an actual doctor and EMT as part of their unit, so there is help available," Major Bluster reassured him.

"Understood. Sir......I am getting strange readings from your Cyberhawk suit… It's like you have an additional… heartbeat?" remarked Captain Unicorn.

"It's just a strange malfunction that I will have someone look at. Betty already informed me of that anomaly," replied Bluster.

"Okay, Sir," replied Captain Unicorn as they got closer to where the new command area was set up for Cyberhawk.

With Betty running the Cyberhawk suit as best as possible, they made a safe landing and were immediately greeted by Dalen Hughes, Dr. Hanni, and Raven Smith. They immediately began working on figuring out how to reopen the suit properly while monitoring her vital signs. Captain Unicorn scanned the suit as it stood there to reassure himself that she was still alive. He could pick up on the heart rate as he did on Major Bluster's suit. It was slow yet steady.

Diana strode over to Major Bluster with a box in her hand and addressed the Military Team commander, "Betty informed me that you required me to assist you with some kind of problem?"

"Yes," replied Major Bluster. "Let's move over here and give them room to work on Detective Ridgestone."

Diana followed Bluster away from the others.

"So, Major, how may I be of assistance?" she asked with that wonderful proper British accent of hers.

"First of all, speak of this to no one. Understood?" he asked.

"Understood. I am very capable of being discreet," she replied.

"Good. I will hold you to your word," he replied, and then opened his face plate. Inside his helmet, squeezed against his face, was a tiny kitten with big eyes that squeaked. "Can you take it out and make sure it is safe until I can retrieve it from you?"

"I certainly can," said Diana, surprised to see the tiny kitten. "That creature should not be away from its mother. Where did you get that?"

He sighed and replied, "I saw a box underneath the freeway ramp near OMSI. I went to investigate it for explosives and picked up life signs. It was trying to get out. Someone had obviously left it in the box. It was closed, so it was not the mother who put it there. I could not leave it there."

"This civilian understands Major," Diana said with a smile as she gently tucked the small creature into the box she brought. She now understood why Betty had requested it. "It will need care soon. It looks like it will require bottle feeding."

"Agreed. I would appreciate it if you looked after it until I can handle the situation myself," said Major Bluster.

"I will do my best," replied Diana as she turned to head back to their command area. "Perhaps some of the ground crews may have some things to assist with this."

Bluster smiled and then popped his face plate closed and went back to check on the progress concerning Detective Ridgestone. Dalen Hughes had managed to make the Cyberhawk suit release her, allowing Dr. Hanni and Raven to examine her. Since they had been successful with that, he decided to head over and see what Captain Davis had come up with regarding the bombs. The group gathered around the monitors seemed to be excited.

"What is the status?" he asked.

"Well, Mr. Knight and Captain Washington found a fourth bomb, which is bad... but Trevor Vermeulen was able to modify one of the energy scans in the HUD system to be able to see where the signals were coming from," said Chris Takahashi. "Captain Davis says that they now know there are only four cluster bombs in that set."

"Okay. At least we know what we are up against... for the most part," commented Major Bluster, still wondering about Detective Ridgestone's malfunction.

"This is good news," commented Captain Davis, coming over to where Bluster was standing. "But we need a fourth bomb expert before we can proceed. And you know what that means."

"Yes, I do," replied Major Bluster. "Call in the spooks."

"Mr. Knight has already requested that," replied Captain Davis.

Overhearing the conversation, Chris asked, "Spooks?"

Bluster turned to the talented pilot sitting at the drone readout table.

"Not the cavalry," remarked Bluster to Chris without answering his question.

CHAPTER 24

"What are we doing now?" asked Fernando, looking at his teammates and taking a moment to wipe his brow with a towel from the first aid equipment. "And does anyone know what happened to Sandra?"

The Cyberhawk Emergency Services Team had been recalled to the command area and had gathered for refueling. They were all taking a much-needed break.

"Something odd happened to her," replied Rafferty, drinking down a container of water. "My gut feelin' is that……something is just not right around here."

"I saw her fall from the air," added Janet. "It looked awful. Not something I want to experience."

"Where is she now?" asked Crane.

"Roy Ekstrand arrived about ten minutes ago with Dr. Eirstone and Dr. Cross. They left with Sandra and Dr. Hanni to go back to our Eugene base of operations," replied Diana, knowing that the others would want to know what happened to their teammate. "Captain Justice is being apprised of the situation in more detail. He is also being briefed on how they plan to deal with the current bomb situation."

"Alright. But where does that leave us? What do we do now?" asked Fernando.

"We wait for our next set of orders," replied Janet Hallman.

"And the best thing we can do is be ready," commented Crane as he waited while a new fuel cell was placed into his Cyberhawk suit.

Dalen finished showing Alejandro how to check for fuel cell damage and then turned his attention to the others.

"I need to check over your equipment. Your team has never used your gear this intensely, so I want to make sure no wear and tear could cause a drop in efficiency," said Dalen. "You also might want to exit your suits to deal with any biological needs and hydration. Drink some water and eat something small. We have noticed that the other users of the Cyberhawk suits can become dehydrated, and some show signs of requiring more caloric intake after extensive use."

"Heck, that sounds like a good idea," said Rafferty, unsecuring his helmet and removing it so he could easily step out of his suit. "I could use a visit to the men's room and something more to drink and eat. I'm famished."

"Well, this is the perfect time to do this. Then we will all be ready for when they need us next," added Janet, stepping into her second-in-command role while the captain was away. "Everyone, take a few minutes to tend to yourselves."

Diana felt like Janet was handling the Gold Team, so she decided to see if Captain Justice or anyone else needed anything to be taken care of. Chris was charging up his drones, and Ellena was taking a break from the VR set. She figured that she might be required to assist in dealing with the bomb that was located under the water level. Lukas Knight had returned to the makeshift command area. The military team was in another location, having their suits refueled and inspected. They were already resting, drinking the prescribed water, and eating energy bars. She then checked the shopping bag that she was carrying over her shoulder like a large purse. She looked into the sack and saw that the tiny kitten was sleeping soundly on a pile of bandages after having some water dropped into her mouth with an eye dropper. One of the local EMTs had brought supplies for rescued animals that were malnourished. It was a formula designed to provide the necessary minerals and energy for recovery. The calico kitten seemed happy with the stuff.

Diana gently re-adjusted the strap so the kitten could continue to sleep safely and then turned her focus to the individuals preparing plans for the deactivation of the cluster bombs. The city police chief, the head of the local fire district, Agent Phan of the FBI, Captain Davis, and Mr. Knight had finalized the necessary steps before the deactivation process began. All personnel within the now restricted danger zone were evacuated, and the ground crews were making sure that the civilian population had also left. The trains and bus systems were on hold, along with the gas lines being shut down. Ships were now blocked from sailing down or up the river. Diana could feel the tension in the air. Captain Justice stood alongside Major Bluster while the strategy was being developed and perfected.

It was at this moment that Diana spotted a man heading towards the group. She walked over to intercept him and to find out who he was and what his business was in the area. As she got closer to the tall man, who appeared to be about twenty-five to thirty years old, she was pleasantly impressed by how handsome he was. He was probably the best-dressed man she had ever seen in her life. He gave her a slight smile and paused before her.

"Excuse me, this is a restricted area due to the emergency," said Diana.

"I am Trevor Howard. Mr. Knight's personal assistant. He requested information regarding a person of interest who had an office in the area affected," replied the dashing man.

Diana had to force herself to stay reserved. She found herself to be utterly smitten by his charming demeanor, polite ways, and good looks. Even his voice was the sound of angels. "Mr. Knight is in conference with other officials right now. Is the information urgent?" she asked.

"I do not know. But I should give it to him as soon as he is free," replied Trevor.

"Well, Mr. Howard," said Diana. "You can come over here and wait with me and some of the other Cyberhawk team members."

"I would be delighted to," he replied.

****

Once Janet saw that everyone on the Gold Team was busy taking care of themselves, she decided to chat with the military Cyberhawk Sandra was partnered with.

She walked over to the group of Blue Team Cyberhawks and asked, "Where is the individual who was partnered with Sandra Ridgestone?"

"He is over there," replied the military Cyberhawk with a strong Eastern European accent and a trident emblazoned upon his pauldron. "The Unicorn."

"Thank you, ...Captain......Trident," she replied, not being able to figure out his name.

"Oh...tak...," he then laughed, looking over at his shoulder as she walked towards the Unicorn.

"Captain Trident over there said you were the one who was working with our Detective Ridgestone," Janet said to the military Cyberhawk with his face plate still down.

"Yes, I am. How may I help you?" he asked.

"I am Janet Hallman. One of her teammates.... obviously........... I saw something just before she fell....and I was wondering if you saw anything. I was down working on one of the other buildings," said Janet.

"What did you see?" he asked.

"You're going to think I am... vraiment cinglè, but I saw a green sparkly light beam... just before she started to hover like she was having a seizure," said Janet, feeling a little worried that these military types would think she was an idiot. "It was as if she were the target."

"Interesting. I didn't see anything, but I was focused on the building. She did say that she had a bad feeling before we headed up to the top. We did a basic visual search for anything or anyone that could be a threat. But found nothing. I will make sure we investigate the data records for that time period. I will request Betty to search for anything that would fit that description during that time frame," he replied.

Janet eyed the white unicorn painted on his pauldron and the captain's bars.

"Do you think it was a system's malfunction or something else?" she asked, knowing the military had more experience.

"I think we all assumed it was probably a malfunction of her suit, but if you saw something that made her the target of an attack or an accidental transmission... then we need to look at things a bit differently. I am glad you said something. Betty... already knows to pull all the data from that moment," replied Captain Unicorn.

"That is good to know," replied Janet, pausing for a moment to think about the implications of such a reality. "Do you know of any group that could attack us in that manner? Our team was not designed for that kind of interaction. We are more search and rescue oriented."

"We need to check the data first before we make any conclusions. Keep a sharp eye out for any additional anomalies," he replied. "Report them like you would for your previous occupation in the RMCP."

"Alright," said Janet, nodding her head and then going back to where the Gold Team was hanging out. He didn't answer her question, but he was correct that making conclusions without more information was unwise. He also seemed to know more about her than she did about him. She could not recall telling him that she had been with the RMCP.

****

Everyone wearing a Cyberhawk suit suddenly got an incoming warning signal. Two Cyberhawks were approaching their perimeter. The Emergency Services Team members looked about and saw no one in the air. Rafferty and Raven had their face plates open and were trying to listen for the sound of the jetpack engines. They could hear a sound, but it was somehow muffled. Chris could see the warning signal on his display for the incoming aircraft to avoid.

"Are you getting that message alert too?" Raven asked Rafferty.

"I sure am," replied Rafferty in his cowboy drawl. He squinted, looking up and about.

Raven looked up and saw how the leafy tree branches shook as a helicopter had passed over them. Chris got up from his monitors to join them, looking up at the sky. And then a shadow appeared on the ground between them and the strategy group. Within seconds, the sound was gone, and two Cyberhawks with armor painted in curious shades of grey appeared as if out of thin air.

"Holy shit!" exclaimed Rafferty.

Raven and Rafferty stood together as they watched the new grey Cyberhawks stride over to the discussion area.

"This is getting weirder and weirder as each hour goes by," commented Rafferty.

"As soon as we are done with this mission, I am going to visit my girlfriend for a couple of days. I think... I need a little more normal in my life," replied Raven.

"Yeah, ... maybe I should go find a girlfriend.......," added Rafferty.

Fernando came up and asked, "Who are those two?"

"We have no idea, but the group that is in charge seems to know who they are," replied Rafferty.

"They literally appeared out of nowhere," added Raven.

"You mean cloaked like Klingons and Romulans?" asked Fernando.

"Yup," said Rafferty.

"That was amazing," said Chris, still gawking at the two mystery Cyberhawks.

"Can our gear do that?" asked Fernando, looking through the systems on his HUD for something that indicated a cloaking device.

"Nah, I think that is for those that hunt the dark, fear-inducing bad guys," commented Raven. "Wendigo and Skudakumooch hunters…"

"I doubt that……more like just bad humans since that stuff does not exist," said Chris incredulously. "Impressive, whoever they are. Did you notice that their engines were not as loud as ours or the military group's?"

"They were less noisy," remarked Fernando, giving Chris a curious look.

Rafferty turned to look at Raven after Chris's comment and said, "I have seen strange stuff in the hills of our ranch… crazy, creepy shit exists. Stuff that makes goosebumps cover your body and takes your breath away."

Chris turned to Rafferty and Raven, "So you two believe in that… ghost type…... supernatural stuff?"

Rafferty and Raven both answered yes at the same time. They both looked at each other.

"I knew there was a reason why we were meant to be roommates," commented Raven.

Rafferty just nodded in agreement.

"I have seen scary stuff too, back in Sacramento….in case anyone cares," added Fernando.

****

The local officials had just left the meeting area when the two new Cyberhawks had appeared. Everyone left in the strategic planning group turned to look at them as they approached.

"Mr. Knight, you requested our explosives expert," a woman's voice said.

"Yes, I did, Agent Koorvert," replied Lukas Knight. "For those of you who have not met the leader of Shadow Team, this is Senior Special Agent Dale Koorvert."

The group all seemed to acknowledge the newcomer. Captain Justice just kept quiet as all this new stuff unfolded before his eyes. He felt like he was in a movie. He had participated in and helped organize rescue missions and fire suppression events, but nothing like this. He felt a bit out of his realm of expertise. He felt like a fledgling firefighter at eighteen, in awe of the older, more experienced people. But some of these individuals were his age or younger. That was the case when Agent Koorvert opened her face plate, revealing a woman a little younger than him with a pleasant but determined appearance.

"Glad you could make it to the party, Koorvert. Did you bring the grungy merc with you?" asked Major Bluster.

Agent Koorvert turned and gave Bluster a sly grin and said, "I brought my whole team with me. Not that you would ever notice…. especially while picking up…...strays."

Major Bluster scrunched up his face and eyed Koorvert.

"Heh," said a male voice with a heavy German accent from the Shadow Team, who popped open his face plate. "It is always fun to come to the rescue of the shiny boys in blue."

"Okay, now that we have the pleasantries over with...... I want Captain Davis to take over this bomb deactivation mission," said Knight. "Those of you who are not part of her efforts will come with me... and Captain Davis, if there is anything any of us can do to assist in this part of the operation, please let me know. We are here."

"Actually," said Captain Davis. "I want the mermaid from the Emergency Services Team. Can you send her over?"

Mr. Knight gave Captain Justice a look.

"Yes, Captain Davis. I will request Ellena Schmidt to come over right away," replied Justice as he activated his HUD comm to speak with Ellena.

Lukas Knight led Bluster, Justice, and Koorvert away from the bomb experts and found Diana dutifully standing with his assistant, Trevor. Both had a look that suggested they were patiently waiting to be of service.

"Mr. Knight, I have those papers you requested concerning Dr. Pierre Arnaud," said Trevor Howard, offering the folder of papers.

"Thank you, Trevor. This is excellent," said Knight, opening the folder and quickly scanning through the contents. The others watched him.

Trevor and Diana left the four of them to have some privacy.

"Your reaction suggests something significant," observed Major Bluster.

"It is. We need to be aware of the potential implications of this," said Knight.

"What is it? I have my people all over the city. If you need something dealt with, we are ready," said Agent Koorvert.

Knight sighed and took a few minutes to gather his thoughts, and then said, "Dr. Pierre Arnaud is a rare, brilliant mind that I tried to recruit for Cyberhawk Research and Development. He was originally working out of Toronto, Canada, but then he felt that he had to move to Vancouver because he told me that people were spying on him. The physicist seemed a bit paranoid and eccentric, but his work on hydrogen plasma-based fuel was inspiring. The concept promised to be clean and efficient. I kept in contact with him because I had hoped to get him to change his mind about working with us. He started moving around to different offices and labs to make it difficult for those whom he thought were after him. He had an office in the building that was imploded. We need to know if he was in the building at the time."

"Do you have images of him?" asked Agent Koorvert.

"One. It is a group photo of top-notch professionals at a symposium," Lukas Knight continued to look through the contents of the envelope, not expecting to find the photo, but there it was. "And Trevor... managed to include this as well." Knight pulled out a photograph of a group of seven scientists who had spoken at the symposium. "He is the one here, second from the left." Knight showed the picture to Agent Koorvert.

She took the photo and, using a specialized device installed on her Cyberhawk suit, took an ultra-high-resolution scan of the picture.

"How many years ago was this taken?" asked Agent Koorvert.

"Approximately ten years ago. It's the only photo I have of him," he replied.

"I will have the AI age him appropriately, and then I will tell my team to keep an eye out for him actively. If he was currently using that office and did not die in the explosions, then he must be terrified and hiding somewhere… unless he was taken prior to the event," suggested Agent Koorvert.

"Now that would make sense," commented Major Bluster. "The destruction of the building may have been done to cover up the abduction?"

"Or possibly theft of his research," suggested Knight.

"This all sounds like something a lot bigger than just terrorists trying to make a point," said Captain Justice, frowning with worry. "I am sincerely concerned."

"And you have good reason to be concerned, civilian," said Bluster. "This level of trouble affects everyone, doesn't it?" Bluster said, turning to the Shadow Team leader.

"Yes. We must also uncover the truth behind several problems that have been brought to light today. Not only do we need to determine the whereabouts of Dr. Arnaud, but also why and who attacked your Emergency Services Cyberhawk. Several of my team picked up an unusual energy signature that hit her, which immediately afterwards caused her to stop functioning correctly," said Agent Koorvert. "I would like to request that Mr. Knight bring in the Black Suit Division for their expertise."

"Dale, do you think this requires their involvement?" asked Knight.

"I do. They have a different perspective on such matters and a broader range of knowledge. We can wait on the analysis of the data concerning what happened to Detective Ridgestone … according to Betty… she is already working on it. Several of the other Cyberhawks have data on their HUD recorders." Agent Koorvert was hearing reports from the sentient AI through her HUD system. She then turned to Major Bluster, "Your Captain…. *Unicorn* has hidden data showing up on his scans. He was not aware of it at the time. Your team needs to actively use the deeper scanning technology."

"I thought that was your team's priority while we handled the combat. Situational awareness is becoming increasingly complex. The Mechanical AIs may need to be upgraded," said Bluster. "When in combat, it is starting to be more difficult to focus on so many tasks. We might need to consider a more integrated submersion of our technology with ourselves."

Lukas Knight frowned in contemplation.

"We don't have enough Bettys to go around, and it would be too dangerous for a Betty AI to travel in one of the suits. She stays where she is," said Knight. "I will get the LabCoat Crew to start working on some advancements for the Mechanical AIs for the suits. As for the deeper submersion, that is a Dr. Elgin Cross question. How safe is it to go farther?"

"I think the Unicorn is proof of how far this stuff can go," remarked Bluster.

"I know...." replied Knight, deep in thought. "But what if he is truly a rarity and not a constant? His situation is unusual to say the least."

"The Unicorn must remain a secret until we know that the general public can handle the ramifications of such a situation," remarked Agent Koorvert. "The unintelligent fringe element is not to be ignored. They can be dangerous. Not only to themselves but to others around them. I have my doubts about the general population."

****

Ellena Schmidt pulled back her wavy blonde hair before making her way over to where the four bomb experts were going through the defusing procedure. She had been asked to assist on many high-tech projects, such as the Aqua Trash Skimmer, but that project did not involve the stressful responsibility of removing an explosive device. She was nervous but ready to help in any way she could.

"Hello," she said meekly, pushing a rogue strand of hair back behind her ear.

"You are the one nicknamed the Mermaid by the Coast Guard?" asked Captain Davis.

Straightening up a bit, Ellena replied, "Yes, ma'am."

"Good. I have heard good things about you. We have four bombs, and one, as you already know, is underwater. One of our experts has experience with underwater demolition, but due to the nature of these specialized cluster bombs, we require precise timing. There is very little room for error. Special Agent Ackermann feels that being underwater and behind the large concrete pylon may impair timely communication. Communication is vital to this operation," said Captain Davis.

"So, these devices need direct communication to work… then how would the bomb behind the concrete pylon talk to the others?" Ellena asked.

"Rogers and Sanchez found a repeater device for one of the bomb installations. We assume there are more, since all the bombs are tucked away under or behind extensive concrete barriers. These devices would have required a great deal of effort to install, so we doubt the bad actors would have been sloppy about ensuring they worked correctly. We discussed the idea of searching for the repeaters, but we do not know when these devices are scheduled to go off. We do not have the luxury of having abundant time. We need to act now," answered Captain Davis.

Ellena nodded and then asked, "What do you need me to do?"

Agent Phan stepped forward.

"We want you to assist Ackermann by making sure he has constant communication with us. You will use the water drone to be a repeater for Ackermann. It's somewhat like having a Wi-Fi access point following you around so you always have a signal," said Agent Phan.

Realizing that the marine biologist might be a bit nervous, First Lt. Archstone added, "You won't have to be anywhere near the bomb."

Special Agent Felix Anton Ackermann smiled leeringly and said, "After all, I would not want such a pretty Fräulein getting hurt."

Ellena just looked at the former merc and rolled her eyes.

"Or too close to… Ackermann," added Archstone, giving the guy a dirty look. He shrugged his shoulders.

"Is the submersible drone ready for redeployment?" asked Davis.

"Yes, ma'am. I can have my teammates put it into the water now," said Ellena.

"That would be fine," said Davis. Ellena took that as an order to get going. She headed off to get her teammates ready to redeploy the submersible drone.

"Agent Phan, we need you to get out of those office clothes and into some rappelling gear. Archstone, please ensure that Phan and I have the necessary harnesses and are wearing them correctly. Ackermann, your suit is submersible, right?" asked Captain Davis.

"Ja, it is," he replied with his heavy accent. "We should make sure we have comm frequencies linked, including the mermaid Fräulein. You and Agent Phan are wearing HUD goggles, so that is three different types of HUD systems."

"Good point. Ellena Schmidt," Captain Davis called through the HUD system.

"Yes, Captain," replied Ellena as she was making her way towards the Gold Team.

"Be prepared that we will be doing a communications test in about ten minutes. Have your VR gear ready," said Davis.

"Yes, ma'am," replied Ellena, picking up her pace to get back to her team to explain and get her VR headset back on.

Ellena found Chris, Raven, Rafferty, and Fernando chatting in a group. Morales was watching the drone monitors for Chris. Crane, Hallman, and Hughes were off meeting with the military team members. Hughes was double-checking the gear and asking questions about improvement needs, while Crane and Hallman were trying to get to know the other team so that they might work with them more effectively in the future. Ellena went up to the first group since they were the closest.

"I need to have the submersible drone back in the water to assist in the bomb deactivation. And I need to be ready on my VR headset for a communications check of the comm system in less than ten minutes," Ellena said to the guys who had all paused in their conversation about sci-fi cloaking devices. "Can you deploy the submersible for me, so I can be ready for the communications check?"

"I can oversee the deployment, Ellena," replied Chris.

"Great," she said, somewhat out of breath. "I will head over to my station and get my VR system back on. Thanks, Chris."

Chris smiled.

The guys watched her head off, and Chris turned to his teammates, "Well, since you three have Cyberhawk suits on, you can go do the heavy lifting."

"I see how you are; you get all the credit for helping the damsel in distress while we do the grunt work," commented Fernando.

"Well, if the shoe fits," replied Chris, laughing.

"Come on, guys, we have a giant banana to deploy," said Rafferty with a grin.

The four of them headed over to where the submersible drone had been placed after it was retrieved from the river. Chris quickly checked it over to ensure it was fully charged and sending all the correct signals. He tapped on his HUD glasses and said, "Takahashi to Schmidt. I have turned the drone on. Are you receiving a signal?"

"Hold on," replied Ellena. "Yes, I am. Is the drone still on land?"

"Yes. I thought it wise to test a few things before placing it into the river," replied Chris.

"Alright. I will quickly run through those tests. Do you see the flippers and fins moving?" asked Ellena.

"Yes."

"Do you see the propellers rotating?" asked Ellena.

"Yes," replied Chris.

"The camera is working, so let's put it into the water, and then I can run the other tests," said Ellena.

"Okay. Guys, let's put this banana into the Willamette," said Chris.

"Good thing we moved further away from the fires and bombs," commented Raven. "The water is closer here."

"Yes, but it will take longer for it to cruise up the river to get to the Hawthorne Bridge," remarked Chris.

"Well, I don't want to do the crazy maneuver that Janet did," replied Raven.

The three Cyberhawks walked the giant banana-like submersible across the parking lot towards the river shore. There was a concrete strolling path with shrubs and vegetation along the shoreline.

"Two of you will have to pick it up in coordinated flight and hover over the water and drop it as close to the water's surface as possible," said Ellena through their HUD system.

"I'll do it for the lovely lady," volunteered Fernando.

"And I'll take the other side. Watch your speed and pay attention to the readouts from the Mechanical AI," said Rafferty.

"Since when did you become an expert?" Fernando asked Rafferty.

"He is an expert compared to me. He has more flight hours," commented Raven.

Rafferty just gave a boyish smile.

"I was doing practices with Crane for the LabCoat Crew one morning, and they had us do this ten times... not with the water drone, but with a crate, which was a lot easier to pick up," replied Rafferty.

"Oh," replied Fernando, making a face. "Next time, I want to learn too. Please invite me."

"No worries. And I will. This is stressful. I think it was simpler fighting fires," replied Rafferty.

"Agreed," said Fernando as the two Cyberhawks slowly lifted the submersible from the ground while holding the large yellow drone's unique aerodynamic handles.

In a synchronized fashion, they engaged their jets, lifted off, gained altitude over the trees, and headed out for the water towards the Broadway Bridge. The water was greenish and appeared deep with a strong current.

"So......what happens if we crash into the water?" asked Fernando, feeling anxious.

"We get wet. Possibly sink," said Rafferty, starting to feel less confident.

Betty suddenly popped up on their HUD system and said to them, "Your Cyberhawk suits have emergency procedures for water immersion, specifically for water over a meter in depth. A flotation protocol will activate to keep you above the waterline. Your gear is both watertight and airtight for flight purposes. You are enclosed in your own environment."

"So, we won't drown," said Fernando, smiling.

"No. You should not unless your Cyberhawk suit is compromised," replied Betty.

"Well, my suit says I am fine. Fernando, yours should say the same. Let's get this beast into the water so Ellena can do her job," remarked Rafferty.

They picked up the pace as they flew, and as soon as they were at the lowest point where both felt comfortable flying, they deployed the water drone just an amazing meter from the surface and on the other side of the Broadway Bridge, shortening Ellena's time to travel up the river to meet with the bomb team.

"Well, that was fun," said Rafferty as they cruised back up and over the Broadway Bridge and down towards the area where the team had set up operations.

"It was. And no crashing into the water," agreed Fernando.

"Yeah, that is a good thing. Damn, I love the view from up here," replied Rafferty.

"So do I," agreed Fernando. "I could get addicted to doing this."

"I think we have found our perfect occupation," remarked Rafferty.

CHAPTER 25

First Lt. Archstone was assigned to the bomb located underneath the Hawthorne Bridge, while Phan and Davis took the locations underneath the freeway on the pillar supports. She would fly under the bridge and hover to work from her Cyberhawk suit, which she had spent many hours working in. She understood why Captain Davis did not wish to try the same thing. The Cyberhawk Military Team had collectively spent thousands of hours in their gear and had developed good working relationships with their experience-enhanced Mechanical AIs. They knew their equipment as if it were part of their bodies, which in many situations had been lifesaving. Captain Davis did not feel that way about the suit she had been assigned. Both Captain Davis and Agent Phan received training in rappelling and other traditional skills for individuals in active military and law enforcement service. Down in the waters of the mighty Willamette, Agent Ackermann was inspecting his assignment. Archstone was glad she was not under the turbulent water.

"I am in position, and the submersible drone is present. Can anyone hear me?" asked Ackermann.

"Affirmative," replied Archstone. She then heard Davis and Phan respond as well.

"Everyone, proceed to your positions and then call in," said Davis.

"I am already in place and have eyes on the... asset," replied the Shadow Team member.

"Patience Ackermann, the rest of us require more time," replied Davis.

"Understood," he replied.

A few minutes later, Archstone called in, "I am in position."

Another few seconds and Phan reported in, "I am now in position and secured. I have eyes on the asset and waiting for orders."

"Copy that," replied Captain Davis as she worked to secure her harnesses into position. She made the mistake of glancing down. "Oh, I hate this," she said to herself. "Give me good old-fashioned weapons of war and don't make me do crazy stuff like this. What I do for my country."

Captain Davis closed her eyes for a few seconds. The automobile with the explosives was down on the street below. It was the one with the enemy's camera watching the freeway support and the bomb. Earlier, a couple of the Cyberhawks strategically dropped material on the windshield to simulate bird droppings, so that the camera could not have a clear view of the events unfolding. She had no idea if it was effective. She certainly was not enthused about putting on a show for the enemy. There was also concern that they might trigger the device if they saw her working to deactivate it. It was unclear if the set of cluster bombs had that feature. When she got up close to it, it did appear to have a designated time for detonation.

Looking at the timer, she guessed that the bombs would go off after most of the cleanup from the fires and the tunnel cave-ins had been completed. It looked like it would be rush hour traffic at noon. It would be extremely congested after having so many streets blocked off and an entire day spent being forced away. Most building occupants would want to inspect their work and home spaces to make sure everything was okay. The instigators of this event were out for as much blood as possible. Luckily, these bombs were somewhat simple, since most of the complexity was in the need to be turned off all at once.

"Alright, team, remember in our study of these devices that the designer used all the same color of wires to make it more difficult to deactivate. Can everyone bring up the schematic we made of each device? Bring up your device's schematic," said Davis.

"Got it," said Ackermann.

"Mine is up," said Archstone.

"And I have mine ready as well," replied Agent Phan.

"Good. Now I want everyone to be ready to cut the wire that we designated as A1. Let me know when everyone is ready to cut," said Captain Davis. She heard three affirmatives. "Good. On my mark, cut the wire designated A1. Three, two, one. Mark!" She cut her wire, quickly looking at how her device reacted.

"Does anyone have anything odd to report?"

She heard three negatives.

"On my mark, cut wire B1. Three, two, one. Mark!" she said. "Anything to report?"

She heard a series of negatives.

"On my mark, cut wire C1. Three, two, one. Mark!"

"There is a light flashing," reported Agent Phan.

"Mine too," added Archstone.

"I have a light as well. It is probably a booby trap wire. We probably need to cut the last one quickly," commented Ackermann.

"Agreed. On my mark, cut D1. Three, two, one. Mark!" said Captain Davis, squinting a little as if expecting the device to go off in her face.

"We are alive still," commented Agent Phan, breathing a sigh of relief. "And there is no more flashing light."

"Alright. As planned, remove the explosives into one of the special container bags and then put the rest of the device in the other bag. Seal them. And get down as safely and as quickly as possible. We have no idea if we have sniper eyes on us," said Davis, taking a deep breath, feeling happy that she was still alive and was going to get off this infernal freeway ramp soon.

"Commander Knight," Captain Davis privately commed Lukas Knight.

"Yes," answered Knight.

"We have completed the mission, and we are still alive," she replied.

"That… is good news. Please come back to the basecamp," said Knight.

"Gladly," she replied.

When Captain Davis arrived back at the basecamp in the small parking lot near the river, she found Lukas Knight, Senior Special Agent Koorvert, Major Bluster, and Captain Justice waiting for her. She had this feeling that she might not like what she was going to hear. The military team driver let her out and then took off to deal with the climbing gear and what was left of the explosive device. The actual explosives had been handed off to Agent Phan's FBI associates, who would take care of the materials. There had been some argument about which agency would be keeping the devices. Davis made a compromise that Agent Phan could take possession of the devices after Cyberhawk Research and Development got a chance to photo-document them. She arranged for Dalen Hughes to do this onsite with Agent Phan present.

"Great job, Captain Davis. Your eclectic team saved the day," said Lukas Knight.

"Well, at least it isn't any worse," she replied, thinking about the collapsed tunnel sections, unstable buildings, and the one that imploded. It would take months, possibly years, before everything would return to normal.

"I have gathered my team leaders together for a private briefing," said Knight.

"And that includes the civilian?" asked Major Bluster, making a head gesture towards Captain Justice.

"Yes....that includes the civilian, who has clearance. He just has never really needed that level of clearance until now," remarked Knight.

Robert Justice kept quiet. He still felt like this was all beyond his scope of knowledge and was not certain he wanted to be involved. This all seemed like a movie to him. He felt he should be with the firefighters on the ground, tending to victims and working on fire suppression and mitigation. He started to wonder what he had gotten himself into. He had a family to worry about. Being a fireman was dangerous enough and had its risks, too, that could leave his wife a widow. Jessica and Ryan counted on him. Knight cleared his throat a little, bringing Robert's attention back to the here and now.

"Agent Dale Koorvert had requested that I bring in the Black Suit Division. Her team members who are here have noticed some disturbing activity. She feels that this could go back to the core of why Cyberhawk Research and Development was created in the first place," said Knight. "One of them is scheduled to arrive...," Knight paused to look at his watch. "In ten minutes."

"Oh, great," remarked Major Bluster, then turning to Captain Justice. "You think I'm an asshole, wait 'til you meet one of them."

"Alright. Alright. I know that they are difficult to get along with, but we are all here for the same reason," replied Knight.

"And exactly what is that reason?" Robert Justice blurted out before he could stop himself.

Lukas Knight turned to Justice and replied, "Basically, to protect and serve the life forms of this planet. Our home. Our people. Our environment. Our plants and animals. Everything about this world. We are building something for the preservation of mankind and this entire planet."

"You make it sound like there is a threat," said Robert, feeling even more concerned.

Knight paused for a moment, collecting his thoughts while the others remained quiet, then he finally turned to look everyone in the eye and said, "I am starting to suspect that there is a lot more to the motivation behind our creation. I have observed things that have led me to suspect a threat, which I have not mentioned to anyone. Over the last few years, a growing sense of urgency has emerged. A feeling like someone wanted......or needed us to be more ready for .... something."

"I agree with you," said Special Agent Koorvert. "Shadow Team has been collecting data all around the world, and we are starting to notice patterns. And some patterns go back hundreds of years."

"What kinds of patterns?" asked Bluster.

"It appears to be some kind of organized force influencing Human behavior," she said cryptically.

"Some kind of organized force?" Bluster repeated. "We need more solid intel. We can't deal with ghost facts or implied threats."

"Not every problem can be solved with a bullet, Bluster," replied Koorvert.

"It makes life easier," said Davis. "But I get what Agent Koorvert is trying to get at. Not all problems can be solved with weapons. It takes brains."

"Well, my brain would like something more straightforward than all that cloak and dagger stuff," replied Bluster.

Robert Justice had to agree with the Major on this point. Understanding the problem clearly and then addressing it made the day go better.

"So, who or what is the Black Suit Division?" asked Justice.

"They are... the individuals that started Cyberhawk Research and Development. I run the company and deal with everyone, but I answer to them. I have often wondered who they answer to," replied Knight.

"So, you don't know?" asked Robert Justice.

"I have some speculations. But no proof and would rather not propagate erroneous information," replied Knight in a final tone.

Everyone respected his response and did not press any further. Captain Justice wondered if the others present had their own ideas as well. He had no idea. He had never interacted with these people. Then, exactly when Knight had said, one of them arrived, a female dressed in a simple black suit, black tie, black shoes, white shirt, and a unique pair of sunglasses, came over to address them.

"So here we are again," said Lukas Knight to the rather stoic woman.

"Yes, Mr. Knight. Here we are. I have already looked over the data collected by your AI, Betty, from the various team members. We have reason to believe that the situation is serious. The Cyberhawks will now all need to run the new energy frequency scanning software on the HUD system. Data must be collected, and your team has the best equipment to provide such information. Secrecy must be adhered to," said the woman in the black suit.

"Are we going to be told what we are looking for?" asked Knight.

"A specific energy signature. It has already been programmed into all the HUD glasses, helmets, and goggles," she replied without really answering what Knight wanted to know.

"Do you have anything else for us that would be useful? Some advice?" asked Knight while his companions remained silent.

She seemed to pause for a moment as if in thought and then replied, "Don't screw this up. Mistakes can be deadly."

Lukas Knight just stared at her. Her expression had not changed. They were always like that. The response she gave could be considered humorous in some circles, but she meant it.

"Is there anything else?" asked Knight.

"Yes. Keep us apprised of the situation concerning Detective Ridgestone," replied the woman in the black suit. She then glanced at those present for the short meeting and then turned and left.

Everyone was silent as they watched her walk away and then get into a black SUV.

CHAPTER 26

"Everyone is talking about how Cyberhawk saved the day, but the instigators for these horrible crimes have not been found," said Sam Tredwall in his smooth announcer voice. "Why did the Cyberhawk team let them go? Is this all a plot to…"

Robert Justice frowned and raised an eyebrow towards the morning news on the small flat-screen television in the kitchen area. He reached for the remote and changed to KGIU News. Percy Roundhaus was doing the weather. Robert breathed a sigh of relief while listening to the short, knowledgeable weatherman describe the incoming cooling trend as a welcome respite from the hot summer weather. Scattered showers were predicted. Of course, that was in Portland, which was many miles away, but the events that occurred there were very close and present in Robert's mind. Jessica was busy making pancakes, and Ryan was excited about the special breakfast they were having. She also made bacon and placed it alongside the pancakes so that when the syrup dripped down, it would fall onto the bacon, creating a delicious combination of sweet and salty. Ryan was very excited.

It had been a couple of days since the events in Portland unfolded. It was difficult to return to normal. It was like the world had changed drastically over a single day. Sandra was recovering in the lab medical bay and was starting to get irritable because she insisted that she was fine. The twins were staying at the

Cyberhawk airbase quarters with the others watching over them. Captain Unicorn had visited Sandra while she was unconscious and was due to visit again today. At least she would be okay, according to Dr. Hanni. Robert wondered why the military Cyberhawk had taken such an interest in Sandra, but the man could have felt responsible for her since they were working together as a team. What disturbed Robert was the idea that Sandra was the actual target of the attack and not the building or the military Cyberhawk. Why would Sandra be the target of an attack, Robert wondered as he waited for his pile of pancakes and bacon.

"Dad, these are the best pancakes ever!" said Ryan as he proceeded to load his fork up with buttery syrup-dripping pancake pieces.

"Well, you are lucky to have such a wonderful Mom," said Robert. "She makes us great breakfasts so we can have energy to do all sorts of wonderful things."

"Like be a superhero in a Cyberhawk suit?" queried Ryan.

"Sure, why not?" replied Robert, not sure they were superheroes. The idea of that and the expectations were a bit daunting.

Jessica brought his plate of pancakes and bacon. He looked up at her. She had that knowing look on her face. She understood. She came back with a plate of pancakes and bacon for herself and sat down.

"A lot is happening. We will get through it all. Ryan is excited that he will get to do extra activities now that we know he is also exceptionally gifted," she said to Robert.

"Yeah, the test results said I'm super smart. Cool, huh?" said Ryan with a smile. "I have always wanted to be smart. Now I can do… extra…ordinary things with the older kids."

"Won't you miss your friends who are your age?" Robert asked.

Ryan paused for a moment and made faces like he was thinking, and then said, "I think I will miss some of them. I like Kip and Tom…...and Heather, but the others not so much. The other kids," Ryan lowered his head and whispered, "were kind of dull."

"Why are you whispering?" asked Jessica.

"Because our teacher told us not to say mean things about others, and… well, saying that the others are dull… is kind of mean," replied Ryan.

"Oh, yes. I can see that," agreed Jessica, nodding her head. Jessica then turned to Robert and asked, "Are you going to work today?"

"Yes, I should. We have a lot to discuss, …. um...so much has changed. Mr. Knight wants everyone to finish their training with the Cyberhawk gear and be ready to start training others. It sounds like they may want to start establishing other groups like ours because we have been so successful," replied Robert. "There may even be a group from Canada that will be started up in a couple of months… and we would train them."

"Wow, that's a big job," remarked Jessica. She sighed and then took a forkful of pancakes.

"What's the matter?" asked Robert.

Jessica made a face and then replied, "I have not been able to find any work that I like. It's retail clerk stuff, and...... I am not into that sort of thing. I'm almost wondering if it would be better if I stayed home and found something else to focus on. I think Ryan and you need me to be focused on our family."

"But I thought you said you were bored and wanted to go back to work," replied Robert, thinking about what she said. "You know, there are a lot of outstanding colleges and universities in this area. I am earning plenty to start a retirement fund and spend a little bit. How about taking a class or two?"

Robert could see the sparkle in his wife's eye as the idea sank in.

"Oh, I like that idea. I never really liked being a hairdresser. I just sorta fell into it after high school. It was stressful, and the chemicals were unpleasant, but I could look for something else... that I would enjoy doing," she replied. She had a look on her face as if the wheels inside her head were turning, as various possibilities lined up in her mind.

"You could just take a class for fun or ...something goal-oriented. You are very organized, which is a good business trait. Most schools have tours or counselors that can advise about what their school offers," suggested Robert.

"I could plan my classes around Ryan's schedule. It gets boring walking around trying to find something to do while he is off," she replied.

"No, plan what you want to do, and we will work around his schedule. I might be able to drop him off or pick him up. You should pick something that you want to do and not because it fits into Ryan's schedule," replied Robert.

"How about this? I will find out which university is collaborating with Cyberhawk Research and Development's educational program for exceptional kids, and I will first look there to see if they have anything I am interested in. Okay?" said Jessica.

"Alright," nodded Robert. "I just want you to find something that makes you happy, …and is interesting to you. I love being a firefighter. I love managing a group of people, so I feel exceptionally lucky to have the occupation I want to do."

****

Sandra eyed the door to the room where she was being forced to stay. She felt like a prisoner. She felt fine. She had already put on street clothes and was waiting for Dr. Eirstone to say it was okay to leave, but for some reason, they wanted her to remain. There was a knock on the door, and she heard someone ask if they could enter the room. There was something about the voice and the cadence. It sounded like the…Captain Unicorn guy.

"Yes, you can enter," she replied as she sat on the edge of the bed, ready to leave.

A man that she had never seen before entered the room. He was tall, with a lean, muscular build, short light brown hair, and pale green eyes. He was wearing navy blue military fatigues with his name on his short-sleeved button-up shirt, along with his Captain's rank and the unicorn patch on his sleeve. It was the military guy that she worked with while scanning the building in downtown Portland.

"Please tell me that your last name isn't really unicorn," she said to him.

He laughed, and his smile brightened his face, making his eyes twinkle with life.

"No, that's just a code name they gave me," he replied. "I wanted to see how you were feeling. You gave everyone a big scare. Myself included. We normally don't incur... paraphysical attacks, so this is all new to us."

He stood, looking slightly uncomfortable. Sandra eyed him.

"That's what they told me. It doesn't make sense, but my kids seem to think otherwise. They seem to think I have some...spooky gift for figuring stuff out," she laughed at herself.

"You do," he replied with conviction.

"How would you know?" she asked, half laughing and feeling a little spooked out about the way he was looking at her. He seemed so familiar. Why did he seem like she knew him?

"This will sound creepy, but I know you better than you would normally think, and that is one of the reasons why I am here. We need to talk," he said.

The way he said *we need to talk* echoed back to years ago, when she and Karl would discuss his work and the required secrecy concerning his job. Being a Navy SEAL was not a small deal, and it meant making sacrifices to everyday life at times. It had been hard to let him go for weeks and not hear a thing. She often worried that he would get injured or worse. Then there was the unexpected divorce. He also said those very same words to her.

"So......what do you need to talk to me about? Is it going to be stressful? Strange? Upsetting?" she asked. "Does it involve our work in Cyberhawk?"

"It could be any of those things. I am not sure how I can even address this topic," he said, looking upset. "I have been hoping to speak with you for a long time, and now that I am here...... I am not sure this is such a good idea."

"Oh, my goodness! Did you know my former husband? Do you know what happened to him? Something odd has occurred, and no one in the Navy will talk to me. I think he might have been killed," she said with her face starting to crumble with emotion. "I thought perhaps they would not tell me because we were divorced. Do you know anything?"

He watched her expression and felt his insides wrench. He was not ready to discuss this with her. He thought he was. He was wrong.

"Damn. I don't think I can talk about this. It's… too upsetting," he said, starting to head for the door.

Sandra got up quickly and grabbed his arm, "Please. Tell me. Did you know Karl Ridgestone?"

He looked into her eyes, resisting the urge to hold her closely, "I did …do…. know him."

Her mouth opened in shock, and then she asked, "Is he alright?"

He thought about her question and then answered, "He is okay…right now…. but that was not always the case. He got seriously injured."

"He is alive! Oh, my goodness, that's good news. I was so worried for him. The kids were upset, too. Can we see him?" asked Sandra.

He felt odd hearing that question and did not know how to answer it. She could see the expression on his face that he was torn up inside.

"I'm sorry. I should be happy to know he is still alive….and okay. His work took him to strange situations that required clearance. Wait, I have clearance now," Sandra said.

"I will have to see if your clearance level is the right kind to know more," he replied. "I can check into that."

"Thank you. I appreciate that. The twins would love to know more," replied Sandra. "They love their father. And they miss him."

The thought of the twins hit him hard. This wasn't easy. He would deal with the rest of this later. Perhaps taking baby steps was wise.

"Well, it's time for the meeting. We should get going," he said, gesturing to the door.

"You mean I can leave now?" asked Sandra.

"Oh yeah......Dr. Eirstone told me... I could tell you that," he replied as he led the way out the door.

The meeting was being held in the downstairs of the Cyberhawk base quarters. The entire Emergency Services Team was present, along with Major Bluster, Mr. Knight, and several members of the LabCoat Crew. Sandra sat down with her teammates while Captain Unicorn stood next to Major Bluster.

"You didn't tell her, did you?" Major Bluster said to Captain Unicorn.

"No. It was a lot more difficult than I had imagined," he replied.

"Uh-huh," agreed Major Bluster. "I should probably warn you; the twins have been staying here while she was in the medical bay."

"Oh, okay. Thanks for the heads up. They probably will not be around for this meeting," remarked Captain Unicorn.

"No. They are civilians without clearance," replied Major Bluster.

Everyone took their seats while Lukas Knight stood up to address the room.

"I have already done a briefing for the other two teams of Cyberhawk, which, during the attack upon Portland, the Emergency Services Team got a surprise introduction. That introduction was originally planned for months in the future, but these events have forced a more imperative-oriented schedule. I have been told that things need to speed up. Fortunately, this team has all the necessary resources to meet that requirement. You all have shown amazing professionalism. I am pleased with your progress, and it appears that I'm going to have to ask you to keep that pace and possibly go beyond that," said Knight, looking out at all the Cyberhawk team members present.

The sunlight poured into the room from the big windows. It appeared to be a beautiful summer day.

"I know that you have questions. Because…… I have questions too. The Shadow Team is currently working with other agency groups to gather accurate information about those responsible for the horrible incident in the city of Portland. We know that the subversive group known as the Action Men is involved."

Lukas Knight saw a hand pop up suddenly out of the corner of his eye. He turned to see Rafferty Lewis with his arm up in the air like a student in a classroom.

"Yes, Mr. Lewis?"

"Mr. Knight, I've never heard of Action Men. What or who are these guys?" asked Rafferty.

"Their origins appear to be some form of a grassroots hate organization, although they did not seem to think of themselves as such. They may have started originally as a group of drinking or hunting friends about twenty years ago. The five original members of this group have seemingly disappeared. We know that two of them died, which may have been the catalyst for the group becoming so negative. There appears to be a vigilante component of the group recruiting others to find those responsible for the deaths of the two original members. It seemed to have a domino effect, and another group, which was essentially a domestic terrorist group, melded with them. That group had ties all over the world and resources. As time went on, their leadership developed an understanding of how to manipulate local male populations to get them involved, and a significant amount of fear tactics were employed. A cell of Action Men in one state may predominantly consist of middle-aged white males, while in another state it could comprise young black males and Spanish-speaking males. The attempt was made in the southwest to recruit Native Americans, but fortunately, that failed. There was a powerful Medicine man who was able to lead the young men away from that thinking. They were lucky. A gang war resulted in San Francisco's Chinatown district. In Canada, a cell has developed around economic disparity. So, this organization will take whatever fear you have and make it your reason for joining them," Knight answered.

Raven raised his hand, and Knight nodded to him, "What was being used against the southwest tribal people?"

"Religious persecution. Fears of being forced into something one did not wish to believe in and taking away traditional attributes of their society," replied Knight. "An example would be... like the forced education of Native American children in boarding schools away from their parents."

"Oh yeah, I can see how that would upset them," replied Raven, thinking about some of the nefarious incidents concerning schools for Native American and First Nation children.

"In a nutshell, the Action Men... are bad business. They promote hate and fear. Mr. Lewis, does that answer your question?" asked Knight.

"It certainly does," replied Rafferty. "They are a bunch of assholes! They are going to ruin what generations have worked towards." The generally genial cowboy folded his arms across his chest in frustration.

"And there is reason to believe that there might be other parties involved in the Portland attack. We need to determine who they are and what their agenda is before making any plans to deal with them," said Lukas Knight.

Captain Justice raised his hand.

"Yes, Captain Justice," said Knight.

"I would like to know why the Action Men attacked Sandra Ridgestone," said Justice.

"They didn't. It was someone else," replied Lukas Knight, seeing the reactions from the group, including Sandra.

"Well, Mr. Knight, why would anyone want to attack me?" asked Sandra, hearing the murmuring reactions from her teammates.

"That is one of our biggest questions. Captain Unicorn was far enough away from you that if he had been the target, you should not have been hit. The attack against you was powerful and completely nonconventional," replied Knight. "According to our data that Betty and the LabCoat Crew have fully analyzed, it is unlike anything we have ever documented before."

"And you are sure…. Detective Ridgestone was targeted?" asked Justice.

"Yes," replied Knight.

"Also, we have seen historical references to stuff like it in the past, and it was not taken seriously in the last two hundred years," added Major Bluster.

"So, what was it?" asked Captain Justice.

"We are currently labeling it as a UAP or Unidentified Anomalous Phenomena," replied Knight.

"Are you implying…... a UFO, ghost, or a witch attacked her?" asked Fernando, making a frown.

"No, it was dark magic," replied Alejandro unexpectedly.

Everyone turned to the usually taciturn Mexican man. He made a face of disgust and reluctance.

"I have seen this before. I looked at the data that was collected. A witch attacked her," replied Alejandro.

Sandra made a frown of concern and confusion.

"Where did you see that?!" asked Fernando.

"Back home. It was a nasty case concerning a specific drug cartel," he replied, starting to shift uncomfortably in his seat. "I don't like to talk about it."

Alejandro got up as the room had become extremely quiet. He shook his head a little. He looked down at his hands, which were shaking, and then walked off to go to the kitchen and splash cold water on his face.

Dr. Hanni got up and walked towards the kitchen to make sure the man was okay.

"Well then,… we are obviously not talking about Harry Potter or Bewitched style witches….," said Fernando, looking around. Everyone looked uncomfortable. Chris seemed to shut down, his arms folded across his chest, while Janet and Ellena looked distressed.

"No," added Diana unexpectedly. "I am wondering if I may have a lead on who or what was involved, but it might be just a coincidence."

"Oh! That weird woman!" exclaimed Sandra, wrapping her arms around herself. "Back at the farmers' market."

"That's right! Diana told us about some weird witch group from long ago," said Fernando, remembering the conversation.

Lukas Knight tilted his head to the side and said, "What are you talking about? What group?"

Diana sighed and replied, "Sandra had an encounter with a woman who could have ties to the Witches of Grüner Nebel. She looked like a woman by the name of Giovanna Bianchi la Ammaliatrice."

Knight raised an eyebrow and looked over at Major Bluster.

"Hey, don't look at me. That's Koorvert's expertise. Remember, I shoot things and blow stuff up," remarked Major Bluster to Knight.

"Okay, this all bears further investigation. Diana, please share all your information with...Shadow Team. I will also require everyone who saw this woman to give statements concerning the incident," said Knight.

"What if we don't recall much anymore?" asked Ellena.

"Just be honest and do your best. Diana, I will arrange for someone from Shadow Team to contact you," said Knight.

"Most of us were wearing the HUD glasses, so maybe something is recorded on those," suggested Janet.

"What do we do in the meantime? How do I protect Detective Ridgestone from......... witches?" asked Captain Justice, feeling perplexed.

Knight sighed with frustration.

"That will have to be investigated... since I have no idea. This might be another project for the LabCoat Crew. But having the data from the HUD glasses might prove valuable. Perhaps some empirical data. Do you recall what day you went to the farmers' market?" asked Lukas Knight.

"I can research that," replied Diana. "It was just after the Cyberhawk clothing had been delivered, and it was suggested that we show the general public that not only men were part of Cyberhawk."

"Oh yes, I remember that," said Captain Justice. "It might be in my notes as well."

"Don't forget that the twins were also there. They might recall something, too," said Janet.

"They'll probably recall details that did not catch our attention," suggested Ellena. "Kids their age have a critical eye for certain things."

Chaos erupted, and everyone seemed to lose focus. Janet approached Lukas Knight and said, "Can we take a break, or are we finished?"

"I have a lot more to go over with you all. You need to know what you have stepped into," said Knight. "Why do you ask?"

"I think Sandra needs some time to process all of this," said Janet, gesturing to Sandra, who was sitting alone with her arms wrapped around herself and her head tilted down.

"Oh. I see what you mean. Take her out for some fresh air, and I'll give everyone else a coffee break…. although at this point, I think we all might need something stronger. Witches…. of the green mist….," he grumbled.

****

Captain Unicorn watched as Janet Hallman escorted Sandra outside. She didn't look happy. He turned to Major Bluster.

"Oh, I have seen that look before," said the Major, looking at the Unicorn.

"I can't leave her like that," he replied.

Major Bluster sighed.

"This is nothing but trouble. You must resolve this by either telling her or going away," replied Bluster. "I could set you up in Koorvert's group. I am seeing this whole operation requiring us to spend more time with the civilians. I need a decision from you."

"I want to stay. I never wanted to leave in the first place. I made commitments. I kept my promise to the Navy, and now it's time I keep my promise to my family," replied Captain Unicorn.

"Alright. I will assign you as the official liaison and trainer for the Emergency Services Team members to learn how to defend themselves. We are stepping into fresh territory here, mixing military and civilians into operations that could turn deadly," said Bluster. "I will talk to Commander Knight about this."

"Thank you," replied the Unicorn. "You know this country was founded by civilians willing to defend themselves against a perceived threat."

The Major scrunched up his face a little and then sorta nodded.

"Go talk to that woman before it's too late," replied Bluster.

****

Captain Unicorn found Janet Hallman and Sandra Ridgestone standing together, watching a small vintage aircraft take off. The taildragger had a distinctive engine sound as it worked itself up to take off into the sky. It was perfect weather for an open cockpit plane to ascend into the bright blue airspace above Eugene. Sandra stood rigid with her arms folded across her chest. He took a deep breath and made his way over to where they were standing. The sound of his crunching steps across the pea gravel caught both women's attention. They turned and looked at him, then back at the vintage plane as it began to arc around and gain altitude.

"Neat old plane," he commented.

"Yeah," agreed Janet.

"We see them all the time, but I never get tired of them," commented Sandra.

"Kinda like the seaplanes that would land and take off in Lake Tahoe. I always wanted to take a ride in one of those," he commented.

Sandra turned and looked at him. He continued to watch the old plane until he could feel the weight of her stare. He looked over at her.

"Really......who are you?" she asked.

"Someone who needs to speak with you about something important," he replied.

Janet eyed the two of them and decided she needed to go back inside. "Hey Sandra, I...uh...need to go back inside. I'm really thirsty. Need anything?"

"No, I'm fine," replied Sandra.

Janet took that as a sign that it was okay to leave Sandra with the strange military Cyberhawk. He was rather attractive. They waited in silence for a few moments while Janet walked away.

"I know what happened to Warrant Officer Karl Ridgestone. He is alive, but he is not the same as he used to be. He was on a mission and was badly injured to the point that he died and was revived by some of the LabCoat Crew. They are under strict orders not to speak of the matter until certain people give permission for you to be told about it," said Captain Unicorn. "It has been deemed that you are now allowed to know what happened to him."

Sandra nodded.

"First of all, he did not want to divorce you."

Sandra immediately turned and looked at him. He did his best to ignore the look and continue to say what he needed to say.

"He felt he had to do so to protect you and your children. The missions he went on were perilous, and you have special abilities that have enabled you to pick up on information that is normally unobtainable unless you were part of the mission. This is why you were such a good detective. You could follow hunches and investigate areas where most police officers would struggle to put the pieces together. Several times, you came close to knowing what some of his missions were about, and the foreign powers that were involved would not think twice about killing you or the kids. It... broke his heart to leave you," said the captain, holding back his emotions.

Sandra remained quiet. Her breathing felt odd. So many thoughts and feelings were going through her head. She turned and looked at the man standing next to her. Her gut instincts were telling her that he was sincere and truthful. If the story was a lie, then he did not know it was a lie. And then there was that aspect about him that seemed so very familiar. She started to wonder about stuff. In this day and age, when people can take pills and have surgeries to change their gender, and reconstructive surgeries are available to help people recover from horrible accidents, then... what if?

"You need to tell me something important......and you are having a hard time.... doing it," she finally said to him. "Why is it difficult?"

"Because I am afraid you will not believe me," he replied without hesitation. "And...... I do not want you to be angry with me."

"And it is.... important to you.... that I believe you. And... not be angry? It's not just a task that you are required to do," she said, searching her feelings, her instincts. It was somehow deeply intimate to him. More so than just an injured close friend.

"No. It is very personal to me," he replied in a matter-of-fact tone, looking back at her.

"Hey! You two! We are about to do the rest of the meeting," Fernando called out to them from the door of the base.

Sandra and Captain Unicorn looked at each other with a sigh of reluctance and irritation and then started back towards the building. Once inside, everyone was settled in the dining area, and coffee, soda, and alcohol had been placed out along with snacks. Alejandro had rejoined the group and appeared to be feeling better, and Dr. Hanni stayed close by. Having someone else who spoke fluent Spanish while Alejandro became more proficient in English was helpful. It was now evident that the former Mexican policeman had endured a mysterious trauma while working back home.

Once everyone had taken seats, Mr. Knight stood up and asked, "How is everyone feeling? I know this is a lot to take in all at once. Our lives are changing."

Robert Justice took another sip of the soda mixed with a little bit of alcohol.

"To be honest, I am starting to wonder if I have the right experience to run a group with this kind of expanded responsibility. Maybe we should be under the guardianship of the military," said Captain Justice.

"Absolutely not. You are perfectly suited for the job and will continue to be the leader of the Emergency Services Team as long as you wish to hold the position. However, we will provide you with training to help you better handle unexpected situations, such as the one that occurred in Portland. The teams are designed to work together. Your equipment is based on the same design as the other two teams, with the same premise: we are here to protect the public. Eventually, there will be a step to expand the teams and perhaps build additional ones," Knight looked over at Ellena and Chris. "There has been some discussion that we should have teams dedicated to water-based operations, drones, and robotics."

Chris and Ellena both smiled with enthusiasm as they looked at each other.

"But before we start expanding, we need our current teams to all be aware that there is a growing danger out there from the domestic terrorist group called the Action Men.

Intelligence sources are no longer certain that they are domestic anymore. They have appeared in other countries, spreading like a virus. These other nations are concerned and are looking to the United States to have answers on how to deal with them, and now the government is turning to us for help," said Knight.

Diana raised her hand, and Knight nodded to her.

"Do you think that the Witches of the Green Mist are working with the Action Men?" asked Diana.

"I have no idea. Witchcraft is not my area of expertise. Nor is the lore and history behind it. We must conduct further investigation before proposing such ideas and making plans of action based on that assumption. Remember, the general public and now the government are counting on us to make good decisions based upon facts. In the meantime, we all need to do our jobs as planned and keep an eye out for these groups and their activities. What we do know now is that someone is after Dr. Pierre Arnaud's work. He is a physicist currently working on hydrogen plasma as a potential fuel source. His secret office was in the building that was imploded. Dr. Arnaud is alive and in hiding. We are still waiting to determine if his notes and materials on his research were stolen or not. The crews going through the wreckage of the building have been swamped by insurance investigators due to the presence of the gems and precious mineral dealers also located in the building. There is a rumor that a batch of old blood diamonds was also stored in the building.

The federal bureaus that oversee that investigation know of our concerns," said Knight, reaching for his glass of water.

"The captain here," Major Bluster gestured to the Unicorn. "He is willing to start training the Gold Team on self-defense, shooting, weapons handling, and flight training using Cyberhawk-installed weaponry. We can't leave them without some means of defense. They're going to be targets."

"We should not have weapons," said Captain Justice. "That will make people afraid of us."

"We carried weapons with us as police officers," remarked Daryl Crane.

"And people are often afraid of the police," added Fernando.

"But you can't arrest violent criminals without having a way to defend yourself. They often carry more weapons than we do," commented Sandra.

"Well, first let's make sure they have the same armor that we do," suggested Captain Unicorn. "And figure out how to provide a weapon that is not so obvious or perhaps so deadly. Other methods can be employed."

Captain Justice shook his head and let out a loud sigh, "I disapprove of firemen carrying weapons. That's not what we do."

"But as long as you are wearing the Cyberhawk gear, you are going to be perceived as a target, civilian," retorted Major Bluster.

"Yes, thanks to you and your military team," replied Justice, making a pained expression.

"But we are wearing different colors," said Raven, joining the conversation. "We are the Gold Team, and they will learn that we are the people who help them get rescued from fires, accidents, and... saving their cats from tall trees.

"They'll also learn that we can't shoot back," added Rafferty. "That's why crazy people shoot up schools. They know there are no weapons to take them out. They take the easy route to cause sorrow and violence. People who think that way just want to cause pain, and they will get more bang for their effort if their victims have no way to defend themselves. You've seen videos where criminals target elderly people; it's because the criminals are cowards. They don't target the big, strong young person who is fully alert and armed. This isn't the Old West with high noon gunslingers having it out."

"Okay," interjected Lukas Knight. "We are getting off target. I will make this decision. The Gold Team will be trained to defend themselves and to carry non-lethal weapons, unless they are former police officers who have received full training in their use. We will institute regular practices to make sure skills and knowledge are up to standards," said Knight.

"What if I don't want to carry a gun anymore?" asked Janet.

"Then you do not have to," replied Knight. "But everyone has to learn martial arts and be instructed on how to use non-lethal weapons properly."

Dr. Hanni raised his hand. He was not concerned about learning military tactics, since all Swiss citizens were required to serve in some capacity and receive training. He did so.

"I have been thinking... and just how do we know who a member of these Action Men is?" asked Dr. Hanni. "And why do they want this hydrogen plasma fuel project of Dr. Arnaud's? It sounds like something that is not readily used, so... these Action Men would have to have someone who does understand this concept."

"To answer the first question... our HUDs have access to extensive databases, and the Mechanical AI knows to keep an eye out for wanted felons and people of interest such as the Action Men members," Captain Unicorn answered.

"And Shadow Team is currently working with the LabCoat Crew on figuring out the whos and the whys of the hydrogen plasma project. We are also trying to get Pierre Arnaud to allow us to protect him," added Lukas Knight.

Dr. Hanni nodded, understanding that these concerns were being investigated. The job had just become more complex and perhaps more vital.

Robert Justice took another sip of his drink and looked about as he listened to the others. It had been almost half a year since the Emergency Services team had been put together, and so much had happened already. Robert Justice hoped he would feel more at ease in this new job. He had the best people to work with and excellent equipment, but something was gnawing at his insides. There was something out there that was unknown. It was unknown and unfriendly. As a firefighter, he was trained to understand his enemy, which was mainly chemical reactions. It did not have a devious mind behind its actions.

CHAPTER 27

Everyone sat down at the conference room table within the enormous diplomatic starship, the *Illuminator Star*, which served as both transportation and home in space while the Illuminators served the Milky Way Galaxy citizenry. Illuminator Four did not require a chair but would often lounge upon what could be best described as a chainmail bean bag, which could accommodate his size and structure. Being a dragon stuck in a starship for long periods of time could be aggravating. He often had to keep his wings folded for long periods, which could be irritating and sometimes painful. Other races had wings, and they had complained in the past that the lack of stretching space was a problem. Sometimes, a visit to the vast hangar bay was necessary. He had replaced a long-revered Illuminator who was of the Fenram race. Fenram are bipeds that stand about two meters tall, have long fur all over their bodies, and wings that fold close upon their backs. They had visited Earth many times, and legends had developed around them concerning their big feet, ability to jump far, make scary noises, and apparently smell bad to Humans. Illuminator Four chuckled to himself, thinking about how funny Humans had been throughout the millennia. His own people had been offered young female Humans to eat, which invariably shocked and revolted the dragons that visited. Often, these young females were taken and brought to another tribe to be cared for by beings that were not idiots.

"What are you chuckling about?" asked Illuminator Three, setting down the datapad that she had been reading reports on, causing her armor to clank a little.

"Oh, …. just thinking how silly Humans have been in the past eons," replied Illuminator Four.

"I can vouch for that," replied Illuminator Two as he finished with the report that each of them had been given. He was tall, blonde, with a lean build, and could be best described as an elf. He looked at his four companions and asked, "So what did you think of the Black Suit Division's report?"

"They have done a comprehensive job as usual," remarked Illuminator One, as he sat back in the chair that was perfectly designed for his smaller and more compact body. He was the senior of the group, although not the oldest chronologically, but elderly for his race. He nodded his grey-blue head and blinked his dark eyes as if he were pondering something important. "I am very concerned. Hopefully, I am not being… overly anxious. Did any of you see aspects about this report that brought forth the Human concept of raising a red flag?"

"Oh yes!" replied Illuminator Five as she swished her grey furry tail about. Her feline features allowed her the flexibility to be comfortable in numerous conference chairs, but not after reading the report by the Black Suit Division. "I felt the fur on my back ruffle up after looking this over. My tail almost went piloerection on me," she complained.

"Agreed," paused the Ar'Kah female, who held the Illuminator Three position. "Not about any hair-raising moments…but this is something to be concerned about. Just looking at the surface, it appears that the enemy is already present on Earth." Illuminator Three started to fiddle with one of the small weapons that she always wore on her armor, which protected her human-like form. Her skin was the color of the richest soil, and her beauty was fierce. She wore her long hair carefully braided back in rows from her face to keep it from getting in her way in combat. It also allowed a scar above her brow to be visible.

"Are we all in agreement?" asked Illuminator One, turning to Illuminator Four.

The golden scaled dragon replied, "That possibility would explain a great many events and behaviors that my people have observed over the many centuries spent around Humans." He sighed. "It is also a worrisome prospect. Does the enemy know we are here assisting the Humans? We need more information."

"Agreed," said Illuminator One.

"Perhaps, we assign a portion of the Black Suit Division on a fact-finding mission. There are some old libraries on Earth and what they call ancient locations that may have some documentation that could be useful in establishing whether they are or have been here… and for how long," suggested Illuminator

Five. "The video recording at the… paper mill… reported by the Cyberhawk member known as Alejandro Morales was disturbing."

The others could see her fur starting to puff up slightly around the edges of her ceremonial short-sleeved tunic dress.

"There are times when I wish we could just go and talk with the Humans," replied Illuminator One.

"Why don't you?" asked Illuminator Three.

"Well….my people don't wear garments like you and Illuminator Two ……… your bodies are almost completely covered. Most Humans find our appearance to be shocking at first. Those that we do meet with require a certain amount of time to get used to that," replied Illuminator One. "They are strangely trained to be ashamed of themselves, but I can understand their need for protective weather garments. Their skin is not as tough or resilient as ours."

"And when most Humans see me coming, they go running," added Illuminator Four, throwing his arms up in the air. "They see horns, fangs, claws, scales… and go nuts. Very few do not react that way."

"Are you using that fear skill you have?" asked the tall Elf, moving a stray lock of hair behind his pointed pale ear.

"No. That is a defensive skill… and it is not always on," replied Illuminator Four. The dragon turned to Illuminator Five and asked, "Didn't your people try to make contact with the Humans?"

"Oh yeah…. with mixed reactions. They either thought we were some large jungle cat to be feared or something to be adopted and brought into the house. My people have reported many strange experiences. At one point, they wanted to worship us, along with the smaller life forms that resembled distant relatives of ours. It was decided to wait until Humans understood better about life off Earth before we attempted that again," replied Illuminator Five.

"I see, so what about my people? Could I speak with these tribal leaders?" asked Illuminator Three.

The other four just looked at each other and got quiet.

Illuminator Three started to scowl, "What is going on? You don't think the Ar'Kah capable of visiting Earth?"

"Oh, we think you are capable," replied Illuminator Two in his typical, serene, aristocratic tone. "But we think the Humans would be so impressed by you that they would try and get your technology from you... Or fear you so greatly and assume you are arriving to conquer them."

"Oh. I see," she replied, disappointed. "I would have gone if you needed me to."

"We know that. You, out of all of us, are the most likely to be accepted by them. We had discussed this idea and realized that insecurity would probably overrule rational thought on their part," replied the Grey. "This is the reason why we have the Black Suit Division."

Illuminator Four got up to stretch a bit as best as he could; he knew that at some point, he would get to the age where he would be too big to fit in the ship and would have to give up his

Illuminator position. He glanced over at Illuminator One and knew he would eventually die or want to retire for a few final years with his family. The Grey people had large, very close family groups, and his time away was a great sacrifice. A few members of his family would stay on the ship with him and then go back home. He was missing out on time with his grandchildren. It was different for the dragons; they lived very long lives and then recycled back into their old life as a baby dragon after their bodies got too old. Fifty planetary cycles away from home was a short time for his people, but not for the others. He had grown fond of his fellow Illuminators and hated to see the day when they would part. Illuminator Two's people also lived long lives and often saw the deaths of friends from other races with shorter lifespans.

He finally turned back to the table and said, "We might need to speed up the Cyberhawk program. If the Sah-tata Keh-shudha are already here, then we need the Humans to be better prepared. We all know what happens to worlds that fall prey to their dark machinations. The Jenfarr, distant cousins to Illuminator One's people, fell under their spell and did horrible things to the less advanced races they visited."

Illuminator One nodded solemnly. He knew the Jenfarr very well.

"They became so corrupted that they started working on viral warfare, and... accidentally destroyed themselves. Their planet is still under quarantine, and... it will probably be that way for several hundred of their years," said Illuminator One sadly.

"They became monsters that we found ourselves fighting against….an enemy…........ but it is still sad to see an entire race and culture go extinct."

"So, this could happen to the Humans?" asked Illuminator Five.

"Yes," replied Illuminator Two.

"It says here in the Black Suit report that the Sah-tata Keh-shudha are known to find the energy created by hate, fear, anxiety, rage, terror, and hopelessness... to be like an intoxicant. How did they find this out?" asked Illuminator Three.

"We provided them with that information," replied Illuminator One. "This was something we discovered from captured Jenfarr. It was described that the Sah-tata Keh-shudha would be interested in a planet where the indigenous life forms could be inspired to emit these emotions. And as we all know, Humans can exhibit all these emotions on a regular basis. Especially when large conflicts with extreme brutality are encouraged... it would be an intoxicating feast for them."

Illuminator Five wrinkled her furry brow and changed the direction of her ears, "That is horrible. Are you implying that they would enjoy Human conflict?"

"Yes, he is," replied Illuminator Two, making an expression of disgust and distaste. "As a race of beings, they *are* monsters. And should not be here in our Galaxy."

"My people are a warrior race with a history of numerous battles and conquests, but we… never sought that kind of engagement," remarked Illuminator Three. "We need to stop them."

"Agreed. We need to expedite the progress of the Cyberhawk Program. It already appears that the various teams, when put together, work well with each other. It may be time to further that spirit of cooperation to extend further out," suggested Illuminator Four.

"What are you suggesting?" asked Illuminator One.

"That the program expands to exist in the lands of other tribal governments," said Illuminator Four.

"I think we can put forth that idea easily," said Illuminator One. "Any other concerns or ideas?"

"I don't like some of the Human social groups that have been described... these witches of the green mist. It almost sounds like they worship the Sah-tata Keh-shudha," commented Illuminator Three. "The Sah-tata Keh-shudha are not a Type III civilization. They must be offering something in exchange for this kind of loyalty."

"We need more information," concluded Illuminator Two. "My people are adept at what Humans call magic. These skills are highly prized among certain fringe groups, resulting in desperate attempts to acquire that knowledge, with individuals doing whatever is necessary to gain it. This, of course, results in some very disruptive and vile behavior. In some cases, insanity."

"Alright. Let's put together a new directive for the Black Suit Division, and this time let's get a report within a shorter period since we are suspecting that the enemy may already have a foothold on Earth," concluded Illuminator One.

www.ingramcontent.com/pod-product-compliance
Lightning Source LLC
Chambersburg PA
CBHW051056030726
47504CB00006B/1650